Final Allegiance

by JS Ririe

Jan Hill Books

Final Allegiance
by JS Ririe
Publisher: Jan Hill Books
ISBN: 978-1-7326612-8-8
Copyright 2019 by Jan Hill Books
Cover Image by: Fotoluminate
Cover Design by William Gensburger

Praise for: Final Allegiance

"A gripping story set in the heart of the Colombian rain forest. This book pulls you in as you anxiously turn each page to see what will happen next. An extraordinary adventure unlike any other told that makes you wonder what choices you would make."
- Elizabeth B.

Synopsis:

Reagan Sinclair defies her family's wishes to join the Federal Bureau of Investigation believing she can make a difference by helping the downtrodden and defenseless. Her motives are pure, but her first undercover assignment proves that true bravery comes from the heart, not just an iron will and concentrated training. Loaned out to the Drug Enforcement Agency to infiltrate a compound in the Colombian jungle and find out what happened to a missing agent, she is forced to face her own mortality when the mission is compromised and she attempts a daring escape without the necessary backup. It's a test of everything she has learned as she fights to keep a promise and survive the ridicule of the only person willing to help.

Dedication:

To everyone who has dreams for accomplishing the unexpected, the seemingly impossible and the impassioned goals that rarely leave conscious thought and make the heart swell. They make living life to the fullest possible.

~JS Ririe

Chapter 1

"I (name) do solemnly swear (or affirm) that I will support and defend the Constitution of the United States against all enemies, foreign and domestic; that I will bear true faith and allegiance to the same; that I take this obligation freely; without any mental reservation or purpose of evasion; and that I will well and faithfully discharge the duties of the office on which I am about to enter. So help me God."

Oath taken by FBI agents

****

"Good morning, Agent Sinclair," the receptionist at the front desk of the impressive building at 935 Pennsylvania Avenue said to me on the Monday of my third full week with the FBI. I'd made it a point to speak to her each day. She was friendly and cheerful, but few people paid any attention to her unless they needed something. "Assistant Director Bridges wants to see you in his office promptly at nine."

"Yes, ma'am," I responded as a rush of excitement caused my heart to race. This was totally unforeseen. To my knowledge, my boss knew less than nothing about me—little more than my name and possibly my badge number—and I hadn't been with the agency long enough to get into any real trouble. This directive could only mean that he had an assignment for me, something unexpected that could turn into the most important experience of my life, and something that could take me from being a newbie with the agency into a genuine field agent. I tried to suppress a smile as I told her that I'd be there.

She smiled back and then resumed looking at the computer screen in front of her. No doubt she was accustomed to telling agents when they were being summoned to the headman's office and knew how to remain indifferent, but this was a first for me. I had shaken his hand briefly the day I'd graduated after 20 weeks and more than 800 hours of training to become an agent at the FBI academy at Quantico, Virginia—that place of learning and preparation that all cadets must pass through and master if they want to receive a badge and the responsibility that came with it.

What an experience in endurance that had been. I had always been a straight A student who prided herself on being physically fit. I had played sports and kept up with my four older brothers, but all of that came to a dizzying momentous stop the moment I met my first instructor, Agent Smith, who put us through a routine of sit-ups, sprints, pushups and running that would have made a Marine wince. His motto was, "It doesn't matter if you have the brains, if you don't have the brawn to back it up." We also had classes in boxing, grappling, handcuffing, tactical maneuvers and safe driving.

And then there were our classroom instructors, Agents Randolph and Kirkland, who knew how to make us feel insignificant and brainless. They had been charged with the task of making sure we knew everything possible about law, ethics, behavioral science, observation, interviewing, reporting, interrogation, forensic science, running counter-intelligence, surveillance, weapons of mass destruction, and investigative techniques.

Added to that hectic and demanding schedule of instruction were field exercises that built on what we learned from personal study, web-based seminars and simulated virtual training before we were taken to the streets of Hogan's Alley—a mock town built and operated by the academy that used paid actors playing criminals and terrorists to help us hone our skills.

At that place of greater learning and heart-pounding experience we were given case scenarios that started with a tip and ended in multiple arrests. If we were killed during the completion of our mission, it was just another strike against us that meant we might not make the final cut, and there was no way we could cheat. Our weapons were paint guns and no one survived a direct hit.

My biggest challenge had been on the shooting range. I understood the need to get inside a criminal's head to figure out what he or she was going to do, but I had never liked guns. I knew they didn't kill, people did, but the thought of aiming my weapon at another human and pulling the trigger was the one thing that almost kept me from completing my training. Taking a life was against everything I believed in, even if it was in self-defense.

We were expected to master three kinds of weapons: our bureau-issued pistol, carbines and shotguns. I spent an incredible amount of time taking my pieces apart and reassembling them until I knew everything I could about the way they felt in my hand to the amount of kickback there would be when a shot was fired. I discharged over 5000 rounds before my training was complete, always hoping I would be one of those agents who never had to release more than a warning shot during their entire career.

There were two men who pulled me through my hardest hours, my partner, Agent Neil Southwick with whom I felt an immediate camaraderie and Agent Banning. Neil was solid, dependable, smart and caring. He always lifted me and made me want to be a better agent. Of course it didn't hurt that he was easy on the eyes, tall and slim, and with none of the obnoxious behaviors I'd noticed in some of the other recruits who liked to push limits and who didn't seem to care whose toes they stepped on to get ahead.

Neil and I had a healthy respect for our instructors who were physically, emotionally and mentally demanding. We might not appreciate some of their tactics, or the maneuvers they put us through, but we understood the necessity of following the rules--

exactly and without complaint or questions. Once we received our badges, the lives of innocent people would be placed in our hands, and we would rely on our training to get us through whatever needed to be done.

The second man I had learned to both count on and admire was Agent Ralph Banning, a supervising special agent and my field counselor who helped us when we got stuck and propelled us towards an area of specialization where we would be best suited. My original intent was to become an analyst inside the bureau walls where I could serve my country without being required to use a gun, but my computer skills—while more than adequate—couldn't rival those of some of my classmates. I had the aptitude to become a first-class field agent. I understood human nature, could assess a situation quickly and accurately, knew how to follow directives and had the ability to remain focused in any given situation. Those were qualities that couldn't be taught, only sharpened into something stronger and more precise, saving innocent lives while bringing the bad guys to justice.

So, after a great deal of self-reflection and despite my aversion to pointing a loaded gun at anyone, I decided to go where I could do the most good. I was thrilled to be selected, along with my partner and a number of other recruits from the class, to join the men and women of the FBI at the Washington D.C. Bureau in helping to protect our country and its citizens whether they were within its borders, or in foreign countries where liberties and safety were being threatened.

I truly believed I was ready to move forward in defending freedom, especially the freedom to worship the only true and living God, the kind and ever-present Heavenly Father I'd first learned about as a small child at home and later in church on Sunday mornings. It haunted me knowing that there were people in the world who didn't know he existed, and it saddened me even more that within my own country many of the religious freedoms my ancestors had cherished were being systematically stripped away.

I feared that the most valiant efforts on the part of good, honest, God-fearing people would not be enough to turn the tide of indifference, self-absorption and greed that caused wars and violence to escalate. But without those same people willingly putting their lives on the line for truth and justice, everything the founders of the country had tried to ensure though the constitution and its amendments would be lost. I was proud to be numbered among them.

Still, it hadn't been easy moving from top of the class at the academy where praise was given for accomplishments, to working with seasoned agents who prided themselves on making newbies feel like they'd just fallen off the turnip truck. But we'd been warned that it would happen. We were green, and it would take time to establish trust amongst our colleagues who already knew from years of experience and working together what it meant to be an FBI field agent in more than name only.

My mind reverted to the present as I hurried across the marble foyer to the bank of elevators that took thousands of people to the floors above. The indicator lights were blinking rapidly. Perhaps this would be my first solo assignment. No, our first solo assignment since I couldn't imagine working with anyone other than Neil. We'd be assigned as longterm partners once our supervisors felt we were experienced enough to be left to our own devises. It would be good to get away from the watchful eyes of the more seasoned agents we'd been assigned to ride with while we were learning the ropes.

I glanced down at my watch, a gift from my parents when I graduated from the academy. They had remembered my propensity for being late as a girl but had failed to understand that I was a changed woman. Everything I had done for the past six-and-a-half years had been based on lists and schedules. Sticking to them had led me to the realization of my childhood dream. It was 7:30 am. I was already at the office, and our day didn't officially begin until eight. Early was my new being on time.

My knees trembled slightly as I walked past the empty desks of other agents in our division. Some of them were out of the building on assignments, while others would start trickling in as the clock ticked closer to the hour. This was going to be either a very good or a very bad day. The knot that had formed in my stomach while I was in the elevator traveled upwards until it lodged in my throat. What if I was being overly confident? Nearly half of the new agents washed out the first few months on the job. There were few nine to five assignments and arrival at work didn't always mean going home at night. Some cases took several days or even weeks to complete, and families couldn't always be apprised of what was going on.

But if this was my first real mission, the actual beginning of a life no one in my family wanted for me - not even my policeman brother, Braydon, who had been on the job for seven years and loved every minute of it—I hoped I was ready. I felt confident with my training and my abilities, but flying unattended would be very different than practicing with a safety net.

"It's a ridiculous field and far too dangerous for a girl, especially a kind-hearted, trusting girl who knows exactly how wicked the world has become, and that it's not going to get any better," my father had told me the day I'd first informed him of my intentions when I was a freshman in high school. "Why don't you become a teacher? It's a good, solid profession that will allow you to work the same hours as your children when you become a mother. That's still part of your plan, isn't it?"

"I don't want to be a teacher," I'd told him.

I wanted excitement, adventure and possibly even forbidden romance - not being stuck in some dismal classroom repeating the same information day after day to students who really didn't want to be there. It would bore the life right out of me. I needed to be one of the people trying to protect innocents who could not do it for themselves.

No matter how valiant his efforts were in trying to convince me otherwise, I wouldn't be dissuaded from my dream any more than he would quit telling me that what I was doing was just plain crazy. Even his more frequent argument that honorable, faithful and good men did not want to marry girls who constantly put their lives in danger failed to persuade me to his way of thinking.

I had thought myself quite grown up at thirteen and quite able to make my own decisions—even if they didn't seem quite logical for a small town girl who'd only traveled out of the state to visit relatives. It was only much later during the course of my life that I came to understand how foolish I had been to think there would be plenty of time to build a career before thinking about marriage and family. Oftentimes, unanticipated circumstances changed the direction a life was heading before the person in question realized what was happening. But I didn't even understand that concept until I'd muddled my way through a vast array of exhausting and dangerous experiences I'd never dreamed of having.

It was the 21st century, and many young women were waiting until later to settle down and have children. They valued education and using the minds they'd been given in pursuit of something worthwhile and fulfilling, and they wanted to experience some of what life had to offer before changing diapers and driving kids to school. Besides, finding the right husband wasn't easy. It's not that I was particularly close-minded or demanding. I'd dated a lot of great guys who would make wonderful husbands and fathers, but I wanted the man I married to make my toes curl and my heart race when we kissed, and that hadn't happened yet.

But most of all, I wanted to do something really purposeful with my life, something I had never been able to quit thinking about. Why couldn't my father understand that I wasn't like everyone else? He'd raised me to think for myself and not to feel pressured into conforming to others' expectations. That's all I was trying to do. Life was about exercising agency, suffering the consequences of poor choices and enjoying the blessings of good ones. I was prepared to learn that important lesson for myself, and if I made a mistake or two, I'd deal with them.

"Hey, partner."

The voice brought me back to the present, and I frowned. My best friend and permanent partner, when our evaluation period had ended, Agent Neil Southwick, was sitting at his desk with a look of hurt and betrayal on his handsome face.

"I've been hearing rumors this morning that you've been summoned to the assistant director's office. I haven't been. So, what gives? I thought we were in this together."

My feelings of excitement quickly vanished. Neil wasn't just my partner; he was my confidant, the man I shared more about my life with than anyone else. If I was being summoned alone that only meant . . .

"I'm sure it's nothing important," I replied, realizing that I'd been off in my own dream world again, just as I'd been so many times in the past. Juicy assignments didn't come to beginners, but dismissal and chastisement certainly did. I tried to recall everything that had happened during the three weeks I'd been on the job, but nothing stood out. I'd simply been trying to learn the ropes like the rest of the newbies.

"He probably needs me to walk the vice president's dog," I retorted. It was the comeback we'd started using at the academy - our way of keeping reality in check when possibilities clouded our better judgment. "You know as well as I do that we haven't earned the right to do anything glamorous or exciting. To tell you the truth, I'm just a little bit nervous. If he wants to see me alone, it can't be good."

"Hell, Sinclair, it might be the opportunity of a lifetime," he responded, taking a sip of hot coffee. "Not every task we get is going to be together, although I'd like nothing more. We'll be asked to go where we're needed."

"But I don't want to go on an assignment without you," I said, sliding my purse inside my top desk drawer. "I like the way we work together. We anticipate each other's moves before we even make them."

"Maybe that's not always such a good thing," he said. "Besides, you know me, I don't even like dogs."

He walked away with his coffee mug in his hand, his shoulders not quite as straight as they usually were. Despite his snarky remark, I could tell he was upset about not being chosen to meet with the assistant director. I knew exactly how he felt. There would always be a certain amount of competitiveness between partners—even those who had survived the academy together and had become best friends - and assignments were not always based on training. Personalities, inherent abilities and talents often played a part. That meant anything could happen. Tomorrow, he could be the one meeting with Assistant Director Bridges, not me.

I wanted to say something more to him, but until I knew why I was being summoned, smalltalk wouldn't help. Neil wasn't the least bit chauvinistic like so many of the other agents I'd met who refused to work with female officers. He appreciated my abilities and told me that often enough, but no one wanted to left sitting on the sidelines if something exciting was brewing.

So instead of following him, I busied myself as much as possible with the assignment I was working on and tried not to glance at the clock every few moments. I wouldn't know anything until nine o'clock arrived and speculating wouldn't help. Whatever I thought the meeting might address would likely be so far off mark as to be laughable.

Nonetheless, by the time I rose my my desk chair, my stomach was churning, and I looked towards Neil for support. But he didn't even glance up from his computer screen as I walked across the floor to the stairs that would take me to whatever lay ahead.

Assistant Director Bridge's secretary was not at her desk. I stood for a few seconds wondering what I should do, but quickly realized that he was likely waiting for me since the summons had come when I first arrived.

Agent Banning, who had given me so much help and support at the academy, opened the door to both of our superior's inner office when I rapped lightly on it. I was surprised to see him there.

"Good morning, sir," I said before walking past him into an impressively large room with an ornate mahogany desk and a great many credentials and citations hanging on the wall behind it. Maybe someday I'd have more than just a desk in the bullpen for myself. The thought made me smile. Dreams were nice to have, even impractical ones.

"Sit down, Agent Sinclair," Assistant Director Bridges said without rising. My superior, who sat behind the imposing desk, was middle-aged, with hard lines between his eyes and a sprinkling of gray in his otherwise dark hair. His voice was filled with assurance and authority, and there was no smile playing about his lips. "How are you adjusting to life with the agency?"

"Just fine, sir," I replied as I swallowed back the nausea that had risen to my throat. Without Neil beside me, I was more than a little intimidated, but I was also a professional who had been trained to expect the unexpected.

"That's good because we've just been approached by the DEA for help with a situation that has arisen in South America. Normally, this would be taken care of internally, but they need a specific type of agent and don't have one available."

I felt the blood rush to my head. The DEA was the Drug Enforcement Agency, a separate entity that I knew relatively nothing about, except the fact that they were dedicated to getting narcotics off the streets by whatever means necessary.

"How does that involve me?" I asked.

Normally, I wouldn't have been quite so impertinent, but with Agent Banning in the room I knew something big was about to happen.

"The answer is quite simple, Agent Sinclair. One of their agents has gone missing, and they need someone who will not be recognized to go in without raising suspicions and find out what happened to her. It's not an assignment I would generally even consider giving to a new agent, but you fit the profile they need and come highly recommended by Agent Banning. He said you were one of the finest agents he's ever trained, and he's confident you have the skills necessary to complete the task."

I glanced over at the man who'd helped convince me that my talents would best be utilized in the field, and wondered if he really felt I was capable of completing an assignment of such magnitude, or if I simply met the qualifications they were looking for. His face was void of emotion, but then that's the way he'd trained us to look too. Good agents maintained control by being able to compartmentalize and not show what they were feeling or thinking.

"Thank you, sir," I replied. "I'm ready for whatever needs to be done."

"You might not be quite so enthusiastic when you know exactly what you're volunteering to do. And volunteering is the only way I'll approve this. You'll be going undercover as an English-speaking governess to Carlos Mendoza's two children at his compound in the Colombian jungle."

My eyes opened with surprise as ripples of wintry cold raced up my arms causing the hair to stand on end, but instead of asking another question, I just sat there and listened.

"Mendoza is a known drug lord who had his wife murdered because she got in the way. Their agent, Maria Gonzales, infiltrated the organization over two years ago as a Spanish-speaking governess. She hasn't been heard from in the last six weeks. She usually checks in like clockwork, and they need to know what happened to her before the next phase of the mission begins."

"My Spanish is far from fluent," I told him; my mind so numb with excitement and apprehension that I'd missed the fact that this might only be the beginning of something more. "I understand more than I can speak."

"Then you're exactly what they're looking for. Mendoza wants a strictly English-speaking governess who won't be tempted to pass on vital information."

"But if they're looking for a new governess, that must mean . . ."

He interrupted my sentence. "Let's not get ahead of ourselves, Agent Sinclair. They don't know anything for certain yet. That's why this operation is so important. It appears that her cover has been blown, and she may have been disposed of. However, the agency needs to know for sure so they can reassess their alternatives. Her placement at the compound was crucial in bringing Mendoza's cartel down."

"I understand," I told him, wishing I really did. There were hundreds of field agents far more qualified than I was to do what was being asked and disguises were plentiful. I wasn't even part of their organization.

"And you still wish to go?"

"I do, sir," I replied.

"In that case, I'm sure you have questions. I'll do my best to answer what I can."

This was the moment that separated me from the rest of the new agents that had just graduated from the academy. I had sworn to "support and defend the Constitution of the United States against all enemies, foreign and domestic." What greater enemy did we have, besides outright terrorism, than the war on drugs that destroyed more innocent lives than great battles ever had? I had given my pledge without reservation; now was the time for me to make good on it.

My knees were trembling as I opened my mouth to say something, anything that would let them know that I really understood what they were asking me to do, but before any words were formed, the assistant director provided further illumination.

"Your file says you come from a large family and have experience with children. That's one of the reasons it was flagged for this operation."

"One of the reasons?" I questioned, momentarily forgetting in whose office I still sat. What they were asking of me was tantamount to a suicide mission, especially if I went into it blind. I knew nothing about how the DEA operated, and I knew even less about Colombia and the drug lords who appeared to be above the law there—even when it came to cold-blooded murder—apparently.

His frown let me know that I was dangerously close to being reprimanded for impertinence. "You'll be assuming the identity of a young woman, a Tess Tremaine, who became indisposed last night. She lived here in the city and was scheduled to be on a plane later this afternoon."

"What happened to her?" I asked, once again forgetting my place in what was transpiring. No one was required to tell me anything. My job was simply to follow orders.

"That information is classified, but I can tell you that whatever happened has paved the way for getting another agent on the inside."

I didn't like what I was feeling. What if the girl by the name of Tess was dead? That seemed almost too convenient, but perhaps the DEA had simply taken her into custody so I could be sent in her place. It was too dark to think they may have disposed of her.

"Your job is to completely immerse yourself in her life; learn everything you possibly can about her before you board that plane. You can rest assured that she's been under constant surveillance by the cartel, and they're very thorough."

"That means there's also a good chance they already know what happened to her."

"What they know is irrelevant, Agent Sinclair. The DEA has asked for our help. Are you still willing to go, or am I wasting my time talking specifics with you?"

I'd been thoroughly reprimanded, but if I walked away from his office for any reason I might as well leave my badge on my desk because I'd never be given another assignment. He wasn't asking me if I felt comfortable with the parameters of the mission, only if I was ready to do it.

"Willing and ready, sir," I replied as my last chance to possibly save my own life vanished. This is what I'd signed on to do, but I had never expected my first undercover assignment to be with another agency.

"I've been assured that the DEA was able to contain the situation before Mendoza became aware of it. For all he knows, she's still alive and well, and will be picked up in Bogotá in the morning by one of his men. So, you can see that we don't have much time."

"No, sir," I replied, although I couldn't help wondering what would possess any young woman to leave her life and family to go to work for a drug lord in the middle of some jungle? She must have been truly desperate.

"I understand that this will be your first undercover assignment, Agent Sinclair, and that you're putting your life on the line without a thorough understanding of what is being asked. I wish like hell I was the one running the op, but the DEA has to take every advantage in addressing a crucial situation. If things work out as planned, you'll be on your way home in a matter of days."

"And a contact?" I asked.

He cleared his throat. "Yet to be determined. Your assignment is to teach the children some English while seeing what you can find out about their missing agent. The DEA will take care of everything else. It's not the way I prefer to work, but sometimes there are no other options."

I wished I could stop my boldness after the reprimand I'd been given, but if I didn't have the background I needed, I'd be hopelessly lost once I landed in Columbia. "What about Miss Tremaine's family?"

"As far as we know, she doesn't have any. That's one of the reasons Mendoza selected her. No one will miss her if she doesn't come back. It's an ugly business dealing with the dregs of society, but if we don't do it, who will?"

"If Mendoza knows what she looks like, I won't be able to fool him."

His brow furrowed ever so slightly as he slid a photo across the desk to me, and I wanted to fade into oblivion. How could I have made so many stupid blunders during my first five minutes with him? He had every right to dismiss me, not only from this meeting but from the agency as well. I had been pushing well-known boundaries from almost the moment I walked into his office. But surprisingly, he let it pass.

I picked up the picture and looked into the face of a young woman who could have been my twin except for the hairstyle and glasses.

"I can see from your reaction that we didn't miss the mark on physical similarities, and you can rest assured that all of their correspondence has been meticulously reviewed but the DEA. As far as Mendoza will ever know, you are Tess Tremaine, born in Trenton, New Jersey, but raised in some of New York City's worst projects. You moved to the city three months ago and haven't been able to find work. You're an only child, have no family, no money, few employable skills and you're in desperate need of a job since you're too proud to accept government assistance. That's why you applied to become a governess to a drug lord's children. All the information we have is in this folder. You'll commit it to memory before you leave the agency at noon. You'll be on that flight tonight."

"Yes, sir," I said as the enormity of what he was asking started to settle. I wouldn't be going back to my apartment, and I wouldn't be allowed to contact my family and tell them where I was going. I had been prepared for that eventuality during my training, but this wasn't a drill. This was reality! What if I didn't come back? Assistant Director Bridges said this was a dangerous mission. Maybe my father had been right. I should have become a teacher.

Agent Banning broke into my reveries. "I know this is a little overwhelming, Agent Sinclair, but you really are one of best recruits I've ever worked with. You have all the training necessary to complete this mission successfully. All you have to do is get in, find out what happened and get out."

"Yes, sir," I replied again, wishing I could think of something more impressive to say.

The assistant director looked at me gravely. "Your safety, and the safety of Agent Gonzales, should she still be alive, depends on your not getting caught. And while it might not sound like it, the less you know the better off you'll be. You won't be hiding anything more than your true identity. I cannot stress strongly enough that you are to trust no one except your contact."

"But how will I know who that is?"

My heart was racing with exhilaration and a certain amount of undeniable fear. I had no real regrets. This was what I'd been dreaming of doing for more than a decade, but now that the time had arrived, I realized that I wanted to get married, raise babies and live to a ripe, old age.

"You'll have to trust your instincts for now," he said. "You're on an information-gathering mission only, and there hasn't been time to put all the pieces in place yet. You will go in without backup or weapons, but you should only be there for a few days before being extracted. All the DEA wants you to do is find out what happened to their agent and get out. From what we've been told, they're in the final phase of organizing a raid on the entire operation. They don't want to endanger your life, and they don't want you to be taken hostage. They just need a better assessment of what they're dealing with. Once you're safely out of the compound, they'll send in the tactical teams."

I wasn't sure I understood exactly what was expected of me, but hopefully I would at least know more about the girl I was impersonating once I'd read the file he'd handed me.

"I'll give it everything I've got, sir," I said before Agent Banning propelled me out of the assistant director's office and into a corner of the room where his secretary still hadn't made an appearance.

"Don't try to be a hero, Agent Sinclair. While I have no reservations about your ability, we have no idea what you'll find when you get there. Just be cautious. If all goes as planned, you should be back by the end of the week."

"I understand," I told him. It seemed those were the only two words I could speak right now, even if I didn't mean them.

"I hope so," he said, smiling gravely at me. "I wish we were the ones running backup for you, but since you'll be working for another agency we have to play by their rules. You can rest assured that you will be carefully watched once you arrive, and like the assistant director said, these people have done their homework. They'll know everything about Tess Tremaine, so memorize all of the details in the folder to the minutest piece of information. You won't be able to carry any of the data with you."

The bright light in the room brought back the nausea I'd been fighting. "I'll do what's expected, sir."

"I just wish we had more time to get you prepped. The DEA caught a lucky break with this one. A new passport, credit card, cell phone and laptop will be given to you before you leave for the airport. You'll need to be there by seven, and you'll be in Bogotá in the morning."

I swallowed hard. This assignment was coming so fast it was making my head spin. How would I ever be able to commit to memory all the information they had gathered? And how could I keep from panicking since I'd be going into the situation blind? I wished Neil was coming with me. I trusted him completely, but I wouldn't even be allowed to see him before leaving the building. The information I'd been given could go no further than the three of us. What we were doing was an incredible risk, but I knew why the DEA was taking it. They needed to do everything possible to make sure their raid was successful. Many innocent lives depended on it.

"You probably think you're being thrown to the wolves," Agent Banning said, drawing me out of my preoccupation again. "That's why the assistant director gave you the option of not taking the assignment."

"But if I hadn't, I might not be given another chance to prove what I can do. That's the reality of the job, isn't it?"

"That's always a possibility. Opportunities like this don't come along very often, but there is another reason you were chosen besides bearing such a strong resemblance to Tess Tremaine and being good with children."

"You don't owe me any further explanations," I told him. "This is the work I've been trained to do."

"That's only partially true," he said. "We don't often work with other agencies, but we do like to be cooperative in case we need their help. One thing the assistant director didn't mention was that part of the reason he even agreed to present this mission to you has to do with your moral convictions. You are one of the few agents we have who is without vices."

My cheeks reddened. I had never talked about my personal beliefs with anyone, not even Neil. I'd only tried to show by my actions what was important to me.

"I'm not a saint, Agent Banning," I said.

"Well, you're the closest to one I've ever seen. While most of the cadets I train don't smoke, I've never had one before who wasn't willing to drink with everyone else at the end of the day, and I've never heard a word of scandal about you. You'd be surprised at the number of cadets who wash out because they get involved with someone they shouldn't, or who say something inappropriate or out-of-line when they've had too much to drink. I'm not condemning anyone for how they live their lives. We're all human, but those assets could very well save your life in a situation like the one you're heading into."

"Then you don't think my lack of experience with the vices in life is a death sentence? You could have easily said I was naïve to the ways of the world."

"You're cautious and you follow the rules, Agent Sinclair. Every agent has to start somewhere. You'll be just fine."

He extended his hand, and I shook it.

"Try not to worry about what may or may not have happened to Tess Tremaine. While I'm not privy to what brought this particular mission about, I trust that the DEA would not do anything to endanger a civilian's life. You have to proceed on the assumption that she has been extracted from what could have turned into a very bad situation for everyone involved."

"I'm sorry I'm not better able to curb my curiosity. I know it's one of the things you tried to drill into us, and I really am trying."

He laughed. It was a most unusual sound. "You are impetuous, Agent Sinclair, and questions aren't always bad. You just need to make sure you're asking them in the right situation. I'm really quite surprised that the assistant direction didn't say more about it, but he knows the makings of a great agent when he sees one. Still, I must warn you that he might not be so forgiving in the future. He expects his orders to be taken literally and completed without question."

I frowned, wishing it felt right to say more. "I suppose this is the point where I leave without a trace."

"It will get easier with time," he assured me. "But from now on, you're Tess Tremaine from the projects of New York City. I can't stress enough that keeping your own identity secret is what will keep you alive."

"What about clothing? Do I have time to go back to my apartment and pack a few things?"

"I'm afraid not. When you leave this building, you'll be taken directly to Miss Tremaine's apartment where you will stay until a cab arrives to take you to the airport. There are two suitcases filled with her belongings packed and waiting. You'll have to leave your badge and gun with me."

So this was what it really meant to go undercover—leaving everyone and everything behind with no opportunity for explanations or goodbyes. My hands were cold when I removed my badge from the waistband of my navy-blue pants suit and then undid the belt buckle that released my holster and gun.

"I'm feeling somewhat naked," I said as I looked at the gun I'd been trained to use, and the badge I'd worked so hard to get.

He didn't acknowledge my fears or offer any more words of encouragement.

"You have a little over an hour to study the documents before you leave, and good luck, Agent Sinclair. I trust we'll see each other again soon."

I watched until the elevator doors closed behind him, and then found a chair and opened the manila envelope the assistant director had given to me. His secretary, who had entered the room while we'd been conversing, looked over at me and smiled. I was more than certain it was part of her job to keep me from leaving the office or talking to anyone else. She looked friendly, but professional, and more than able to take care of herself and her duties should I decide to bolt.

According to the information, Tess was barely twenty and had been attending a small community college in Family and Child Development in New York City until she'd unexpectedly dropped out a few months earlier. She was introverted and shy, and reading was her favorite pastime. She'd been in love with a Luke Everett, but he'd broken her heart by becoming involved with her roommate, Jill Terry. Perhaps that was the trigger that had caused her to abandon her goals, move to another state and look for work out of the country? Every drastic move had one.

Her favorite color was purple, she liked yellow roses, and she attended the Lutheran Church occasionally. When I looked at her picture, it gave me chills. We had the same blue eyes, dark hair and full lips. She had a small mole on the left side of her nose that I didn't, but it was something most people wouldn't even notice once makeup was applied. And even if they did, I could easily say I'd had it removed for either cosmetic or medical reasons.

The door leading into the outer office where I sat reading suddenly opened, and a young woman with her blonde hair pulled severely away from her face entered the room.

"The assistant director told me to give these to you," she said without emotion. "There's a bathroom at the end of the hall where you can change, and you might want to let your hair down. It will definitely help with the illusion."

I took the small bundle of clothing she put in my hands. They smelled faintly of a perfume I didn't recognize. I instinctively knew they had belonged to the young woman whose life I was assuming. There was a white blouse with puffy sleeves, a multi-colored peasant skirt and a pair of tan sandals that laced around the ankles. There was also a light sweater I could put on should the evening become cool. The outfit was about as opposite to what I was used to wearing as anything could possibly be, and I wondered if she had purchased it so she could more easily fit into her new life. My closet consisted mostly of suits and professional attire.

Sadness enveloped me when I pulled the skirt on and secured the button at the waist. Tess should never have had to leave everything behind for this operation to take place. I wished I knew so much more about her. Certainly, there was someone who would grieve if she'd been taken into custody and given a new identity, but I couldn't worry about that now. I needed to stay focused on my assignment if I was going to come back and resume a life of my own.

Assuming someone's identity and flying thousands of miles away from Washington, D.C. to find an agent who had gone missing in a drug lord's compound in the Colombian jungle was the last thing I'd ever envisioned doing, especially as a first solo undercover assignment. I thought I'd be spending most of my time with a wire in my ear protecting dignitaries who came into the country and investigating political scandals or terrorist activities. This was entirely different than that, and my reservations were returning at an alarming rate.

Who did I think I was anyway? I had yet to be released from working with a training agent, and still I was being sent deep undercover with nothing but my wits and my instruction to keep me safe. I needed a handler like Jennifer Garner in the "Alias" TV series to monitor my movements and tell me what to do next. Watching that show as a teenager had convinced me that I wanted to be just like her, even though I realized that television wasn't real life and missions couldn't be completed in forty-six minutes.

Wearing fashionable and trendy clothes, traveling to exotic places and having to rely on my instincts and abilities had seemed nothing short of exhilarating back then and even during my training. Now, I wasn't quite so sure I'd made the right decision in going against my families wishes. I had never envisioned myself being sent anywhere totally alone.

When I looked in the mirror after letting my hair fall in soft ripples down my back and putting on the dark-rimmed glasses that had been supplied, I didn't even recognize the reflection staring back at me. I resembled someone left over from the hippie generation of the 1960s, a real flower child with the clothing to match.

"I can do this," I bravely told myself as I continued to scrutinize my appearance, but I was about to learn that self-assurance, personal strength and the best training available couldn't erase fear and moments of doubt when standing alone with no place to go and no visible means for survival.

I returned to the outer office to finish my reading, grateful that I'd never had trouble retaining important information. That's one of the reasons I'd been qualified to enter the academy. The restrictions were harsh, the work intense and the dropout rate higher than the number of cadets that actually made it.

The file I'd been studying was filled with small trivialities about her behaviors and likes that would only have been known if she'd been within the DEA's radar for an extended period of time. I wondered just how long they'd been monitoring her, and how they'd even found out that another governess was being sought if news wasn't getting in and out of the compound with at least some regularity. But there wasn't time to pursue my own investigation into anything right now. I had to continue under the assumption that I'd been given the best and most complete profile possible. Committing each detail to memory was what would keep me alive.

According to the documents, Tess Tremaine was gentle and intelligent, not prone to outbursts or excess questioning, and a real peacemaker who hated confrontation. But she was also a person who wanted to make a real difference in the lives of people who were less fortunate than she was.

I could only assume that information had come from the correspondence she'd exchanged with Mendoza, but I couldn't imagine being less fortunate than having no one around who cared. No wonder she had been chosen by a drug lord to be governess to his children. She was a loner, too quiet and unassuming to make any waves, ask compromising questions or defy authority. If she could handle the children and teach them something, she would be perfectly safe, unless she got caught in the crossfire of a raid.

I was her complete opposite in almost every way, having been raised with four older brothers who liked to torment, but who would also give their lives to protect me. They had taught me to stand up for myself, take chances and fight back when necessary. I also had loving parent who supported me even when they disagreed, sisters-in-law who had become some of my best friends, and several nieces and nephews who often taxed my patience but who made me realize just how much I wanted children of my own some day.

But what had actually prompted the inconspicuous, kind girl I'd been reading about to willingly leave the country of her birth to go to work for a drug lord? She had to have known that she might never return, but perhaps she'd been driven to point where she no longer cared. It was hard not blaming her friends who had so cruelly betrayed her, but I wasn't judge and jury for anyone.

Maybe when I returned, I'd put some of the pieces to the puzzle that was Tess Tremaine's life together and find answers that would satisfy my natural curiosity. Believing as I did, I knew that each person on earth was a child of God--a person of infinite worth with a special mission to complete. I didn't understand what Tess had been sent into mortality to do, but I would try not to mess up the legacy she'd left behind.

I just hoped I was adequately prepared for the mission I was about to undertake. Having been relieved of both my gun and my badge made me vulnerable, as did not knowing the identity of my contact or even the area where I was being sent. But I'd been raised to live by faith and trust that my Heavenly Father was always near. That was something most of my fellow agents did not have.

I tried to calm my racing heart after giving my own clothing to the agent who'd brought Tess's to me. Then I walked back to my chair, picked up the folder and continued to read.

Chapter 2

It was well after noon when two agents I had not seen before entered the small, windowless room outside the assistant director's office where I'd been sitting alone for nearly two hours reviewing the file that I was supposed to commit to memory. I didn't know why they were late, and I hadn't learned a great deal of particularly useful information about the woman I would be impersonating, except that she had been raised in three different foster homes after her parents had been killed when she was eleven. The reason for their deaths was sketchy, but apparently, they had been victims of a drive-by shooting. Drugs had most definitely been involved, and she'd escaped injury since she was sleeping in the back bedroom at the time. No family had come forth to claim her, although the authorities had searched for months.

She had lived with the Russells, the Boswells and the Hatches before graduating high school, when she moved in with Jill Terry to attend a local community college. That's where she'd met and become involved with her only boyfriend, Luke Everett. She worked as a waitress, making barely enough on which to subsist.

I closed the file and held it to my chest. Now that I was dressed in some of her clothing, I could feel her pain, her hopelessness in searching for love and acceptance, and the desperation that had led to her choice to travel to a foreign country from which she was likely never to return.

"If you'll follow us," one of the agents said. "We'll take you as far as we can, then it will be up to you to make it to Miss Tremaine's apartment where you'll wait until your taxi arrives at four this afternoon to take you to the airport. We'll have eyes on you the entire time, but there will be no direct contact."

"Understood," I replied, picking up the purse I had been given and putting the strap over my shoulder. I left the file on the chair where I had been sitting.

I was led down back stairwells and through tunnels that had been rumored to exist but were only used for emergencies or top-secret missions. I wondered what both my supervising partner and Neil had been told when I didn't return to the bullpen. The two agents leading me didn't say anything until we reached a doorway that opened into the subway system. I had no idea where we were, only that we had walked what I knew must be more than just a few blocks from FBI headquarters.

"This is where we leave you, Agent Sinclair," the taller of my companions said. "Her apartment is thirty or so blocks north on the left." He recited the address, and I committed it to memory. "Good luck. Hopefully, we'll see you in a few days."

I felt the enormity of my decision as they walked away. Part of me wanted to turn and run after them, back the way we had come to the safety I felt inside the FBI building with my partner working beside me. I could tell my superiors that I just wasn't ready for such a dangerous assignment, but that would end my career, and the DEA might never find out what had happened to their missing agent. This was what I had signed on to do by taking the oath of office, and just because it wasn't what I had expected, it didn't mean that I couldn't do it.

So, I took a deep breath and pulled the handle on the heavy, green, metal door inward. It moved with a nerve-grating sound. The subway was filled with people, but I took a moment to quiet my beating heart before joining them. Then I moved quickly into the crowd, grateful I knew how to blend in with other individuals. This was the first step of my journey, and it took every ounce of willpower I possessed not to glance over my shoulder or peer into the masses to see if I could detect the faces of other agents who had been put in place to protect me until I was on the plane and bound for the truly unknown.

I rode the cars until I came to the location where I'd been told to disembark. The sunshine outside the subway tunnels warmed my body.

"What would Tess Tremaine do on her last day in the city, in America?" I asked myself as I moved onto the sidewalk in the direction of her apartment. I couldn't answer with any degree of certainty, but I knew she would have to eat. Her file said she loved both Italian and Mexican food. I couldn't go wrong if I went with one of those for lunch, but she wouldn't go anywhere expensive. That much I had learned from reading her file.

On my way to her apartment building, I ordered a taco and a drink from one of the street venders. My stomach was tied in one of those proverbial knots people often talked about, although the physiology made no logical sense when one understood the human anatomy. The man taking my order smiled but didn't say anything. I wondered if Tess had purchased food from him before and if she had ever smiled in return. Her imprint on the city would be small as far as most of the residents went, but I would make sure her essence wasn't forgotten. In spite of where she was now, she'd had enough compassion for motherless children to be willing to travel thousands of miles to take care of two of them.

The sun did little to cheer my soul as I walked down streets she would have traveled on her way to and from her home. There was no way of knowing where her abduction had taken place. I refused to believe that anyone would have her killed just to gain an advantage over the enemy but knew that was always a possibility. I thought I detected black tire marks that only happened when a vehicle stopped suddenly but realized that a snatch from either government officials or the enemy likely wouldn't have happened so close to where she might be recognized.

If the DEA had her in custody, they would have removed her in the most inconspicuous place possible, and that was likely why I had been left in the subway to find my way back to her home. I reached inside her handbag to make sure the keys I'd been given were still there. I couldn't afford a screw-up. If members of the cartel were watching her every move, they would have me in their sight by now.

I wished I dared do a little sleuthing on my own to find out what had really happened to her, but remaining in the open, stopping to look around, or asking specific questions where something small could give me away might risk exposure and lead to detection.

With that in mind, I walked while I ate trying to remain calm and enjoy the day as I assumed she may have done since everything I'd read about her suggested a person who thought deeply and wasn't prone to outbursts of any kind. I needed to get inside her apartment and stay there until my taxi arrived. My natural curiosity would serve no good purpose now. I just hoped I wouldn't meet any of her neighbors going into the building. I might be able to fool a complete stranger in South America, or even some thugs watching from a distance, but anyone who had known her personally wouldn't be fooled by my attempt at impersonation.

The area of the city where she lived was mostly residential; three-story brownstones with concrete steps leading to the front doors and pots of annual flowers hanging from the porches. The buildings were old, but well preserved, and the sidewalks and streets looked as if they had been replaced in recent years. There were few cracks and no sign of weeds anywhere. Tall trees stood at intervals, and mom and pop establishments for dining out, groceries, dry-cleaning and hardware supplies were sandwiched in-between the apartment buildings and a few stately homes with balconies, short driveways and iron fences. The entire neighborhood brought feelings reminiscent of a more peaceful, less chaotic time.

It crossed my mind that she must have come to city with some financial reserves to live in such a neighborhood, or else she knew someone who resided there, but once again, my inquisitiveness had to be stilled. I'd been given what I needed to know for now. Everything else would have to wait until later.

There was no security at the front door. The keys I held in my hand were meant to open anything that stood between me and her apartment. I didn't like the idea of invading her private space, but it was only part of what my job required. So acting as if I had every right to be there, I inserted the first key in the lock, and took a deep breath before advancing into her brownstone and down a short hallway to the left. Her living quarters faced the street so I wouldn't have to wait outside for the taxi's arrival.

I was still having trouble wrapping my mind around how someone as young as Tess Tremaine had become so disillusioned with life that she had basically sold her soul to the devil just to get away from the pain, but then intense grief could cause an otherwise rational person to do something completely out of character. Perhaps she didn't know that her employer was a vicious drug lord who had likely killed his own wife because he was either tired of her or was afraid of betrayal since she knew too much. Going into a situation like that wasn't something most women wouldn't do unless they truly didn't care what happened to them.

The apartment she lived in was spotlessly clean and must have come furnished with the bare essentials since she had only been there a few weeks while looking for work. The living room furniture consisted of a tan sofa and chair, a scarred wooden coffee table and a four-shelf bookcase. There were no pictures on the walls and no collectables; just a couple of lamps that didn't match and heavy curtains that would allow no light to enter the room when they were drawn. There was absolutely nothing that defined her as a person, and the landlord would have zero to dispose of before renting it to someone else.

The two suitcases waiting by the front door contained all the worldly possessions she had left. It was apparent that she had no intention of coming back, and anything she may have collected over the years had been given away or thrown out.

The refrigerator and kitchen cupboards had been emptied of their contents, and there was nothing sitting out in the bathroom except for a toothbrush and the personal items that would be needed until she left. She must have cleaned and packed the day before because even the sheets had been stripped from the bed. There was an old blue blanket draped across the back of the sofa in the living room. She must have planned on using it her last night in the city.

I sank down on a kitchen chair in a room that suddenly seemed anything but hospitable. Where had she been so late the night before? According to the reports I'd committed to memory, she had no friends in the city, and like me, she didn't drink. That cut down significantly on the places she could have gone after dark. Maybe she'd simply taken a walk to clear her head as I was now trying to do. She'd disappeared from the streets about eleven, but fortunately for me and the mission I was now on, no one had seen it happen.

I suddenly pulled my bottom lip into my mouth and bit down hard. Here I was, doing it again! Trying to solve a puzzle when the most important pieces were missing. I might want to know what had occurred in the past, but it wasn't relevant to my current situation. I needed to do as Agent Banning had suggested—get my head in the game and keep it there. For what it was worth, I could find out everything I wanted to know about Tess when I got back. The government knew everything about us anyway—where we lived, who we talked to on the phone or contacted through texts or emails, every purchase and financial transaction, along with every relationship that left any kind of paper or Internet trail. It would terrify the public at large if they knew just how closely all their movements were being monitored, and I had access to all of it.

Still, I wished I had more practical information work with. It only stood to reason that if the United States Federal Government knew Tess Tremaine's exact moves, then so did the Mendoza cartel since she was about to become part of their organization, albeit only indirectly. At least that's what I was counting on. They relied on secrecy to keep their operations going and on threats and violence to take care of problems when they arose.

If Carlos Mendoza had any idea of what had just taken place, he would know I was a plant before I even arrived in Colombia. But even as my heart began to race again, I knew I couldn't give in to speculation. I had been trained to rely on facts and to trust my superior's judgment. The DEA must believe that the switch had been made unnoticed, or they wouldn't be taking such a calculated risk by involving another federal agency. And Assistant Director Bridges must have agreed with them, or he would never have allowed one of his rookie agents to become part of the mission.

Still, as hard as I tried to remain calm and objective during hours that seemed to drag on forever, my mind kept exploding with flashes of foreboding and dread. Just how much of the decision made to send me on this undercover assignment was due to my natural ability and training, and how much of it was simply my strong resemblance to a girl who had the made the choice to walk into a drug lord's compound in a foreign country where there would be no resources or help if the need arose—even if she didn't know what I did.

I wanted desperately to call my parents and let them know what had happened, but it was against the rules I had agreed to follow when accepting my badge. Mendoza's men could easily be watching my movements and contacts. That's why it had been necessary for me to alter my appearance before leaving the agency and why I'd been taken through tunnels instead of front doors. Any misstep on my part could mean detection, put an end to the mission and quite possibly my life.

So to help calm my nerves, I did the only thing I could. I sank to my knees in front of the worn sofa and prayed that God would protect me while I was on this perilous assignment, and that he would give comfort to my family when they found out that I was gone. Oh, how I wished I could see each one of them again before leaving and sit on the striped sofa in the family room eating popcorn, laughing and watching old movies.

I wouldn't even mind my brothers' constant teasing. Braydon, the cop, who tried to tell all of us what to do since he was the oldest and knew from experience just how bad the world had become; Austin, the contractor, who couldn't understand why some women preferred a career when they could stay home and raise children; Scott, the school teacher, who preferred coaching football to actual classroom work; and Adam, who had just begun his residency in hopes of being a heart surgeon someday.

We were all so very different, but we loved each other completely, just as we loved our parents, Tom and Julia Sinclair. The thought of never seeing them again pierced my heart with such force I almost cried out in physical pain. What if my father had been right all along? Placing myself in danger by choice was far different than having it happen by chance. What if I got into trouble I couldn't handle and my supposed contact wasn't around? What if I became the next Jane Doe in a faraway country where no one knew who I was or where I came from? Or even worse, what if I simply disappeared? My family would be heartbroken, never knowing what had happened to me.

Assistant Director Bridges would only tell them that I'd vanished on an undercover assignment. There would never be any closure until I was home or my body was found. The people I loved would just go on hoping, praying and worrying because family was everything to the Sinclair's. But then how could I ever have anticipated receiving an assignment that would take me out of the country with an agency I had not joined?

Stopping the spread of drugs was part of what I had been trained to do, but not in the way a member of the DEA had. They infiltrated organizations and were specifically educated in the tactics necessary for staying alive, whether they were dealing with cartel leaders, rebel forces who terrorized the locals, or government officials who had been paid handsomely to look the other way.

These swirling thoughts made my knees unsteady as I rose to my feet, so I sat down on the sofa with nothing to do until the cab arrived. It was a ground floor apartment and the street in front of the building was clearly visible from where I was sitting with my back erect and my feet planted firmly on the floor. I wondered who might be outside watching me. I couldn't seem to rid my mind of the idea that the cartel already knew that I wasn't the real Tess. That meant this assignment was going to be a game of cat and mouse where only the people with the most diabolical plan would win.

I tried to assess every aspect of what my mission might entail from landing in Colombia to the jungle and compound where I would be staying, but without documented information my thoughts were purely speculative. It would be easier carrying out the charade if I knew the identity of my contact. Working with a partner had become second nature, but relying on my instincts alone would be a new adventure I might not be prepared for.

While my thoughts were still in disarray, Tess's cell phone rang. The sudden, jarring sound made my heart race, and I felt the heat rush to my face. Would my superiors expect me to answer it? While we might resemble each other physically, our intonations would most certainly be different, and it might be a call from someone who had not been mentioned in her file. So, I waited with almost baited breath until the call was picked up by voice mail and then listened to what had been said.

"Why won't you return my calls?" a man said. "I'm worried about you, and so is Jill. Please get in touch with one of us so we can explain. We never meant to hurt you by falling in love."

I was tempted to pick up the phone, hit redial, and tell Luke Everett—the man who had supposedly broken Tess Tremaine's heart —exactly what his betrayal had cost the woman I was now trying to impersonate. If she hadn't felt it necessary to run away from an unbearable situation, she may never have dropped out of school or accepted a job with a drug lord in South America, but it would serve no useful purpose and could endanger what I'd begun. So, I took what pleasure I could in knowing that a little worry might do him a world of good.

I had been given a carry-on bag before leaving the agency but had yet to look inside. It was hard trying to reconcile what I was doing right now with how I'd been raised. Each life was precious to God and deserved to be honored, not exploited, but my job was to become immersed in Tess's life, even if her approval to do so had been forced. Besides, I'd have to open it at the airport anyway, and it would look suspicious if I had to fumble around for what I needed.

Tess's laptop was sitting on the top, but most of the hard drive had been wiped clean. That was standard operating procedure and made it easier for me because I would never have to explain the websites I'd visited or the e-mails I'd sent. Naturally, I knew that even deleted items were not completely gone. Any capable computer technician could find them in a matter of minutes, but I doubted that would become an issue now. Mendoza had hired her because he trusted that she would be loyal to him, and I seriously doubted there would be any form of satellite or electronic communication in the jungle.

There was a romance novel I would only read under duress since I wasn't into fantasy, a one-way plane ticket, traveler's checks that only amounted to a few hundred American dollars, a passport and all the other documents Colombia required so I could remain in that country and work. There were also a few toiletries, a tube of mascara, several granola bars and a diary. My heart almost skipped a beat when I flipped open the cover and saw her first entry in handwriting so neat it looked like calligraphy. I closed it rapidly not wanting to intrude on her private thoughts. At this point in my charade, I was having enough trouble just internalizing the fact that she had disappeared, and I had taken her place.

I wished there had been time to grab the book of scriptures I kept in my desk drawer at the agency, but I had been required to leave everything of a personal nature behind. I loved the feel of a book in my hands, especially since it was covered with soft leather and contained the Word of God. It would be hard not having anything besides faith, hope and prayer traveling with me. I hoped that would be enough.

While waiting for the cab to arrive, I played a few free games on her cell phone and paced the floor almost relentlessly. I even forced myself to look through her suitcases, but all they contained was clothing meant for a colder, damper climate, a few pieces of costume jewelry, a photo album with names and dates written on the backs of the few pictures it contained, a windup alarm clock, and a small statue of Christ and the Virgin Mary wrapped in paper and then put in the folds of one of the dresses she'd packed. There was one pair of jeans, some sturdy boots, a heavy jacket, and other items of clothing that could be layered as necessary.

The cabbie was cheerful when he loaded the suitcases I would be taking with me into the trunk of his car, but I was grateful the pane of glass that separated us during the drive had been closed. I was much too frightened to carry on a conversation with a stranger and glanced out the window several times to see if we were being followed, but it was rush hour, the freeways were busy, and vehicles were moving at such a rapid pace that keeping track of just one or two was nearly impossible. Either Mendoza's men didn't know about the switch, or they were waiting until I was no longer on American soil to do something about it. I paid the cabbie and then pulled the two suitcases through the front door into the terminal where I located the airline my ticket specified and got my bags checked for the flight.

It was hard making it through the security checkpoints without flinching, and then gathering up Tess's belongings once they had cleared the scanner, but I managed to do it. I knew at least two other FBI agents were at the airport with me. I spotted them just as I entered the building, but they were left behind the moment I proceeded to the gate where I had an hour to wait before boarding began.

I thought I noticed a look of concern from one of them as I stopped at the food court to grab a sandwich and a bottle of water, but I let it pass knowing that they were only doing their job, and I couldn't afford to look uncomfortable or conspicuous. I didn't feel much like eating again, and since it was an International flight we would be served a meal at some point, but I needed to be doing something with my hands. Once I left the United States, I would be at the mercy of whoever was there to pick me up. I even bought a magazine to read so I'd look more like the other travelers.

The terminal was filled with people, and I tried not to examine each new passenger that walked into the area where I was waiting for my flight. I was curious by nature—a trait I knew I had to curb if I wanted to stay alive—but no one appeared to give me more than a cursory glance or a simple smile. If this was to become a game where the winner took all, it may have already begun, and I was at a definite disadvantage because I didn't know any of the players. All I had was the name Carlos Mendoza running through my head.

It was more than a relief when boarding started, but once I found my seat and decided that the man sitting next to me was no risk, my circular thoughts began and didn't ease up as each hour in the air brought me closer to an uncertain future. They drifted from my lack of real field experience without known backup to the very real possibility that I might never return home to my family. I consoled myself with the knowledge that I knew where I had come from, why I was here, and where I would be going when I died. Those extraordinary resources of strength and solace alone were comforting, but I also had the companionship of the comforter given by Christ himself to direct my footsteps—if I was willing to listen and move when inspiration came.

My cover was solid, and if I didn't deviate from the task I'd been sent to do, I had every reason to believe I'd be safely home in a few days. I simply had to look at this as an experience every recruit hoped for—a chance to prove what he or she was worth to the bureau. Assistant Director Bridges would not be sending me into the field alone if he didn't believe I was ready, and I would find out who my contact was when I got there.

I managed to close my eyes and rest for a portion of the journey, even though the jet was large and people all around me were talking and milling about. I'd been given a window seat, so I knew the exact moment the South American Continent came into view. I had never seen anything so green. I'd looked up a few facts about Colombia on Tess's computer during the flight. It was one of the most biodiverse countries on the planet with 50,000 classes of plants and 18 percent of the world's bird species, most of them indigenous to the country.

With its vast tropical rain forests, it was a perfect place for the cultivation of coca, and unfortunately, that's what it was most known for. Four square meters of rainforest had to be cleared for every gram of cocaine processed. Cultivation of these illegal crops had led to the destruction of 2.2 million hectares of forest. I didn't know how large a hectare was, but the literature said it was larger than the country of Wales. That seemed significant to me.

The Colombian Minister for the Environment said he was tired of having images of violence describe his country. He wanted tourists to enjoy its beauty and to understand that the destruction of the rainforests was a travesty that could potentially impact the climate worldwide, in addition to causing the extinction of hundreds of species of plants and animals. It was a scenic country worth visiting and should not be thought of only as a place where the drug culture thrived.

I wished I was coming here for any other reason as we flew over the densest foliage I'd ever seen—miles and miles of mountains and green—a place to get lost in – a place to lose everything in. No wonder the drug lords had chosen the country to establish their empires. With its humid climate and land too rough to cross, unless one knew exactly where one was going, it was a place few people would venture, and I was soon to be part of it.

I felt a moment of panic when the pilot announced that it was time for passengers to return to their seats for the initial descent into Bogotá—Colombia's capital city. Had I been going there on a journey of discovery concerning some of the lost civilizations I'd studied about, instead of heading directly into the presence of a drug lord, my feelings might have been very different.

Still, a rush of excitement engulfed me as I looked down on the red tile roofs of houses and the steeples of tall ornate churches. In a few minutes, I would be walking the land of ancient civilizations where powerful societies had flourished, acquired great wealth and eventually succumbed to the baser instincts of man and lost everything. Pride, hatred, wickedness and waring were as much a part of our lives today as they had been centuries ago. That's why I was here now. Wanting enough money to live comfortably on wasn't wrong, but the obsession to acquire it by any means possible certainly was.

Where primeval cities and highways had once crossed the length and breadth of the land, now there were coca farmers, Marxist guerrilla bands, local armies, and drug lords ruling their own private kingdoms. It saddened me that people couldn't seem to learn from the past, but the fight between good and evil would continue until the end of the world. In some ways, I wanted to be alive when that happened, but I wasn't a huge fan of plaques, natural disasters and pain. And Armageddon didn't sound like a whole lot of fun.

The skies were overcast and a drizzle of rain was falling when the pilot landed. Along with all my other misconceptions, I'd always thought of South America as being hot and humid. I had the humid part right, but the city of Bogotá was far from being warm. It sat too high in the mountains and was too far away from the coast to be overly pleasant most of the year. And while I loved the rain, what I would experience here was nothing like Virginia since the average temperature was 57 degrees.

The sense of security I'd felt on the plane evaporated as I fought my way through the terminal, surrounded by people speaking dozens of languages I couldn't understand. If I were being totally honest with myself, I'd have to admit that despite the pep talks I'd been giving myself on the last part of my flight, I was scared. Scratch that! I was terrified!

Walking into the unknown had always produced an adrenalin rush, but in the past I'd had people around to turn to if things got rough. I just hoped my contact wouldn't keep me in waiting in suspense for too long. Without a way to protect myself, I was hopelessly vulnerable and ill prepared.

Nonetheless, here I stood in a city of over seven million strangers - any one of whom could be part of the enemy camp— waiting for Tess's suitcases to come down the conveyer belt. The assistant director had given me a sign with her name written in bold letters to hold above my head once I exited the terminal. I wondered if I would even make it that far.

What I was doing was so far on the other side of sanity that it was almost laughable. I watched as my fellow travelers retrieved their luggage, many of them smiling and chatting happily with the people nearest them. Mine would be easy to recognize. Fluorescent green ribbons had been tied around the handles making it easy to distinguish from among all the other black suitcases on the flight. I was almost shocked that I could call it mine, but I couldn't act surprised about anything. For all intents and purposes, I was now Tess Tremaine, born in Trenton, New Jersey, and on her way to take up the post of a governess.

While I stood in the open waiting for my luggage to arrive, I thought about the note I'd left in my office drawer for my family the day I started my job with the agency. It was a sort of final will and testament in case the unthinkable happened. I wanted my family to know how much I loved each one of them, and that I never wanted to do anything that would disappoint or bring them disgrace.

I had divided what few personal possessions I had amongst my brothers and their families, according to what I thought they might value most. Not that I had much to leave anyone other than a few books and some childhood toys and souvenirs, but I hoped what I'd left behind would help them remember how much I valued life even with my rather unconventional career choice.

My final act had been to write my personal thoughts and beliefs. I'd always been a religious person, having grown up in a home where the scriptures were regularly read and prayers were offered on more than just food. I loved my Savior and wanted to emulate him in every way. I knew my few words would never be enough if I didn't come home, but at least my family would know how I really felt inside. I believed that my vocation would help make the world a safer place, but I also believed that I had a responsibility to share Christ's message with anyone who was willing to listen. I couldn't do that very well in a world where chaos reigned.

Chapter 3

My sign had been in the air less than a minute when a man in a white shirt, tan pants and holding a wide-brimmed, straw hat in his hands approached me. I wondered why he wasn't wearing a jacket. I felt chilled to the bone even after putting on the coat Tess had zipped into the top of one of her bags.

It was impossible to guess his age, probably his mid-thirties, but he smiled reassuringly before speaking. He was handsome in a somber, brooding way with deep-set eyes, a straight angular nose and a cleft in his chin. His skin was dark, but not as dark as that of most of the people on the street outside the terminal. The shoes on his feet were worn and dust-covered.

"Miss Tremaine," he said in a voice that had lost much of the Spanish accent usually associated with native speakers as he surveyed my less than comely appearance. I almost wished I could remove the coat I'd put on. It seemed a little excessive now that I was standing next to him. "My name is Jorge Santos. Carlos Mendoza sent me to bring you to the hacienda."

He picked up my suitcases and started to walk away before I had time to reply. I numbly followed him as the seriousness of my situation washed over me again. I was in a foreign country, friendless, unarmed and headed into the jungle with a man I didn't know to the home of the head of one of the largest drug cartels in Colombia. I was carrying a fake passport, had no idea who oversaw the DEA or the American Embassy in this part of the world, had yet to find my contact, and only two men in Washington D.C. who knew where I was. But if I acted worried or upset, it would be a dead giveaway that I was not who I was pretending to be.

I stood silently in the cold mist as he put my bags in the back of what I could only call a ramshackle jeep with peeling paint, numerous dents and a cracked front windshield and then opened the passenger door for me. "I'm sorry, but you will have to ride up front with me."

I clutched the bag that held the personal papers I'd been given close to me as Jorge Santos walked around the front of the jeep, and then climbed in beside me and started the engine. The noise reminded me of the backfiring of a motorcycle, and I inadvertently jumped.

He smiled but didn't look at me.

"I trust you had a good flight. Señor Mendoza is anxious for you to arrive to teach his children."

"Is it a long drive?" I asked while my heart beat more rapidly than it ever had before. It seemed like a safe question, and I didn't want him to think of me as being totally helpless, even if I was supposed to be unassuming and shy.

"Oh, Miss Tremaine, it will be several hours before we get there. I will take you to a private airstrip about two hours outside of the city. The hacienda is far up in the mountains. There will be a short plane ride and then another hour over some of the worst roads in all of Colombia. But you do not need to worry. You will be perfectly safe with me."

His words were almost laughable. He was one of Mendoza's men, and as such, I didn't feel perfectly safe at all. Trusting him with anything other than a little polite conversation was a mistake I couldn't afford to make.

"I hope so," I whispered to myself as I looked down at my hands that were clasped so tightly together around the bag I had been carrying that my knuckles had turned a pasty-looking white. I should have relinquished it to the floor of the jeep, but it was the only lifeline I had left. For all intents and purposes, I was now at his mercy.

I watched from a side window as the tall white buildings of Bogotá turned into a rural landscape where farmers were at work in their fields of coffee and corn, wearing broad brimmed hats despite the lack of sun. I was glad I'd come in the summer. I couldn't imagine the country in the winter. In just the short distance we had traveled, the unequal distribution of wealth was clearly evident between the haves of the city and the have not's outside its border. No wonder so many people in the country turned to the cartels for a living. The drug trade was far more profitable than farming or other manual labor.

Jorge whistled as we rode along in silence, but my mind was never still. I'd researched the Colombian jungles during the flight, and I had more to fear than the human animal in the compound if I wasn't extracted as planned. Every body of water contained leeches, piranhas, crocodiles, electric eels, canderas and thousands of other flesh-eating creatures. The land wasn't any better. There were large predator cats, vampire bats, and poisonous spiders that had been known to bite through boots. There were hornets, bees, wasps, army ants and mosquitoes that brought malaria, typhus and yellow fever. There were also poison tree frogs and hundreds of poisonous snakes like the coral, cobra, pit vipers, and bushmaster.

Thinking of all the potential dangers, it was hard to remember that Colombia was also the home to anteaters, sloths, several species of monkeys, speckled bears, deer, giant turtles, orchids and other fragrant, delicate flowers, and more than 1,500 species of birds like the toucan and hummingbird—all things that visitors traveled thousands of miles to see. I hoped that during my brief stay, I would only come in contact with the latter.

I tired not to look worried or distraught and we bounced along a road that was much in need of repairs. No wonder his jeep looked like it did. I was afraid we might hit a pothole and lose a tire, if the whole vehicle didn't fall apart first. I wanted to think of something clever to say that might give me an indication of what I could expect when we got to the hacienda, but I knew the real Tess would already have that information and observance was my best defense at present.

So we drove for over an hour and a half without saying anything, and I was more than a little hungry by the time we made it to a small airstrip somewhere on the exterior of the jungle. My escort had offered me nothing to eat or to drink, and I was too afraid to ask for any considerations. Jorge Santos seemed harmless and friendly enough, but he still worked for Carlos Mendoza. That meant I needed to be both cautious and watchful. One unfortunate slip with him, and my assignment could well be over for good.

Fortunately, the fact that I was still sitting in a rickety, old jeep meant that my deception had not yet been uncovered. For if it had, I would not have made it out of the city alive, unless they were planning my demise in a much less populated place. His words about the dangers of the jungle road we had yet to travel had not gone unnoticed. I imagined that an accident of any sort could happen quite easily and could be readily explained to his boss—especially if any kind of pretense was suspected.

"Welcome," said a man in soiled, wrinkled clothing who was missing one of his front teeth when he came out of a small wooden shack to greet us.

"Thank you," I replied, pushing the glasses I was wearing up on my nose. They were uncomfortable but part of the disguise. Luckily for me, the lenses had been exchanged for clear glass, or it would have been impossible to see through them without getting a headache or eyestrain.

He extended a grimy hand in my direction. There was grease underneath his fingernails and in every crease. I was taken aback by his overall unkempt appearance but took his offered hand anyway because it seemed like the right thing to do.

"It's a fine day for flying," he continued, shaking my hand enthusiastically. "I have the plane ready to go, but there is hot coffee inside if you would like some while Jorge and I get the luggage on board. There is also a bathroom around back for your convenience."

I was amazed that he spoke English, even with a very pronounced accent, and I was grateful for his kindness. But I'd never tasted coffee and wasn't about to start drinking it now. A large fly touched my cheek. I frowned and brushed it away.

"If you think the flies are big here," the man laughed. "Just wait until you get to the hacienda. Everything grows much bigger, higher in the mountains."

"Don't listen to him," Jorge said with a toothy smile that made him look more like a jungle cat than my escort. "He's never even been there. He just wants to impress you. Beautiful women don't come this way very often."

If Jorge Santos and the man at the small airstrip were trying to flatter me into revealing something I shouldn't, it wasn't working, but I smiled demurely anyway before lowering my eyes to the ground. It was what I imagined Tess would do. She would find it hard to trust men after her boyfriend's betrayal and being away from them might be one of the reasons that brought her to the jungle where she would only have to deal with children.

My stomach was doing somersaults as I made my way around the building. The room that stood ready for my use was filthy, from the nearly black-stained toilet to the sink with dripping water. I tried not to touch anything without a paper towel in my hand. This was not the way I'd envisioned the journey. Drug lords were powerful, wealthy people. They could afford the best accommodations possible, so why all the squalor? Maybe it was meant to drive me away before I even got there.

The two men had the suitcases aboard the small plane by the time I came back to the clearing. My eyes quickly took in my surroundings from the faded exterior of the metal - roofed shack that housed both the living quarters and the office of the man who took care of the landing strip, to the jeep without a hard top that we'd arrived in, to the nearby trees and foliage that was so thick it was impossible to see inside. It was the perfect place to dispose of a body, if that's what they intended on doing with me. I pulled Tess's coat closer around my chest, wishing I had something on my feet other than sandals.

"Are you ready?" Jorge asked as he sipped hot, brown liquid from a cup, and eyed me with a curious look I didn't understand. "We could wait a few minutes if you'd like some coffee. I'm sure food is being prepared for your arrival, but it will be a few hours before we get there."

I forced a smile I did not feel. "Thank you both for your generosity and kindness, but I'm not sure my stomach would handle it right now."

Jorge laughed, and the shorter man, who was standing not a great distance away from him, snorted in amusement. It sounded as though what I had said brought both of them a great deal of enjoyment. I wondered just how many people had been taken to the compound this way, and how many of them appeared as frightened as I did. It certainly lent credibility to my ruse.

"You don't have to be afraid of the plane, Miss Tremaine," Jorge said. "Looks can be deceiving, and I'm a very good pilot as you will soon see."

"I'm sure you are," I told him, as I tried not to stare at the small aircraft that would soon be flying over the mountain ridges with me inside. From its color and design, it must have been built during World War II and had not received the best care during the interim of years, but I had to believe it was safe, or he wouldn't be willing to take up - with or without me in it.

Jorge threw the remainder of his coffee onto the ground and then handed the cup to his companion. "We'll see you in a few days. I'm sure the boss will have another errand of one kind or another for me to run."

"All will be ready for your arrival," the man replied.

Jorge then motioned for me to climb inside. I thought he might offer assistance like he'd done at the airport, but apparently chivalry had been left behind in the city. I wondered if the law of the jungle really was every man for himself as I'd been led to believe.

The propeller on the nose of the plane made an awful noise as Jorge Santos started the engine, but the grinding sound didn't seem to bother him.

"Don't worry," he told me as he taxied onto the short runway that began and ended with trees and underbrush. "I've flown this plane a hundred times. It's perfectly capable of getting us over the mountains, and I'm sure you'll soon agree that it's far preferable to spending nine additional hours driving. The roads are barely more than trails, and they can be treacherous after even the slightest rain."

I wasn't sure of anything at that moment, except that my chance to turn back was over. Once I got to the hacienda, I'd be at the mercy of a truly ruthless and evil man who might already be behind the deaths of numberless people, including his wife and quite possibly one of the DEA's undercover agents.

I closed my eyes and said a quick prayer as the airplane's wheels left the ground with a sickening thud, then I looked out of the small window at the man who was waving his hat in the cold, muggy air. Oh, how I wished I were back on the ground with him, but I had promised to serve my country, and I never went back on what I had committed to do. We hit an air pocket before we cleared the trees, and I inadvertently screamed.

Jorge shot me an impatient glance. "Just sit back and try to relax, Miss Tremaine. The mountain air is unpredictable."

I closed my eyes again and tried not to let what he'd said bother me. There was no need to pretend that I wasn't afraid. The real Tess Tremaine would be equally as frightened flying over the tops of trees with no houses or people in sight, in a rusty two-seater aircraft that was being flown by a man she knew nothing about.

I had hoped that my contact would make a connection before the city was left behind, but of the two men I'd met, neither appeared to be anything other than what they appeared--loyal employees of a very dangerous man. Their fluency with English was a little surprising, but Carlos Mendoza would pick his men carefully. He would want to make sure that those in key positions understood what was going on around them, and since America was his biggest place of distribution, it only stood to reason that he would want them to speak English.

"I'm sorry I screamed. It just caught me off guard," I told Jorge Santos a few moments later, after the blood had quite pounding so unmercifully in my head. "I've never been in a such a small plane before."

"Not many people have," he replied, checking gauges and knobs on the instrument panel. "Relaxing the body does help. It won't take long to arrive at our destination. Mendoza was going to send for you in one of his choppers, but they were needed elsewhere."

"Does he have many of those?" I asked, not really surprised that my safe arrival was not high on his list of priorities. After all, I wasn't a business partner or even a valuable contact, I was merely a teacher for his children.

"A few. Our employer is a very rich man."

Oh, how I wanted to pump him for additional information, but my orders had been clear. Find out what happened to Agent Gonzales and get out. I couldn't do that if I aroused suspicion before I even arrived at the hacienda where she'd last been seen.

There was nothing below us, but dark, green vegetation. I couldn't tell where one mountain ridge ended and the next one began, and there wasn't a single landmark visible to help me establish in which direction we were headed, or how we would ever get out of the jungle unless it was by plane or helicopter.

"I'm glad we're not going by jeep after what you told me about the perils of traveling that way," I said. Even Tess Tremaine would not be indifferent to her surroundings, and the difference between where she had come from and where she would now be living was immense. Besides, a little conversation might keep me from worrying so much about the safety of the ramshackle plane I was flying in.

"It is wise to be aware," he said without taking his eyes from the murky sky in front of us. We were above the tree line, though not above the clouds. "But you don't have to worry as long as you stay inside the compound and do as you are told. There are guards posted everywhere. No one and nothing enters or leaves without being noticed."

I wondered if he was warning me that escape was futile, regardless of the reason. Perhaps my superiors had been a little premature in telling me that I could leave as soon as I found out what had happened to their missing agent. If her cover had been blown, she would never have been allowed to get away. And even if she had managed to get out of the compound—which seemed highly unlikely—she would never survive for long in the jungle. Between Mendoza's henchmen and the wild animals I knew so little about, it seemed very unlikely that she was still alive.

The DEA could have proceeded on that premise rather than involving me, but perhaps her careful placement in the household was crucial for the planned raid. If that were true, there might be a great deal I needed to learn before my own getaway was orchestrated, including the safety of the young charges I had yet to meet.

After what seemed an eternity in the air, I saw the red roofs of several buildings encircled by a brick wall. We were too high and far away to see much of anything else.

"Is that the hacienda?" I asked, quite forgetting in my relief that the flight was almost over that he'd already told me another jeep ride was necessary before we arrived at our final destination.

"No," Jorge said with a chuckle. "That's where the workers live. We're about five miles from the hacienda, but we'll set put down here and go the rest of the way by jeep. It's the closest place to land."

I was going to ask him what they did, but no one in the twenty-first century could be that dumb. They couldn't be farmers or herders unless planting and harvesting cocaine counted. I wondered if they fully understood what they were helping a drug lord do. While coca leaves had been used for centuries in religious rituals and as medicine to alleviate pain for the South American Indians, other people were using it to alter reality, and in so doing, countless lives were being destroyed and lost. It seemed a senseless travesty to me.

It also made me realize that Tess Tremaine must have known exactly the kind of life she was entering. She was neither obtuse nor naïve, but it seemed entirely out of character from what I'd read about her. She went to church each Sunday, attended Bible classes, and she didn't drink or smoke. There had to be more to her story than I'd been led to believe. Being cheated on was not reason enough to enter the criminal world. She had to have been recruited by either the DEA or Mendoza himself. Nothing else made any sense.

We circled twice before landing. Like the airstrip we'd flown from, this one was surrounded by heavy vegetation that made me wonder just what lived inside its borders since it was so close to the village and how foolish I would be if I stepped inside of it to see. I was amazed at Jorge Santos ability to take off and land in such a tight space, but he made flying a plane look easy.

After what I'd been through since my arrival in Colombia, I wasn't prepared for the reception I got when we left the plane. I expected to see more men like the one I'd met at the airstrip, but instead, a dozen barefoot, smiling children ran out to greet us. Some were carrying wildflowers, others had bananas or a type of citrus fruit I didn't recognize in their brown, unclean hands. They were dancing around and chattering happily in a heavy dialect that was totally unrecognizable, even with my knowledge of the Spanish language.

"What are they saying?" I asked Jorge as he put my two suitcases on the bare ground beneath our feet.

"They are welcoming you to their home, although you won't be staying here with them."

"I wish I could," I told him as a second child added more flowers to the ones I was already holding. Their dark-skinned, smiling faces brought tears to my eyes. It was so apparent that they lived in poverty with their tattered clothing, dirty bodies and bare feet, but they were still infused with the purity of childhood.

"Where are their parents?" I stupidly asked as I tried to put my arms around all of them at the same time. It seemed an appropriate thing to do since I'd come to Colombia to assume the role of a governess, but it was more than that. These little ones were God's children, whether they knew it or not.

"They work in the fields in the daytime."

"But who takes care of them? They shouldn't be left alone all day."

"Things here are not like where you come from. The old ones look after the children when they're not sleeping."

There were goats, pigs, chickens and old mangy dogs running around the fenced off yard, a few even came out of the buildings that must have been the homes of the people who lived there. Since there were no doors, I noticed that while the houses might have roofs, the floors were earthen and there was no heat or plumbing. It was cold and damp and would only grow worse as the night came on.

Apparently, drug lords didn't care how the people they employed lived.

But it was the children themselves who tugged at my heartstrings. My eyes sought each upturned face as little boys and girls stepped away from me. Every essence radiated complete joy and a willingness to share—meager though their possessions might be. Would I find the same light of Christ when I met Carlos Mendoza's children at the hacienda? I certainly hoped so. They must never be held accountable for the kind of man their father was.

"Oh, how the Savior must love these little ones," I thought as they followed me to the jeep on the far side of the small courtyard. I shivered despite the sun that was trying to peak out from beneath the gray, clouded sky. It was even colder in the mountains than it had been in Bogotá, and the children were wearing thin clothing with no shoes.

Jorge must have noticed my frown. "Don't worry about them," he said. "They know how to keep warm. You'll soon find out that no one goes outside after dark. It isn't safe anywhere in the jungle, and those dogs you see running around do more than offer companionship and food."

I felt another cold wave wash over me. Perhaps my senses were heightened because of the place I was in, but once again, I wondered if Jorge was giving me another warning.

"I'll remember that," I told him as I forced what I hoped would not be interpreted as a false smile. "You must get a lot of rain. Everything is so green."

It was a ridiculous thing to say, but he didn't chastise me as my own boss had done so recently.

"We get enough," he said as he motioned for me to get in so we could be on our way. This jeep didn't have a front window for added protection and was coated in so many ayers of dried mud it was impossible to tell what color it was. My suitcases had been thrown unceremoniously behind the two seats.

I held onto the door as we drove past the children who were now waving at us. Oh, how I wanted to take all of them home with me and find loving families that would provide them with something other than just the bare necessities of life, but this was the way they had always lived. I might not understand but interfering wasn't wise.

We bumped along what appeared to be nothing more than an unkempt trail. The vegetation was so close to us that every minute or two I had to duck or be caught across the face by a vine or a branch that needed to be cleared away.

"Is this the only way in and out of the compound?" I asked, before realizing how dangerous to my safety the question might be.

He looked at me from the corner of one eye. "Someone not accustomed to our way of life should never be overly inquisitive," he said. "It isn't healthy."

My heart nearly missed a beat. He was too articulate to be one of the planters and harvesters. Most likely, he was a member of Carlos Mendoza's inner circle of thugs and thieves and was looking for something that might give me away. Only someone who had proven his loyalty would be charged with the task of escorting the new governess to a place of secrecy.

"I'm sorry if I said something out of line," I replied. "I hope you can understand that this is my first time outside the United States, and it's all a little overwhelming."

"What made you come to such a place?" he asked. "It has been my experience that no one comes here unless they're hiding from something or from someone."

The directness of his question startled me.

"I'm not sure what you're implying," I replied. "I came because I love children. Is that so hard to understand?"

"Nothing surprises me, Miss Tremaine, and I understand human nature far better than you might think. I have been at the hacienda for many years and know exactly how Señor Mendoza conducts both his personal life and his business enterprises. You would do well to remember that his home is his castle, and nothing goes on within those walls that he isn't aware of."

The jeep hit another deep pothole that forced me up and out of my seat. I gasped but didn't cry out as I had done on the plane. I had not forgotten the look of impatience and distain he had given me then.

"I didn't mean to offend you, or your position in his household. It's just that I'm anxious to find out more about my new home and the people I'll be working with."

"Your restraint when it comes to curiosity would be to your advantage," he responded, but did not look in my direction. "While our employer is a generous, tolerant man, he is not fond of questions. He expects the people who work for him to do exactly as they are told, and he will not tolerate anyone snooping around. He demands complete loyalty, or consequences will be executed."

This warning was even more compelling than the last one. Did part of Jorge Santos' responsibilities include getting rid of irritating problems? He might seem civilized on the outside, but everyone had secrets and pretense was a game many people enjoyed playing.

The heaviness in my chest made me turn my attention back to the rutted road, the isolation and the task that loomed ahead. I had to find out what had happened to Agent Gonzales and then figure out how to get away from a compound I had yet to see, but suddenly, that simple strategy seemed to have more holes in it than a spaghetti strainer. I couldn't just walk off the job as had been implied when I met with the assistant director. I was hundreds of miles away from civilization, and there was no one around to watch my back.

I felt more alone and vulnerable than I had when the assignment had first been offered. My training was supposed to prepare me for anything, but so far it only served as a reminder of just how much I didn't know and how ill-prepared I was to be in the field without a partner I could depend on.

"It won't be long now," Jorge said, and I noticed that his fingers were gripping the steering wheel tighter than they had before. "I hope you'll find exactly what you're looking for here."

His statement intrigued me. Could he possibly be my contact and was just keeping a low profile until the time was right to reveal his identity, or was he simply saying that I deserved anything that happened to me since I'd been stupid enough to come?

"I'm sure I will," I said, staring straight ahead. "I've always loved children."

That was true. I did love children, and I spent all the time I could with my nieces and nephews. That's what happened when one was the youngest child and only girl in a larger-than-normal family. I'd changed plenty of diapers, read hundreds of stories, and had given horseback rides more often than I could remember, but the children had mostly gone home with their parents at night, except for the occasional sleepovers where my mother had taken over all the hard work. I'd mainly been around to make sure everyone had fun.

Something hit my cheek, and I swatted it away. Reality check! My mother wasn't here to help me, and this wasn't a casual sleepover with people I knew and loved. I had never met the children involved, and I wasn't sure they would even like me. The only thing I knew was that I already loathed their father.

And then I saw the tall iron gates in front of us. To each side was a tower, and inside each tower was a man holding a machine gun with a strap of ammunition hanging over his shoulder. I involuntarily shivered as Jorge stopped the jeep and called out, in Spanish, to the man on the left tower.

"Tell Juan to open the gates. I have the new governess with me."

Another man carrying a machine gun appeared from behind the compound gates and pushed them open. When I looked up, I noticed that guards with additional automatic weapons and plenty of bullets had been stationed at intervals along the top of the compound walls for as far as the eye could see. There were others on the ground that watched as the jeep moved forward. I could feel their eyes on me.

I had been sent on a suicide mission. The DEA must have known what would happen if I arrived at the compound unprotected, but they'd issued their request anyway. As for me, I'd been so determined to prove my worth that I'd walked into a situation without adequate preparation. Even if my contact materialized, I wasn't sure I'd ever leave the compound alive.

We drove past several large buildings that could have been used for anything from housing members of the cartel to storing coca leaves or carefully measured blocks of cocaine. But their contents didn't really matter; my assignment began on the inside of the house. I had to clap my hands together to keep them from trembling when Jorge stopped in front of a lovely, white, stucco house with a courtyard that was filled with flowers and blossoming trees. One of the gardeners glanced up but went right back to his weeding.

"It's lovely," I said as I pushed opened the jeep door and planted my feet firmly on a dirt driveway that had been hard-packed by constant use. I was tired, dust-covered and famished, but I was not about to say anything when a man in shirtsleeves and riding pants walked out of the front door and across a flagstone patio towards us.

"Ah, good Jorge," he said, cracking his riding crop against the palm of his hand. If the movement was meant to disarm me, it certainly did. "I see you have found our new American governess."

He reached for my hand and lifted it to his lips.

"It is so good you have come this long distance to teach my children, Miss Tremaine. Their mother, God rest her soul, was taken from us several years ago, and their former teacher has become, what you Americans might call, indisposed."

My new boss had obviously been educated abroad. His English was excellent, and his accent hardly noticeable. I tried to focus on what he was saying, rather than the movement of the guards that had joined him on the front portico of the hacienda.

He wasn't particularly tall, just a few inches taller than me, but there was something about him that commanded more than respect. This was a man to be feared. I had no doubt that he was capable of anything, even killing the mother of his own children. His lips were curled into a welcoming smile, but the icy gleam in his eyes made me want to shrink away from him, and I could ill afford to do that when I'd been the one to accept his offer of employment.

"I'm very happy to be here," I said, hoping there wasn't a note of apprehension or fear in my voice. He would detect it like a Bloodhound searching for little foxes. "Will I be meeting the children soon?"

"Soon enough," he said.

He'd been looking at me from head to foot with the practiced eyes of a predator. It would be easy to get caught up in his spell of intrigue. I wondered if that was what had happened to Agent Gonzales. Indisposed could mean anything.

"But first," he said, extending his arm to me. "I trust you could use a hot shower and some tea. I will have Rosa show you to your room. We dine at seven. I have permitted the children to eat with us this evening since it is such a special occasion."

I allowed myself to be escorted across the flagstone to the ornately carved front doors of what might become my last place of residence.

"The flowers are very lovely, Señor Mendoza," I said.

"Ah," he said, stopping to break off one of the red roses that was just starting to unfold. A thorn pricked his finger, but he didn't respond like most American men would have done with a curse. He merely looked at the blood on his fingertips as if he was used to seeing far more of it, and then casually rubbed it away.

"Roses are truly beautiful," he said, extending the flower to me. "But it pales in comparison to such a lovely young lady as yourself. Your photo did not do you justice, Miss Tremaine."

"Thank you, Señor Mendoza," I replied, fighting back the feeling I had of a fly being lured into a spider's web. I pushed the unfamiliar glasses higher up on my nose. I wondered if that might have been what the real Tess Tremaine would have done had she been the one standing here instead of me.

He opened the door to the hacienda, and the opulence, order and warming light nearly took my breath away it was in such stark contrast to the earthy and murderous feeling outside. But I knew better than to be taken in by such peaceful appearing surroundings. Tess Tremaine's boss was a monster who would not hesitate having me killed if I got in his way.

Underneath my feet was rose-colored marble, and I was standing in an entry the size of my entire apartment. A wrought-iron staircase dominated the center of the room and curved slightly to the right and upwards until it connected to a balcony that was at least 30 feet higher than the main floor of the house.

To the right, a door stood open, exposing a large, formal dining room with a mammoth bouquet of fresh flowers in the center of a dark, wooden table. To the left, a double set of heavy mahogany doors kept hidden whatever stood behind them. A crystal chandelier hung from the ceiling with an elaborately carved table underneath, and a tall marble statue of a partially clad woman stood on top of it.

The walls were made of whitewashed adobe and numerous portraits and landscapes with small lights illuminating them had been masterfully hung individually or in small groupings. It was a residence fit for a king, and I had no doubt that Carlos Mendoza viewed himself as such. Even the way he stood with his riding crop still in his hand let me know that the drug business was booming, and he had the loyalty of everyone who surrounded him.

He watched me until my expression told him I was suitably impressed, and then he pulled on a velvet cord, releasing the sound of a bell that could easily be heard most any place in the house if the stucco walls weren't sufficiently thick. It seemed ostentatious and a little old fashioned, but then I was in a different world where modern conveniences had been given up so complete control could prevail.

A Spanish woman with her hair braided and wrapped around her head like a halo came out from behind a less noticeable door to join us. She was wearing a black, silk dress and looked every bit as formidable as the man who was now my boss. She inclined her head in his direction but only glanced at me.

"Is this the new governess?" she asked in English that was far less fluent than that of her employer, but easily understood anyway.

"It is, Alma," he replied. "I hope she meets with your approval."

"Time will tell," she said, giving me another quick glance that I was more than certain missed nothing about my appearance or my demeanor. "Her room has been prepared as requested."

"Very good," he said. "Perhaps you can have Rosa show her the way since I am sure you are busy with other matters."

I was puzzled by their interaction, but I was given no explanation or formal introduction.

"As you wish," she said, clapping her hands loudly together.

Another door, somewhere out of my line of vision, opened and a young woman also dressed in black, but wearing a white apron, came hurrying towards us. She looked far more approachable than the people I had already met, but there was a look of fearful apprehension in her eyes that made the knot in my stomach tighten. She might be loyal, but she was afraid.

"Rosa, show our new governess, Miss Tremaine, to her rooms and draw her a warm bath," the formidable Alma ordered.

"Sí, madame, I will take her there directly," she responded.

The wave of Alma's hand was nonchalant, and I was certain it meant dismissal for both of us.

"If you will follow me," Rosa continued in her halted English as she looked quickly in my direction.

I turned to thank my new boss, but he had silently and almost mysteriously disappeared, as had the woman named Alma, so I followed Rosa up the staircase and down a long hallway. She opened the door at the end and then stood back so I could enter the tastefully decorated room that was to be my new home.

My bags were sitting on the floor at the end of a dark wooden bed with a snowy white coverlet on it. White draperies had been pulled back, exposing French doors that led to a second-floor balcony.

Rosa pointed to the armoire where my clothes could be put and then escorted me to the bathroom where warm water was already filling a stand-alone ceramic tub supported by claw feet that was both quaint and charming.

White towels had been laid out for me to use, and lavender oil had been poured in my bath water. Its distinctive smell permeated both the bath and the bedroom.

"Is there anything else you might need?" she said in a tone that was meant to reduce the intensity of her accent. She was a small woman, barely five feet in height and had the saddest, dark eyes I had ever seen. I instantly wanted to make her life easier.

"Everything is perfect," I told her with a smile. "Thank you so much."

"Put your soiled clothing in the basket on the floor, and they will be washed and ready for you in the morning."

"Thank you," I said again as she began opening the first of my suitcases. I was about to tell her that I could do the unpacking myself, but something told me that was one of her duties, and it would only make her job more difficult if I didn't adhere to their practices and customs.

Had I been in such a lovely place under different circumstances, I might have felt like a pampered princess. The rooms I was meant to enjoy were spotlessly clean, and when I stepped onto the balcony, the smell of the tropical flowers in the garden below filled the air with the sweetest fragrance imaginable.

I could see stone walkways, fountains, perfectly trimmed grass, and shrubs and flowers of every hue imaginable. It was like a storybook land. Then suddenly the heavy clouds of the day darkened, and a mist of rain that would turn into a downpour began.

I wrapped my arms around my body, stepped back into the room and closed the doors. Suddenly I was cold, colder than I had ever been before. The dampness of the air outside and the rising fear inside of me made my knees so weak I could barely walk across the room.

What had I done? I was in a heavily guarded prison with a man who killed people who disobeyed. Agent Maria Gonzales was likely one of them, and if I wasn't perfectly convincing in my role, I would be next.

In the past, I had often engaged in idle chatter to pass time and get to know people better, but every word uttered from this point on had to be carefully selected. I hoped I could do it, but the reality was that if I didn't, I would never see my family and friends again. That was a very sobering thought.

Chapter 4

It felt good to be clean and warm again after I climbed from my bath, and I desperately wanted to drop down onto the bed and sleep for hours, days if possible, but just as I finished dressing in one of the outfits I found among Tess's clothes that had already been hung in the wardrobe for me, I heard another bell ring. Glancing at the alarm clock on my nightstand, I saw that it was fifteen minutes to seven. Carlos Mendoza would soon be waiting for me downstairs.

But before leaving my room, I took my passport, traveler's checks, and the other important papers I had been given by the agency and slipped them far underneath the armoire where I hoped no one would ever look. Those documents were my lifelines to home. Without them, I would never be able to leave Colombia.

Rosa was waiting outside my door. I wondered if her duties included making sure I was never left alone. She escorted me down the marble staircase, through the double doors that had been closed at my arrival and into a massively impressive study where more books than could be read in a lifetime lined most of the walls.

Carlos Mendoza had dressed for dinner in a black suit, edged with red piping, along with a white, ruffled shirt that was open at the neck. It was just like the ones I'd seen in old Spanish westerns at the cinema. He was standing in front of a blazing fire with a goblet of red wine in one hand, watching the liquid as he tipped the glass back and forth. In his other hand was a brown cigarette of some kind. The smell was unpleasant, but not intolerable if I didn't have to endure it for long.

"Ah, Miss Tremaine," he said in a honey smooth voice. "Could I pour you some wine? Dinner will be served when the children arrive."

"No, thank you," I replied, clasping my hands together behind my back so they wouldn't betray the nervousness I felt inside.

"Ah, what a shame," he said, peering intently at me from over the rim of his glass. "I own some of the finest vineyards in the country, and my wines . . ." He brought his thumb and index finger together and kissed them with an outward thrust. "What can I say, other than they are truly superb? You do not know what you are missing."

I forced an unfelt smile. "I'm afraid the quality of your very superb wine would be lost on me since I have nothing to compare it with."

"That is too bad," he said as he threw the remainder of his cigarette in the fireplace and took a step towards me. I felt every hair on my body bristle with apprehension and disgust. "I understand that you drank none of the tea that was taken to your room earlier. Are you to refuse every beverage we have to offer?"

It was only then that I remembered the tray that had been sitting on the round table in one corner of my room. I had been too anxious to even look at what it contained before it was removed.

"Not all, Señor Mendoza," I replied. "I hope I haven't offended you already."

"I am not easily provoked, and it is not every day that a young woman, such as yourself, leaves the country of her birth to take up residence in a foreign land. I am sure there has been much to occupy your mind. Besides, gluttony and excess are sins to be avoided."

I almost choked on the irony of his words. If anyone had chosen to indulge in a life of hedonism, it was the man standing in front of me now. But it occurred to me that if I was going to survive the evening meal and remain true to myself in the process, he might as well know about the other things I refused to drink. It would be one less thing I had to worry about in trying to maintain my cover.

"Then I hope you will not be upset when I tell you that I do not drink coffee or tea in addition to any form of alcohol. It is purely a personal choice. I suppose that sounds rather odd to you."

"To refuse all our most important exports, yes! But I find it rather quaint and charming. It tells me you have both courage and conviction since you are willing to stand up to me when we have just met. Those are traits not to be taken lightly in the care of children. You see, Miss Tremaine, I remember from your resume and letter that you do not drink alcohol, but it has been my experience that most people can be swayed into doing anything if the enticement is right."

My brow furrowed. He'd been testing me. Had he done the same thing with Agent Gonzales?

"You frown, Miss Tremaine, but I was only seeing if you were to remain true to your convictions once you left home. I can tell already that you will be a good influence for my children."

"I hope so," I said, more than grateful that my ruse still appeared to be intact. "Children are precious and deserve special care."

I thought about all the barefoot children I had met only hours earlier when the plane had landed outside their small village. Who was there to protect them when all the adults were either working or sleeping?

"You are so right, Miss Tremaine, the blessed Virgin watches over all children. Mine are no exception. We have few modern conveniences like television, phones and the ever-important Internet, but our religion is very important to us. Father Francis lives in one of our cottages and comes several times a week for confession and communion. I understand that you do not share our religious beliefs, but you will be expected to attend services along with the children and the rest of the staff."

"Of course," I said, wondering how such an evil and ruthless man could consider himself religious. As for his children, my heart ached for them already, and I hadn't even seen their faces.

"I hope you will be happy here, Miss Tremaine," he continued, as I stood there wishing the time would move more quickly.

I didn't like nor trust this man. He might appear charming, but I knew who he really was, and I was going to help bring him down.

"Most people find the jungle oppressive and harsh, but there is nothing to fear as long as you stay inside the compound and do as you are told," he continued.

There it was, another warning. Had Agent Gonzales not listened to his warnings, and was that the reason she was missing and presumed dead?

"I would never take the dangers of the jungle lightly," I told him.

"That is good," he replied. "Everything you could possibly need will be supplied. All you have to do is ask Alma or one of the other servants. There will never be any reason for you to leave the hacienda, unless it is under my supervision, of course."

"Of course," I said again, making sure I did not look away from him, even though I knew the real Tess Tremaine was much more reticent than I. Carlos Mendoza needed to know that while I respected him as my employer and would do as he said, I was still my own person, and my individuality would not be stripped away by either coercion or fear.

Fortunately, the children came into the room just then, rescuing me from more conversation with my repugnant boss. They were beautiful, truly glorious descendants of the earliest inhabitant of the continent, and I found myself immediately drawn to them as both a protector and a friend. They deserved so much more than being forced to live in a compound with a drug lord for a father, completely cut off from the rest of humanity. I wondered if they had been born there and what had possessed their mother to become involved with such a truly evil man.

"Come Isabel, Luis," Carlos Mendoza motioned for his children to move farther into the room. They seemed to be hesitating in the doorway. "I want you to meet your new governess. Miss Tremaine has come to us from the United States. I want you to use your best manners and show her just how good your English is. Miss Tremaine does not speak Spanish so you will have to be patient with her while she learns our ways. They will be new and confusing to her at first."

Clearly, that was another threat, sugarcoated to sound innocent, but I understood its meaning. I had no rights, no friends and no way to escape except through a jungle filled with wild animals, dangerous reptiles and war-faring guerrillas with machine guns. I was completely at his mercy and would have to do exactly as he said if I wanted to remain alive. Oh, how I wished I had never come.

"Yes, Father," they said in unison as they walked closer to me.

Isabel was the oldest—a child of seven with luxurious, dark hair that had been brushed until it shined and a look of grim determination of her face. Luis was two years younger with his hands hanging at his sides and sad, brown eyes that told me he couldn't remember what it felt like to be truly loved. He must have been no more than a baby when his mother died. I wasn't sure when Maria had come to take care of them.

"I'm very happy to meet both of you," I said, trying to slow my speech so I could maintain control. Words tended to slip off my tongue rapidly, especially when I was nervous, overwhelmed or afraid. "I look forward to getting to know both of you as we work and study together."

How I wanted to take them in my arms and kiss away the pain, the loneliness and the sorrow but remembering my precarious place in the household, I extended my hand instead. Luis shook it, but Isabel curtsied in a most charming way. It would be such a delight to nurture and guide them if I were their real governess. I somehow knew that they would give their whole hearts if shown a little kindness.

Without saying anything more, Carlos Mendoza led us across the magnificent entry hall to the formal dining room where tall, tapered candles had been added to the table decor. The children advanced to their places at the table without having any physical contact with their father and without being told.

I wasn't sure if they were in awe of him or just plain frightened, but their behavior was beyond reproach and their manners impeccable. They spoke politely when addressed, and their replies were no more than a sentence long.

"Miss Tremaine," Carlos Mendoza said, once the main course had been served. "Perhaps you should tell the children about yourself. They need to become acquainted with the woman who is to be with them each day."

I swallowed the bite of roasted beef that was in my mouth. Did he bait all the people who worked for him the way he was baiting me, or was he simply trying to start a conversation? Either could spell disaster. I was not used to lying, and I had no idea how much he really knew about Tess Tremaine. The file I'd read had given me very little to go on, and any embellishment could prove deadly if he knew more about her than I did.

"My life has not been that interesting," I replied when my mouth was empty.

"Ah, but everyone has a story to tell, Miss Tremaine. Something led you to my compound where there is virtually no contact with the outside world. The reason behind such a decision is a story in itself since few young women would willingly do so."

Once again, I knew I was being warned that my motives for coming had better be pure. Carlos Mendoza ruled his part of the world, a place where federal agents from any country could not touch him without a great deal of effort and favorable luck.

While he stared at me from over the rim of a crystal glass, I thought back to what I had read in Assistant Director Bridge's outside office about Tess Tremaine's life. The details had been brief, tragic and very foreign to my own, but comparing my life to hers - if only in my mind - might prove deadly. I had to become who I was now only pretending to be.

"My parents died when I was young," I told the children whose eyes had not left my face since their father had asked the question.

It made my heart ache to lie to them when they were innocent in every way, but deception was my only protection. Their father, or someone else, would be listening closely to every word I uttered, comparing it to what was already known and looking for any indication that I could not be completely trusted.

But if I had to watch everything I said like I was doing now, I'd be lucky to make it through the next twenty-four hours, let alone the amount of time it would take to find out what had happened to Agent Gonzales and make it out of Colombia alive. There was no way every piece of correspondence could have been covered in my brief introduction to the woman I was now trying to impersonate.

"I was an only child," I began again as my feet started to twitch underneath the table. "After my parents died, I was raised in the foster care system. That's where children who have no other family are placed."

"Ah, yes," Carlos Mendoza interjected. "Are you not grateful, my children, that you have such a secure and beautiful place to live? You are truly more blessed than Miss Tremaine has been. But please forgive my interruption and continue."

I glanced from him to Isabel and then Luis, but their expressions had not changed, so I resumed as Mendoza had asked me to. "I loved being around other children, but it is not always easy being on the outside, and I was moved around quite often. I suppose that is the main reason I applied for the position here. I wanted to be part of a family that needed and wanted me for more than just convenience or a paycheck. There was also the added incentive of seeing places I had only read about in books."

I waited for my employer's reply with nearly bated breath. If he was looking for something more specific he would have to ask more direct questions.

He cleared his throat moment later. "Well, I hope you will not be disappointed, Miss Tremaine. I too, am an only child—an only boy, that is—and I value family greatly. There is nothing I would not do to protect what is mine."

His smile was anything but reassuring. Could anyone be more obvious in letting me know that I was now under his command?

After the children had finished their dessert of fresh fruit, Señor Mendoza rang a bell that had been conveniently placed to the right of his china plate, and the woman named Alma came into the room.

"It is time for the children to be put to bed," he addressed her.

She nodded, and Isabel and Luis obediently rose to their feet.

"Goodnight, Papa," Isabel said, taking her little brother, who was already showing signs of weariness, by the hand and leading him away from the table. "It was very nice to meet you, Miss Tremaine. I am glad you have come from so far away to teach us all about America."

With every fiber of my being I wanted to get up from the table and take them in my arms. They were the saddest children I had ever seen. Strict obedience to orders could not be equated with love. They feared their father. It was evident in every move they made. They did not even hug or kiss him goodnight.

"I will see both of you later," I said, wishing I knew what later was. Nothing I had read gave me any indication of what my responsibilities towards the children would be other than teaching them during the day. What was I supposed to do with the rest of my time? It would be futile to start snooping around so soon after Jorge Santos had warned me against it. I was just about to wish Señor Mendoza goodnight myself when he rose from his chair at the head of the table and invited me back to the library for an after-meal aperitif.

"I know you do not drink, Miss Tremaine, so I have taken the liberty of telling Rosa to bring you a glass of fresh pineapple juice. I hope that is to your liking."

"Very much so," I said as I followed him to the far left of the marble entry and through the doors I had entered less than two hours earlier—before the children had arrived for dinner. I'm not sure why I hadn't noticed before that the shelves of books extended from floor to ceiling on two walls only. Most of them had Spanish titles, but their worth was evident in the soft leathers with which they were bound. The third wall was made of tinted glass and looked out upon the back gardens I had seen from my balcony, and the fireplace on the remaining wall was so tall a person could walk right inside. It was the most spectacular room I had ever seen. I stood looking at the leather-bound books on the shelves closest to me while he poured himself a goblet of brandy.

"What an amazing room," I said. "I've always had a passion for reading."

"Then consider this your personal library while you are with us."

My heart jumped at his insinuation. What he'd just said could mean anything.

"If you will look closely, you will find that not all of the books are written in my native tongue. I was educated in the United States. My father thought it was important for me to learn everything I could about the world and how it runs. He was a great exporter of fine coffee. Do you not believe that is a noble ambition for any father to want for his son?"

"Education changes lives," I said. "And thank you for your generosity in allowing me to use your library. Some of your books must be very valuable."

"You have an eye for quality," he said, smiling at me from over the top of his goblet like a fox waiting to pounce on an unsuspecting chicken. "But of what value are books if no one reads them?"

"I quite agree," I replied as Rosa came into the room with the promised glass of pineapple juice on a silver tray.

"Come sit," Señor Mendoza said when I had the glass in my hands. "We have much to discuss."

I had no choice but to take the chair he offered. It was so close to his I could see the pores on his face. Some of them were deep, as if he'd had severe acne as a youth.

"We live a simple but ordered life," he said. "Everyone has a job, and I expect it to be done without question or delay. Your every need will be taken care of as long as you are teaching my children and do exactly as I say."

I took a sip of the pineapple juice. It was fresh and tasted wonderful. "Exactly what are your expectations?"

"You are a direct young woman, Miss Tremaine. I like that very much."

He smiled at me again. It was very disarming.

"You will see to all my children's educational needs. The schoolroom is on the second floor next to their chambers. You will be responsible for them during the day. Alma will see to their needs at night. If you require anything of a personal nature, or for the schoolroom, just tell Rosa or one of the other servants. The children are allowed to enter the back gardens during the daylight as long as you have cleared it with Alma first. She is the final law when it comes to them." He paused, but only momentarily. "Under me, that is."

"I understand," I replied.

"In all fairness to your inexperience, I do not believe you do, Miss Tremaine. You will remain quite safe from all danger if you remain inside the hacienda, do exactly as instructed and follow every rule I have made. The jungle is a different story. It is vast and merciless, and you have more to fear than just predatory animals. It is a lawless state of guerrilla warfare."

Oh, how I was beginning to hate all these warnings, especially from the master himself. "But I saw nothing of concern on my drive here, only the men in the towers by the front gates."

"They are experts at keeping themselves hidden, but do not suppose they are not always close by. You were safe because you were with Jorge Santos. You might not be so lucky next time."

"I'll remember that," I told him. "Not just for my own safety, but for the safety of the children. Do they ever get to play with others their own age?"

"They have each other, and now they have you. Children do not miss what they have never experienced."

He smiled as he moved to the fireplace and threw another log onto to the embers causing the flames to dance. For being such a cold and dreary night, the library was stifling hot.

"You see, my dear Miss Tremaine," he said as he turned around to face me again and removed the goblet from the mantel so he could take another sip. "Things are very different here. The jungle has its own set of rules. We live by them or we die. It's as simple as that."

"You make it sound very savage and violent."

"Mark my words, Miss Tremaine, since I will not repeat them. Danger is all around us, but you are under my protection for the time being. Should that change, I can only say that I would not want to be walking in your shoes. Now, it is getting late, and I know you have had a long journey and must be tired. Your bed has been turned down and your breakfast will be brought to your room at seven. You will join the children in the schoolroom at eight. It is required that you are punctual."

My cheeks were quivering, but I managed a weak smile at the man who held everyone around him hostage.

"Lunch will be served in the schoolroom at noon and dinner at five. You may eat with the children at that time or in your own room. Unless I ask for your company in the evening, the time is yours for preparing daily lessons or browsing through my library when it is not in use. Rosa will show you the back staircase, but you must ask permission before leaving the second level of the house. I often have visitors and prefer keeping my family life separate from my business affairs."

He was leaving little room for me to accomplish my mission. How was I supposed to find the answer I was looking for if I was not allowed to leave the confines of my own exile? He'd already told me that he had guards posted everywhere, and they would be watching me. I had to assume it would be continually. Powerful men didn't become that way by leaving anything to chance, and he would be overly cautious if Agent Maria Gonzales had indeed betrayed him.

"Understandable," I told him; grateful I would not be forced to see him unless he summoned me. "Is there anything else?"

"Not at the moment," he replied. "New supplies for the schoolroom should be arriving shortly. They were ordered by the previous governess."

Oh, how I wanted to ask him what had happened to her, but doing so would be disastrous since he'd already laid the ground rules for my continued existence under his roof. So instead of saying anything more, I simply excused myself and left. Rosa was waiting for me in the hallway, but instead of showing me the back staircase as I had been told she would, she escorted me back to my room the way I had previously come. I couldn't help but wonder why.

Despite my physical exhaustion, I lay wide awake in my bed in the beautiful room I had been given and thought about my family back home and how crazy I'd been in thinking that I was ready for my first big undercover assignment.

My motives were pure. I wanted to make the world a better place for everyone, and now that I had met Isabel and Luis Mendoza, those desires had focus. I desperately wanted to protect them from the man who was their father, in addition to finding the missing agent, but how to do that eluded me. I was caught like a mouse in a maze with no visible way out.

Fighting through feelings of both desperation and fear, I wondered if my family even knew I was gone. We usually talked several times a week, but they understood that if they couldn't reach me, I was on an assignment and would get back to them as soon as I possibly could. I prayed with all the strength of heart I possessed that I'd be allowed to be with them again.

Chapter 5

I was both mentally and physically exhausted when the alarm went off at six the next morning. I had done little more than doze for a few minutes at a time the past 48 hours and hoped I could stay alert enough to catch any clues that may be hidden in this oppressive but luxurious house.

I ate the breakfast meal Rosa left for me while getting dressed for the day. Although she was not as intimidating as Carlos Mendoza and the overly disconcerting, head-servant, Alma, her presence disturbed me, as did everything else about my present situation. Her movements were stealthy. She came and went so quietly and quickly that I wouldn't even have known she had been in my room unless something had been left or removed. If the rest of the servants moved the same way, I would be in a constant state of nervous awareness whether I was awake or trying to sleep. There was no lock on my bedroom door, and the hinges moved both quietly and easily.

From everything I'd observed within the compound, Carlos Mendoza ruled with cold, meticulous indifference to the needs of his employees, unless it suited him to do otherwise, and had planned for every contingency. What had Agent Gonzales done to give her identity away, and whom would she have passed any information to if she indeed had a contact within the household? Teaching the children would have given her little access to what was really going on if she'd been assigned to the same rooms I had and had been given the same warnings and instructions. Something else had happened, but I couldn't figure out what it was if I wasn't allowed to move about a little more freely.

I left my quarters at seven-thirty, wanting to get to the classroom before the children arrived so I could prepare something with which to occupy them during the morning hours. I had no idea what a governess was supposed to do, but I was good at reading situations both promptly and accurately. If nothing else, I could try to ascertain what they already knew and build from there.

The hallway was dark and menacing since the compound was surrounded by thick jungle, and there was little chance for the sun to get inside, even if it happened to be shining. Nothing illuminated my path from bedroom to schoolroom except gas powered wall sconces that hung at intervals along the hallway and gave off a muted, dismal light. Each door on the floor was recessed, making it easy for someone to hide in the shadows and observe.

I had checked my entire room for listening devices the night before and had found two—one in the lamp by the bed and one behind the edge of a frame that enclosed a picture of colorful flowers and birds. I'd left them where they were. Either removing or destroying them would be tantamount to admitting who I really was and why I was there. I hadn't found any sign of a camera, but that didn't mean there wasn't one. A powerful, ambitious and suspicious man like Mendoza would have access to the most sophisticated surveillance equipment available. I was caught like a rat in his diabolical trap with no apparent means of escape.

My eyes rapidly scanned the corridor as I walked the few steps between my bedroom and the classroom, taking mental notes as to where each chair, small table or potted plant stood. Ornately framed pictures hung on the walls, scenes depicting the jungle— some were beautiful; others, violent and cruel. There was no need looking for hidden cameras here. They were clearly visible, suspended from the corners of the ceiling at designated intervals so there would be no lapses in coverage. The only question was whether they were being continuously monitored, or if they had been installed simply as a means of keeping the servants and other employees from stepping out of line.

Something moved in an alcove on the other side of the hall just as I got to the classroom door. Every nerve in my body jumped to a sickening awareness as I glanced over my shoulder and saw a woman standing in the shadows. She was dressed in a loose, black covering with a simple veil shielding both her hair and her face. Her belly was swollen, and she looked very close to delivering her child. I willed myself to be calm since her condition alone would prevent her from inflicting much harm.

"Good morning," I said, taking a step in her direction, but that only seemed to make her recoil further into the murky darkness. "I'm Tess Tremaine, the new governess."

"You should not be here," she fiercely whispered. "Go away while you still can."

Her dark eyes bored into mine, but the gauzy fabric kept me from seeing her face clearly.

"But why?" I asked, keeping the tone of my voice light. "The children are lovely, and the house is equally so. It's like living in a palace in paradise, except for the walls and guards outside, but then every job has a few drawbacks."

"Do not be naïve," she almost hissed, peering ever so slightly down the hallway in the direction of the main staircase. "This place is far from what you believe it to be. It will destroy you as it has done me. I cannot leave, but you still have a chance."

I was going to ask her what she knew, and if she was my contact, but before I had time, a swooshing sound made me realize we were no longer alone.

"You came," Luis said as he stepped into the hallway, and then ran towards the mysterious woman and threw his arms around her neck as she bent down to return his embrace. "I have been praying to the Blessed Mother that I would see you again. I am not going to like having a new governess."

The woman's voice was low and her words in Spanish, but I could still hear and understand.

"You must not talk like that, Luis. Miss Tremaine is a very good governess, or your father would not have hired her. You will soon grow to love her, and she will love you just as I do."

"But it is not the same," he said, and I could see that there were tears in the corners of his eyes as he remained clinging to her in the dark.

"Life changes, my precious one," she said. "You must learn that so you can make the right choices as you grow older."

Compassion filled my heart as I looked at the beautiful Spanish woman whose hair hung loosely down her back to below her waist. She was being careful not to step directly in front of one of the cameras, but it was obviously that her feelings for Luis were real. Quite suddenly I realized that this must be the missing agent, Maria Gonzales. Was her pregnancy the reason she was no longer the children's governess? But why should that prevent her from making contact with the agency unless . . .

My speculations were interrupted by her next words. "Run and find your sister, Luis. You do not want to be late for class. Your father will expect you to treat her kindly just as you did me."

Her choice of words surprised me, but when I looked back to where she had been standing after watching Luis retrace his steps to his own keeping quarters she was no longer there.

I made my way back across the hallway feeling more than shaken. If what I suspected was true, everything about this mission may have already been compromised.

It was hard concentrating on lessons when I so desperately wanted to talk to the mysterious woman who had warned me to leave. How had she disappeared so quickly, and why couldn't she leave unless the baby belonged to Mendoza? That thought made me physically ill. My employer was a man who wouldn't hesitate to ensure that what belonged to him remained his.

"Miss Tremaine," Isabel was saying in practiced English. "Are you sick? You look very strange."

"I'm perfectly fine," I told her, fighting back a rush of nausea. "I was just thinking about all the things you have here to help you learn. Your last governess must have been very special indeed."

"Father told us not to discuss her with anyone."

"I'm sorry. I didn't mean to pry," I replied, looking at the faces of my new charges. Apparently, I needed to be cautious even around them. They might be innocent as to who and what their father was, but I could not make light of their allegiance. Even if they feared him, they would tell him the truth if he asked.

And if the woman in the hall was indeed the missing agent as I now suspected, I had the information I had been sent to acquire, but what was I supposed to do with it if my contact didn't surface? Something truly horrid was going on in this household, and I needed to get both Maria and her child to safety, if that's what she wanted. I couldn't be sure that her cover had been blown since she appeared to be able to walk around the hacienda at least somewhat unsupervised. But how could I find out for certain when I didn't know where she had gone, if I would ever see her again or how much time I had until the raid occurred?

"Should I send for Alma, or perhaps even father?" Isabel was saying when I forced my mind back to the present and my beautiful, young charges.

Her words froze me to the core. The last thing I needed was to see Carlos Mendoza again. As for the illusive Alma, who was supposedly in charge of the children at night, I didn't want to meet her again at all.

"No, Isabel," I told her with a smile I didn't feel. "I'm just a little tired. It's a long way from the United States to your home. Would you like me to show you where I lived in America?"

That piqued her interest, but Luis still seemed distressed after seeing the lady in the hallway. How could a father keep his own children away from someone they so obviously loved? Being pregnant didn't mean she couldn't continue her responsibilities as a governess. There had to be something more that had taken her away from the children. Could it be possible that she was going to be their new mother?

"Let's look at the world globe," I said, forcing back my own sobering thoughts and removing it from the teacher's desk that was situated next to the window. The children followed my movements with their eyes as I put it on the table in front of them. "Who can show me where North America is?"

Isabel spun the globe around with the tip of a dainty finger. "Maria showed us once, but I can't exactly remember."

"That's okay," I told her, wondering if she really couldn't remember or was just testing me. "There's plenty of time. You speak very good English."

Her little chest puffed out in pride. "Father expects that. Why else would he hire a teacher who cannot speak Spanish?"

"You're absolutely right about that," I told her.

She was not trying to be rude. She was simply stating the obvious since I'd been told that even my limited Spanish could not be overtly used on this assignment, and the real Tess spoke no Spanish at all. I was beginning to think that might be the only advantage I had in this household. If people thought I couldn't understand, they might let something important slip.

"Why don't you come over and join us, Luis," I asked the young boy who was sitting on the other side of the table looking like he was still about to cry. "It's important to know where other countries in the world are located. Your father told me last night that he attended school in America. Perhaps the two of you will do that when you are older."

"I'm not sure I would like that," Isabel said. "I have never been away from the hacienda."

"Were you born here?" I asked.

She gave me a curious look. "I do not know where I was born, but Luis was born here. I remember looking inside his cradle in the room next to where my mother slept when he was baby."

The temptation to ask her where that room was located since it might be where Maria had gone was great. Houses like this had to be filled with secret passageways since Mendoza would want a means of escape if his enemies came in through the front door, and Maria had both appeared and disappeared without using the hallway, but involving the children could mean putting them in danger.

"It's a lovely place to live," I said, forcing myself to think like a governess instead of a federal agent. "Maybe you can show me where on the globe you live before we talk about anything else."

"I can do that," Luis said as his eyes squinted in thought. In less than a moment, he was pointing to the entire South American continent. "Maria said we live in the most beautiful country in the world."

"It is a beautiful country, and you're a very bright young man. You live several hundred miles away from Bogotá, right in the heart of Colombia."

"Maria lived there once," he continued. "She promised to take us to see all the people and cathedrals, but now she is having a baby."

"Maybe she still can. Babies won't stay little forever," I told him, excited that at least one person in the compound was being somewhat forthcoming without being prodded.

"But she can't! Father said so," Isabel insisted. "He also said she might have to go away once the baby is born. I don't understand why. She said she loved us."

My heart ached for these two motherless children who were so obviously in need of compassion and love. The schoolroom contained more than just books. There were games, puzzles, toys and art supplies that meant Maria was doing more than just teaching them to read and write. If I worded my questions correctly, they would give me whatever information they had.

"I'm sure she loves you very much," I told them. "Perhaps you just misunderstood what your father said."

Isabel shook her head defiantly. "No! Our mother left us just like father said she would. The same thing will happen with Maria."

"Not necessarily. Maria isn't sick. She's just going to have a child."

"Our mother was not sick," Isabel said through narrowed eyes.

"I'm sorry," I replied as goose bumps raised every hair on my arms. "I didn't know."

Dare I ask for confirmation as to what I'd just been told? The walls in the schoolroom could indeed have ears just like my bedroom. I should have arrived earlier to look for hidden surveillance. Carlos Mendoza would demand on knowing exactly what was going on everywhere within his domain, especially when a new member of his staff arrived to take care of his children. He might not be a fatherly man or the least bit affectionate towards his offspring, but he would make sure that his heir was properly insulated from influences that might lead him to question his destiny as part of his father's empire.

"Father said she went to live with the angels because she fell over the railing and died," Luis said, explaining his sister's statement. "That is why we are never allowed to go anywhere alone."

Horror penetrated my very soul. Their mother couldn't have fallen over the balcony unless she was pushed, or had intentionally jumped. The top railing came nearly to my chest. Mendoza was using her death to force his children into compliance.

"It must have been very hard for you to lose your mother like that," I said hoping to cover what I was feeling inside. I wanted to help bring Mendoza down if for no other reason than the way he was emotionally and mentally abusing his children. He would leave physical punishment to someone else.

Isabel's eyes penetrated mine. "Father said we should not be sad. She is with Jesus and the Blessed Mother."

Her back was straight and her eyes clear, although I could detect a great deal of sorrow behind her blank stare. She had been carefully taught how to keep her emotions hidden. Luis was still in the process of learning how to do that.

"I'm sure she is, and we don't have to talk about anything unless you really want to. I just want you to know that I'm here for you, and I care."

That was true enough. I wanted to save these children as much as I wanted to save Maria, who had obviously become involved with the most evil man I had ever met. But I was here to do a job, and getting sidetracked through emotional involvement would only make it more difficult for me to leave. I couldn't take everyone with me when I left, even if I managed to find my contact and get out of the compound alive.

I had them read to me from the books that had been laid out on the table before our daily lessons began, then we did some simple math computations and practiced drawing letters until Rosa brought our lunch into the schoolroom on a silver tray. There was a plate of tamales and fruit for each of us, along with milk for the children and a glass of pineapple juice for me.

The afternoon went by much as the morning had done, with the exclusion of any personal conversations, and we were almost finished for the day when Rosa returned to the schoolroom. She looked flustered and carried a note addressed to me in handwriting that was bold and perfectly lettered.

"From Señor Mendoza," she said, placing the heavy piece of cardboard that had been folded in the middle into my hands.

"Thank you," I told her as she turned to leave without uttering another word.

"Join me for dinner tonight," I read. It wasn't a request; it was an order. *"I'll be waiting for you in the library at seven."*

More fingers of fear traveled down my arms. I had dined with him the night before. Why was he summoning me again?

I was surprised that the children didn't ask any questions. My nieces and nephews certainly would have, but perhaps they were used to notes being delivered to their teacher. Maybe this was the strategy he had used to start Maria's downfall. She was both young and beautiful, and he most certainly would have been interested in conquering her, but how could she have become involved with such a repulsive and evil man? The same thing would not happen to me.

I returned to my room to wait

Once Alma had come for the children, I returned to my room. She mystified me. Her face betrayed nothing, but it was obvious Mendoza trusted her. I needed to figure out why.

How I wished there was someone I could talk to. I had never felt more alone, but I was beginning to doubt that my contact would ever find me. What if something had happened to that person as well? No one entered or left the compound without Mendoza's knowledge, and now he wanted to see me again. That certainly couldn't be good.

I fell to my knees by the side of my bed once the door had closed behind me and began to pray. I couldn't utter a word aloud for fear of being overheard, but my heart was full and my need for help and direction great. So I poured out my concerns and worries to the only person I could and then waited to see if I would receive any answers. But all I got was a troubling stupor of thought. Maybe I wasn't asking the right questions, or maybe I didn't have enough information for a feasible answer yet.

I dressed carefully and then waited until five minutes before the hour for Rosa to escort me to the library. My nerves were raw, but my tardiness would most certainly be noticed, and I didn't want the evening to start with subservient and apologetic behavior on my part, so I checked to make sure I couldn't see her coming down the hallway. It made no sense that I was being left to my own devices after the numerous warnings I'd received the day before, but instead of remaining in my room like I probably should have done, I took a calculated risk and nearly ran down the iron staircase.

There was no one visible in any of the alcoves, on the staircase or in the large and spacious entry hall that separated the library from the dining room. It was almost as if I was being tested again, but where would I go if I left the hacienda? The house may have been cleared of guards to see what I might do, but the rest of the compound was swarming with them. I would ask to be shown the back way all the servants used the next time I saw Rosa, but for now, I would go on the assumption that I had not made some colossal error since I was dining with the man who had hired me.

I had paused momentarily on the balcony to re-examine the railing. The height was substantial and the bars too close together for even a small child to get through. If Mendoza's wife had fallen to her death, she had most definitely been pushed. Was Mendoza planning the same ending for Maria once his child was born? It hardly seemed prudent in light of what his other children already knew, but they were young and anything could be covered up by a man who had plenty of henchmen to do his bidding. More than likely, he would simply have her taken into the jungle and shot. He would never risk her making it to the village where one of his workers might be willing to keep her concealed until someone arrived to help.

The ruler of the kingdom was sitting in his accustomed chair in front of the fireplace with a glass of clear liquid in his hand.

"I hope you will not mind if I stay seated," he said. "It has been a long, grueling day with many hard decisions to make. I hope you had a pleasurable time teaching the children and that they were well-behaved."

"It was very pleasant, and the children were wonderful," I said, hesitating, if only momentarily, in the doorway. It would be hard walking into that room again knowing no one would be coming to run interference as they had the previous evening. I felt like a hunted animal. One slip and the snare would tighten.

"Come now, Miss Tremaine," he said, motioning me to move forward. "I promise not to bite you."

He smiled, and his teeth glistened white just like Red Riding Hood's wolf.

"I'm sorry," I said, advancing a few steps closer to him. "This is all very new, and you are my employer. I'm not exactly sure what I'm supposed to do."

"Even more reason for us to get well-acquainted," he replied. "After all, I have entrusted my children's education to you."

"And I will teach and care for them as if they were my own."

He swirled the clear liquid in his glass. "Then I trust I will find their improvement more than adequate."

He gave me another look I didn't understand. If he was trying to break me as he had broken Agent Gonzales, it wasn't going to work.

"Come, sit," he said, indicating the winged back chair I had sat in the night before. "I have had Rosa bring some grape juice—non-alcoholic—of course."

"Thank you for both your kindness and generosity." I said, deciding not to say anything about Rosa not coming to escort me, unless he bought it up.

His lips curved into a sardonic smile. "Kindness is not an adjective most people would use to describe me; ruthless and cruel, but never kind. It would be good for you to remember that. I am, after all, a businessman first and foremost."

I had been warned again, and the reason for that warning was made even more clear in his next words.

"I understand that you met the children's former teacher in the hall this morning. That is most unfortunate since it must raise questions I am unwilling to answer at the moment."

"It was a very brief encounter," I replied, adjusting the glasses that always seemed to be slipping down the bridge of my nose. "The children seem to adore her."

"It is not healthy for my children to form emotional attachments to their teachers, Miss Tremaine," he said, swirling the liquid again before taking another sip. "Miss Gonzales would be gone if it were not for the fact that she has something of mine that I want."

So, the baby was his! How could a federal agent ever have become intimate with him? He was a monster! A murderer! An evil man who preyed on the innocence of others! But perhaps I wasn't being fair. If he had wanted her, no amount of resistance would have stopped his advances. They would have only made him more intent on owning her.

I needed to get out of the compound before he tried something with me. I would fight to the death to retain my virtue, but from what I already knew about him, he was not a man to be denied his pleasures, and he liked to play games with other people's lives.

"You have nothing to say, Miss Tremaine? I am sure your inquisitive eyes did not miss the fact that she is carrying a child I cannot allow to leave this compound. She, on the other hand, is permitted to leave anytime she wishes, once the child is safely delivered, that is."

I knew he was lying, and somewhere deep inside I knew he was aware of that, but I was at his mercy now. There was no way anyone could leave the compound without his permission and assistance, and he would never let Maria leave of her own volition. She knew too much about him.

"I'm sure things will work out satisfactorily for everyone involved," I said.

"You are a young woman of tact," he replied. "I admire that, and it will serve you well as our relationship progresses. I like to get to know my employees well—the most important ones anyway. It brings a sort of understanding and fondness."

If he thought I'd ever look at him with anything other than contempt, he was sorely mistaken. I had to remain aloof and confident, even if that was not the impression he'd received from his exchanges with Tess Tremaine. I needed to read her diary. It might provide information that would help me keep him at bay. Right now, all I knew was that her heart had been broken by the only boyfriend she'd ever had. Maybe he thought that would make her easy game for another tryst like the one he'd already had with Maria.

"I'm sure that could be the case in many instances, Señor Mendoza," I said, trying to watch what I said as carefully as I could. This might be the only chance I got to gain any helpful information from the man I was more determined than ever to help bring down. "But if you will remember from our correspondence, one of the reasons I am here, other than my love for children, is the fact that I have recently been betrayed by people very close to me. I have no desire to put myself in another situation like that."

He rose to his feet and closed the short distance between us, resting his hand on my shoulder. My heart began to race as if a freight train was rushing through it, and I almost spilled the glass of grape juice I had yet to taste. Was this what he had done to Agent Gonzales on her second night at the hacienda? He was far from subtle in his intentions to make a woman his conquest.

"I, too, have been the victim of betrayal, but not all men are insensitive to a woman's needs and desires." His hand traveled over my shoulder and down the top part of my arm in a way that made me want to retch. "You are very young, and you will have many lovers. Do not let one man deprive you of the joys that are found in the bedroom. Perhaps you should consider a man, not a boy, as your next aficionado."

I moved forward in my chair, my eyes ablaze with repugnance and anger, but he only chuckled as his hand fell downward.

"I did not mean anything by my advance, Miss Tremaine," he said. "Only that you are a very attractive young woman, and there will be many men who will want to own you. Though you are right in assuming that you will be safe here. I would not allow any of my men near you, and I would never force myself on a woman who does not desire me."

I looked up at his swarthy face as he stood next to me. His words may have been meant to dissuade my fears, but his body language told me that his pursuit had just begun.

"Thank you for saying that, Señor Mendoza," I replied with as much temerity as I could muster. "I want to believe that love could happen again someday, but right now, I just want to be a good governess to your children. They are bright and articulate, and I believe we can learn much together."

He returned to his chair across the multi-colored carpet that lay underneath our feet. If I had made him angry, he never let on.

"Yes, my children are quite extraordinary, and they deserve to have every advantage. It is difficult being a single father, would you not agree? That is why I take great care in selecting who will be with them while I am involved in other matters."

"I shall do my best to prove worthy of your confidence," I replied.

"I am sure you will, Miss Tremaine. Life is not easy in the jungle. I have several other residences where my children often stay, but I like having them where I am working, and at present, I am needed here. If you remain with us long enough, you will no doubt visit some of my other homes."

Here was another warning, and an outright lie if what Isabel had said about never having left the hacienda was true, but I steadied my fears by looking at a picture of a white, quaint mansion on the wall. I wondered if he suspected that I wasn't who I claimed to be, or if he took a special interest, similar to this, in many of the new female members of his staff who had come to his compound willingly. It wouldn't matter how his advertisement for employees was worded, anyone with half a brain would know exactly what kind of business he was in.

"That would be lovely," I said. "I have a great desire to travel and see new things."

"Then we must see that it happens. Now, if it would not be too offensive, I would like to escort you into dinner. It is not often I have the pleasure of dining with a lovely young woman. Most of my associates have far less breeding than you."

Surviving that meal without trying to escape took all the willpower I possessed. He was affable and asked few questions, but the way he still looked at me made it almost impossible to swallow even a mouthful of food. He told me about growing up on some of the largest coffee plantations in the country and how his father had insisted that he attend school in New York City since men who wanted to make something of themselves needed a solid education in more than one area of life. America was a land of great opportunity and had given him connections and experiences that assured he would become a wealthy man.

I had no doubt that many of those associations still existed. It took people working on both sides of the border for the drug cartels to flourish. He may have even recruited Tess to work for him knowing the kind of life her parents had lived and how easy it might be to convince her into doing more than the job she'd agreed to.

"What else did your father do besides export fine coffee, Señor Mendoza?" I asked, knowing the risk I was taking by asking a personal, family question when we'd just met but also recognizing that I might not have another chance. "He must have been a great man to have such high expectations for his son. I'm sure he's impressed with the kind of life you have made for yourself and your children."

"My father is no longer with us, but in the eyes of everyone who knew him, he was a great man. I am only trying to follow in his footsteps, as will my son when he is old enough," he replied, lacing his fingers together as we waited for the plates to be cleared so dessert could be served. "My father raised coffee beans, some of the best in the country. That is all you need to know about him."

"Surely not here in the mountains. Isn't it much too cold?" I responded, hoping a foolish question would help negate the one I had just asked. Perhaps his father really had been into coffee beans, and it was only when Mendoza went to the United States that his ambitions had changed. One kind of empire could easily be converted into another if there was enough motivation and backing. He hadn't said how long his father had been gone or how he had died.

His laugh was methodical. "I see that your education in that area has been neglected, though I am not surprised since you do not drink the beverage. Do you mind if I ask you why since it has been proven to have as many healthful benefits as wine?"

"Suffice it to say, Señor Mendoza, that I spent my most formative years in foster homes where it wasn't served. As you said last night, one does not miss what one has never had."

"Then perhaps you should try some and decide for yourself. You might find it enjoyable. Most people do."

"Perhaps I shall, but right now, I would like to know more about my new home," I replied, hoping I wasn't being too liberal with my answers. "It is quite the loveliest place I have ever seen."

Why couldn't I just quit talking? This was the second personal question I'd asked this evening. The ice was going to crack, and I was going to drown.

Carlos Mendoza's eyes wrinkled around the corners, and the lines around his mouth hardened. But I couldn't allow him to see that I realized I had made another horrible blunder, perhaps even a fatal one since I already knew that his home held at least one deadly secret he didn't want revealed.

"No expense was spared in its construction. I have always loved beautiful things. Perhaps that comes from being poor as a child. We had to rely on the generosity of extended family until our first fortune was made."

I didn't believe a word he was saying, but somewhere in his lies there had to be a grain of truth. If I listened carefully enough and made just the right comments maybe I would find it.

"In that respect we are much the same, Señor Mendoza," I responded. "You must know from our correspondence that I came from very humble beginnings, but unlike you, I had no other family to turn to."

"Alas, that much I do know. My father was an honest but not an educated man who spent a good portion of his life working the fields many kilometers south of here. Still, he knew what must be done to get ahead and took what was made available and turned it into something any son would applaud. I repaid his generosity and sacrifices by becoming a successful businessman he could be proud of."

I almost choked. No honest man could be proud of a son who was nothing more than a mercenary, unless he'd been part of the same kind of life. While Mendoza was an entrepreneur in many ways, he would have needed help in amassing the fortune and position he now so clearly enjoyed. If that help hadn't come from his family, then someone else had helped pave the way. But that was something I didn't need to know right now. It would not help with my escape.

Fresh fruit and a kind of wafer were served at the conclusion of the main course. He didn't ask me to return to the library with him after dinner. A man, whose voice I recognized as belonging to Jorge Santos, came to the door of the dining room and motioned for him to come into the front hallway. With a quick glance over my shoulder, I saw that he had his hat in his hand and his body language told me this wasn't the first time he'd disturbed his boss's meal. He had to be part of Carlos Mendoza's closest circle of confidants, and I would do well to avoid him.

I sat where I was at the table, straining to hear what was being said, but they were too far away.

"Excuse me for cutting our evening short, Miss Tremaine," my employer said when he momentarily returned. "I have urgent business that must be attended to this evening. Rosa will escort you back to your room."

He didn't wait for her to arrive before leaving the dining room again, but something told me to stay where I was. I fidgeted in my chair wishing I knew what had happened. If only my contact would materialize, I would be only too happy to feign an illness that would necessitate my being taken away. There was more than the cultivation and movement of drugs to fear here. Carlos Mendoza was a dangerous man in every possible way.

When I returned to my room, I saw that my bedcovers had been turned back as they had been the night before, but I wasn't ready to climb underneath them quite yet. I needed to figure out exactly what I was up against, and what connection, if any, the real Tess Tremaine had with Carlos Mendoza. I didn't want to invade the privacy of her thoughts, but the time had come for me to read at least part of the story she had written in her diary. It had been tucked away in one of her suitcases, and I hadn't even known it existed until Rosa had done the unpacking for me. She had left it on a small, corner table with the laptop I would never be able to use for anything that required the Internet.

I took it from the drawer in the nightstand by my bed and opened the front cover. Tears filled my eyes before I even read the first entry. Undercover work was not the reason it had been written.

"I don't know why I bought this book today. I've never wanted to remember any of my past, or ponder on what the future might bring. The present is filled with so much heartache and disappointment that I wish I had the courage to end everything, but I know I would be condemning my soul to hell by taking my own life. It says so right in the Bible, and I choose to believe in that since there is nothing else to hold on to.

"I thought I had finally found something important and lasting when Luke told me that he loved me, but that was a lie just like everything else in my life. My parents told me they would never leave me, but they did. My foster parents said they would cherish me as one of their own, but they threw me away when I disappointed them. Even my foster siblings blamed me when their parents found out they were using illegal drugs.

"But I never touched drugs! Not ever! And I had plenty of opportunities to. They surrounded me from the day of my birth. My earliest remembrance was sitting on the floor and watching my parents tie strips of elastic around their arms and insert needles into their veins. Sometimes they would be happy and laugh for hours, and sometimes they would simply slump back on the sofa and not say anything for the longest time. I would get so scared because they wouldn't wake up when I was hungry or afraid. The night would come, and I would hear strange noises both inside and outside the doors to wherever we might be living. I would cover my head with my blanket and lay on the floor at their feet with my stomach aching from hunger and hoping that everything would be better when morning came again."

I sat down on the corner of the bed while I continued to read. What an awful life Tess must have had. I could sympathize, but I certainly couldn't understand how alone and frightened she must have been. My own home had been filled with laughter, and I had always known that I was loved and my needs would be met.

"I think I always knew that they were pushing dope, especially as I got a little older. Strange people were constantly at our house in the projects. I was always told to go to my room whenever anyone knocked on the door, but my parents seemed to forget that even though I might not see what was happening, I could still hear. There were clear packages of white powder in the freezer, inside of drawers and underneath their bed. I was told never to touch any of it or bad people would come and kill all of us.

"I knew they weren't kidding. I peeked through the keyhole in my door sometimes and saw the men and women who came. They were never well-dressed or soft-spoken. They were thugs and transients; some old and some young, but all with glassy-looking eyes and money held tightly in their hands.

"When I was not much older than a little child, I would walk through the neighborhoods just a few blocks away, past large, fancy houses with clean walks and flowers in window boxes and wish I lived there. But it didn't take long until I realized that the people who appeared to have so much were just as involved in the drug culture as my parents.

"I would be dressed in a little, brown uniform with a ribbon in my hair and be told that I needed to deliver small boxes of cookies or candy to some of the finest homes in the nearby neighborhoods. It was a service project to help raise money for our family. I was to knock politely on the front door and ask to speak to the man or lady of the house. Then I was to wait to hand over my package until I had been given a certain amount of money.

"I must have been about eight when I realized what those packages contained—carefully measured amounts of cocaine—or whatever other substance my parents were selling."

I closed the book and lay back on the bed, even though I was still wearing my daytime clothes. I had gone through hundreds of scenarios at the academy on how to tell when drugs were being distributed, but this was the first time I'd read about a child, dressed as a Brownie scout, being used to distribute them.

I didn't want to continue my reading, but something told me I couldn't stop where I had. Tess Tremaine might have been handpicked as a governess simply because Carlos Mendoza knew about her past. Not that she could be prosecuted for things she had done as a child, but a threat could go a long way towards ensuring compliance.

"I can't say that I was surprised when I heard the guns fire into my house the night my parents died. Drive-by shootings were common in our neighborhood. It was almost as if no one really cared what went on. We lived in the projects where the affluent never went, and the police who tried to protect the innocent were spit at and beaten with bats when they tried to interfere.

"I remember going into the living room and looking at their blood-soaked bodies and wishing I could feel anything. They had given me life, but they had never been true parents. Their lives revolved around drugs, and more often than not, I was left to fend for myself. It was a pitiful existence."

"No doubt," I thought as I sat up and put the book on the table beside the lamp. It was incomprehensible the amount of child abuse that went on, undetected by the people who had sworn to keep children safe, but then I had been raised in a predominately white, middle class subdivision where people were expected to obey the law, not tenement housing where everyone looked the other way. The trouble with both worlds was that no one ever knew what really went on behind closed doors.

I prepared for bed while I let what I had read sink in. Tess had been a victim since the day she was born. I had to admire her tenacity and strength in rising above the life she had been born into and trying to become something good and positive. I almost loathed Luke Everett and Jill Terry for taking away her future and forcing her to make a decision that my have destroyed her life.

"Is everything all right?" I heard a voice from the hallway ask as I left the bathroom wearing one of the nightgowns Tess had packed. I hated wearing her clothes because I knew that wherever she was, she had to start over again.

"Everything is fine," I replied, drawing the door open since I recognized the voice. Rosa stood in the hall with a cup of warm milk on a silver tray. "Was my light disturbing someone?"

"Yes, Miss Tremaine," she responded. "Alma saw it as she passed by. Lights must be out by ten. It is a rule that must be strictly obeyed."

I shook my head. "No one told me. I'll remember that for the future, but you could have just knocked and told me. There was no reason to bring warm milk."

"My orders were clear, but I will take it back to the kitchen if you do not want it."

"Thank Alma for her thoughtfulness, but I don't like warm milk unless there is chocolate in it."

Rosa smiled. "I will remember," she said.

Chapter 6

I wasn't commanded to dine with Carlos Mendoza the next two evening and was grateful, but I still carefully watched every word I uttered in front of the children. Isabel and Luis were clever and rather eloquent when it came to their studies, and I doubted they often saw their father, even though he wanted me to believe that he was concerned about their education and personal welfare. They had been raised to obey every command, and I knew they were neither old nor wise enough to figure out what kind of a home they lived in, what had really happened to their mother, or what Maria's fate would be once her child was born.

Despite every luxury money could buy, they still lacked the one thing necessary for growing into confident, productive, caring adults – a loving parent who could show them the way. I tried not to dwell on the fact that it would be nearly impossible to leave them behind when my own extraction came. They were well-mannered and not given to outbursts like my nieces and nephews who laughed and screamed like banshees when they were around each other—with or without adult supervision. Perhaps that's what made me want to protect them most. They were more like little adults than children. They were quietly obedient, which I couldn't complain about since it was trial and error when it came to teaching them, but they seldom smiled. Their sad, dark eyes haunted me, even when they were out of my presence at night.

My evenings with nothing to do were the worst. As much as I accepted that my first responsibility came to the task I'd been given to complete, I had yet to meet my contact, and I had been at the compound for over 72 hours. That thought tormented me almost as much as Isabel and Luis' eyes. What if the DEA had gotten all of their facts wrong? They'd made me believe that an attack was immanent, and I would be on my way home by the end of the week. It felt more like the truth had been completely misrepresented to me. What if Agent Maria Gonzales had defected to the wrong side and my contact disposed of? It wasn't such a stretch considering the length of time I'd been here, and the fact that I had learned nothing that would lead me to believe anything was going forward as planned.

I hadn't seen her since the morning after my arrival, and I'd been unable to learn anything of real value since then either. Guards roamed the perimeter of the house at night, and I knew they were doing the same thing indoors. I had listened at my door on several occasions when sleep would not come. There were always soft voices talking, or the movement of feet as they walked across the highly polished, wooden floors in the hallway at very precise and short intervals. I was too far away from the main part of the house to hear what was going on there.

Leaving the second level of the house was impossible even during the daylight hours. If I ever went past the schoolroom door, there were servants to ask me in their halted English what it was that I needed. I was trapped like an animal, even if I was in a very luxurious cage. I wasn't even sure I'd be allowed down the back stairs once Rosa showed me where they were. In fact, I rarely saw her. It made me wonder if she was being punished for my disobedience in using the main staircase without permission. I had no personal contact with the fear-inspiring Alma, but I saw her lurking in the shadows quite often, her hair pulled severely away from her face and her eyes as cold and penetrating as the day we had met. I was more than sure she didn't trust me.

The box of supplies arrived. There were sketchpads, markers, watercolors, clay and workbooks on every subject imaginable, but I didn't need more materials to keep the children occupied. I could take care of their learning with what I already had. What I needed was a way to escape from my keepers so I could do some exploring on my own. The quiet normalcy that seemed to permeate the premises was as unsettling as any unrest could be.

I took only one occasion when it presented itself to approach Alma with what I thought was a simple request about taking the children outside for a walk after our morning lessons had ended. It wasn't raining or particularly cold, but she gave me a look that could have frozen water in the hottest desert before informing me that she would be the who decided when the children would leave their rooms. I was to teach them how to speak, read and write in English. Other than that, they were not my responsibility.

And if that wasn't enough to convince me that I was a nothing more than a prisoner, I had to contend with the fact that Maria (I had come to think of her in a more personal way now that I knew at least part of her reason for losing contact with the outside world.) was being kept away from the children intentionally so they would be used to not seeing her, and it would come as less of a shock once the baby was born and she was removed from the hacienda permanently.

There were so many things I wanted to ask her if the opportunity ever presented itself again. The most important question being why she hadn't she tried to get away when she first found out she was carrying Mendoza's child? It would have been much easier then, and the DEA most certainly would have assisted had they known what she was up against.

But then maybe I had it wrong when it came to what had really happened. It wouldn't be the first time an undercover agent had fallen in love with someone in the organization they were infiltrating. Perhaps she had believed Mendoza's lies when he came on to her as he had tried to do to me. I didn't know what her background was, why she had joined the agency, or what she really needed to be happy. I only knew that she had stopped communicating with her contact. It could have been by choice or by force.

I tried to recall everything that had been said during what I thought was only a chance encounter so she could see the children. Regardless of her position in the household now, she still had limited freedom, and that had to mean something. Otherwise, she would not have been able to navigate the security devices that existed most everywhere.

She hadn't volunteered anything about her identity, what quarters she occupied, or the real reason she was no longer working with the children. She had only warned me to leave because it wasn't safe to remain. That could have been for any number of reasons, but there was no one I dared ask about her. I was already under constant surveillance and living in fear that someone would come to my door and take me away before my assignment was complete. All this waiting around was the last thing I had expected when I told Assistant Director Bridges that I would accept this mission with the DEA. He was going to owe me big time, if I ever made it home again.

And so I got up on the fourth morning of my mission, ate a small breakfast, and then joined the children in the classroom for lessons. Nothing out of the ordinary had happened since my arrival, and I was feeling somewhat more confident that while I had not yet discovered the identity of my contact or when the raid that had been mentioned would take place, at least my cover was still intact.

Luis and Isabel never questioned anything I said. They simply followed my lead, even when I was showing them how to play some simple childhood game like hide-and-seek. Once or twice, they even cracked a smile when I allowed myself to be caught and acted surprised by their cleverness in finding me. I was growing to love them, but if I could not maintain my distance, I would fail at what I was supposed to be doing. I would still be expected to leave them behind when my extraction was arranged.

We shared dinner in the schoolroom that evening. Alma arrived promptly at six to whisk them away. I wanted to ask if we could spend some extra time together just reading or playing more games, but the hard set of her jaw and the harsh lines around her eyes prevented it. She was a puzzle, not quite one of the family, but not a servant either. There was no doubt that she knew everything that was going on inside the hacienda. The question I had not yet been able to answer was why she was allowed so much freedom when everyone was so closely monitored.

After writing down a few ideas for the next day's lessons, I retired to my room to contemplate, yet again, how I was going to get out of the mess I'd allowed myself to be drawn into since no one else seemed to be concerned about my safety.

My mind had always moved quickly from one task to another, and I had been blessed with the ability to compartmentalize and to recognize and remember easy-to-forget details. That's partially why it was so difficult for me to remain idle when there were so many things I needed to find out, understand and do. I'd spent as much time as I dared on my balcony scanning the area for any possible means of escape, but my room faced the back of the house, with a garden beneath and a high rock wall surrounding it.

There were guard towers on each corner, and beyond that lay the jungle with all its beauty and danger, stretching for thousands of miles in every direction. There was no way I could traverse it to safety. If one of Mendoza's men didn't shoot me before I made it out of the compound, I was sure to meet my death from some predatory animal or deadly insect long before I made it back to civilization.

I knew that someone from the DEA would eventually come looking for me, even if my contact didn't. Still, I'd been off grid for five days, and it seemed highly suspect that an inexperienced operative would be left in the dark for that length of time unless something unexpected had happened. But in taking my oath to serve and defend my country, I had been stripped of many of the rights most Americans took for granted. I was in Colombia on an undercover mission with a fake identity, and if the DEA was close to taking down the operation, they wouldn't hesitate to leave me exactly where I was. If I didn't survive, it would simply be an unavoidable loss.

But I didn't want to be a casualty in the war against drugs. I wanted to return to my family and my own future. That wouldn't happen if I just sat back and waited for my contact to reach out to me. I needed to be better prepared. Where would I take the children to keep them safe if the house exploded with bullets, tear gas, or other kinds of combustibles? I couldn't rely on any of the servants to help. They'd be busy fighting back or trying to find safety for themselves.

I had to learn more about the hacienda and the people who lived and worked there, and I couldn't do that if I was afraid to leave my own room. Carlos Mendoza had said I was free to visit the library at my convenience, if it was not already in use. Certainly, that implied a certain amount of supervised freedom, despite his indirect threats.

I'd even asked Rosa about the back way to the main floor of the house the last time she had come to my room to return clean laundry. She had reluctantly admitted that the stairway in question was through the door across the hall and to right of the schoolroom, but her demeanor intimated that it would be best if I didn't use it.

That was one warning I couldn't take. I needed to make at least one trip to the library on my own without waiting for an escort. It seemed to hold many of the answers I was looking for with its big, impressive desk, locked cabinets and possible private exits. No drug lord would construct a fortification without a way to escape, but finding those portals would be next to impossible. I had no idea where his personal suite of rooms was, or if he had a private office. So far, the only parts of the house I'd seen, other than the schoolroom and my personal bedroom and bath, were the entry, the library and the dining room.

It would be to my advantage to learn as much as I could on my way there as well. Carlos Mendoza would be dining alone, or with other members of his cartel, since he hadn't summoned my presence, and Alma would be busy with the children. It shouldn't be that difficult to avoid the remaining servants who would be engaged with tasks of their own. If one of the guards saw me, I would feign ignorance and, hopefully, be escorted back to my room with a warning not to leave it again.

I checked for guards upon opening my door. For once, no one appeared to be watching me, so swallowing back whatever fear remained over being caught, I hurried down the hall and soon found myself at the top of a flight of narrow stairs where exposed bulbs hanging from the ceiling lighted my way downward. The wooden steps were slightly scarred in the center as if thousands of feet carrying heavy loads had traversed them.

At the bottom, I came upon a hallway that extended in two directions with a number of doors spaced evenly going both ways. The one to my left was shorter than the other, and even though the staircase had included several turns, I realized that I was now standing almost directly below my suite of rooms. That meant the door at the end of the short hallway led outside. What lay beyond it would remain a mystery because I had no intention of alerting anyone to what I was doing.

I listened intently for any sound that might indicate I was about to be discovered, but another quick glance in both directions told me I was still alone. The first door I pulled open was a spacious storage closet with shelf after shelf of white, folded linen; the second, a large laundry room where a worker was busy taking cumbersome sheets or tablecloths from the dryer. She didn't hear the door open, and I managed to close it before she looked up from her work. The third opened onto another staircase leading down into the damp darkness. It smelled pungently of fermented grapes. This had to be the wine cellar. I stored that information away. It was a place where an escape route could easily be hidden.

I hurried back to try the doors on the other side of the hall, but before I could open the first one, a girl stepped through it into the hallway. I turned abruptly and pretended to take a step backwards. She bobbed her head but didn't say anything. Perhaps she was kitchen help who didn't speak English and who would be too timid to mention that she had seen me. I caught a glimpse of the cavernous room behind her before the door closed. There were other people inside who did not have guns strapped to their bodies. It had to be part of the servant's quarters.

The girl walked directly to the door at the far end of the hall. When she pushed it open, the din of noise it released let me know that she had entered the kitchen. My heart was beating rapidly, but I had come too far to turn back now. The other doors I opened revealed a large pantry and a cold storage facility with racks of butchered animals hanging from the ceiling. Carlos Mendoza certainly enjoyed the finer things in life.

The first of the last three doors was locked; the second was a small office with a desk, a file cabinet and two chairs, and the final one brought me into a short hallway where people were scurrying everywhere. A servant carrying a silver tray stacked high with dirty dishes was making her way across the floor and nearly collided with a colleague who was coming from the opposite direction. They said nothing to each other; only hurried on their respective ways.

"Can I help you?" The voice was so near it made me jump. Alma was standing behind me, her arms folded across her chest and her face set in a hard mask no one would be able to read. She was responsible for the children at night, so what was she doing so near the kitchen?

"I'm sorry," I told her as I forced my breathing to slow the way I'd been trained at the academy. "You startled me."

"You should not be walking around the house at this hour unescorted. It is not something Señor Mendoza would allow."

"I'm sorry," I replied again. "But Señor Mendoza told me I could use the library whenever it wasn't occupied. I wanted to find something to read since I still have a few hours until the lights are required to be out. I didn't want to inconvenience anyone by asking for an escort during Señor Mendoza's dining hour."

This woman made my skin crawl with apprehension. She moved silently from one part of the house to another, always undetected, like a snake waiting for its next victim.

"It is not your place to make assumptions of any kind, Miss Tremaine. Señor Mendoza does not like his routine disturbed, nor does he like insolence from his employees. You should have rung. I would have accompanied you had no one else been available."

"Pardon me, but I thought you were with the children at night," I responded.

The hostile look in her black, beady eyes let me know that I was going too far, but she didn't come after me as I supposed she might.

"I see that you remember at least part of what you have been told - although incorrectly. I get the children settled in the nursery, but they have both day and night nurses that attend to their needs outside of the classroom."

If that was true, why had I never seen them? This place was like a fortress with mysterious people placed at every portal. Carlos Mendoza might run the cartel, but I was beginning to believe that this woman with the unreadable eyes and hair pulled so severely away from her face that I supposed she must have a continual headache ran everything else.

"It won't happen again," I assured her.

"That is wise," was her reply. "Now, if you will just follow me."

I had no choice except to walk behind her into the kitchen where one cook was stirring a pot on a long, cast iron stove that had eight burners, and another was putting the finishing touches on a frosted cake. Several other servants, all female, were scooping a rice dish onto china plates, scraping the remains of personal salads into a trash can, and washing what appeared to be a small mountain of dirty dishes. It was a place run with precision like every other operation in the house.

From the kitchen, she led me into another hallway—one that bypassed the dining room—and on to the main entrance of the house. It was still a beautiful room, but I was no longer in awe of its splendor. Even the decorations on the walls seemed to be glowering at me now that I knew I would never escape unless someone came to get me.

"I trust you can find your way to the library now, but find what you are looking for quickly. Señor Mendoza is entertaining and will want to use it for after-dinner entertainment."

"I won't be long," I assured her. "Am I to summon you when I am ready to return to my room?"

"That will not be necessary, Miss Tremaine. I will have Rosa wait for you in the entry to escort you back the way you came. I will let this indiscretion go for now, but please do not assume that you have any rights in this house. You will not leave your rooms without permission again. Do you understand?"

"I do," I replied. "And once again, I apologize for causing any undue concern."

"It is my job to make sure things run smoothly. You were hired for a very specific job. Do not think that just because Señor Mendoza asked you to dine with him twice that your rights are greater than any other servant here. You can be dismissed at his pleasure, or at mine."

She turned and left the room, leaving me to realize that my situation had just gone from bad to worse. Alma didn't trust me, and she was more dangerous to my safety than any of the cameras or listening devices that had been installed to keep track of the movements of everyone in the house. She might only be a higher servant, but I knew without even asking that Mendoza would defer to her wishes if push came to shove.

My fingertips scanned the first row of books I came to. Any one of them would be sufficient for my needs if it was written in English, but that was not why I had taken the risk of coming to the library.

I walked from one bookcase to the next not really seeing the titles, although the covers told me that many of the volumes were costly and perhaps very rare. What I was really searching for was some lever or knob that would lead to an opening in one of the walls. I studied the pictures, wondering if a safe had been secreted behind one of them. I moved several small statues and pulled out a few books but nothing changed.

I stood in front of the locked gun case trying to decide if there was some way I could get into it without being discovered. I needed something with which to defend myself, but even if I managed to pick the lock, nothing in it resembled the weapons I'd been trained to use. These were antiques, worth an incalculable amount of money, but virtually worthless to me except as a battering ram. Mendoza didn't use these for protection. His arsenal of weapons must be in one of the buildings we'd driven past on our way to the hacienda.

Without warning, and before I had selected anything to read, I heard someone softly clear her throat. "Excuse me, Miss Tremaine," Rosa said. "Dinner is finished, and I must escort you to your room."

"Just a moment longer," I said, grateful that she had given me an indication of her presence. I only hoped she had not been standing there observing what I had been doing for long. While I hadn't seen any cameras, that didn't mean she wouldn't report any irregularities in my behavior to her boss if she noticed them. "Señor Mendoza has many beautiful books, and an amazing collection of guns. Do you know where he got them?"

"No," she responded, but her eyes never left my face. "I do not ask questions, and I do not take liberties."

I wasn't sure what she was implying but had the feeling that she wouldn't report anything she might have seen.

"Nor do I, Rosa, but it is hard not to admire so many interesting things.

I picked a book that was close at hand. It was "Jane Eyre". I wondered why he had an old English romance novel by one of the Bronte sisters in his collection, but then it was leather-bound, likely an original. That would make it valuable to him.

When I found myself back in my room, I realized I would never read the book in my possession. I was facing unwanted despair. I didn't want to die before I'd had a chance to really live, but escaping was impossible without help. What if something really had happened to my contact? The DEA certainly didn't know everything. Otherwise, they would have known that Agent Maria Gonzales was carrying Carlos Mendoza's love child.

I had unquestionably chosen a hazardous profession. It wasn't the least bit glamorous like in the movies or on television where escape clauses had been written into the script. Most undercover work was isolating, longterm and took more patience than I had at present. If something didn't happen soon, I was afraid I would make a lethal mistake.

It was early the next morning when Alma rapped briskly on my bedroom door and informed me that I was expected to be at Mass at eight. Heaviness settled in my chest as she handed me what looked like a lace doily to put on my head as a sign of reverence for what they believed and for Father Francis whom I'd yet to meet.

Attending the religious services of other denominations was not new to me since I lived in what was considered part of the Bible Belt. There were contemporary and more established churches on nearly every street corner in the business section of my small home town, and most of my friends were affiliated with some Christian sect. Still, it had always been a rather strange experience when I went with them, whether there was a paid minister, a priest in ornate robes or what could only be described as a rock band playing music that talked of Christ but did not express reverence or a true understanding of what it meant to be one of his disciples.

I'd been able to handle each of those experiences since I knew that agency was all part of God's plan, but today's experience would test everything I'd been taught about leading by example and sharing what I knew in a kind and loving way. I was in a foreign country working for a man who had a Catholic priest at his beck and call but who didn't live even the minutest precepts of a Christian life. He might take the wafer and wine and say all the right things to Father Francis, but the moment he was out of the chapel it was back to business as usual. That meant destroying the lives of people who had become addicted to the cocaine his employees grew, processed and sold, and killing anyone who got in the way of his continued financial and power-driven success.

Carlos Mendoza had been tolerant when it came to my odd proclivities that included not drinking alcoholic beverages, but a blatant show of disrespect in front of everyone in his household would not go over well. I had the uneasy feeling that my position on his staff was anything but stable, and I was nowhere nearer discovering the identity of my contact than I had been the day I arrived. It momentarily crossed my mind that Father Francis might be the person I was looking for, but I wasn't about to say anything that could be misinterpreted and put me immediately in front of a firing squad.

I dressed in one of the long skirts and sweaters Tess had packed, all the time wishing I could feign a headache or some other malady that would keep me from attending. But even if I didn't go to the service, I couldn't leave my room to do any exploring without being seen. The guards in the hallways were heavily armed and had very specific orders. Taking me captive or even shooting me if I got out of line was most likely one of them. Besides, I might learn something useful if I remained alert and watchful since I was going into a part of the hacienda where I had not been allowed to go before.

"Miss Tremaine," Señor Mendoza said as I stepped through the doorway and into the hall that led to the wide staircase I had used only twice since my arrival. He was coming from the opposite direction. Perhaps his quarters were in reverse to those occupied by the children and me. It was the first time I'd seen him anywhere, other than in the library or dining room.

"Good morning, Señor Mendoza," I responded, though the words nearly stuck in my throat. He looked cheerful and confident in a black suit with gold trim.

"I am glad you will be joining us for Mass today, Miss Tremaine," he continued, taking a few more steps towards me. "Please feel free to walk with me on this one occasion. We take our religious convictions seriously, though I fear you may not be comfortable in the situation since you do not drink wine, even my best."

"I am sorry, Señor Mendoza. I hope my abstinence won't be a problem."

He smiled at me in the way I had come to abhor. He knew just how to keep the people around him guessing as to what he would do next.

"Not at all, Miss Tremaine. I find your peculiarities rather endearing. I have instructed Alma to make certain there is grape juice so you can join us in our service. Father Francis has agreed."

"Thank you for your consideration. I would never want to offend anyone."

He extended his arm in my direction, and I had no choice except to slip my hand through the crook of his elbow as he led me down the staircase and then turned to a hallway directly behind it. We walked along silently until we came to a wooden door with heavy brass hinges.

The room behind it was small with a crucifix on the wall above a dais, where a man dressed in a flowing red robe, and with a tall, jewel-encrusted circlet on his head stood in front of the children. He held a Bible in his hands and looked very solemn. Señor Mendoza took me directly up to him.

"Father Francis, this is the new governess, Tess Tremaine, from the United States."

He gave me a quick visual assessment before speaking in practiced English. "I am glad you are here for the children, and I want to extend my services for your religious edification, although Señor Mendoza tells me you are not of our faith."

"All religions that teach of Christ are to be respected. Is that not right, Father Francis?" I asked with just a hint of a smile that I hoped would take some of the sting of my words away since I was supposed to be a Protestant who faithfully attended her own church.

It seemed an eternity until his brow furrowed and he spoke again.

"Yes, it is true that we are all God's children, despite what we believe. Perhaps you will become converted to the truth while you are here."

"Perhaps," I replied, but the only truths I wanted right now were what had happened to my contact, and whether I would make it out of the compound alive.

Isabel and Luis looked up at me with solemn eyes as I was escorted to a bench behind them. Señor Mendoza sat beside his son, but made no gesture of affection towards him. Moments later, I heard the heavy doors open again, and I turned my head to see all the household servants file quietly in and sit in the back rows of benches. It was easy to see which ones were more valued in the Mendoza household. They sat in order of trust and importance.

Jorge Santos, the man who had brought me here, stood silently just inside the door with his hands clasped together. It might be a house of God, but I could see the revolver in the holster on his belt. Alma stood next to him, always watchful, and just as dangerous as any man there.

The service Father Francis conducted was in both Latin and Spanish, and it was hard for me to stay focused since Latin was basically a dead language, and he spoke so rapidly I missed ninety percent of what he said.

My eyes scanned the room and its occupants as much as possible without turning my head too far in any direction. The walls were made of white stucco like the rest of the house with no decorations, pictures or artifacts to detract from the meeting, except for the one that had been hung behind where Father Francis stood—

a gleaming gold crucifix. It seemed a little ostentatious considering the needs of most of his fellow countrymen, but money was no object to him. So why the starkness of the chapel that was meant to be a home for God, unless he didn't want any of his treasures destroyed should he be forced to make his way through the room in a hurry with a bunch of DEA agents following him.

The wall where the crucifix hung was slightly indented, but it was impossible to tell if there might be something beyond it. Candles that gave off a great deal of haze lighted the room, and I doubted I'd be allowed close enough to determine if my supposition might be correct. But it would certainly be another excellent place to hide a secret passage.

I watched Carlos Mendoza carefully, but he simply sat where he was and pretended to be listening to what the priest on his payroll said. It seemed preposterous that a man who claimed to be a servant of God could stoop to such a low level, but perhaps he'd been left without a recourse. And maybe he wasn't even a real priest. Perhaps he was only playing a part because Mendoza knew his servants needed something to believe in. I wished I knew far more about him.

After finishing his monologue, Father Francis blessed the wafers and wine. There were two goblets with liquid in them. I was grateful Señor Mendoza was allowing me grape juice instead of wine. I took a sip of it when Father Francis stood in front of me and offered me the goblet, but I could not make the sign of the cross like everyone else did. Gratefully, no one questioned me about it.

And then it was over. The servants left the chapel and just the family remained, along with the ever-disturbing Alma. Isabel and Luis did not smile as they timidly bowed before the priest. He touched each of their heads, and then Alma took them by the hand and led them to the back of the chapel. I was about to follow when Father Francis detained me. The expression on his face was impossible to read.

"I do not know what you believe, Miss Tremaine," he said. "But while you are here, please feel to call on me with anything you might need. God is no respecter of persons, and I am only here to do his will."

"Miss Tremaine is still in the process of learning her place," Carlos Mendoza interjected before I could ask Father Francis if he resided in the hacienda like the rest of us.

I doubted that he lived in the village where we had landed, but that didn't mean there weren't other lodgings nearby. He may even be brought to the compound in one of the helicopters Mendoza had for his personal use. I heard their blades whirling often enough when the other sounds of the jungle weren't playing out their constant song of life and death.

"Perhaps our new governess will soon learn that working for me means complete allegiance," Mendoza continued, and I knew he wasn't speaking in a religious context. "God may be more inclined to forgiveness than me."

About three the next morning, I was awakened by what I perceived to be movement against my bedroom door. I bolted upright in the dark as the blood rushed to my head and a heavy knot of foreboding made it difficult to breathe. I had been in a constant state of anxiety since my arrival and had slept very little because there was no lock to keep intruders out of my room. I knew it was just another of Mendoza's tactics to keep his employees in line, but it seemed highly invasive since no one who knew what he was capable of doing would step out of line. I had been sliding the back of a chair underneath the handle so I would be alerted if anyone tried to get in but knew my feeble attempt at self-preservation wouldn't stop an invader if he or she meant to do me harm.

Nonetheless, instead of returning to my pool of warmth underneath the covers and hoping whomever it was would leave, I picked up the heavy candlestick on my nightstand and moved cautiously towards the door. I was grateful the floor was carpeted and the floorboards didn't creak. When I got to the edge of the doorframe, I tipped the chair upright and raised my hands in the air, but the person waiting on the other side must have heard what I thought were very stealthy moves.

"I am not here to hurt you, but you need to let me in quickly before the guards return," a soft voice whispered.

"Who is it?" I asked as I pulled the chair back and inched the door open just enough to see out. Perhaps my contact had finally felt it necessary to break the silence and get in touch. There was no one else in the hacienda who would risk being seen by one of the guards wandering the halls at night.

A white hand shot out and clutched my wrist. I felt my heart plummet until I saw Maria Gonzales hold a finger to her lips. She didn't say anything but quickly brushed past me into the room. I closed the door behind her while she moved hastily towards the glass doors that opened onto the balcony. I grabbed the top cover on my bed, wrapped it around my shoulders and followed. My jaw shook at the first blast of cold. It was raining outside, but a slight overhang protected us from the downpour.

"I'm sorry if I scared you, but I had to be sure I wasn't being watched," she said softly, pulling her own light covering more tightly around her slim shoulders. "Carlos has spies everywhere. Most of the rooms in the house are bugged, and his men are always patrolling the halls."

I knew that already. The question was how had she managed to get past them? It hastily crossed my mind that this might be a setup to see if I was really who I claimed to be. I had been told to trust no one, but did that include the woman I had come to find?

"I can only stay a moment," she continued. "The guards pass through these halls every fifteen minutes, and they seem to know if we are not in our rooms."

"Why are you here?" I asked.

"There is no time to explain, Miss Tremaine, but you must trust me. You do not know what goes on around here, or you never would have come."

"Then enlighten me," I said. "I am here to teach the children, something I assume you were doing not so long ago."

"I cannot explain the reasons for the situation I am in. I only came to tell you that you must leave immediately."

"But why?" I asked her. "I just arrived, and there is no way to leave unless Señor Mendoza approves of it first."

"Please," she said, grabbing my arm again. "I understand that you have no reason to trust me, but I know you were sent here by the DEA to find out what happened to me."

"And what makes you think that?" I asked.

"Because I still have a few friends here,   despite what I have done."

My moment of indecision had come to an end. It was hard to believe the woman standing beside me could be an enemy. Instinct or inspiration told me to trust her.

"But there are still so many things I don't understand."

"Your questions will have to wait. You must be ready to move when the signal is given. There will not be a second chance to get away."

"Are you my only contact?" I asked.

"No. Our agency does not work that way."

"Then please tell me who else I can trust."

"You have met him already," she replied. "He is a good man and knows how to do his job."

The only man I had met besides Carlos Mendoza was the man who had brought me here. I couldn't believe that I'd spent the better part of a day with a DEA agent and had suspected nothing. Jorge Santos was Mendoza's right-hand man. If he really was a government agent, why hadn't he rescued Maria long before now or at least gotten word to the officials about her status at the compound?

As if exorcizing my questions, Maria said, "Things do not work swiftly here. Our job was to bring Mendoza down and that has taken the better part of three years. We could have crippled him much sooner, but that was not the mission. One must become part of the inner circle to find out what is going on, and then many plans must be made. I chose to stay here and complete my assignment after things began to unravel. That is all you really need to know right now."

"But you can't stay here in your condition."

"I have made my choice; now you must make yours. The men in the house tonight are all big players in his cartel. They are celebrating the beginning of the coca harvest. That is why I took the risk of leaving my room. Most of them are very drunk by now, as are some of the guards."

My head was reeling with more than a few additional questions. Not the least of which was how she could sacrifice her life and the life of her unborn child for a job - important as it may be.

Maria's grip on my arm increased. "Please do not be distressed for me. I knew what I was doing, and what consequences might have to be paid. You must make yourself ready to go. It will not be an easy extraction. Our governments will raid in two days. The plan is to get you to safety before that happens."

"But why can't we just wait until then and all leave together?"

"If something goes wrong, Carlos will have all of us executed. My fate has already been sealed, but yours does not have to be. I tried to leave when Carlos first discovered I was carrying his child, but I could not involve our friend. It would have meant sacrificing everything we have worked for. Carlos knows I am an agent, and he suspects you are too, or he would not have invited you to dine with him two nights in a row."

"Why hasn't he confronted me?"

"Carlos likes to play games. Besides, he knows that no one can escape his compound without help. Anything suspicious would put too many innocent lives in danger and stop what we have sacrificed so much to accomplish. You have no idea how it feels to be hunted. I did what was necessary to get the answers I needed."

It was too dark to see her eyes, but I could tell from the tone of her voice that she had experienced many grave hardships during the time she had been at the compound. But sleeping with the enemy was something I simply couldn't understand. Making love was supposed to be a beautiful, sacred experience between a husband and wife who had promised to love and protect each other forever. Anything less seemed like a travesty to me, but then who was I to judge? I had not walked in her shoes, and would I really choose to die rather than give my virtue to a criminal in order to save my life? I hoped it was not a decision I would ever have to make.

"I must go," she said, turning around to leave. "You will be contacted, but I cannot tell you how, when, or where."

"You will think about leaving with us."

"No promises," she replied. "They bring nothing but unhappiness since most of them are impossible to keep. You will learn that soon, if you have not already."

I wondered if she was thinking about Isabel and Luis, but she couldn't control what happened to them anymore than I could. We were at the mercy of a very evil man who cared nothing about the lives he destroyed.

She opened the glass door and then glided across the carpeted floor in her soft slippers as gracefully as a ballet dancer and disappeared into the hallway before I had time to ask anything more.

I pondered on the relationships she had formed since her arrival as I slid the chair back underneath the door's handle. From the way Luis had greeted her in the hallway the morning after my arrival, I knew she loved the children. So how could she just give up and accept her fate? She should be willing to fight for her former charges, and for her unborn child. If I had more information about the takedown, I might be able to help. But while I now knew who my contact was, there was no way of reaching him, and I doubted Maria would risk another trip to my door.

Perhaps I should have felt better knowing that my extraction was about to take place, but there were still too many questions without answers. Besides, how could I ever feel good about leaving innocent children and a pregnant woman to defend themselves? Luis and Isabel might be kept from harm, but Maria certainly wouldn't be. She simply had to agree to come with us. She would be killed if we left her behind.

I crawled underneath my covers again, but sleep would not come. Through my mind floated visions of all the smiling children who'd given me flowers and hugs when I'd gotten off the unsound plane before the last leg of my journey to the compound. If their parents no longer had work to support them, how would they survive? They barely had the necessities of life now with no running water or electricity. It hardly seemed fair that they should be the ones suffering for the actions of the adults around them. But that's how it always happened! The weak lost what little they had while the powerful and rich took what they wanted—regardless of the cost.

Since Maria had indicated that most everyone in the house was inebriated and sleeping, I momentarily contemplated leaving my room to see if I could discover anything more on my own. But drawing attention to myself and possibly upsetting plans that had already been set in motion wasn't the way to do it. I needed to sit tight, play the hand I'd been dealt and hope for the best. If Mendoza already suspected my duplicity, he'd have me exterminated the first time I made any waves.

Chapter 7

It was difficult staying focused on the children's lessons the next morning when I knew I wouldn't be with them much longer. I had grown very fond of them during the few days we'd spent together, and it pained me greatly knowing they were not receiving the love, attention and guidance they deserved. But my hands were tied since they had been born into a life where there was no escape.

If their father was captured during the raid, they might have a chance for a more normal life, provided there was someone on the outside who would take them in knowing who they really were. If it was unsuccessful, they'd go on as they always had, being cared for by governesses and servants who were all too afraid of Carlos Mendoza to oppose him. Either way, it didn't seem like much of a life to me.

"What is wrong, teacher?" Isabel asked in her direct way as I listened to Luis recite his ABCs. "You have that funny look on your face again. Do you not like being here with us?"

My heart filled with pain as I knelt on the floor between my two young pupils and put my arms around their shoulders. They sat stiffly upright in their chairs as they always did, not understanding the dangers that lay around them, but fully comprehending the loss of tenderness and caring.

"I love both of you very much," I told them as I suddenly realized just how much I wanted to keep them safe and see smiles on their faces.

"Nobody tells us that anymore," Isabel said, sniffing back what I knew was the beginning of tears she would never let fall. "It used to be different when our mother was alive. She would hold us and tell us stories. She would kiss us goodnight and help me with my prayers."

"Maria told us that she loved us," Luis interjected.

"That is different," Isabel replied. "She was brought here to take care of us when you were a baby. You do not remember our mother, but I do."

The timeline was still unclear, but I couldn't help wonder if Maria's arrival had been the catalyst for the poor woman's demise. If that were the case, it would help explain her reluctance to leave the compound. Guilt alone would make her want to stay and watch out for the children that had been left behind.

"There are many people who love you. I want you to always remember that," I told them. "And they don't always have to be with you physically for you to feel their love."

"You mean baby Jesus," Luis said. "Father Francis told us all about him and the blessed Mother. He said we can turn to them whenever we want to, but it is not the same."

Isabel looked intently at her little brother. "He said there were many saints like St. Augustine and St. Jerome looking out for us too, but I do not care about any of them. I just want my mother back, and that is not going to happen because she is dead. People we love always leave, so it is best not to get attached."

"Who told you that?" I asked.

"Alma! She said she was the only one we could ever really trust."

"But that's not true, Isabel."

"Yes, it is," she firmly replied. "She told us Maria was going to leave us, and she told us the same thing about you."

I felt a sudden chill of menace. Was there nothing Alma did not know, including what was intended for me?

"When did she tell you that?" I asked.

"This morning when she came to wake us. She said you would not be here much longer. Why are you going away?"

I felt tears come to my own eyes. Alma had a reason for telling the children that my brief stay was about to end, and if she was that willing to confide in them, it was only because she felt she had their loyalty, regardless of how it had been obtained. But my greatest fear was that Maria's coming to my room had been discovered. If that was the case, we might not make it to the raid. Each moment we breathed might truly be our last.

"Alma must be mistaken," I said, even though I knew it was a lie. Whether I left of my own volition or was terminated, I would not be an employee in the Mendoza household much longer.

"But Alma is always right," Isabel insisted. "She told us that our mother was going to die, and that Maria would no longer be our teacher before it even happened. Alma knows everything. It is why father allows her to look after us."

Her last comment was puzzling and made wanted to ask her what else Alma had said, but I couldn't involve either of the children any more than I already had. They were innocent puppets in some very diabolical plans. I couldn't begin to imagine all they had suffered. I just wanted to take them away from the madness and give them a home and a family they could count on—like the one I had left—but that wasn't my call. Nor was it why I was here.

"Let's not talk about sad things that haven't happened yet," I told her, willing the heaviness in my own heart to go away. My leaving, regardless of how it happened, would only further prove to my young charges that Alma was all-knowing and the only one they could completely trust. "We still have a great deal to learn today, and we haven't even looked at all the wonderful things Maria ordered for our studies."

I took the box from off my desk and carried it to the table. I had glanced through it's contents but had never shown anything to the children. They were most excited to see all the art and craft supplies so I tore open a few packages of colorful clay and told them to create their favorite animal. They looked at me for guidance since it was obvious they had never played with anything like it before.

"You can start with either the head or the body," I told them as I took a pinch of yellow clay and rolled it into a ball that could be used for a head.

Luis followed my example, and Isabel soon joined us. I absentmindedly continued to make what I hoped would resemble a monkey, but my mind was on Alma and how and why she knew things before they happened. That seemed a little reckless for a man like Mendoza, who appeared to want supreme power and control, unless she was responsible for carrying out some of the sinister deeds that occurred inside the hacienda. She was certainly in a perfect position to push the children's mother over the railing. And if Mendoza had been the one to suggest it, she knew she would never be punished for her crime.

There was no justification for what their father had done to any of the women in his life. Someone had to stop him. I just wished I could truly be part of the team in place to take him down. But I had to keep those thoughts to myself and concentrate on making what time I did have with the children count. I wanted them to have some happy memories of the time we'd spent together when I was gone.

I looked over at their beautiful faces as they tried to create little animals with unskilled but willing fingers. "Never forget that God loves you very much, and he has given us a beautiful gift in being together now. I feel very lucky to get to spend time with both of you, teaching you things that will help you become wise, caring adults."

"Please stay with us," Isabel pleaded before doing a very uncharacteristic thing. She rose from her chair, put her arms around my neck and hugged me. It tore at my heartstrings as I returned her show of affection. Although they'd been told I was going to leave, she still wanted to believe that I cared enough to stay.

"I will stay for as long as I possibly can," I said as I held her close to me for just a few moments longer.

Luis, not wanting to be left out of anything, threw his small arms around both of us; only he added a kiss to my cheek.

"Oh, my," I said, after our hugging had ended. "There's a whole lot of love in the room this morning, isn't there?"

"You are funny," Luis said. "Maria never talked to us like that."

"Well, she should have," I said, giving in to a moment of weakness and bravado. "Children need to know that the adults in their lives love them. Someday, both of you will be far away from here. You'll see beautiful cities, clear expanses of sky, eat many kinds of foods, and meet wonderful people who will see just how special you are."

I wanted desperately to tell them about my own family, and what it was like to be around people who were not afraid to express how they really felt, but Tess Tremaine was an orphan who had also been raised in a home where drugs took precedence over everything. She would understand how alone and frightened the children were, and that filling their heads with too much hope might not be the kindest thing to do. Children could not find a new way to live unless someone was willing and able to help them.

"I think it's time for me to read you some stories," I told them. "Why don't you pick your favorite book, Luis, and then Isabel can pick hers."

They spent a few minutes rummaging through the shelves of books in the schoolroom while I situated myself in the teacher's chair. Isabel was wearing a white, frilly dress with a large pink sash around the waist and a ribbon of the same color in her hair. She had on white tights and black patent leather shoes that glistened in the soft overhead light that was powered by a generator somewhere within the compound. Luis wore tan pants and a blue polo-style knit shirt. Girls and boys in America seldom dressed that way anymore, unless they were in a private school or going to church.

When they found the books they wanted, they came running back to me, but instead of having them sit at my feet like they had done the few days before, I gathered them into my arms and held them on my lap. It was rather awkward trying to hold them and juggle a book, but even if we didn't make it through either of the stories, I'd accomplished something important. For just a few moments, they knew that they really mattered.

It had quit raining by the time we finished our noon meal of tortillas, rice and fresh fruit.

"Why don't we go outside for a few minutes?" I asked them as they were getting ready to sit down at the table to study their numbers. In all my anxiety over what was going to happen in the next couple of days, I'd forgotten that Alma would never allow a trip outdoors unless she approved of it first, which was highly unlikely even if she hadn't branded me a traitor.

"Alma says it is not good for us to go outside. It is too cold," Isabel said. She was back to being the intense, obedient child.

"Not if we bundle up and stay in the back garden. It would only be for a few minutes. Aren't you tired of being inside?"

"I want to go," Luis said. "Please, Isabel. You will not ruin your shoes or your dress since it has stopped raining."

Threatening young girls about ruining their clothes, and the punishment they would receive if they did was just another technique used to train them into submission. Americans did that too, but generally not for the same reasons. I had no doubt that someday she would be married off to someone of her father's choosing, and Luis would be trained to take over the family business, if his father was not put behind bars first. Mendoza had basically told me that much already.

"But Alma said we were never to leave the hacienda without permission. She said something awful would happen to us if we did," Isabel lamented.

I frowned at my lack of judgment and carelessness. If Alma had already told the children that I wouldn't be there much longer, I already had a great deal to fear and couldn't justify putting the children at any risk.

"I suppose it would be best if I ask her first," I relented. "Not because anything bad would happen if we took a simple walk outside, but because it's right to follow the rules."

"Even if they do not make sense?" Isabel asked. "I really do love smelling all the flowers and looking for monkeys. Sometimes they slip over the wall, and we watch them play from our room until someone takes them away."

"Do you think there is one outside now?" Luis asked, his eyes bright with hope. "I would love to see a monkey or even a lizard or a speckled frog, though we have to be careful not to touch them since they could be poisonous."

"I'm not sure what's inside the garden today," I told them. "But I think we should find out. Why don't the two of you get your coats while I find Alma and gain her permission?"

Luis immediately pulled his jacket from the hook by the door and took an umbrella from the closet where the school supplies were kept, but Isabel hung back.

"What's wrong?" I asked her.

"I do not want to get in trouble," she said. "I hate bread and water, and I hate being locked in my room all day with no one to talk to and nothing to do."

I looked down at her frightened face. "Does that happen often?"

"Sometimes, when I will not drink my milk or get too tired to say my prayers. Then Alma says I must be punished for being horrid."

"Surely, she understands that you're just a little girl, and little girls aren't always thirsty, and sometimes they get very tired."

Isabel looked down at the floor. "Alma said I have responsibilities. Father expects me to learn how to be a proper Colombian lady so I can find a suitable husband and rule a great house."

"I don't think going outside is going to endanger that," I replied. "Even great ladies need to be aware of their surroundings, and not everything can be learned from books."

I hated the fearsome Alma even more for subjecting these delightful, loving children to physical and mental abuse simply because they were not being compliant, little adults. She needed to be stopped just as much as their father did.

"It is okay," she said. "You just wanted us to have some fun. Maria tried that once. She took us on a game of hide-and-seek in the house, but Alma found out and Maria was sent away."

"A game of hide-and-seek?" I asked, trying not to sound overly inquisitive. "Like the one we played here in the classroom?"

"Sort of like that," Luis added. "Only we got to explore more of the hacienda. We looked behind doors and even went into the kitchen. It was the only time we have ever done that."

"And Alma found out and punished Maria for taking you out of the classroom?"

"Only because she was already going to have a baby and could not stay with us much longer anyway. Why should she be sent away for that?"

Why indeed! I pondered as I looked down at my two young charges. They were expected to live by a set of rules they were too young to understand, but perhaps Maria had been trying to find another way out. That meant she might not be as resigned to her fate as she'd led me to believe. If she would just contact me again, maybe we could figure something out together.

"I'm sure there were other reasons because she isn't completely gone," I said. "Luis and I saw her in the hall the morning after I arrived."

Isabel's eyes grew large and frightened. "She is not supposed to come to our rooms. Father and Alma forbade it. She is supposed to be resting until the baby is born, and then she will leave us."

This time I couldn't stop myself from asking the question that had immediately come to mind. "Where did your father or Alma say she was going?"

"Probably to heaven like our mother," Isabel replied with resignation. "It is difficult to have babies in the jungle. Not many survive."

"And why not? Certainly, there are doctors to look after you when you become ill."

"There is a doctor who comes to see us when we need him, but it is different when babies are born."

I didn't have the heart to question her further. Once again, she was being fed half-truths and outright lies to keep her from asking any difficult questions about Maria's impending disappearance. Childbirth was always a risk, especially when there wasn't a hospital close by, but Luis had been born at the hacienda and survived.

Carlos Mendoza didn't care about anything other than enlarging his own empire, or he would make sure that the mother of his soon-to-be-born child had proper care. Would he even be bothered with the infant after she was gone, or was he keeping her alive simply as a means of torture for having deceived him?

"Perhaps we could do something else," I suggested as they continued to look up at me.

"Like what?" Luis asked. "I want to go outside and bounce my ball. I promise not to splash in any puddles."

I smiled at him. He was a little boy who should not be confined to the house, but then, neither should his sister. Children needed fresh air and exercise, even if it was damp and cold, and I wouldn't keep them outside long enough to get chilled. I just needed to figure out how to approach Alma so she wouldn't take anything out on them. They would have enough to deal with in coming hours.

"I do want to look at the birds and flowers," Isabel pouted, and I knew that the draw to nature was only being suppressed because of fear. "I picked some beautiful ones for Maria once. She said she would keep them forever."

"Then I'm sure she will," I responded, wondering just how long forever on this earth would be for any of us. Things were looking mighty bleak right now. "Why don't I see if I can find Alma? I'm sure she's not far away."

She must have been listening at the door because I had taken no more than a step in its direction, when it literally flew inward and two cold, black eyes focused on us.

"Where do you think you are going?" she demanded, ascertaining the situation with one scathing glance.

Luis dropped both his coat and the umbrella to the schoolroom floor, and Isabel looked as miserable as if she'd been caught with her hand in a forbidden cookie jar, but that didn't stop our adversary's attack.

"I believe I made myself clear when I said there would be no leaving the house without my permission."

"You did," I replied. "I was just on my way to find you. It isn't raining and the children need some air."

"You forget your place, Miss Tremaine. I am the one who will decide what is best for the children."

Her cool voice sent chills down my spine, but I didn't flinch a single muscle. She might have me killed, or even do it herself, but I would never beg for mercy. That was one thing she did not know how to give.

"I do apologize, but I have been hired to take care of their educational needs, and sometimes a trip outside the classroom is necessary for them to learn more about the country in which they live. Besides, it's musty and dry inside the classroom, and I am certain that is equally as detrimental to their health as a few moments in the fresh air. I assure you that we have no plans to leave the garden."

I was being incredibly bold, and I noticed that both Luis and Isabel had sought protection behind my back. They were terrified of this forceful and cruel woman who had been given such complete control over their lives.

"I'll make sure they stay on the pathways, if that's what you require," I hurried on, even as I felt my jaw begin to tremble. "It isn't raining, and I would enjoy a closer look at the back gardens myself. They appear to be quite lovely from my balcony, and I thought the children could tell me about all the birds and flowers, in English, of course, since they have lived here so much longer than I have. It would be a wonderful exercise for their education."

She eyed me with hostility, but I didn't much care. She needed to know that her scare tactics would no longer work on me, even if she did think she knew who I really was and had begun making plans to get rid of me.

"Make sure you are back in the schoolroom by three. I will check for myself at a quarter past," she suddenly relented. "Señor Mendoza has business acquaintances at the hacienda and does not want to be disturbed by any household matters. They will probably stay the night again."

I looked at my watch. It was 1:30. She was giving us far more time than I'd ever anticipated. Maybe she was just busy with other things since there were guests in the house, and maybe it was simply my final reprieve, but I decided to take it anyway.

"Thank you," I replied. "I'll make sure the children are back at the requested time."

"Just make certain you do not leave the back garden. Its walls are high and thick. I will have one of the gardeners there to assist."

"Thank you again," I said, knowing that more than a gardener would be watching us. The guards in the towers would not miss anything, and they had been trained to shoot to kill.

The children hurried with their coats and gloves before she could change her mind. I made sure their buttons were fastened, and they were both wearing hats that covered their ears. Then I ran to my room to secure my own coat while Alma waited outside my door with her arms folded and the children within reach.

She led us down the back staircase and into the kitchen where the cooks and their staff were busy preparing the evening meal. They didn't look up from their work. Rosa was polishing silver. I tried to catch her attention. She was the only servant in the hacienda who had been remotely friendly, but she kept her face down. Was there no one in the house who wasn't afraid of Alma? She ruled with an iron fist and got the results she wanted. Perhaps they were only too aware of what would happen if they disobeyed. Death could come very swiftly in the jungle.

That evening, I ate my dinner of tortilla soup and fruit in my room. Alma had insisted the children eat alone. It was punishment for my insubordination, but I was still glad I had taken them outside. They had been thrilled walking among the roses, hydrangeas and orchids and watching the brightly-colored birds as they flew effortlessly from tree to tree. Over the wall, we could hear monkeys chattering and the sound of frogs. There were other sounds I didn't recognize, sounds of death and carnage like wild animals attacking their prey, but the children seemed oblivious to them. Maybe they were used to the resonance, and maybe they were too closely supervised to even know what they were hearing.

Before we returned to the house, I was certain I heard a machine gun fire a few rounds. It made my blood run cold. These people would stop at nothing to protect their realm. I felt suddenly frightened for any of us who attempted to get in their way. If the raid didn't happen as planned, we'd all become victims to merciless lust and greed.

Nonetheless, once my meal was finished, and I'd had time to rethink my current situation, I decided to return the book I had borrowed to the library. I hadn't read so much as the opening sentence, but if I was going to die in the next few hours it would be on my own terms, not waiting in my room like a coward. I was going to be bold as I had been trained to be. It hardly mattered that Carlos Mendoza was still entertaining his cronies; I would learn nothing if I stayed where I was.

It had been sixteen hours since Maria had appeared at my door, and the evil man who had hired Tess Tremaine and got me instead must be laughing my inexperience and incompetence as an agent. Well, I'd give him something to ponder because I wasn't about to die without a fight. I'd concentrate on getting Maria to safety and leave everything else in God's hands.

My decision made, I rang for Rosa and then made sure everything I needed to get out of the country was still available. The jungle might be a dangerous place, but if I could come up with a weapon and find a means of escape, I'd take my chances with any wild animal or poisonous reptile or insect. I wasn't going to be careless or disrupt my extraction, but if something fell through I needed a plan.

When Rosa appeared at my door, she looked flushed and hurried.

"Yes, Miss Tremaine, what is it that you need?" she asked, looking over her shoulder as she did so.

I felt sorry for her. She might well be a good, honest woman who had been left with no recourse except to work for a man like Mendoza. She was certainly not cold and indifferent like some of the people in the hacienda, and she seemed genuinely frightened. I wondered if she had family close by—perhaps even in the village where I'd landed. She appeared to be about my age, but that didn't mean she couldn't have a child or two of her own.

"I'd like to return this book to the library," I told her. There was no need to explain my actions. She had been trained to follow orders without asking questions so it wouldn't have mattered anyway.

"Follow me, but we must go quickly," she said. "Señor Mendoza is dining with his guests. They will retire to the library once they have finished."

"I'll be quick," I told her, suddenly wondering if my need to become proactive would put her at risk. If Mendoza were already planning my demise, he wouldn't be lenient with anyone who befriended me.

We went down the back stairway, just as I had done with Alma and the children earlier in the day, but instead of escorting me to the library as she would have done, a young girl, not more than twelve or thirteen, grabbed her arm and began speaking to her in rapid-fire Spanish.

From what little I could understand, she was Rosa's sister and had been summoned to the compound to help with the celebratory meal. She had dropped something valuable and was afraid of being beaten if her mistake was discovered by one of the other servants. She needed help desperately.

Rosa looked totally bewildered as she looked from me to her sister - whose large, frightened eyes told me that she was just about to cry.

"It's okay, Rosa," I told her. "If I open the door leading into the entrance hall, I can see the library from here, and I'll make sure to hurry since Señor Mendoza will want to use it after dinner. I won't do anything to get you into trouble. I know how important this job is for you."

The look on her face told me that she was weighing the advisability of leaving me alone for even a few seconds since I would have to pass by the dining room to get to my destination, but an angry voice coming from inside the kitchen made the decision for her.

"It is important," she said. "I send money each week to my family. They need it to survive. My sister has a chance to work here."

"Then you must make sure nothing will jeopardize that," I replied.

"You are very kind, Miss Tremaine, but Señor Mendoza will not be happy if I disobey an order and leave you alone. He is not a kind man when crossed."

Her pleading should have made me reconsider my actions, but this might be the last chance I had to help myself out of a very precarious situation by learning something useful. Besides, there had to be an object in the library with which to defend myself, other than a gun from his costly collection. I just needed a few moments to find and secure it without getting caught. I no longer felt like I could wait for Jorge Santos' help. He might forget about assisting me if something more pressing came up.

"I'll be out of there in a flash, and I promise to take all the blame if I am caught," I assured her.

"I do not know, Miss Tremaine," she lamented as her sister pulled on her arm again. That seemed to help her make a very difficult decision. "Just hurry! They will not be long. Dessert has already been served."

More of my heart seemed to crumble as I watched them hurry away. Good people shouldn't be put in bad situations, but it still happened everyday. I pushed open the door leading into the short hallway that ran parallel to the dining room. The portal to the room from which much laugher was coming was only slightly ajar. If I stayed close to the far wall no one would see me pass.

It shouldn't have mattered so much if my presence was detected, but I didn't want to be stopped from securing a weapon. My bare hands and jaunty repertoire would not stop my fate from being sealed.

"This will be our best harvest ever," I heard a masculine voice say as I crept closer to the dining room doorway. I knew I shouldn't stop to listen, but the words he spoke next made it impossible for me to move forward.

"The local authorities and their American allies must be sleeping. There has been no talk of a raid."

"Never underestimate your enemy, Miguel, " Mendoza cautioned. "I have reason to believe another agent has been placed in our midst."

My breath caught in my throat. Maria had been right. Mendoza had never bought my cover story, so why had he allowed me to stay? Maybe he'd simply decided it wasn't worth the trouble of getting rid of me until after the harvest was complete. What harm could I do if I never left my room, and he did need someone to teach his children?

"But surely they would not be stupid enough to send in another plant this soon? I thought we had taken care of their interference with Agent Gonzales."

I recognized the voice immediately. It was Jorge Santos, the man who was supposed to be my contact.

"Ah, Maria!" Mendoza said. "I was actually very fond of her. Too bad she betrayed me. I was thinking about asking her to be my wife."

His wife! I mused, and then looked quickly around to make sure no one was watching. I was being foolish tarrying so long in a place I shouldn't be, but if surveillance equipment was in use, they would know what I was doing without eyewitnesses anyway. And if I was going to die, the only thing likely to change would be when and possibly how.

"Yes," Mendoza continued. "It will be sad to kill her after my son is born, but traitors must be dealt with. That includes her recent replacement."

"Surely, you don't think the DEA would use the same cover twice," Jorge Santos said with complete disdain. "The woman I brought from the airport seemed too young and inexperienced with life to be a federal agent. She was literally trembling in her shoes when she saw the plane she was to ride in." A few men laughed. "But I suppose anything is possible since few Americans understand our way of life."

"Stupid or smart, it makes no difference, my dear Jorge. Anyone who betrays me will suffer the same fate."

The rapid beating of my heart made my head start to swim. What had I done to give myself away? I had talked to no one besides the children, Rosa, Alma and Mendoza himself since arriving at the compound, except for Maria. Had one of his henchmen seen her entering or leaving my room the night before? Or had they simply known about the switch from the beginning?

"This Miss Tremaine, she is too cool," Mendoza went on. "She says little, but observes all. It should not be too hard to catch her in a lie if that would make you feel better about killing her, Jorge."

"I am at your command," the man who was supposed to be helping me said.

"I have never doubted your loyalty, Jorge," Mendoza responded. "Just make sure it never wavers. I have come too far to let anyone stand in the way of my becoming the most powerful and feared cartel leader in all of Colombia; perhaps even all of South America. But no more talk of this, gentlemen. Our Miss Tremaine cannot escape the compound, and if she does, Jorge will take care of her just as he has the others who have tried to cross me. After all, the hunt is the most exciting part of any game."

Oh, how I wished I was back in my room. Maybe Maria was wrong about Jorge Santos. If he was in charge of executions, he certainly couldn't be our contact. But during the brief moment I spent contemplating that thought, I heard chair legs scrape across the wood floor in the dining room.

I should have turned around and gone back the way I had come, but I was almost to the entry of the hacienda. If I could just make it to the library, I could feign getting caught up looking for a new book, but what difference would that make if they already knew who I was? Quite likely, it would only hasten my execution.

My feet carried me quickly though the doorway and into the cavernous room where the propane-powered chandelier with hundreds of crystal droplets cast a unearthly glow. I was no more than a foot from the library when a calm, but deeply penetrating, voice stopped my forward motion.

"Why, Miss Tremaine, what a surprise."

I turned to accept my fate, but it was not Mendoza who stood in the shadows. It was Jorge Santos, but not the scruffy Jorge Santos in sandals and work clothes who had picked me up at the airport. This man looked like an aristocrat in his black suit, with his hair combed back and his facial hair neatly trimmed.

"Good evening, Señor Santos," I said as I took a tenable step towards him on the marble floor. "I was just on my way to the library to find another book to read."

If they could play games, then so could I. His dark, flashing eyes studied me intently as he moved towards me, and I felt like a caged animal about to be devoured by a ravenous wolf.

"Then perhaps I could escort you there. I am sure Señor Mendoza would not mind if you took a moment or two to find a book. You should not have to make a trip down the stairs for nothing."

He had to have known that the grand staircase was not the way I had come. Everyone in the house followed the same rules, but before I could say anything, Mendoza came through the same doorway, along with his other dining companions. There were six of them, equally as well dressed, and equally as dangerous. They looked truly sinister in the dim lighting. Generators that powered the complex were cut to half-power from early evening until the sun came up.

"What have we here?" The man I so greatly loathed asked as the flat tone of his voice made my blood jell. "I see that the children's new governess has decided to disobey one of my cardinal rules by leaving her assigned quarters unaccompanied and without permission again to skulk around my home under certain flimsy pretenses."

He didn't have to come right out and say it, but this was all the proof he needed to order Jorge Santos to get rid of me. I'd played right into his hands by taking a stupidly calculated risk, but I wouldn't try to defend myself by telling him that I had followed protocol. Rosa and her sister did not need to be drawn into this.

"Is there something we can do for you, Miss Tremaine?" he continued. "I am sure our business can wait a few minutes longer."

His coldness penetrated to my very soul, but he had nothing to lose by continuing with his game. I would never get out of the compound alive anyway.

"I was going to return this book," I replied.

"Surely you have not finished it already. You just got it last night."

"I was in the mood for something lighter."

"Then by all means, we must help you find something simple and light-hearted. Every life needs some levity before it is over." He held out his arm to me. "I would never want to be remembered as anything but gallant."

Remembered? Was this just another one of his sick perversions, baiting people he would soon have eliminated? Still, I had no choice but to slip my hand through the crook of his arm. I was still alive. That meant there was still hope I might stay that way. Jorge Santos had not betrayed me, and he knew I hadn't been entering the library from the main staircase.

"I won't take long, Señor Mendoza," I assured the evil man at my side. "I thought I'd have time to find another book before you finished eating."

"But of course, my dear Miss Tremaine. We cannot have an illiterate governess, now can we?"

He patted my arm and a wave of revulsion swept over me. How could Agent Gonzales have become intimate with him? He was as repulsive as a death-inflicting serpent.

"Take as long as you like. We are in no hurry. I would offer you some brandy, but I know you do not partake of the finer things of life."

My smile was anything but genuine as the men he'd been dining with passed by us and gathered in front of the fireplace. I had no idea who any of them were, but they were not fieldworkers. Their skin had not been hardened by hours in the wind and the rain, and their hands were free of calluses and stains. A tray of goblets filled with amber liquid was sitting on one of the small tables that had been carefully placed around the room.

I looked up to see where Jorge Santos was. He was in the middle of the group of men chatting amiably. It was as though he'd forgotten my presence.

"Perhaps I could help you find what you are looking for, Miss Tremaine," Mendoza continued instead of joining his comrades in their after-dinner drinks. "There are some marvelous books about Colombia. Perhaps you were looking for something that would explain more about our jungles, and the possibility of traversing through them on your own."

He was still baiting me, like a cat with a field mouse. Maybe I wouldn't be shot if I tried to escape. That would certainly make his explanation to his children easier. They already knew that no one survived for long in the jungle. He would only have to say that I'd wandered away from the compound and had become lost.

"I really have no preference, Señor Mendoza, all books bring edification, especially the classics." I glanced down at the book in my hand. "But I do feel like reading more of a comedy tonight."

"The *Taming of the Shrew*, perhaps," he said, retrieving the leather-bound volume from my hands. "I see you have a fondness for the Bronte sisters. I haven't read any of their work, but my late wife enjoyed them immensely. She was from a very prosperous family and had received an extensive education. I was hoping the same would happen for my own children."

How could he speak of her so casually when he had been the one responsible for her death? But he was not like any man I had known before. It was almost as if he was devoid of conscience.

"I'm sorry I never got to meet her," I said.

"Her life ended so unfortunately. Perhaps that is why I prefer the tragedies, Miss Tremaine, from Greek myths to Shakespeare. Who cannot get caught up in the story of a Trojan horse or a mad king? They are the things legends are made of."

Did he consider himself a legend? It wouldn't surprise me. Evil people reveled in power and glory. Wasn't that exactly what the Father of all Lies wanted, deluding and sustaining his supporters in their visions of grandeur until their souls were lost? Then he would desert them and move on to someone else. Carlos Mendoza might win this war on drugs, but he would lose big when the time came for him to stand before his maker.

"I'm sure you have more important things to do than pick out reading material for a simple teacher of children," I told him, no longer wanting to be part of his perverted games.

"There is little of more importance than education. Had I not gone to your country to study, I would never be the man I am today. You Americans have a great deal of money, along with habits that need to be indulged. It is easy to find people who are willing to take a few risks. Generations of associates are found that way."

I was tired of his riddles and innuendos. They were making my head swim. He had already decided to eliminate me. Why was he even bothering to be cordial? I'd be dead in a few hours anyway, and it would be business as usual unless the authorities that were supposed to be coming in the next few hours caught him. But at least he'd answered one of my questions. Tess Tremaine had not come to his compound by accident. She had been recruited.

"But you are right," he continued. "I do have other more pressing matters tonight. A man does not remain on top by allowing distractions to keep him from what needs to be done."

He walked over to one of the rows of books my fingers had touched the last time I'd been in the library.

"Here is one you should enjoy, even if you have read it before," he said, holding out another leather-bound volume towards me. It was identical to the one I had just returned except for the title on the spine and cover. I had read *Little Women* as a young girl, but knew that any objection would be pointless. I would be lucky to make it through the first chapter before one of his men came looking for me.

"Thanks for your generosity in allowing me to use your library," I told him. "I am sorry for having disrupted your evening. I should have come down earlier, or not at all."

"Never apologize, Miss Tremaine. It shows weakness. You must be aggressive, even cruel, if you are going to survive out here."

There was no doubt about his message. He was lord of his empire and would squash anyone who got in his way, but it did make me wonder if he was challenging me to try to escape.

"Perhaps I should escort Miss Tremaine back to her room," Jorge Santos said with just the right amount of derision to be convincing. "We would hate for her to get lost again, and there is much to be discussed."

I held my breath waiting for Mendoza's reply. I could be marched out the front door and into the night when it came.

"But of course, Jorge," he said. "One mistake a day is enough for anyone, and my children's education is still very important to me."

It was hard being submissive to a man who had already decided my fate. I no longer questioned my supposed employer's complete lack of scruples. He was a sociopath with no aversion to killing. He likely even enjoyed it.

I left the room without looking back. Mendoza held all the cards in this game of chance, but it was Jorge Santos who kept a firm grip on my arm and almost pulled me up the stairs without saying anything. There was nothing I could do, except try to keep from falling in our haste, until we arrived at my bedroom door. We had passed no servants and only one guard on the way.

"Thank you for escorting me, but it was hardly necessary. I know my way back to my room," I told him before opening my door.

He released the pressure on my upper arm and I automatically pulled away. He might not have revealed the way he had found me in the entry, but that didn't mean he wasn't going to kill me. He was dressed for the evening and likely didn't want to ruin his good clothes.

When I forced myself to look up at him, he only scowled. "I am sure you are aware of a great many things, Miss Tremaine, besides the way to your room. Too bad you ever decided to leave it tonight. Rules are in place for a reason. I believe I told you that on our way here."

"I take my work here very seriously," I told him. "I was only looking for something more interesting to read. The evenings can be very long when one is confined to her room."

"Sometimes, we are our own worst enemies, Miss Tremaine. You should have stayed home where you belonged."

I tried to keep my hands from shaking as I pushed open my door. I was about to step inside when his voice stopped me.

"Excuse me," he said in a tone that gave nothing away. "But it appears that something has dropped from your book."

I opened my mouth to protest as I looked down at the floor, but he was already bending over. When he stood upright, he handed me a folded slip of paper.

"Thank you," I replied. "I should have been more watchful."

My heart was beating wildly. It had to be a note from him. I would have noticed if the book had opened even slightly. I was gripping it so tightly I thought I might crush the spine.

His movements were always methodical, and his face and voice betrayed nothing. Perhaps that was why Mendoza still trusted him, along with the fact that it he took care of some very ugly business. I could never be a trained assassin like him, even if it became part of my job, and my only means for staying alive.

"I must be returning to the other guests," he said, taking a step away from me. "I trust you have everything you need and will not leave the comfort of your room again until morning. The night is lengthy and dark, and disagreeable things happen to those who do not obey. Too bad you did not listen to my earlier warnings. It would have saved me a great of trouble. I do not enjoy being forced into doing things because of others foolish errors."

His words chilled me. Was he telling me that plans had already been made to remove me from the hacienda? Mendoza obviously knew who I was, and Jorge Santos took care of problems for him. If I was his next problem, then why the warning about staying put? But then perhaps executions only took place in the morning, once the sunlight had made it to the top of the stately, tropical trees outside the compound walls, and everyone could see what disloyalty cost the betrayer.

I stepped inside my room, closed the door and then listened to his footsteps as he made his way back along the parquet floor until he reached the marble staircase before opening the note he'd given me.

"Tonight!" was all it said.

It took a moment for the relief to wash over me. The note could only mean that I was being extracted before the raid occurred, and I needed to prepare. But how, and who would be going with me? I doubted Jorge Santos would be willing or able to leave since he'd worked for years to see this cartel brought down and was likely in a key position to make sure it happened. As for Maria, she had already expressed her decision to remain since her baby was about to be born. But how could I leave knowing what her fate would be? In his own words, Mendoza had condemned her to death.

I needed to find her and persuade her to come with me. It wouldn't be easy since I had no idea what our escape would entail or who might be leading it, but anything had to be better than just waiting to die.

Tears clouded my vision as I knelt beside my bed in a house filled with danger and thought about all the great men and women who stood up for truth despite tremendous danger. What I needed a miracle, and not the small ones I'd been used to all my life. I needed something huge like Moses parting the Red Sea, or Daniel being delivered from the lion's den, or David meeting Goliath on the battlefield. Nothing else would do right now.

I was in a terrible situation – one brought on by a choice I had willingly made - but that didn't mean my selection of a vocation had rendered God's power in my life ineffective. It only meant that I had to rely on him more than ever right now. So I prayed for deliverance from my enemies, and not to lose faith in the presence of fear, even if my safe return home to my family and friends did not happen.

When I rose to my feet, my trepidation had vanished. Thanks to God's goodness and guiding light, I knew what to do. I dug through my drawers and closet for the warmest clothing I could find. I would have to wear several layers since I had no idea what it would be like in the jungle or how long I might be there. Then I secured my passport and what little money I had left in the button-down pocket of the shirt I was wearing.

I took the time necessary to pack all the medical supplies I could find in the small knapsack I'd brought with me, along with the diary Tess had written. I felt it might be important someday. Then I added a couple of towels, filled my water bottle and put the last of the protein bars I'd brought with me from the states inside the knapsack and zipped the flap shut.

There was no need to worry about a weapon. There wasn't even a butter knife in the room, but I'd included the razor I used to shave my legs, a fingernail file, and a pair of tweezers. Anything sharp would be better than nothing, and then I sat down on the edge of the bed to wait.

It seemed like I remained in the dark for hours listening for the slightest sound that would indicate I'd be leaving the compound. When I'd just about decided to lie down and try to give my body a chance to decompress, I heard something brush against my door. But this time I waited for the visitor to open the door instead of rushing towards it.

A moment later, Maria stepped inside. She was dressed in the black nightgown she'd been wearing the first time she'd come to my room. She didn't say anything until she'd crossed the short distance to where I was now standing. I stood almost a foot taller than her, and my height alone made me want to protect her, even if she was the more experienced agent.

"You must go now," she whispered. "Jorge will be waiting for you outside the gates. I will show you the way to the tunnels."

"The tunnels?" I questioned. If escape was this easy, why hadn't they tried it before?

"He drugged the wine after dinner. He said there was no other way of getting you out of the compound now that Carlos knows who you are and has asked that you be executed at first light. He is not happy leaving until the authorities get here. The raid is to take place in the next few hours. He has given everything to this cause over the past few years, but if he remains he will be executed himself since Mendoza will know he is a traitor too. Jorge has done many things he is not proud of, but he would never risk the life of a fellow agent, especially one who never should have been sent here. Everyone inside the hacienda who has power to raise an objection is asleep, but the effects will not last long. You should have time to get inside the jungle if you hurry."

I took her hands in mine. "You have to come with us, Maria. You deserve to live and be free and so does your baby. Mendoza has every intention of killing you once the child is born."

Her voice choked. "I deserve to be punished. I broke the most important rule of all. I got involved with the man I was sent to bring down. I have no excuses for my actions. I knew he had killed his wife and would do the same to me if he discovered who I was, but I thought if he trusted me we could obtain the information we needed sooner ..." her voice drifted off.

"He used you, Maria. He is a powerful and ruthless man."

"You don't understand, Miss Tremaine. I am dead no matter what I do. My family will reject me the moment they know who the father of my baby is. I come from a strict Catholic family, and I have betrayed both God and the blessed Mother, not to mention my superiors and my country."

I couldn't begin to understand the depth of her guilt and anguish, but I couldn't leave her defenseless to die at the hands of a man as cold-blooded and ruthless as Carlos Mendoza.

"I come from a very religious family too," I told her. "But my parents would never disown me because I made a mistake, no matter how big it was."

"Then you are very lucky," she said. "My great-grandmother was killed for cheating on her husband."

"But you didn't do that! You were forced into the relationship."

"Part of me enjoyed it. Carlos is a very sensual man."

I could hear the sorrow in her voice, and I reached out to her again in the dark. She was such a small, delicate woman. Her head came just above my shoulders, and her body trembled as I put my arms protectively around her. Then she started to cry. I knew at that moment just how alone and frightened she really was, despite her show of acceptance and bravado.

"Please come with us," I pleaded. "You're not alone anymore. I won't let anything happen to you or your baby. We'll escape together, or we'll go down fighting. If you decide to stay, then so will I."

My determination was unwavering. If we both stayed, we both died, and Mendoza and his men might never be brought to justice, but I simply couldn't walk away. My family would never know what had happened to me, except that I had died in the line of duty, but I could never live with myself if I let an innocent baby die.

"Do you really think we can make it, Miss Tremaine? My baby could be born at any time."

"My name is Reagan," I told her, hoping to dispel some of the fear by revealing my true identity. "And we'll never know if we can make it if we don't try. We are in this together."

"Then I will come," she answered with a heavy sigh of relief, but I must change my clothing and gather up a few of the things I've been making for my baby. Please follow me."

My relief at her coming with us was short lived. I bent down long enough to retrieve my jacket and pick up the knapsack on my bed. When I stood erect again, she was gone, and Jorge Santos was standing in the doorway, his eyes mere slits in his angry face.

"What the hell is going on, Miss Tremaine?" he seethed. "You were supposed to meet me five minutes ago. We don't have a lot of time."

This Jorge was a different man than the one I'd conversed with only hours before. He was strong and confident. I liked that. It meant we might have a fighting chance, if he could keep from unleashing more of his anger on me.

"Wait a minute," I whispered at his back as I followed him out of the room. "We can't leave yet. Maria is coming with us."

"Damn," he swore. "Why couldn't she have decided that earlier? I'm not prepared to drag a pregnant lady through the jungle."

Any admiration I had for him quickly faded. "Well, I won't go without her."

"Then you are a fool in addition to being an incompetent agent," he raged through clenched teeth. "Women should never be sent on missions like this. They should be home tending to their babies, or doing whatever useless assignments are given to them."

I wanted to tell him exactly how I felt about his intolerance, but he didn't give me a chance. He moved swiftly down the hall until we came to a staircase that was deftly hidden behind a screen and a potted plant. He had obviously been this way before. It wasn't something to be found in the dark unless one already knew it existed, and it was likely the way Maria had gone when she'd disappeared so quickly the morning we met.

The stairwell was cold and damp, and I had to hurry not to lose sight of him. He was moving more than quickly down slippery, rock steps in the inky darkness. When we'd made it down several short flights that twisted and turned, he pushed back a partition and stepped into a dimly lit hallway.

"Maria's room is the third door on the right. You get her, and I'll make sure we haven't been followed. But I must tell you upfront that she's your responsibility, and you must make sure she keeps up. We only have a couple of hours before all hell breaks loose around here."

"Why can't we just wait for the raid?" I asked. "We're on the same side."

"Because thanks to your total lack of competence, your cover has been blown to hell, and I was given orders to have you executed before morning. Mendoza isn't one to offer leniency to anyone, and that includes me."

"Does he know who you are?" I asked.

"Not unless I decide to continue with this farce," he snarled. "These are bad men, and it's taken me nearly four years and a whole lot of things I'd rather not admit to having done to bring them down. How dare you expect me to be pleasant when I end up babysitting two bungling women instead of completing my mission? Our troops should be here before first light, but I'm not about to risk executing a woman - even if she might deserve it. There wasn't time to notify the DEA about a change in plans."

I knew better than to try to defend myself to a man who had every right to hate me. He'd invested everything he had in this operation, and I'd ruined the victory for him. But for the life of me, I couldn't understand why he hadn't been able to get word to the DEA about Maria. If he'd just told them what had happened to her, I would never have been sent here, and his raid would have happened without incidence. Nothing about this operation made any sense to me.

Chapter 8

Maria had put on a long dress and a heavy jacket, but I was worried that she wouldn't be warm enough in her condition. She should be wearing close-fitting clothes and heavy boots that would help protect her against whatever we might find outside the compound walls, if we were lucky enough to make it that far. From where I stood, Jorge Santos seemed perfectly capable of changing his mind and leaving us to escape on our own.

"I'm sorry, but I have nothing else to wear," she apologized, looking down at her protruding belly. "I did not mean for this to happen."

Obviously, she'd had no intention of becoming pregnant while on assignment, but still it had happened, and I knew getting her and her baby to safety was a long shot at best. She had a small bag in one hand.

"You need to leave that," "Jorge Santos told her, the contempt in his voice obvious. "It's only going to slow you down."

She looked up at me with pleading eyes. I knew the bag contained the things she'd made for her baby.

"I'll carry it," I said as I took it from her. It was too heavy to be filled with only linens, but I wasn't going to question either her actions or her motives. She had the right to carry away anything she wanted to after all the suffering she'd endured. A few expensive things would come in handy as she tried to reestablish herself in a place where Mendoza would never be able to find her—if such a place could even be found.

"Thank you," was all she had time to say before we were both following our reluctant escort down another flight of stairs into a room that smelled of moss, damp dirt, and fermented wine. We were in Mendoza's well-stocked wine cellar, but we had come to it from an entirely different direction than the one I'd found.

"This way," he said as we rounded the first aisle of shelves. "The entrance to the tunnel is at the far end of the cellar."

I was shivering as much from fear as the cold dampness. Why couldn't we have just gone out one of the doors? But then Mendoza's servants hadn't been drugged, and they seemed to be everywhere whether it was day or night, as were his guards, who were stationed at intervals along the brick wall that surrounded the compound. I wondered what had happened to Alma. She was always skulking around somewhere.

"How are you doing?" I asked Maria who was just a few steps in front of me. I could hear her softly panting, and it worried me. Our journey had barely begun.

"Do not be concerned about me," she said. "I will keep up. I am doing this so my baby can be free."

Santos had a flashlight shining its beam on the rock wall by the time we reached him. He was a tall man—well over six feet tall with broad shoulders and a determined gait—very unlike the other men I'd observed as they made their way from the dining room to the library for drinks. They were much shorter and their skin was a shade or two darker. I was beginning to wonder if he was even Spanish as he pretended to be.

"Not so high," Maria told him. "I have been down here many times. The lever should be just about here." She reached out her hand until it touched what looked like just another stone to me.

How had she known the access to the tunnel if she hadn't had Mendoza's complete trust at one time? Oh, the web of lies that are created when people try to deceive, even for the right reasons.

"Right here," she said as she pushed against the rock with all the strength her small body could give.

There was a loud, grating noise as rock moved over concrete revealing a passageway into more black, dank darkness.

"Take this," Santos said as he threw a flashlight towards me. "I don't know what might be in this tunnel since there was no time to investigate. I don't suppose either of you brought something with which to defend yourselves."

"Not exactly," I replied as I caught the flashlight and followed them into the overpowering obscurity of the tunnel.

It was a surreal experience, and I forced myself to think about the relief I would feel once we were outside again. The tunnel curved and twisted with passageways leading to both the left and the right. Had I been in the lead, we most certainly would have become lost. This maze was designed to keep people inside. No wonder Maria had not used it to escape. I feared there was more than one body lying within its confines.

I couldn't bring myself to look down at the floor, sideways at the walls or upwards for fear of screaming. I kept my flashlight focused directly at the back of Jorge Santo's head. I didn't want to be separated from him, even though he loathed me right now because my very presence at the hacienda had forced him to make a decision that meant leaving over three years of hard work, commitment and skeletons behind.

There were sounds and movements everywhere, but it was hard to focus on anything other than my rapidly beating heart. I hated the dark, and I hated creepy crawling things even more. Nothing pleasant ever dwelt where the sunlight could not penetrate. More than once, small feet scampered across my boots. Rats, most likely, I told myself, since I wasn't sure what other small rodents lived in tunnels in the jungle. But when the rush of air above my head brought something in contact with my face, I couldn't muffle the shriek of terror that escaped from between my clenched teeth.

"What the hell happened this time," Santos snarled, stopping so abruptly Maria almost crashed into his back. He turned his head and glared at me; looking more than a little sinister in the focused beam of light that made his brow and cheek bones more prominent than ever.

"Nothing," I said as I tired to settle my frazzled nerves. This was not an experience I had ever contemplated having as an FBI agent, but I would not let this man, who had every reason to hate me, know that I was afraid of things "that go bump in the night."

"It was only a bat," Maria whispered as we moved forward again. "They are everywhere, but they are mostly harmless."

Mostly, I pondered as we moved slowly onward. If I was this afraid in a tunnel, what would it be like in the jungle? Perhaps I'd been rash in almost forcing Maria to go with us when I had no idea what we might have to face, but I tried to calm my rising concerns because anything had to be preferable to absolute death. At least this way we had a chance.

Our time in the tunnel was relatively short, but I was still shaking when we came to another door. Jorge Santos leaned into it.

"Damn," he swore. "There must be something blocking it."

I was just about to volunteer to help push when he braced his feet on the uneven ground and rammed his shoulder into it for a second time. It took three additional tries before it moved. The hinges growled and moaned from rust, but soon gave way to the weight, and we looked out of the chilly, dark tunnel into a starless night.

The wind was blowing, and it felt like rain. Jorge Santos kicked at the brush surrounding the outside entrance to the tunnel leading back into Mendoza's lair.

The light from my flashlight was ineffective in the heavy haze that soon covered the glass that protected the bulb inside. I had to keep brushing it away with the sleeve of my coat. Maria was standing next to me, her small frame quivering.

Santos threw one of the two backpacks he'd been carrying towards me. I wondered if he'd missed the fact that I was already wearing one, and I was carrying Maria's bag too.

"We have to keep moving," he said. "The sedatives I put in their drinks will wear off soon. Mendoza will have his band of guerrillas after us the moment he realizes I've betrayed him."

"Where are we going?" I asked, my teeth knocking together so loudly I was sure neither of my companions could miss the sound.

He gave me a look of complete contempt. "Not to the village! That will be the first place he'll look. There's a jeep stashed about ten miles down the mountain. I've had it there for some months in case the unexpected happened, but it won't do us any good unless we can make it through the coca fields before the workers get there. Most of them are loyal to Mendoza because he provides for their basic needs, and they see nothing wrong with the work they do. It suits their way of life because little is demanded, unless they step out of line and are punished. They don't much care what happens once the harvest is over and the crops are prepared for transport, as long as their bellies are full and they have a place to sleep."

I wished I could argue the point with him, but the day laborers were only doing what their ancestors had done for generations. Mendoza and his associates were the ones profiting by turning the plant into cocaine, a lethal and much sought after substance that destroyed millions of lives each year from the pushers and users to the people who loved and tried to help them.

The sides of the hillside had been cleared and rows of bushes that reminded me of the Blackthorn bush had been planted for as far as the eye could see. From my reading, I knew that the coca plants could live for up to 40 years and could grow with their straight branches to a height of 6 to 10 feet with small white flowers that turned into red berries. This must have been one of the newer fields since few of them had grown that tall yet, but the thin, opaque leaves that tapered at the ends and had been missed in the initial picking looked healthy. Everything else had been harvested and stood ready for shipment - if the raid didn't occur on time.

The enormity of the empire Mendoza had built was momentarily awe-inspiring in an evil, vindictive and horrid way if he really had built it on his own. This was likely one of his smaller fields since it was set high in the mountains and only certain strains of the coca plant could survive at this altitude. He must have dozens of similar fields spread across his domain, and the harvesting must be a constant source of worry and ecstasy. I wondered if he had overlords at some of the other locations. There was a reason he had his family stowed away in the jungle. Perhaps he felt it was the safest place for them or the place where he could more easily control them.

I hoped the authorities would burn every branch to the ground, but that wouldn't slow the production of cocaine. For every field the government burned, dozens would spring to life in a matter of days. There was no stopping the greedy, merciless men and women who had power and wealth as their only goals and who had the connections and resources to get away with any crime necessary to secure what they wanted.

We had been walking briskly for almost an hour through tall plants whose leaves and stems had to be brushed away with every step before we reached the trees and low climbing vines that framed the edge of the jungle.

Santos stopped abruptly. "Did you hear that?" he asked.

I listened and so did Maria, but all we could hear was the cawing of colorful birds and the twittering antics of monkeys as they played in the branches above our heads.

When neither of us answered his question, he glanced around again and then frowned. "I suppose the circumstances surrounding this pathetic attempt at escape have made me a little more paranoid than usual. I know what Mendoza is capable of doing when he gets crossed, but perhaps we should take a moment to catch our breath. This has been the easiest part of our journey."

Maria lowered her swollen body to a fallen tree. She was sweating profusely, regardless of the fact that the thickness of the trees and the dark, gray clouds of early morning were hiding any glimpse of the sun. The humidity must be nearly a hundred percent. We'd barely begun our trek, and it was already taking its toll on her. Perhaps my boldness in insisting that she come with us would only backfire, but if she had remained behind, her death was a certainty, and it might come even before her baby was born. Mendoza was unpredictable, and his rage at finding Santos and me gone could easily poison what little humanity he had left.

I handed her the bottle of water I'd brought from the house. She smiled wearily. "Thank you, Reagan," she said. "You have been very kind to a woman who is doing nothing but slowing you down."

"Nonsense," I tried to reassure her. "This is hard for all of us."

Jorge Santos glowered over his shoulder at me and then pulled a long, gleaming machete from his belt. "Getting through the coca fields is a cakewalk compared to what we'll find once we get inside the untamed jungle. We'll have to cut our way through from now on, and I can't predict what will happen to any of us. If Mendoza doesn't get us, it's quite likely some animal or insect will."

"He's not going to get us," I shot back at him through narrowed eyes. Being boorish and shouting insults would not help when we were all doing the best we could. "We just need to pool our resources and work together."

"Now, that is laughable," he said in a voice dripping with sarcasm. "Maria is about to give birth, and I have no idea who the hell you are, except that you've managed to singlehandedly destroy what I've been trying to accomplish for the past four years."

"I was sent here to do a job, just as you were," I retorted, surprised that I was able to stand up to him at all. Despite what Maria had said about him being a good man who would not leave an agent behind, he seemed haughty, uncommunicative and dangerous to me. I doubted it would take much for him to renege on his promise to see us to safety and return to the compound where he would simply have to tell Mendoza that he'd been taking care of both the governess and Maria since they had been the ones plotting against him.

While my own thoughts were swirling, he gave me another hostile look. "Your coming here was a mistake. We didn't need some newbie agent who wasn't even part of the DEA messing up our plans."

"I came because an assignment was given," I replied, tired of the insinuations that I was a liability instead of a partner. It wasn't my fault I'd been kept in the dark until it was too late to be of any help. "And for your information, I did exactly as instructed: find out what had happened to a missing agent, keep a low profile and wait to be extracted. I didn't even know you were my contact until a few hours ago. Why didn't you tell your superiors what had happened to Maria weeks ago? Then my coming would have been unnecessary, and your precious raid could have gone off without a hitch."

"You don't know what the hell you're talking about!"

"Then enlighten me! You had the flexibility to go into Bogotá to pick me up at the airport. How hard would it have been to contact the DEA at some point before my arrival?"

He shot me another venomous look. "That comment proves just how little you know about working undercover. Mendoza keeps his employees on a short leash, and anyone who opposes him or becomes even the slightest threat to his empire is dealt with immediately."

"And that's where your services came in."

"I did what was necessary to maintain my cover and stay alive, but now isn't the time to get sidetracked in what I may or may not have done that might upset your childish view of morality. I didn't even know Maria had gone off the grid until I was informed that a new governess had been hired, and I was to pick her up at the airport. I couldn't exactly return to the compound empty-handed, and I wasn't about to lose everything I'd worked so hard to accomplish over a slip of a girl who should have been stopped before she even arrived. Hell, I didn't even know you were an agent until Maria told me."

I wasn't sure I believed him. He was a member of Mendoza's inner circle and was most certainly privy to a great many things, but he was right about this not being the time to cast stones or ask unnecessary questions.

"Perhaps I don't understand the law of the jungle," I relented. "But if I had been informed a little earlier who you were, I might have been able to help."

"Help!" he exclaimed. "Mendoza had you pegged as a counterfeit the minute you got to the compound. He may have even known before you left the United States since his contacts are as plentiful there as they are here. How would confirming his suspicions have helped any of us? I had to play it the way I always had or risk being executed myself, and I'd worked too damned hard to let that happen."

"Please do not take your anger out on her when you are only mad at me because of the way things turned out," Maria interjected.

"Like hell," he snapped. "What happened between us was a huge mistake and completely unprofessional, but you didn't have to jump right into bed with Mendoza."

I was glad our would be protector and guide had turned his wrath away from me. Still, I wished I could close my ears to what they were saying, but standing next to them in the narrow strip of land that separated the coca fields from the jungle made that impossible.

Maria's eyes were large and tear-filled when she responded to his more than insensitive remarks. "If I had not been so inexperienced, you would not have felt it necessary to comfort me in a time of weakness. We do not always do what is wise, but that does not make us bad people. What happened with Mendoza was a way to ensure that my cover remained intact. He had fancied me from the moment I arrived, and I was not unaware that he had killed his own wife because he no longer trusted her. Nonetheless, I did what I needed to survive and was able to find out a great deal of useful information that contributed to the upcoming raid, but I am not proud of what happened with you or with him. It destroyed all I held dear, but God-willing, perhaps someday I may be allowed to make amends. I only pray my child will not be forced to suffer for the sins of his mother. That is why I agreed to come with you. He must not be raised by the horrible man who is his father."

I was grateful neither of them was looking at me because I knew my face registered more than just surprise at their admissions. Being undercover for indeterminable amounts of time came with untold dangers, and it must have been very difficult living in isolation and sharing the same big secrets month after month, but it was still hard not to be a little judgmental after what had been said about me. They'd both broken innumerable DEA rules while I'd simply been trying to do my job.

"We don't have time to air all our dirty laundry," Santos said as his brows furrowed, and he glanced in my direction. "We need to keep moving, or asking pardon from Father Francis or some other priest for all our indiscretions will be useless. You'll find a gun and ammo in your backpack, Agent, whatever your real name is. I just hope you can use it."

He stomped off towards the dense, jungle foliage before I had time to open the backpack and see what kind of a weapon he'd provided for me.

"Do not mind him," Maria said as I pulled her to her feet. "He has much on his mind. I could have refused Carlo's advances, but I had come too far to pull back just because I did not like what I might be asked to do. I am glad the same thing did not happen to you. Going home in disgrace will not be easy. I will lose my position with the DEA, and the respect of my family, but Father Francis helped me understand that I could make no restitution for my sins if I did not first confront them."

"Father Francis knew what happened?"

"He would never betray a confidence. He is sympathetic to both causes. Not the distribution of cocaine, but the unfortunate lives of the villagers who work the fields. They do not understand that what they are doing is wrong. The coca leaf has been a great help to my people in many times of need."

"I'm sure it has," I said, regardless of the fact that I could make no sense of the world I had entered. Priests could not absolve all sin, and taking certain risks in the hopes of gaining pertinent information while on an assignment just wasn't worth it to me. Still, I could understand the need to support one's family and keep from being put to death.

No wonder Agent Santos was so angry. He'd spent the last few years working with an inexperienced female field agent who had obviously disappointed him, but I doubted that was the only reason for his anger. He wanted to be there when the cartel was brought down, and he deserved his moment of glory after all the time he'd invested trying to make sure it happened. Not that Mendoza would be out of business for long even if he was captured alive. His pockets ran deep, and he'd buy off anyone who could help him reclaim his freedom.

"I can't judge anyone," I told her as we fell into line behind him. "I leave that up to our Savior and our Eternal Father. They are the only ones who know the true intent of our hearts."

"So, you are a Christian," she said as we made our way past another clump of undergrowth.

Mosquitoes and other flying insects were fierce now that the night was wearing off, and that wasn't good. They carried dozens of diseases from malaria and typhus to yellow fever. Even if one didn't become ill from their bites, they could be painful and must itch something awful. Santos was definitely right in saying that if Mendoza or his men didn't get us, there were thousands of other things in the jungle that could—things we couldn't kill with a machete or a gun.

"Yes," I told her, trying to push back the thoughts that were trying to engulf me as I swatted at another bug that was attempting to take a hunk of skin from the side of my neck. There was blood on my palm when I looked down at my hand. "And I believe there is a plan for each one of us."

"Do you come from a big family?"

"I have four brothers, three sisters-in-law, two nephews and five nieces. I guess that makes us a fairly large family."

"Mine also," she replied. "I have three sisters and two brothers. As the oldest, it was my job to help care for them. That is why I became an agent. I could send money home. They still depend on me."

"I'm sure they will be very happy to see you when you return."

"I fear they will not be able to overlook the disgrace I bring. If my baby's father were any other man . . ."

Suddenly, she stopped moving. "I cannot go on," she said. "I must go back."

"It's a little late for that," Agent Santos said, stopping in mid-swing with his machete. He had very good hearing when it suited him.

"You do not understand, Jorge," she said with a sigh that came from somewhere deep inside. "Carlos will have my family killed when he finds out I have tried to escape. I must go back before that happens."

"Mendoza will not spare them anymore than he will spare you if you are foolish enough to do go back," he said. "Your only hope is to get them into protective custody before he goes after them."

"We can do that?" she asked.

"The government can, but let's not worry about that right now. We have more pressing problems at hand."

I took her hand reassuringly in mine. He was right. If we didn't make it out of the jungle, none of us would return to our families. Maria would not be able to keep hers safe, and mine would never know what had happened to me. That thought alone would keep me putting one foot in front of the other until I was no longer able to move.

Had the circumstances been different, I might have enjoyed the trek through the jungle. The colors of the birds were amazing from the tiniest of hummingbirds to the highly-colored macaws and parrots with their dazzling reds, pinks, blues, yellows and greens. They filled the trees with their presence and the air with their songs. Closer to the tree line, I could see larger vultures and eagles, predatory birds who circled until their prey was close to death before coming in for the final kill.

There were butterflies and moths; larger and more rich in color than any I had seen in the United States, and glorious flowers like delicate purple orchids and sweet-smelling, pink bromeliads. But this was not a nature walk where God's creations could be enjoyed and admired. We could be spotted at any moment and killed before we were able to defend ourselves.

My eyes continually scanned our surroundings, although it was impossible to see more than a few feet into the thick foliage that surrounded us so closely on every side. I watched Maria and tried to help her climb over or push past every obstruction we encountered. There were moments when we came to complete standstills as Santos tried to clear a path large enough for us to move through. I had no doubt that anyone who came after us would have no trouble discovering which way we had gone. We were leaving a trail of crushed leaves and cut off branches that would be impossible not to detect. Our only hope was that the Colombian Police and the DEA would arrive before Mendoza discovered we had gone and sent his guerrillas looking for us with orders to shoot on sight.

Every so often, I caught sight of a lizard or a tree frog. I even saw a giant armadillo with its gray, spiny covering, but the most amazing creatures in the jungle - to me anyway - were the monkeys who swung from branch to branch over our heads calling out playfully to their companions in neighboring trees. Luis loved the White-footed Tamarin and the Colombian Woolly, but my favorite would always be the Longhaired Spider Monkey with its penetrating eyes, happy chatter and entertaining antics. We were moving too fast to pay much attention to any of them, but I knew they were close, and that gave me comfort since I knew they were some of the few mammals or reptiles that wouldn't harm us.

I wasn't so concerned about my own death since I had always tried to do what was right. It was the thought of what my family would go through not knowing what had happened to me that caused the most anguish. They didn't deserve the uncertainty, and I would miss not meeting the right man and having children of my own. I had wanted that from the time I was small—regardless of the work I'd chosen to do—but I had to believe I would be protected until it was my time to die.

We had been fighting our way though heavy foliage and damp underbrush for quite some time when we unexpectedly heard the sound of helicopters flying above our heads.

"They're here," Agent Santos said, looking upwards, but we were completely hidden beneath a canopy of trees. No one would see us unless they were in the jungle following the path he'd cleared.

"How many are coming?" I asked.

"If the local authorities and the DEA are both involved, there could be a hundred troops. If not . . . Let's just say that I'm not sure the good guys will stand a fighting chance. I should have been allowed to remain behind and finish my mission as planned. We have very few friends anywhere in these mountains, and no one involved in the cultivation of the crops is going to help us once their livelihoods have been destroyed. For better or worse, I'm afraid we're on our own now."

I felt complete nausea rise to my throat. He could blame me all he wanted for disrupting his mission, but it wouldn't help our situation, nor would it help the men who were arriving to try to take down the members of the cartel inside of the compound.

"Please, Jorge," Maria said. "Do not blame Reagan too much. She was only trying to do her job. There are others inside those walls who will help. Rosa will make sure the servants are safe, and her sister will make sure both the front door and the one outside the kitchen are unlatched."

So, I had not been wrong in assuming that Rosa was different than the other servants at the hacienda, but would she and her sister be safe? There were no doubt a great many places to hide, but bullets could penetrate almost anything, and there was Alma to consider. That woman frightened me every bit as much as Mendoza did.

The whirring of the blades was almost deafening it was so close, and then the first explosion sounded. Maria jumped in fright.

"Are they dropping explosives?" she cried out. "What about the children?"

"Try not to worry about them. Our team will try to lure as many of Mendoza's men into the open as possible before storming the hacienda. Though you can be sure that the great man himself will not be among them. I know his every route of escape. He'll want to get one of his own choppers off the ground before it's too late."

"That cannot happen now," Maria said.

"Probably not since the airspace above the hacienda is being overrun as we speak. My job was to make sure Mendoza was captured alive—with as little bloodshed as possible—so he could be interrogated. His dynasty does not stop at the compound walls. He has dozens more operations like this scattered all across the country. We were hoping to get information from him on a great many things."

"All does not have to be lost," Maria said. "You know many of his people, and I have made the acquaintance of a number of his most valued confidants as well. I was not always housed in the dungeon. I attended a great any parties while I was still in his good graces."

"We could spend forever making lists of people who are involved, but little good that will do us if we cannot find them."

"You are just upset, Jorge," she responded.

"Damned right, I am," he replied, looking at me with derision again.

I hadn't disrupted any of his plans intentionally. I'd only been following orders with no one around to help me. But all the self-justification in the world could not stop what was happening now or the repercussions that might ensue. The DEA did not know that Agent Santos had been forced away from the compound before the raid began so the lives of two inexperienced, female operatives could be saved.

The helicopters with their explosives and machine guns were dropping their bombs and firing round after round at the men who stood on top of the walls. The din of noise was deafening, making it impossible to tell exactly what was going on, but I could clearly picture in my mind the men dressed in bulletproof vests with DEA or Policía printed in bold letters on the front, jumping to the ground or trying to climb down swaying rope ladders without being killed. They could be inside the compound, trying to gain admittance over the walls, or bursting through the front gate, armed with guns and rounds of ammunition, already engaged in the battle that would end in far too much slaughter.

More gunfire! More blades whirling!

Were they storming the hacienda? Were they in the great entry hall that had so impressed me just a few days earlier? Were they firing into the library with all the beautifully bound books? Were Mendoza and his men fighting back? Were the children and servants safe, or had they become innocent victims in the not so innocent war against drugs?

I thought I heard screaming. Perhaps it was only the mimicking Macaws, but the sound was enough to make my blood freeze. There would be casualties, no doubt about that.

"We've got to keep moving," Jorge Santos said as more gunshots erupted.

I looked down at Maria. Tears were rolling down her cheeks. She didn't even try to wipe them away.

"It's going to be okay," I tried to comfort her, but I knew that many innocent people would lose their lives today.

"Perhaps," she said as she inched forward. "But I should have stayed behind. I might have been able to help."

"How?" I asked.

She didn't respond, but the immediate rounding of her shoulders let me know that her remorse for past actions was great.

Santos angrily swung his machete at the vines that grew profusely in all directions. Why had I ever agreed to come to South American? I wasn't ready for a field assignment of this magnitude, especially one with an agency I knew nothing about. They should have picked someone with more experience or gotten their facts straight. If they had, I'd be home right now, not fighting my way through a jungle with a pregnant woman and a man who hated both of us. There was no way all of us would survive.

The popping sounds were becoming louder. That meant the fighting had moved from the compound to the fields. Had all the workers arrived? Were they fighting back? And what about Mendoza and the men who had eaten dinner with him the past two nights? Had they still been drowsy from their induced sleep when the first attack came, or had they been at least somewhat prepared, regardless of the fact that they hadn't known the raid was coming.

It wouldn't surprise me if Carlos Mendoza tried to escape through the tunnels just as we had done, leaving the other members of his cartel to take the fall. He might act like an all-powerful drug lord, whom everybody feared, but inside he was a coward. Wasn't that the reason he surrounded himself with dozens of armed guerrillas? They were meant to fight his battles, but how would they feel when they realized he'd taken the easy, less honorable way out?

I doubted that more than a select few even knew the tunnels existed, but he wouldn't have had them constructed without intending to use them if the need arose. Would he try to take his children with him or leave them behind in Alma's callous care? Surely, she would be able to protect them, unless she left when he did. I had not been able to figure out her role at the hacienda. She was more than just a servant because he appeared to listen to her, but how much more was beyond me.

Oh, how I hated to think about what might be happening behind those impressive walls. The adults in the compound had chosen their fates. Hired soldiers knew they could be killed, household servants came and went at their master's whim, and farm workers were just doing what had been done for hundreds of years by cultivating a crop that would give them a better livelihood than raising coffee, bananas or corn, but children were innocent until they had reached the age of accountability and understood the difference between right and wrong.

As unrealistic as it was, I understood why Maria wanted to go back. Luis and Isabel would be heartbroken when they found out that both of us were gone. They needed our protection and care, and it would not be easy never knowing what had happened them.

The toe of my boot caught a vine that was too close to the ground for Santos to have removed. I wobbled precariously for a moment before moving on. I had to stay focused if I was going to live, but it was hard to ignore what was going on behind me.

In many ways, I deserved Santos' wrath for taking away his glory in being at the forefront of the raid he'd spent four years helping to plan. I couldn't begin to imagine the amount of energy he'd invested, or the number of horrid things he'd done to ensure his place in Mendoza's inner sanctum. I could never be an undercover DEA agent who was expected to do immoral and unethical things to get a job done. I wanted my actions to remain transparent and virtuous as I fought for the truths I had pledged to uphold.

My own jaw was clenched so hard I thought it might lock as I inched my way forward. In its pure form, coca leaves were chewed to relieve fatigue and hunger, and to help conserve body heat; all things I knew Maria was suffering from now. I wished there was something I could do to do help her, but the few granola bars in my bag needed to be saved until we really needed them.

"They're getting closer," Santos whispered. "We've got to move faster."

I looked back at Maria, who had somehow fallen behind. Her face was red, and she was sweating profusely.

"I cannot move any faster," she panted.

She was clutching her swollen belly as if she was in a great deal of pain, and my concern for her safety quickly heightened.

"Are you okay?" I asked, stopping in the narrow, green pathway Jorge had cut to wipe the perspiration from my own forehead so she would have time to catch up.

"I do not think my baby likes all this walking. He is being overly active right now."

Her anxiety must be far greater than mine since she so close to delivering her child. I could only pray that she wasn't going into labor because physical exertion and mental stress could certainly bring it on. We'd lose both mother and child if that happened before we found shelter.

"So you're going to have a boy," I asked, waiting until she closed the few steps between us. I could hear the swooshing of Jorge Santos' blade as it lopped at the vines a few feet ahead.

"Oh, yes," she said. "The doctor Carlos engaged for the delivery confirmed it. He said I was carrying my baby too low for it to be a girl. He should be returning to the hacienda any day now."

"Is he there often?" I asked as I brushed away another insect that had touched my face.

"Only when he is needed. Alma takes care of most of our medical needs."

"Is she a nurse?"

Maria shook her head. "I am not sure what credentials she has. I only know that Carlos has a great respect for her many talents. I am just glad that my son will never be left in her care."

"You must be very excited," I told her. There was no reason to torment her further with more questions concerning Alma since she obviously knew very little about her. "I've heard that most women want to have a boy first."

"Oh, yes," she said. "My son will be strong and beautiful, and now that he can be born free, there is much to rejoice about."

I looked down at her beautiful face with its dark, frightened eyes. It was important that she not lose hope. It was the only thing that would keep her moving forward.

"I hope I'm there to see your baby come into the world," I told her, praying that we'd make it to civilization long before that happened. I had no idea how to deliver a baby, and I doubted that Jorge Santos knew any more about it than I did.

"Oh, you shall be," she replied, breathing deeply, even though the air was too heavy to fill anyone's lungs. "In fact, I want you to be my son's godmother. If you had not convinced me to leave, my baby would be born at the hacienda, and I would not be around to see him grow up. Carlos would see to that."

I was grateful that our conversation had given her something more productive to think about than the gunfire that suddenly seemed less constant.

"I'd be honored to be your baby's godmother," I told her, although I had no idea what it actually meant. From the movies and TV shows I'd watched, I gathered it was being there in case something happened to the child's parents and being included in special occasions like birthdays and weddings. That seemed highly improbable since I lived in another country, but I knew Maria was extending the highest privilege possible when it came to having a child, and I couldn't deny such an earnest request.

Jorge Santos had stopped chopping. He swung around and gave us another furious look. We were no more than five yards behind him.

"What's the matter now?" he demanded. "We're far from being safe."

"Maria needed to rest for a moment," I told him. "We've been walking for a very long time."

"Not long enough," he said, taking a few steps towards us with his machete gripped tightly in one hand. I had no doubt he would like to use it on me after what I'd cost him, but I knew he wouldn't hurt Maria. I could see the concern he had for her in his eyes. "In case you've forgotten, we have an army of men who could descend on us at any moment."

"We haven't forgotten, but the gunfire has let up considerably, " I replied, biting the inside of my lips. "Perhaps they're all in custody now."

"Stupid girl," he said, wiping the sweat from his own brow. "Have you learned nothing since your arrival? Mendoza will not stop until we are all dead."

The muscles in his arms were rock solid. That was easily discernible now that his shirt was clinging so tightly to his body. He'd removed his coat earlier since he'd been cutting a path for us through the underbrush. I'd removed mine as well, but Maria was still wearing hers and continued to look as if she was freezing.

She was not wearing heavy boots like Santos and me. Her feet were covered with the same soft slippers she'd been wearing inside the hacienda, and they were soaked. I wondered if Mendoza had taken all her heavy clothing away as a means of keeping her from trying to leave, even though he knew she would never make it anywhere by herself on foot.

"And just for the record," he continued. "I'm Agent Sam Fielding of the DEA, not Jorge Santos. That was my cover to get close to Mendoza. I guess if we're risking our lives for each other we might as well be honest about who we really are. None of us will be going back to the compound anyway."

"Agent Reagan Sinclair, FBI," I volunteered, grateful we were all taking a moment to catch our breath. I didn't want Maria's baby arriving while we were walking and climbing over every obstruction imaginable. If the raid had been successful, maybe we could stop at the village with the happy children and get some help, but my hopes were dashed before I'd even uttered them aloud.

"I wish we could take more time to rest, Maria," he was saying. "But we need to put as much distance as we can between us and the compound just in case Mendoza wasn't captured."

"I understand," she said, but the words had no more than slipped out when she started to sway backwards. I thought she was going to collapse, but Agent Fielding caught her arm before I had time to move.

"Damn it," he swore. "We can't stop here on a trail any fool could find, but there's a brush house not too far away. It's more secluded."

I took Maria's other arm. "Will you be able to make it that far?" I asked.

She swatted rather helplessly at the nits and flies that were swarming around her face. "I can make it," she said, taking a tentative step forward. "I am so sorry for slowing you down. You would be miles away from here if it was not for me."

Agent Fielding shook his head. "We're not going to leave you behind, Maria. You're one of us. I'll carry you out of this damned jungle if I have to."

Fortunately, he wasn't glancing in my direction, or he would have seen the look of shock and disbelief on my face. A few minutes earlier he had been cursing our very existence, and now he was offering to carry Maria for miles over some of the roughest terrain I'd ever seen. Who would clear the path if it came to that? It took a great deal of strength to render blows hard enough to cut through live foliage, and it would take me ages to accomplish what one swing of his arm could do.

"You won't have to carry me, Jorge," she said. "I will always think of you as Jorge. We made good partners before everything became so complicated."

I held my breath, not wanting to hear any more confessions unless they facilitated our flight out of the jungle.

"Yes, we did," he responded, almost smiling at her. "But we're different people now, and that was a long time ago. But come . . ." He pulled her forward. "Let's get you some rest. The remainder of the journey is going to be much harder than what we've already experienced."

He handed me the machete and practically propelled her forward. The blade was heavy and cumbersome, but I followed as best I could as we moved away from the pathway he'd been making into the interior of a tropical forest with branches and vines that seemed determined to take off of one of my appendages. I didn't know how Agent Fielding was moving forward at all without chopping a pathway first, but he obviously didn't want anyone to know where we had gone. I wondered how long we might be able to stay there. Maria needed more than rest; she needed a safe and sterile place to stay until her baby arrived.

Chapter 9

The shack we came to after the most difficult hike of my life where I was slapped across the face with branches and water-soaked leaves and struggled to get the small suitcase and machete I was carrying through some very risky gaps in the heavy foliage without dismembering a part of my body was much shoddier than anticipated. There was nothing but a hard, dirt-packed floor, crumbling brush walls held upright by crudely cut poles, and the remains of what had once been a table, a cupboard and a few wooden chairs. Had the entire structure not been supported by thick vegetation that had grown through the openings that were meant to be windows, I was more than certain it would no longer be standing. From the pungent smells that still lingered inside, it must have been used as a place to process or store coca leaves. We wouldn't be safe here for long, even if Mendoza hadn't left the compound the way we had.

Agent Fielding lay his coat on the ground so Maria could rest. Then he eased her down to a reclining position. She smiled her thanks and immediately closed her eyes. He brushed her hair away from her eyes and waited.

Once her breathing had slowed, he rose to his feet and motioned for me to follow him outside. A quiver of cold settled over me, although a sliver of sun was peeking down on us from above the highest trees. The rain and the dampness of the early morning hours were starting to burn off, and I noticed that the strange and fearful sounds of the jungle were much louder now that we were no longer walking.

"I didn't want to say much in front of Maria but getting this far really was the easy part. I have a jeep waiting not far from the river. At least it was there a few days ago. I wanted to be ready if things went south at the raid."

"I'm sorry for messing up your plans, Agent Fielding," I said as the hopelessness of our situation washed over me again. "I was told this was a simple fact-finding mission. All I had to do was get into the compound, find out what had happened to a missing agent and get out. I should have realized it was more complicated than that when they couldn't even tell me who my contact was, but I came anyway because DEA was in enough of a bind to ask the FBI for help."

"So you're not even a member of our organization."

I looked over at him wishing I could see him as a true fellow agent and not just someone who held three lives in the palms of his hands.

"That would have made this endeavor far easier for everyone involved, but the only reason I was asked to assist was because I so closely resembled the real Tess Tremaine, and the DEA was out of options. I wasn't even told what happened to her. I was simply given some of her clothing and a couple of hours to familiarize myself with what little information they had about her life."

"That's a hell of a way to become involved with the DEA," he replied. "Why didn't you just refuse?"

"Let's just say that I considered the alternative and made the only choice I could. But I still don't understand why the DEA was willing to take such a risk. Maria may have been off the grid for a few weeks, but information was getting to your superiors somehow."

He looked at me and frowned, but I was tired of his accusations and tongue-lashings. Everything that had happened before this moment was in the past, and we needed to resolve our differences and learn to trust each other if we were going to survive. I already knew how he felt about me, but I wasn't incompetent, gullible or obtuse. I simply hadn't been given enough of the facts to be effective.

"This really is your first undercover assignment, isn't it?"

I twisted my lips before replying. "Yes, but I was at the top of my class at the academy."

His snort of disapproval let me know that he wasn't interested in excuses. "The exercises given there are child's play when compared to what happens in the real world. There are no rules here. Mendoza, and hundreds of others just like him, control their empires. What they say is law, and those foolish enough to get in the way are terminated."

"You've already explained that part to me."

"Then you obviously weren't listening. The DEA suspected something may have happened and had to take advantage of an opportunity when it arose to get another agent inside. People do not leave the compound voluntarily, and Mendoza selects those who enter his kingdom carefully. You can rest assured that he knew everything about Tess Tremaine before he ever hired her. He may not be much of a father, but he expects Luis to take his place some day, and that means whomever he chooses to be with them must be willing to do anything he asks."

His comment made me realize just how futile this mission had been since the moment it was assigned, but there simply had to be a way out. I refused to die like some animal in a jungle where my body would never be found. I might not be as seasoned and capable as Agent Fielding, but I knew how to do my job. I simply needed a little help because there was no way Maria and I would make it on our own, especially if she was going into labor, or if someone decided to come after us.

"In case you hadn't noticed," Agent Fielding proceeded as my thoughts continued to swirl. "Mendoza has eyes and ears everywhere, and it wasn't like Maria and I saw each other every day. I didn't know anything had happened to her until Mendoza told me that she would be terminated for betraying him once the child was born."

"But how did he figure out who she was, and how was information passed to anyone if she was never allowed to leave the compound?"

"You ask too many questions. We each had our own job to do."

"But there must have been other contacts at the compound who were able to elude Mendoza and his men. Word was getting to the authorities somehow."

"You're not going to let this go, are you?" he asked.

I looked up at him without flinching. "I think I deserve a few answers after risking my life for the greater good."

His eyes studied my face for a few moments. It made me feel more than exposed. "I only know that she used to talk to one of the deliverymen a little more than was prudent. I went in a year and a half before she did. Maria was sent to help out because Mendoza had me so busy doing his dirty work that I couldn't get a feel for what was going on inside the actual residence. We needed to know where the weak points lay, and she supplied that information. Empires have been won and lost in the bedroom. I thought she may have gone over to the other side after seeing what Mendoza could give her."

"Maria would never do that."

"And you know people so well after all your years of experience in the field," he mocked.

"I'm a pretty good judge of character. Maria may be drawn to powerful men, but she would never betray her mission."

"Perhaps I underestimated the strength of her loyalty, but I couldn't afford to take any chances when we were so close to reaching our objective. I'm not a callous man, Agent Sinclair, regardless of what I've been forced to do, and I've only disrespected my badge once. The circumstances surrounding our indiscretion don't really matter. I was the senior agent and knew better. I just hope you'll keep what you heard to yourself when we get back. I'll take care of any repercussions in my own way, if the need arises."

His jaw went rigid, and I knew better than to pry any further into a topic that was obviously distasteful to both of them. What had gone on at the hacienda before my arrival was really was none of my business.

"What's our next move?" I asked.

"Do you mean are we just going to stay here and take our chances?"

"Not exactly! I was simply hoping that the lack of constant gunfire meant that the authorities were able to catch both Mendoza and his men."

"I wouldn't make a wager on that," he replied. "Men like Mendoza don't get caught, and they don't get their hands dirty unless it's unavoidable. Why do you think he's been wining and dining his partners the past few days? He's setting them up to take the fall for him if necessary. That's how he's survived this long. As sure as I'm standing here, he's escaped the compound just as we did, and once he finds us, we'll all be dead unless we see him coming first."

My heart was beating so rapidly I thought it might explode. "That means he really might be just a few minutes behind us."

"You're finally starting to see what we're really up against, Agent Sinclair. There are many ways through the jungle, and I'm sure he has several contingency plans ready in case one or more fails. No doubt he has an additional chopper waiting somewhere that even I am unaware of, but that doesn't mean he won't opt to take us out first if he knows we're in this together."

"But you can't be sure he knows we're gone. The DEA attacked before dawn."

"Time means nothing at the compound. Between the guards and the servants, nothing goes unnoticed. At best, we can only hope that the attack slowed them down. He knows both you and Maria are agents, and since I'm the only one of his men not accounted for, he can safely assume I'm a traitor as well."

"So how much time do you think we have? Realistically?"

"Realistically, none!"

"Maria can't go much farther in her condition. I'm no expert, but that baby is about to come."

"Then I suppose that means we may have a few tough decisions to make."

"You already told her that you'd carry her out of the jungle if you had to. She's counting on you. We both are."

"And I'll do my best not to disappoint, but the truth is, she might end up a casualty of this war, regardless of what we do."

My total dislike for him instantly returned. "It's not her fault she got pregnant. Mendoza must have forced her into a physical relationship. He was hinting at doing the same thing to me, even if he did suspect I wasn't who I claimed to be."

His forced laugh was more like another chortle of disapproval. "I suppose you would have succumbed as well, given time."

"Never! I found him to be one of the most loathsome men on the face of the earth."

"Then you are the exception to every other woman I've met. I knew the spell he held over her from the moment she got to the compound. Despite what he does for a living, he can be a most charming and captivating man."

"Not to me, but I'd rather not discuss him right now. I know there isn't much time, but in case we do make it out of this alive, I'd like to know what gave me away. I don't want to ruin another mission or endanger anyone else's life."

"Are you sure you can handle my assessment of the situation? I am a very blunt man."

"Maybe that's what I need since my training officers led me to believe I could become a very good field agent, given time."

"We're not always allowed the luxury of time. But aside from the fact that he likely knew you were a plant before you even arrived, your entire demeanor was suspect, as was your apparent lack of interest in the new home you were traveling to. Either you really were a shy girl running away from life, or you had yet to gain enough field experience to access the situation accurately."

"But you told me it was best not to ask questions."

"I was testing your ability to follow rules."

"So I did everything wrong. Is that what you're telling me?"

"Not everything," he replied, giving me just the hint of a smile. "You wouldn't leave Maria behind. That shows you have a heart. The other things can be learned with a little practice and a little more exposure to the seedier side of life. You can't really believe anyone would accept the fact that you don't drink alcohol unless you wanted to keep a clear head because there was more at risk than just keeping a new job. A little wine never hurt anyone."

I was just about to tell him that according to what I had read the real Tess didn't drink either when I saw his hand move slowly towards the gun that was holstered around his waist.

"Don't move," he said in such a quiet voice I almost didn't hear him. "There's a puma in the brush right behind you."

My breath caught in my throat as every nerve in my body poised for flight. I'd been so concerned with Maria's fragile condition, my animosity towards Agent Fielding and the idea that Mendoza or his men might find us that I hadn't even seriously considered all the dangerous animals that lurked in the jungle.

I can only say that my life truly did flash before my eyes during those brief seconds as I listened for any sound that might indicate how close I was to being mauled or eaten alive. Not that Agent Fielding would let it go that far if he got off a clear shot, but which would be fastest, the bullet or the puma?

How still and quiet everything had suddenly become. It was as if every bird and creature was hovering in suspense, waiting for the attack that would bring certain death and a veritable smorgasbord of leftover flesh and internal organs.

Agent Fielding's eyes never left my face, and I would never forget the hard set of his lips, the stubble of facial hair on his cheeks and chin or the small scar above his left eyebrow. Then I heard crushing twigs. I steeled myself for my last moments on earth, but instead of coming closer, the sound was retreating.

Neither of us moved for the longest time as we waited in animated silence for what might happen next. I was acutely aware of how foolish I had been to instigate a   rather meaningless conversation when we needed to stay focused on our surroundings. It would not happen again.

"You must have an army of guardian angels watching over you, Agent Sinclair," he finally said as his fingers twitched so close to his gun I was surprised it hadn't gone off by accident. "I've never seen a wild animal walk away from easy prey before. By all rights, you should be dead. Even I couldn't have gotten off a kill shot in time, and I'm a damned good marksman."

His words sent a chilling, yet grateful, sensation throughout my body. All of God's children had angels surrounding them, but I was far luckier than the masses that didn't understand how intimately connected to each one of us they were. I had just received the mighty miracle I'd prayed for while on my way here. I just hoped I would not need another one.

"How close was it?" I asked when I was finally able to speak again.

"Ten yards, maybe. He was all set to pounce. Damnedest thing I've ever seen. They never walk away like that."

"Maybe he wasn't hungry," I retorted, knowing that I was only alive because it was what God wanted. "Or maybe I really was being protected."

"You sound like you believe in a higher power."

"I do," I told him. "I believe in God with all my heart, don't you?"

"Never really thought about it much until now."

"Why not?" I asked.

"Why should I? I've been able to handle things on my own just fine. Relying on something that can't be seen is for weaklings."

It was another jab at my incompetence, but I had learned my lesson about becoming distracted. Besides, no good ever came from arguing with a man who knew everything - even when he didn't. I turned my back on him and took a few steps in the direction of the hut, but he reached out and gripped my arm, stopping me from moving any further.

"I'm a realist, Agent Sinclair," he said, his eyes blazing with more than anger. "I've been in this jungle for nearly four years and have seen plenty of death and dying. What just happened may be unexplainable by common logic, but you have no idea what other dangers we'll have to face before we get out of this place."

"Then enlighten me," I said, trying to keep my lips from quivering. Whether he liked it or not we were in this together, unless he chose to leave us behind.

"Well, let's start with the small things. Those mosquitoes you keep swatting at are the most dangerous things in Colombia. Not only are they prolific blood suckers, they are carriers of some of the most devastating diseases in the world, especially to people who can't afford to be vaccinated. I'm sure you've heard of malaria and typhus. Those are just two of the things that kill thousands of natives every year, and there's no way to treat them out here. Then, we have all the lush, green foliage that can be so hazardous to your health, but I doubt you know much about the poison tree frogs that live everywhere. Some of them are so small you can hardly see them."

I swallowed back a new onslaught of fear. I hadn't noticed any of those things. I'd been too worried about getting Maria and her baby to safety.

He released my arm, bent over and picked up a twig. "See that spider?" he asked, holding it towards me where I could see it more clearly. "It's a poisonous banana spider. They're all over, and it's nearly impossible to avoid them. So, you see, Agent Sinclair, we have more to fear than just Mendoza or some big cat that may or may not have been hungry."

There was nothing I could say in response to his poignant demonstration of my naïveté. Reading about something and experiencing it were two entirely different things. Our situation was more than dangerous; it was pretty much impossible.

Maria's eyes were open when we walked back into the hut.

"How are you feeling?" I asked her.

She forced a weary smile. "I will be okay," she said, pushing her body up with her hands, "Did anything happen while I was resting?"

"Nothing important," Agent Fielding assured her, giving me a look that let me know I'd better keep quiet about everything we had discussed and what had just happened with the puma. "But then we're not likely to know anything more than we do right now unless Mendoza or some of his men catch up with us. If we don't want that to happen, we have to keep moving."

I offered Maria my hand and helped pull her to her feet. She was in pain; anyone could see that, but we were out of options unless we wanted to take our chances with a man who wasn't averse to killing all of us.

We followed Agent Fielding back into the jungle. "Why would anyone choose to live or work in a place with so much inherent danger?" I thought as a low-hanging branch caught the top of my head. I held it back so Maria could pass by me.

"Thank you," she whispered. "You have no reason for being so kind to me. I am not sure I would be so accommodating if our roles were reversed."

"We're fellow agents, and we're in this together," I said as she almost tripped over a trailing vine that Agent Fielding hadn't removed with his machete. In fact, he wasn't using the machete at all right now. He was just moving forward expecting us to come after him as best we could. "You did what was necessary for survival."

She turned her head in my direction and gave me a sweet, sad smile. "That is what I thought until I knew I was carrying his child."

Saying anything else was pointless. Maria had accepted the consequences of her actions and had tried to keep us from becoming involved. Like Agent Fielding, she knew what Carols Mendoza was capable of doing. I was the one who had forced the issue, but I wasn't sorry for doing so. Even an agent who knew she could lose both her job and her family deserved the chance to make things right.

It was getting warm even at such a high altitude, and the flying insects were worse than intolerable. They swarmed around the bare skin on our faces, arms and necks and swatting at them did little good. For every creepy-crawly we managed to kill, dozens more swooped in to take its place. I had been inoculated against most things before leaving the academy, but I wasn't sure the shots would cover everything I was being exposed to right now. The jungle was one place I'd never expected to be, unless it was part of a carefully planned vacation.

I wanted to think about something other than our safety. The colors and sounds around me were truly amazing, but I couldn't enjoy anything about the situation we were in. There was no way to calculate how far away from the compound we were or even in which direction we were traveling most of time. The sun was largely obscured from view, leaving a sick coldness that penetrated deep into my very soul. I had had prayers in my heart before, but nothing so intense as what I was experiencing right now. My pleadings with my Heavenly Father for help and safety had not stopped since I'd left the assistant director's office nearly a week ago.

When I took a moment to glance at my watch, I saw that it was only 9:15. We had been gone from the compound for over five hours. No wonder we were all tired, thirsty and hungry. An occasional gunshot in the distance could still be heard.

And then it happened! Maria screamed, doubled over and fell to the ground.

Agent Fielding turned around and swore. "Damn it all! What's wrong now?"

I was already kneeling beside her.

"She's probably in labor," I told him.

"It is not that," she whimpered. "I think I may have been bitten by something."

"But what?" Agent Fielding demanded.

"I am not sure," she moaned, trying hard to hold back another cry of pain.

"Not bitten! Shot!" Mendoza exclaimed, along with a truly evil laugh. He was coming into view from behind us.

We should have heard his approach, and his sudden appearance made my world start to go reel. The gun Agent Fielding had given me—the one I hadn't even looked at yet—was in the backpack slung across my shoulders. It would do me no good now. Why hadn't I put it on my person while I had the chance? I let the small suitcase I was carrying for Maria drop to the ground.

Agent Fielding raised his machete high in the air, but he wasn't fast enough to strike. Mendoza had already turned the barrel of his automatic machine gun on him knowing that Maria and I were no real threat since neither of us appeared to be carrying a weapon.

"Such a shame, Jorge," he said, looking at him with the coldest eyes I'd ever seen. "You could have been a very wealthy man."

"I never wanted your money, Mendoza. You deserve to be put away where you can't hurt anyone else."

Mendoza laughed, a cold, unearthly sound. I felt for the zipper on the backpack now that his focus was elsewhere but knew it would take another miracle for me to get off a shot, even if I managed to retrieve the gun. It was sitting in the very top, but any sound would alert our captor as to what I was doing.

"And you, Maria," he said, without taking his eyes off Agent Fielding. "You really believed you could take my son away from me? I should shoot you in the head right now, but you have won a short reprieve. That is why I aimed for your shoulder. You will suffer with that while you await the birth. Then you will be killed as the traitor you are."

I looked over at Maria. She was holding her arm, and blood was running between her fingers.

Immediately, I dropped the backpack I'd been trying to unzip to the ground, ripped off the bottom of the cotton shirt I was wearing and held it against Maria's arm. I knew the pressure wouldn't stop the bleeding for long unless the bullet had only grazed her. If it had penetrated the flesh and become imbedded, she would need a doctor before it became infected or she bled to death.

"You are a monster and a coward," I shouted up at the madman who held our fate in his hands.

He laughed sardonically. "No, my dear, Miss Tremaine or whatever your real name is. I am a businessman and have no intention of losing what is mine. My partners and associates knew what to expect when they joined my cartel, and they were paid handsomely for their services. I will have a new operation going before the buzzards have stripped your carcasses of their flesh. Have no doubt about that."

Maria reached out and softly touched my arm before looking up at him. "Please let them go," she pleaded. "It is me you want."

"That may have been true a few hours ago, but that was before the man I trusted like a brother betrayed me also. To drug the wine, really Jorge, do these women mean that much to you? You will all be executed. No one crosses Carlos Mendoza and lives."

Maria slumped back against my arm. There was a sad, accepting look in her eyes. She was ready to die, but I wasn't. If anything, I was more ready to fight than ever. Mendoza might have a machine gun, along with several other firearms, but there were three of us. Surely, we could think of something that would switch the balance of power in our favor. An idea was forming that might give Agent Fielding time to get the machine gun away from him.

I turned my fury back on the evil man who'd just shot the mother of his child.

"We need to get Maria to a hospital, or she might die before the baby comes. But then what do you care about the lives of your children. You never have any contact with them unless you want something. Even now, you have left Isabel and Luis to the mercy of the authorities. You care more about power and money than you do about your own flesh and blood. How will they react when they find out that you killed their own mother?"

I was going to include both Maria and me in my tirade to get his attention, but further words were unnecessary. My point hit home and he swung his free hand in my direction, striking me so hard that I fell to the ground.

"You will die for saying that," he threatened, aiming the machine gun at my head.

But that one brief moment gave Agent Fielding the chance he needed to gain control of the situation. He lunged at Mendoza, and in the second it took for me to open my eyes again, both men were on the ground fighting for their lives.

I crawled towards the machine gun Mendoza had dropped. If I could get just one clear shot this whole ordeal would be over, and we could get out of this jungle the way we'd come—through the village where all the happy children played.

With the machine gun finally secure in my trembling hands, I forced myself to my feet.

"Stop it!" I shouted at the men who were rolling over and over, crushing vegetation as they continued hitting each other with their fists. I aimed the gun in their direction but was afraid to fire they were changing positions so rapidly. I didn't want to accidentally hit the man who had been trying to save our lives.

"I mean it," I shouted again. "I will shoot."

"I think not," a deep and penetrating voice said.

The words were spoken with forceful clarity, and I felt the barrel of another machine gun come to rest against the back of my head.

"Surely, you did not think that Señor Mendoza would come alone."

The very oxygen seemed to leave the air, but I didn't move. That would be just the excuse he needed to pull the trigger.

"Now I suggest you drop that gun and get down on the ground before I kill you first."

Complying was the last thing I wanted to do, but I still lowered the machine gun, and the man behind me kicked it far enough away that it.

"Stand down, Jorge," he shouted. "Or you die right here, and your lady friends with you."

Agent Fielding looked away from Mendoza. He had a large gash above his left eye where the small scar had been visible just a few minutes earlier, and his clothes were torn and dirty. Mendoza didn't look any better—not that it mattered. We were going to die, and my family would never know what had happened to me.

Maria was sitting up, and I cautiously inched myself towards her since she was no more than a foot or two away.

"What took you so long?" Mendoza asked the man.

When I looked up at him, I recognized him immediately as having been in the library the night before. His eyes were even crueler than Mendoza's.

"It took longer to get away from the compound than expected. I had to make sure there were no witnesses left to tell the authorities where we had gone."

I thought about the servants and the children. Had they been discarded just as we would be?

"And the policia?" Mendoza asked.

"Burning the fields and processing houses."

"Minor details," Mendoza laughed. "Just how stupid do they think we are? This is not our only base of operation. We will be up and running as if this raid had never taken place by this time next week."

He laughed again as he picked up his machine gun. "I am going to the airstrip. Shoot all of them before you join me. What do I care about another bastard child?"

I watched as he walked away, taking his weapons with him. He was truly an evil and degenerate man who saw nothing wrong with killing for pleasure. If he and the man holding us captive were the only ones to escape the raid, that meant he had sacrificed the rest of dinner companions to get away.

"You will get to watch the others die," he said, kicking me in the side with the toe of his boot after Mendoza had disappeared.

I willed my fear to stay hidden as the pain from his kick intensified. I was almost certain I had felt a few ribs crack, but I would not beg for my life.

"You're a fool, Fernando," Agent Fielding told the man with the machine gun in his hands and the bullets hanging around his shoulder. "Do you really think Mendoza will ever allow you to be anything in the cartel other than a paid assassin? You are of no more use to him than a lapdog."

"You sound so brave for a dead man, Jorge," he countered.

"Perhaps, but at least I know when my end will come. You will spend the rest of your life looking over your shoulder. And who's to say that Mendoza will even wait for you to arrive after you kill us. He already has a head start, and he doesn't like loose ends."

"He will wait for me. He knows I am loyal."

"If you believe that, then you are the fool. Mendoza trusts no one but himself. You see how easy it was for him to sacrifice his own children. He will do the same to you."

Agent Fielding was stalling for time, but what did he expect me to do? I was too far away from the machine gun to reach it before I was shot.

Quite suddenly, I realized that it wasn't me he was counting on. While we had been occupied, Maria had secured the weapon from my backpack. She aimed and fired at Fernando, dropping him to the ground in a single shot. By the time Agent Fielding pushed at his still body with the steel toe of his boot, blood was gushing from a hole in his chest.

"Nice shot, Maria," he said.

"I only did what was necessary," she replied as the gun dropped limply into her lap.

I must have looked horrified by what had just happened because he turned his attention to me once he'd retrieved the machine gun Fernando had been carrying.

"Don't take it so hard, Agent Sinclair, watching a man die isn't easy, but one gets used to it after a while."

"I will never get used to it," I replied as I glanced at Maria again. The look on her face told me that she was in shock. This must have been the first time she'd been forced to take a human life. "I know he was a bad man and would have killed us."

"Tortured and then killed us," he corrected me. "These men are trained assassins and take great pleasure in their work. They have no mercy."

I could have talked to him about real mercy, the kind extended by our Heavenly Father and our Savior, Jesus Christ have, but now wasn't the time or the place. We still had a jungle to survive.

"Pick up the gun and fire it, Agent Sinclair," he instructed. "And do it quickly. If Mendoza hears only one shot he might come back and try to finish the job himself."

Now was the time to prove to the man who blamed me for everything that I wasn't totally useless. So with my jaw set, I picked up the gun and fired two additional shots. I didn't want to be wasteful since we might need a weapon again, and the kickback from firing a machine gun would be intolerable with cracked or broken ribs.

"That should keep him satisfied for a few minutes, but he will be back to investigate if Fernando doesn't join him soon," Agent Fielding said. "Or I suppose he could leave without him. The one thing I know for absolute certainty about Mendoza is that he only cares about himself. You were not wrong in your comment about his children. Born or unborn, they are little more than a liability to him."

I rose to my feet and watched as Agent Fielding helped Maria to hers. She seemed to have gathered strength and picked up the small suitcase I'd been carrying for her with the arm that had not been injured. It was impossible to understand how they could both remain so calm after a man had been killed, even in self-defense. The nausea had risen so high in my throat I was afraid it would spew forth if I opened my mouth. This was my first encounter with death in the line of duty. All the drills at the academy had used paint guns and blanks.

"If it wouldn't be too much trouble," Agent Fielding said as I bend to retrieve the backpack I'd been carrying. "I could use a little help getting Fernando's body covered. The wild animals will get to his remains soon enough, but we don't want to leave an open invitation in case Mendoza sends someone else after us."

He was already dragging the man's limp body by the shoulders into the dense foliage that crowded the edges of the pathway we'd been trying to make.

I moved towards him as rapidly as I could. "Do you really think Mendoza would do that?"

"He would if he had any reason to believe we were still alive."

I had Fernando's body by the feet and was trying to inch forward carrying my end of a cumbersome burden while Agent Fielding pushed back the vines and leaves with his head and shoulders. Something slithered over my boots, but I didn't even look down. I was helping to carry the body of a dead man, and that was the most upsetting thing I had ever done.

While we piled dirt, dried leaves and vines over the body, Maria covered the drag marks his body had made by breaking off leaves on a small bush and running them over the ground and pools of blood. I marveled at her capacity to compartmentalize and do what needed to be done even after being shot and killing a man.

"Listen, Reagan," Agent Fielding said, using my given name instead of my title. "I know this is hard. Hell, I don't like killing another human either, but sometimes we have to it. There are a lot of evil people in the world, and drug lords are some of the worst. You see how easy it was for Mendoza to walk away from his own child after keeping Maria locked up. He only cares about his empire. To hell with everything else, and that includes his own flesh and blood."

"So he is capable of walking away from Isabel and Luis and not looking back?"

"He's capable of anything if it affects his freedom. His own wife wanted to help us she was so frightened of what he might do to their children. When he got suspicious, he killed her. I watched him do it."

"There was nothing you could do to stop it," I asked as I put my last armful of rotting leaves on top of Fernando's body. It was hard to comprehend that just ten minutes earlier we had been the intended victims and now he was the one who was dead.

"Isabella was a courageous woman. She knew the risk she was taking when she opposed her husband and began helping us. That's why I knew about the tunnels. She wanted to get away and take her children with her. I would have helped her had there been time. I was standing in the entry when her body left the railing. I was the one who had to bury it while Alma took care of the blood and the calmed the servants. Mendoza never mentioned the incident to me. It was almost as if it had never happened."

"I'm sorry," I said. "I didn't know."

"There is much about this life that I hope you will never have to know. Living with demons isn't easy. Maria has now discovered that. It's kill or be killed for most of us."

When we were finished, we made our way back to where Maria had now sunk to the ground again. I'd always been taught that all people had been given the light of Christ, but power and money could turn anyone into a monster. It had certainly done that to Carlos Mendoza. Luis and Isabel did not deserve to be used and abused by the man who had helped give them life. I hoped they were okay. I should have made plans to bring them with us. But the past could not be undone, and the question still remained as to whether or not I could do any better with Maria and her unborn baby.

"Let's go," Agent Fielding said as I brushed the dirt from my hands on the legs of my jeans. They were covered with brown, musty fragments of rotting leaves, and it seemed like the smell of mold had penetrated every cell in my body.

"Can you walk?" I asked Maria as I pulled her to her feet again. She looked frail and haunted despite her brief burst of energy just moments before. She didn't even reach for the suitcase again, and for the first time since I'd convinced her to come, I wasn't sure she was going to make it.

"I will be fine," she said, gripping my hand.

"Not with a bullet in your shoulder," Agent Fielding said. "We need to get it out."

"I know someone who can do it when we get out of here," she replied. "And he will not tell anyone."

I felt so sorry for her and her unborn child. Even if they survived, she'd be left alone to raise her baby in constant fear since there was no way of knowing when Mendoza would find her again, even if she went into hiding. His circle of influence wasn't confined to Colombia. He had people everywhere—people who were trained to kill.

"Let's not worry about that right now," I told her. "Let's just put a little more distance between us and this awful mess."

"You are very kind, Reagan," she said as she stood rather wobbly on her feet again. "You would be a far better mother to my son than I will ever be."

"Nonsense," I told her as we fell into step behind Agent Fielding. I wondered why he didn't insist on trying to remove the bullet before we went any further, but perhaps he felt it was less dangerous than what might be coming from behind. "You're tired and wounded. Things will seem much better once we're safe from Mendoza and his men."

"I will never be free of him," she sighed. "He will come after me. Even if he doesn't want his own son, he will never leave me in peace. I know too much about him and his operations all over the world. It is easy to get men to talk once you have made love to them."

My face turned red underneath all the dirt and the sweat. I had never been where she had, and hopefully never would be, even with my career as an FBI agent—black suit, sunglasses and all.

"Does he have a lot of other compounds?" I asked, not so much for information right now, but to keep her mind occupied so she might not notice her pain quite so much.

"Three that I know of—one of them is far to the south. It is where his father lived. There is a picture of it in the library. He always said we would go there someday. It is on the bank of a beautiful, peaceful river, with lots of sunshine and fresh air."

"It sounds lovely," I replied.

"But it was all a dream. I knew he would never take me there. I was not his wife. He killed her before I even arrived. She told Jorge most of what she knew about his operations. She wanted him stopped. He would beat her when he was displeased, and she feared for her own safety and that of the children. I just wanted to keep them safe."

"Did he suspect who you were from the beginning like he did me?"

"One never knew what Carlos was thinking, but if he did, he did not want to believe it. He wanted to control me in every way. He was a very persuasive and sensual man. I tried to fight him for such a long time, but even knowing what I did, it was impossible. He knew exactly what to use against me."

"Did he threaten your family?"

"Not directly! His threats were more subtle, but I knew exactly what he meant. I do not come from wealth, but my family is proud. I wanted to do what was best for them. That is why I joined the agency. I knew the danger, but there are not so many things a young, peasant girl can do without help. My benefactor offered me a solution, and I took it."

"Your benefactor?" I asked.

"The man who rescued me from a life of poverty and gave me a chance."

I wanted to ask more questions, but every step was becoming a struggle for her, and I wasn't sure how much longer she could keep putting one foot in front of the other. It angered me that Agent Fielding had dismissed both of us as injured women who might need help but understood that someone had to remain in control. He was trying to remove what impediments he could, but he was doing it in a way he hoped would not make a clearly identifiable trail.

We had been walking for about forty minutes when Agent Fielding stopped and put his finger to his lips. The air felt and smelled different, moister, more humid and putrefied. We were getting near water.

He retreated a few steps closer to us so we'd be within whispering distance. He looked disturbed.

"The jeep I have stashed is on the other side of the river, but there's an Anaconda between us and there. I saw its body move through the brush. We've got to get Maria a safe distance away from here in case it decides to head this way. Where there's one, there's bound to be more."

"But where," I only mouthed the words as the blood pounded in my head.

I wanted to believe he was kidding. This was like some nightmarishly awful action adventure where the director was trying to fit every conceivable scenario into the plot. Three times in as many hours, we had been in imminent danger, and there wasn't a safe place in the jungle where we could hide. Mendoza or one of his men might be trailing us from behind again, and any wild animal or reptile could smell fear. It was part of their genetic makeup. I took a tentative step backwards.

Maria glanced up at me with wide, frightened eyes. "Just shoot it, Jorge," she said. "It cannot hurt us if it is dead."

But he lowered the machine gun from his shoulder. I knew he was more worried about giving our location away than having a dangerous snake in the vicinity.

Suddenly, Maria let out a scream and clutched her swollen belly, nearly doubling over in pain. "The baby's coming," she cried out.

"That's not all," Agent Fielding seethed as the brush moved behind him. I could see a forked tongue darting rapidly back and forth. The snake had changed course and was now moving in our direction.

The olive green of its body was overlaid with black blotches. Its head was narrow compared to its body width with a distinctive orange-yellow stripe on either side. Its eyes were set high on its head, as was its nose, so it would have no trouble seeing out of the water without exposing its body. I couldn't see how big it was yet, but I had read that boas were some of the largest snakes in the world, 20 to 30 feet in the length and weighing up to 550 pounds.

They usually floated beneath the surface of the water where they could move rapidly, but when they were hungry, they moved across the jungle floor or even into the branches of trees looking for something to eat. Their diet consisted of deer, wild pigs, caimans and even jaguars, but not humans. And they could go months between feedings if their last meal was large enough.

The one coming towards us now must be ravenous, and it must have smelled the blood on Maria's arm. It would strike and then slowly wrap its body around its prey until all life was gone, and then it would unhinge its jaw and swallow its victim whole.

I had my gun in my hand and had fired off a shot before I realized what I had done. We most likely could have outrun it, but I hated snakes and didn't want to take that chance. I hit it right between its two black, flint-like eyes. It slithered forward a few additional feet, and I stood mesmerized watching until it quit moving. It was the first living thing I had ever killed.

"Good going," Agent Fielding said, his voice a mixture of admiration and disdain. "I wasn't sure you had it in you to actually pull the trigger, but now everyone in the jungle knows exactly where we're at."

I wanted to say something hurtful, mocking, but it wasn't the time because the brush leading to the water was shifting again. I moved quickly to Maria's side as two crocodiles left the water and literally raced in our direction; no doubt smelling the death of the snake I'd just shot. I stood transfixed as one, then two pairs of gnashing teeth tore into the flesh of a large, cold Anaconda that was lying on the ground just a few yards away.

Maria let out another scream and sank to the ground as Agent Fielding poised the machine gun for action.

"Get her out of here," he shouted.

I sidestepped, twisting my ankle in the process, but I didn't fall to the ground and I didn't scream. He let off a round of bullets, and I watched as reptile parts spewed forth in every direction.

"They won't give us any more trouble," he snarled, turning back to face us in an incomprehensibly short amount of time. "But we sure as hell can't stay here now. They aren't the only creatures in the water, and if your shot wasn't heard clear back to the hacienda, mine certainly was."

I grabbed Maria around the waist and pulled her to her feet. "Don't worry," I whispered. "We're not going to let anything happen to you or your baby."

The dead animals would provide a feeding frenzy for the ones left in the river. That would give us time to get away. I just wished I knew where we could go. We were hours away from the rest of humanity—even the good ones who would be willing to help us—and Maria didn't have much time before her son made his appearance.

"It's just one thing after another with the two of you," Agent Fielding complained as he pushed past us.

It wasn't a very gallant thing to do since it put us between him and the river, but I understood where he was coming from. We'd be more than a little lucky if we escaped from the jungle at all, and not just because of Maria. It seemed like even Mother Nature was working against us now.

I pulled her forward while Agent Fielding continued his tirade.

"I don't know what you women expect me to do? I don't see a hospital or even a shaman around to help, and I know nothing about birthing babies."

Maria slumped forward, and I nearly dropped her. She was sweating profusely, and even in the semi-darkness of the jungle I could see that her face had taken on a peculiar grayish hue. We stopped walking, and I tried to comfort her, but the truth was that there was no longer any comfort to give.

"My water has broken," she panted. "I cannot go any further."

"You have to," I prodded. "I'm sure we'll find shelter soon."

"It is no use," she whimpered, slumping to the ground, despite my attempt to keep her upright. "My son is not going to wait to get somewhere safe."

"What's happened now?" Agent Fielding demanded at hearing the commotion behind him. The bodies of the dead reptiles were just a few yards away. "We can't stop. There isn't any shelter, and we have no idea what might be coming for dinner."

"That may be true, but she can't make it any farther on her own," I told him as I looked back at the snake I had killed. "We'll just have to do what we can here."

"Damn it," he swore again, coming back and kneeling beside us. "That isn't an option."

"I am afraid my son does not know the disagreeable situation are in," she said, screaming out and clutching my hand until a pain shot through it. "I cannot go any farther with or without help."

I was looking at Maria, and Agent Fielding was looking around trying to assess the situation, but all we could see in any direction was leaves, flowers, trailing vines and tall trees. The jungle was suddenly very quiet again. Even the birds and the animals seemed to know that something else was now in distress.

"Listen," he told her. "I get it that you can't walk right now, but you can't stay here either."

"There is no other choice, Jorge," she said. "I have made my peace with God. You and Reagan can leave me here knowing you have done everything humanly possible to help and protect me. I am not afraid to die."

"No one is going to die," he stormed, pushing the machete he was carrying behind his back and deftly picking her up in his arms as if she weighed nothing at all. I had no idea where he would take us but trusted that my reluctant partner had something in mind. He could have deserted us and gone after Mendoza, but he'd opted to stay. Perhaps he wasn't as uncaring as I'd thought.

Chapter 10

My clothes were completely soaked - and I was in a great deal of personal pain - by the time we made it back to the half-shelter of the hut I'd hoped to never see again. It was an unearthly place that held no pleasant memories, but evidently, there had been nothing closer where we could find refuge.

Mendoza would not hesitate to kill us if our paths crossed again. Our only hope had been in putting miles between us, but that wasn't going to happen now. The shots fired had let anyone who heard them know that we were still alive, and now we were right back at the place where he'd found us just a few hours before.

The insects were swarming inside the partial enclosure. The cool of the day was making them even more active. I swatted at them trying to keep them away from my face. Despite the heat generated by moving so swiftly and the ever-present humidity, I was glad I'd worn jeans, heavy shoes and a long-sleeved shirt. But my face, neck and hands were covered with red, swollen and itchy bites.

There were tears in Maria's eyes as Agent Fielding lowered her to the ground where I'd spread his coat out for her to lie on. Dozens of crawling creatures scurried away. The bile in my stomach rose to my throat. This was so far from the kind of assignments I thought I'd be given as an FBI agent as to be almost laughable. I could die right here and no one would ever know what I'd endured. Not even

Neil who had been so upset because I'd been the one summoned to Assistant Director Bridges' office, not him.

"Try to rest," he told Maria as he patted her good arm like he would have done to comfort a small child. "We'll figure something out."

Maria smiled her thanks, but her face immediately distorted in pain. She was trying hard to be brave, but her eyes told me how frightened she really was.

"I need to speak with you outside again," Agent Fielding said to me, and I could see the concern etched into every feature of his face.

"You do not have to go outside to talk on my account, Jorge," Maria whispered. "I know I will not make it out of this hut, but you must do everything possible to save my son. He does not deserve to suffer for my sins."

Agent Fielding went to her side and knelt on the ground, taking one of her dainty hands in his larger, more powerful ones. She looked truly beautiful, like a Madonna about to give birth. No wonder Mendoza had desired to possess her and hadn't killed her upon discovering her betrayal. I still didn't know what she had done to give away her true identity, but if we didn't survive, it wouldn't really matter.

"You don't need to concern yourself about anything, Maria," he said. "You and your baby are not going to die. All you have to do is lie here and be brave. Agent Sinclair and I will take care of everything else."

He kissed her on the forehead, and she smiled weakly up at him. "I will try, Jorge, but it hurts so much."

Tears were glistening in her eyes as she fought another contraction. I would have gone to her too but somehow felt that they needed this time so the hurts of the past could heal.

"That's my girl," he said, brushing her damp hair away from her forehead before motioning for me to leave the hut.

I did exactly as he instructed, wishing that someone was there to comfort me. While they were busy conversing in whispers, I turned away and lifted the edge of my shirt. A grossly-colored bruise the size of football extended from the small of my back to the middle of my stomach. I gingerly pressed to see if I could detect the extent of my injuries, but there were no protruding bones or any conclusive signs of internal bleeding. It might be difficult to breathe, but my life was in no imminent danger from having been kicked.

After several minutes he joined me. I had moved as far away from the hut as I could so they would have the privacy they both seemed to need and want.

"Did you really mean what you said to Maria?" I asked him.

He was standing with his back to the hut door, staring at something deep in the foliage that I couldn't discern.

His voice was hard and controlled when he spoke to, but didn't look at, me. "I said what I had to. She needs to believe everything will be okay, or she'll quit fighting."

"She's strong, and she wants this baby very much," I replied, looking at the side of his head and wishing I knew what he was trying to hide. "She'll do everything within her power to make sure he's okay."

He suddenly whipped around and glared at me. "Don't tell me you fell for all that load of crap I just gave her. Without medical attention, we'll lose both of them before sunset. She's got a bullet in her shoulder and a baby about to be born. Unless you're a doctor in a very pitiful disguise, there's not a damned thing we can do to help either of them. I checked her pulse. It's far too weak. I'm afraid we're losing her already."

I brushed at the tears that had filled my eyes. I didn't want the inevitable Agent Fielding was talking about to happen. Maria didn't deserve to die in a place like this and neither did her baby.

"Dear Heavenly Father," I silently pleaded. "Help us find a way to save them both."

But my spoken words came out slightly different. "We can't just give up, Agent Fielding, even if it seems impossible. She's one of us."

"I'm not giving up," he said, glaring at me again. "I'm going for help, and you're going to stay here and try to keep her alive until I get back."

The shock I felt must have shown in my face. His demand had filled me with more terror than when I'd felt the machine gun pushed against the back of my head. He was asking me to stay and watch a woman and her child die.

"You can't be serious," I said. "Maria is about to give birth, and I can't help her by myself."

"I've never been more serious. You think things are tough in the jungle during the daylight. Well, you haven't experienced anything until you've survived a night here. That's when all the predators come out, and they can smell blood and fear for miles."

"Then we need to work together to get her out of here before then. We could build a stretcher and carry her."

"Sure, we can," he said, his voice dripping with disdain. "We can build one out of all the branches and trees around us and bind it together with the clothes we're wearing. I'll get right to it with my machete, or better still, why don't we just make one materialize by magic!"

I looked down at a colony of ants that was moving several twigs across the ground near my feet. They worked together to accomplish the seemingly impossible. Why couldn't Agent Fielding just give us another chance? Maybe Maria would be able to travel a little further once she'd rested a bit. Some women were in labor for hours, even days, before giving birth. Perhaps we were just overreacting because her water had broken, and we had never been around someone in her condition before.

"Listen, Agent Sinclair," he said, disrupting my fanciful and unproductive thoughts. "I don't like the idea of leaving the two of you alone out here with the possibility of Mendoza coming back, but I don't see that we have any other recourse. She and the baby will both die if we don't get help. At least she has partial shelter if the baby decides to come while I'm gone. Taking the time to build a conveyance is pointless. She'd be dead before we got it constructed. I can go for help much faster on my own, and I can bring back the things we need to get both of you out of here safely."

I wanted to believe him just as Maria had pretended to, but the knot in the pit of my stomach was telling me that things were not going to turn out the way he predicted. All of our lives were in God's hands now.

"I'll do my best," I told him. "Just how long do you think you'll be gone?"

"There's no way to predict that. This was not part of my plan, but the village we landed in should be just a few miles away to the east. I'll hurry as fast as I can, but it will be a few hours, and it's going to be dark before I get back."

Oh, how I wanted to go with him, and I wanted Maria and her baby to go with us too. But he was right, she was in no condition to travel, and we couldn't leave her alone. I had to be willing to stay behind and do what I could. It was the only chance she had.

"Things could be worse," he continued, taking a step towards me. I fought back the desire to flee even from him. "There's a clean towel in my backpack, a knife and more water, but nothing for the pain. And just for the record, I am sorry for being so rough on you, Agent Sinclair. You never should have been sent into the field before you were ready, and most certainly not by another agency. Even seasoned operatives have trouble remaining under cover for extended periods of time. That's why so many of them lose their way."

The soft edge to his voice left me feeling strangely consoled, but I couldn't afford to be complacent about anything. I had never felt more alone, and without him, our chances for survival were diminished beyond belief. My training had prepared me for a great deal, but not something like this. All I could do was remain vigilant and never give up on my prayers. We would most certainly need any help we could get to make it through the next few hours.

"We'll be okay," I told him. "Just hurry!"

"As fast as my feet can carry me. It should only be a few hours. I wish I could be more specific, but there's no way of knowing what I might have to face before I get back."

"Are you thinking that Mendoza or his associates might still be in the area?"

"I'm fairly confident that he's miles away from here by now. He would never allow himself to get caught, but he has some loyal workers, and they won't be happy that their livelihoods have been taken away. You saw how poor they are. Empty bellies can turn even good men into killers."

I thought about the beautiful, barefooted children I'd seen in the village when we'd landed. I didn't want them to suffer because the adults in their lives did horrible things. But once again, I couldn't control anything that happened. I couldn't even control what I might be forced to do next.

"Listen," he said, squeezing my upper arm. The sheer force of his grip made me wince, but I was fairly certain he didn't notice. "I wish things were different, but they aren't. Just stay inside the hut and don't be afraid to use your gun on anything or anyone that comes near. There's plenty of extra ammo in the bottom of the backpack. I'll be back as soon as I can."

I watched him walk into the jungle. My heart grew heavier with each crunching step he took, and then even the air around me was silent. The sky was getting dark. It looked like more rain, and he'd taken the machine gun with him. Not that I would have been able to use it if he'd left it behind. It was far too cumbersome, and a single shot would be more effective, unless a small army were after us.

When I stepped back into the hut, I saw that Maria was curled up in a fetal position, despite her swollen belly and the bullet in her shoulder. I wished I dared take it out. I'd watched training films on extracting them, but I could do more damage than good. She'd be dead within minutes with no way to stop the bleeding if I hit an artery, and we had nothing for the pain. No wonder Agent Fielding had not been willing to try. He knew his limitations, and perhaps in his own way he was expressing hope that we'd get her to safety in time. All I could do was try to keep her comfortable until he returned.

Her eyes were filled with tears when she looked up at me in the semi-darkness of the hut that provided less than adequate shelter from anything. I believed that Agent Fielding would return, but if it took more time than he anticipated, it was highly doubtful that we'd all still be alive.

I sat down on the dirt floor beside her. "How are you doing?" I asked.

"Not good," she muttered. "Where is Jorge? I need him. I cannot do this alone."

"You're not alone," I told her. "I may not be as good as Jorge, but I won't leave you. I promise."

"He said that I was a strong, brave woman and he was glad we had been there for each other. He said everything would be okay."

"And it will be! He went to the village to get help. He should be back in a few hours."

"I might not be here that long," she replied, looking away from me. "I can feel the angel of death coming for me even now."

"Nonsense," I told her, forcing my voice to be light as I took her hand in mine. It was cold and clammy. "You're going to be just fine, and who knows, you might even have your baby ready to meet him when he gets back."

She started to whimper. "No, that will not happen. I only pretended to be okay with Jorge because I did not want him to remember me as being a coward like Carlos, but I am not okay and neither is my baby."

"You're just tired and scared. Women have babies every day. You'll know exactly what to do when the time comes. We're very lucky God made us the way he did. We might not know exactly what to do, but your baby does."

"I used to believe in God," she said. "But I have not thought about him much for a very long time. I guess I have been afraid to. I have not been to confession for months. Father Francis used to be very sympathetic towards me, even after he had learned that I was going to have a child."

"You were fighting for survival and trying to do your job. No one can condemn you for that."

Her hand dropped to her side and came to rest limply on the edge of the soiled coat she was resting on. "If only that were true. I turned my back on God by not remembering who I was. I slept with a horrible man who had killed his own wife, and I have Fernando's blood on my hands. I do not think even a merciful God can forgive me for that."

How I wished I could ease her mind of the burdens she bore, but decisions—right or wrong—always brought consequences. And feelings of guilt and remorse were just the first step in trying to make things right again.

"You only did what was necessary, Maria. Fernando would have killed all of us. You shot him in self-defense."

"Perhaps my own death is the only way I can atone for my sins," she responded. "I cannot give my baby anything—not a home or family. He will be on the run for the rest of his life if Carlos finds out he's alive."

"But he said he didn't care about the baby."

"He was trying to hurt me because he knows how much I love my son, despite who his father is. Carlos is a vicious and ruthless man who will stop at nothing to get vengeance. My baby will only be safe if he is dead, or . . ." she paused. It was only for a moment, but the look on her face suddenly softened, and I knew she was about to present another possibility. "Maybe you could take him to the United States and raise him as your own. Then no one would ever know what had happened to him. I trust that you would be a good and loving mother."

"You don't even know me, Maria!" I exclaimed, wondering how she could even ask something like that of me. I wasn't prepared to be a mother to my own child, let alone the mother of a child who might well be hunted for the rest of his life. Besides, no one would allow the baby out of Colombia, even if we happened to survive our time in the jungle.

"I know that you are brave and loyal and have a good heart. Otherwise, you would not have insisted that I leave the hacienda when you knew I would only slow you down."

"I wasn't going to leave you behind."

"That only shows that you have compassion and love for others. That is very rare, but it lets me know that you will be the best mother for my son. It will not be easy to raise him never knowing when Carlos might come after you, but you are the only chance my baby has."

"That's not true," I said as panic rose to the surface once again. I'd only thought about getting Maria and her son to safety. It had never crossed my mind that she might not make it, and I would be left to decide the fate of an innocent child.

"But it is," she said. "I will not make it out of this jungle. My body is too weak. Already the infection is setting in. I can feel it eating away at me, but my son still has a chance. Please vow to me here on my deathbed that you will protect my precious baby with your own life if I am not allowed to raise him. I need to know that he will be safe before I return home to God. It is my only solace after the life I have led. Carlos believes in heaven and hell and does not care where he ends up as long as he has what he wants here. He will have my son killed to punish me—even after I am gone. He does not care about the child. You heard that from his own lips."

Yes, I had heard Carlos Mendoza's threats against all of us. He was a monster and must be stopped, but keeping a baby away from him, even one he did not want, would be nearly impossible. Maria was right! He'd stop at nothing to inflict the most pain imaginable on the people he considered his enemies, whether they were dead or alive.

When I didn't say anything, she continued. "He is to be named Samuel. I have already made documents stating that he is not to remain in Colombia if I am gone. No one need ever know who his father is. Please keep him safe for me. It is my one dying request. The papers you need are at the bottom of my bag. I put them there before we left the compound."

Her request left me not only speechless but stunned and heavy-hearted as well. She couldn't possibly be serious asking me to raise her son. Her own family would be much better equipped to do that, even if they were poor and possibly angry with her for having a child fathered by a drug lord. Besides, it was totally illegal, and I could never take a child that wasn't mine out of the country without permission. I simply wasn't that kind of person.

As I sat there contemplating the treacherous vow she had asked me to make, her thin fingers closed around my lower arm. I was surprised at how strong they were in her weakened and painful condition.

"Promise me," she pleaded. "I know it will be difficult, but there is no one else for me to trust."

"What about your family?"

"That is the first place Carlos would look." She was struggling to even remain coherent, but to her great credit, she wasn't giving in to all the pain. "They know nothing about the baby, and he would kill all of them for trying to help. You do not fully understand the kind of man he is if you think he would be kind to anyone for long. Sometimes I believe he is the devil incarnate."

"I don't know, Maria. That's a promise I'm not sure I could keep. There are laws."

"And ways to get around them. Please, you do not want the blood of my child on your hands."

I most certainly did not, but I couldn't make a promise that could never be kept. It wouldn't be right, even if it was her dying request.

"There's no need to talk about this now," I stalled. "You're going to get well, and Agent Fielding and I will make sure you're set up in some place safe where you can be together."

She sank back against the ground. "At least you did not say 'no'. That gives me reason for hope. You will make a wonderful mother to my son if God requires my death to compensate for my sins."

"God isn't vengeful like that, Maria."

How could anyone who had been raised as a Christian believe that God was anything less than a loving parent? It made no sense, even if they had moved away from him in their hearts and actions.

"He is just," she said.

"Yes, but he loves all his children equally, regardless of what they have done. That's why he gave us a Savior."

"The Blessed Mother's Son! I do want to believe that my baby will not be condemned because of the way he was conceived. He did not ask to be born. Perhaps I should have ended his life when I first found out. There are many ways to do that."

"But none of them would have been right. You knew that. That's why you let him live."

Oh, how my heart ached for her, but what could I do to erase her fears or the shame she bore for the things she had done? Her baby was innocent, and whether she believed it not, he had asked to be born. We all had! It didn't matter the circumstances of our birth or what we might be ask to endure. We needed a mortal body, along with the chance to prove our intrinsic worth.

That's where things always got a little hazy for me. We couldn't remember the life before this one, but I believed that everyone had been given the light of Christ to help show them the way, even madmen and murderers. They had simply chosen not to accept it. Maria was not like that. She was a good woman who might have done things much differently had she been given the chance.

"Oh, it hurts," she suddenly cried out, thrashing from side to side in agony.

I reached out and touched her forehead. It was hot and dry. She was running a fever, and her eyes looked almost vacant and glassy. If Agent Fielding didn't return soon we'd be left with another body to bury, and I couldn't imagine doing that.

"Take a sip of water," I instructed as I tilted her head up and held the canteen to her lips. "It will help you feel better."

She didn't argue but could only swallow a sip or two before writhing in pain again.

"Why does my baby not come?" she sobbed. "I have not felt him move in the longest time. What if he is already dead?"

I squeezed her damp, clenched fist wishing I had an answer that would give her added courage and strength. Agent Fielding was right in saying that if she lost the will to live she would never survive.

"It will be okay, Maria," I tried reassuring her. "Baby's don't move all the time."

"Mine did," she protested. "He was always active. That is why I know he wants to be born, and he wants to live, even if I do not. He must be given a chance."

Everything she said just made me feel more guilty for not easing her mind by making a simple promise, but she had no idea what she was asking. People didn't take children out of foreign countries without authorization. It was called kidnapping, and I was a federal agent who had sworn to uphold the law.

"Perhaps he's just conserving strength for the delivery," I said.

"You do not understand the bond between a mother and her child yet, Reagan, but you will someday. Mine is in trouble. He needs to come now."

"He will come when he is ready," I replied, knowing that wasn't true. Babies died before birth all the time, and if that happened, I'd lose both of them before Agent Fielding got back, if he ever did. There was a lot of dangerous ground between the hut and the village, and he wasn't certain what his reception would be once he got there. But I couldn't think about that right now. I had to stay focused on the situation at hand and trust that we were going to make it because no matter what happened I would never leave her alone.

Still, I had to do something to distract her from all the pain and self-reproach she was feeling. I was saving the few tablets of Ibuprofen I had brought with me for the delivery—not that they would help much. Frankly, I was surprised she hadn't passed out already. A bullet in the shoulder had to hurt far more than she was letting on, and remaining in a heightened state of anxiety and fear wasn't helping her baby.

Quite suddenly, I knew there was only one way to help her now. She must be taken to a place of peace and safety like I had been trained to do whenever I needed to clear my head and refocus my attention.

"Tell me about your childhood, Maria. It must have been a wonderful time since you were surrounded by so much family and love."

The faintest of smiles played about the corners of her lips. "We lived in a very small hacienda where I shared the same bedroom with all my sisters. My father worked in the fields mostly, but there were always enough tortillas to eat, and my nanna would tell me wonderful stories about our ancestors who used to be wild and ferocious but who built amazing cities and highways. I should loved to have seen some of those remains before I died."

"Where are they?" I asked.

"Oh, they are everywhere," she replied. "I have seen many pictures in magazines and books and have always dreamed of discovering one of my own where I could take my family and we would know peace. Even the small village where I was raised was controlled by the gangs who fought continually with each other over territory and cocaine. No one was safe outside at night, and the daytime was not much better. I suppose that is part of the reason I agreed to this assignment. I hate drugs in every form, but the violence they breed is worse. The government would like to see visitors come to our country for the beauty it has to offer."

"Maybe someday that will happen."

She shook her head sadly. "I had hoped to see many parts of this great land with Luis and Isabel, but we were never allowed to leave the hacienda, except to walk in the back gardens when Alma would allow it."

"What is Alma's story?"

Getting sidetracked was not my intention, but it was impossible not to think like a federal agent at least part of the time, even in a dire situation like this. I needed to find out what Maria knew while there was still time.

"I did not ask questions about her, even when Carlos and I were sharing a bed. She frightened me, and every interaction I saw between them only led me to believe that they shared some secret I was never meant to know. She was the only one who had any personal freedom. I would often find them talking in hushed tones that would cease the moment they suspected anyone was near."

I had noticed that during my few days inside the hacienda as well, but she had been there for over two years. it seemed unlikely that she hadn't heard something that might facilitate his capture, and Alma was most certainly a person of interest. The closer the servant was to the master, the more he or she knew.

"You never overheard what they were talking about?"

"Not often. Despite my relationship with Carlos, I was never part of his circle. I was allowed to dine with his business associates occasionally, but only when I was looking my best, and I was never allowed to be part of their after dinner conversations. I was whisked away to my bedroom and had to remain there. If there had been a disagreement between us I was forced to stay in my quarters, and Alma would instruct the children."

"Did he beat you?" I asked.

Tears suddenly welled-up in her eyes. "Carlos is a man of force passion and no self-restraint. I soon learned that my survival depended on remaining as inconspicuous as possible."

"That must have made it nearly impossible to do your job."

"I found out what I could by playing games with the children, listening at doors and searching his quarters while he was sleeping or in the shower, but I was never allowed to walk about the hacienda at will. Carlos uses people for his own amusement or what they have to offer, but he trusts no one."

"Did he suspect who you were?"

"Almost from the moment I arrived, but he was lonely and needed a diversion from his daily business affairs. He knew I could not escape. That gave him all the leverage he needed until I was no longer able to entertain his guests the way he expected me to."

"Was there no one you could talk to, even Father Francis?"

"He only came to conduct Mass and confessions occasionally. Carlos wanted everyone to believe he was a religious man, but he did not believe anything Father Francis professed about loving others and treating men fairly."

She was becoming agitated again. I chided myself for not keeping her attention focused on the distant past where there were a few fond memories she could turn to. No doubt everything she was telling me now had already been given to the authorities, and it didn't really matter anyway because this base of operation had been dismantled. "Did you attend church often as a child?" I asked.

"Oh, yes," she replied as her eyes closed. Apparently, her last contraction had completely subsided. "There was a beautiful cathedral in our village with stained glass windows. We went several times each week. That is where I learned to love Jesus. I am glad you care about him too. I want my son to know about the blessed Virgin's Son."

Perhaps she wouldn't be saying that if she knew I did not believe exactly as she did, but right now that didn't matter. We were sharing a spiritual experience, and my heart was filled with love and compassion for this beautiful woman and her child who both lay so close to death's door.

Besides, if Agent Fielding didn't return soon, neither of us would leave the jungle alive. I had no idea where we were and trying to find the trail we'd made when leaving the compound would be virtually useless since he'd given up trying to clear our way long before we found the hut.

But even as my thoughts turned to more silent prayer, she screamed out in agony again. "Please do not leave me! I am so afraid."

"I won't," I promised, running my hand down the side of her cheek. It was incredibly hot, and I didn't even have a cool compress. "Just lie still and try to conserve your strength. Agent Fielding will be back soon with help."

"We don't know that," she said as the height of the contraction started to ebb away. "We both know the chance of returning to civilization alive is next to nothing. Jorge knows that too. Maybe that is why he has not come back. He does not want to be bothered with us any longer. We ruined everything he has been working for, especially me. You should have left me at the compound."

"You're talking nonsense, Maria. No agent would leave another one behind, no matter what the danger was."

My words sounded hollow even as they left my mouth. Could Maria be right? She knew Agent Fielding far better than I did, and he'd done nothing but show contempt for me since we'd left the compound. Walking away from me should be relatively easy for him after the kind of life he'd lived, but I doubted that even he was heartless enough to leave Maria and her unborn child to die in the jungle. They'd been partners, and that created a certain bond, regardless of the fact things had not gone according to plans. He'd even carried her back to the hut when she couldn't make it on her own any longer.

"You should have gone with him," she lamented. "I am going to die, and I am okay with it. But you should take my baby and leave now while there is still time. Just cut him out of me, and then he will have a chance to live."

"That's not going to happen," I replied.

The very thought was horrifying. I wasn't in charge of who lived and who died, and even if I had the medical training to do it, I wouldn't. It had to be the pain and fear talking because no rational woman would suggest something like that. Maria loved her unborn child dearly and would never do anything to intentionally harm him.

"It is the only way," she said.

"No, it isn't, Maria! Agent Fielding is coming back, and we're all going to leave this place together."

"You make me want to believe that, but we both know it is not going to happen. My time on earth has almost ended, but you still have a chance."

She reached out and clutched my hand. I thought another contraction must be coming, but she simply needed human contact.

"You are a good person, Reagan. I wish we had known each other sooner. We might have become good friends."

"We're friends now, and that's all that matters."

"Perhaps," she said as her voice trailed off. It was then I knew that if something didn't give her the incentive to go on she'd simply quit trying. I couldn't allow that to happen on my watch. I had not come this far to fail.

"I'll tell you what, Maria," I said as tears dampened my cheeks again. "If you'll promise to keep fighting, I'll promise to raise your son if you don't make it."

"You really mean it?" she asked.

"With all my heart! Your son will know an earthly mother's love, and he'll know that his birth mother loved him so much she gave her life so he could be born."

"You do know that a solemn promise like that must never be forsaken. I will hold you to it even when I am in heaven."

I swallowed back a hard, bitter lump that was threatening to choke me, but I couldn't take what I had said back. I would do what I had promised, regardless of the obstacles placed in my path if it came to that, but I wasn't going to let Maria die. Agent Fielding would come back, her baby would be delivered, and we'd all walk out of the jungle together. It simply had to happen that way. I wasn't prepared to deal with the alternative.

I gave Maria another drink from the canteen Agent Fielding had left. The water was nearly gone. By morning there would be nothing left for either of us. He simply had to return soon. The sky was growing darker. I looked down at my watch to see what time it was, but the face had been smashed. I couldn't remember that happening, but then most of the day was pretty much a blur to me now that I had nothing left to do but think and watch over a dying woman and the baby she already believed might be dead.

"Do you feel like telling me more about your family?" I asked, hoping that recalling a few of the more positive times in her life would help the time go by faster for both of us. "It must have been fun having sisters. I have four brothers who did nothing but torment me while we were growing up."

Her eyes were closed, and she didn't immediately respond. I felt a moment of alarm, but then her chest moved, and I knew she had not left me alone.

"It is difficult to talk, but nothing in my life means more to me than my family. That is the one thing I will miss when I am gone. I have not seen any of them for over two years. That is a long time to be away from the people one loves. Perhaps that is why I did not follow the rules as I should have."

"We all make mistakes. That's just part of life."

She shook her head. "You do not understand what it is like here. I should have allowed myself to die before falling into the bed of a drug lord. My two brothers joined one of the local gangs before I was old enough to understand what that meant. Edwardo did not live to see his his eighth birthday, and I do not know what happened to Ricardo. It broke my parent's hearts. They are good people who did not want to see their children's lives destroyed by drugs."

"I'm sorry for your loss."

"We were not alone in that. Few children in the villages escape a life of violence and crime. It is not easy to survive by working in the fields. I feared my sisters would become caught up in the only life available for them if I did not to something to give them a chance for an education."

I knew the kind of life she was talking about—servitude to some pimp who would supply her all the food and fancy clothes she desired until she was no longer a valuable commodity to him.

"You were very brave to leave everything behind so they could have a better life."

"I was young and believed I could make a difference, but life seldom goes as planned. I thought I would be living in Bogotá which is very close to my family's village. I saw them often the first few years, and then I was sent to the jungle. I do not even know if they receive the money I send home to them. The cartels have people in every branch of the government who leak information and steal from those who can least afford it."

I couldn't imagine living in a country where all the freedoms I took for granted were only dreams but that was Maria's reality. I couldn't blame her for any of the choices she had made.

"We don't need to talk about this anymore if you don't feel up to it," I told her. She seemed so weak and hadn't had a contraction in the longest time.

"My family is kind and they love each other very much. That is why I cannot burden them with my problems. They have worries enough of their own and no way to protect anyone. They know what I do is for them, but they will never understand the situation I now face. The disgrace of my actions will cost them what is left of their dignity. That is why I am so grateful you agreed to take my child. There is no one in all of Colombia who can protect him. The orphanages are filled with children no one wants. They receive adequate food and shelter, but there is no love. I cannot bear to think of my son in a place like that."

"Please try not to worry about that right now," I told her. "A lot can happen in a few short hours."

She sighed deeply and closed her eyes again. I knew she was right in everything she said, but doing what I'd promised weighed heavily on my mind. I couldn't take on the responsibility of a newborn infant if she didn't make it. I didn't have the resources, the time, or the inclination to do so. She simply had to live, and then I'd make sure that both she and her baby were taken into protective custody. The DEA would keep her in hiding with a pension to live on if necessary. It was done all the time.

I watched the slight movement of her chest until the darkness settled, and then I reached for the flashlight I'd slipped inside my backpack before leaving the compound the night before. I hadn't slept for over thirty-six hours and was beginning to feel the effects now that Maria appeared to be resting more comfortably.

The light I shined in her direction did not have the calming effect I had hoped it would. Instead of seeing her face without waking her, I saw several black, hard-shelled bugs with wings and pincers making their way up her body.

"Shoo!" I fiercely whispered.

Now that I could no longer see anything that was not within my beam of light, we were at the mercy of the night and the creatures that did their hunting then. I prayed that the flashlight batteries were strong enough to last until morning while I picked up my gun and settled down to wait.

It was eerily silent except for the occasional chatter of monkeys, the hoot of an owl or call of one animal to another. The things I could hear did not bother me, but I was terrified of anything that moved stealthily like the snake we'd run into earlier. There was no way to prepare to either fight or flee if an enemy remained unknown. Any wild animal could get into the run-down enclosure, and it would be impossible to see it in the heavy darkness that now encompassed the jungle.

I knew I had to stay awake. Still, my eyelids were heavy now that the adrenaline had quit pumping so hard. I wanted nothing more than to slip into the oblivion of dreamland where I knew that when I awoke my world would have fallen back into place, but I couldn't afford to do that. For better or worse, I was our protector now that Agent Fielding was gone.

Oh, how I wished Neil were with me. He might not know his way around the jungle, but he would never be insulting or condescending. He would give me the encouragement and support I needed and would not leave me alone to defend myself. Together, we would figure a way out of the situation we were in because neither of us had become hardened by the job the way Agent Fielding had done. And our commitment to honoring the oath we had taken would keep us from ever crossing any departmental lines. I knew I could trust him with anything, especially my life.

Maria remained almost motionless for what seemed like hours as I sat vigil on the damp ground at her side trying to mentally prepare myself for what might come next. The coat I had worn when leaving the compound was laying on top of her swollen abdomen, and I was freezing. I rubbed my arms every few minutes trying to restore some of the circulation, but it did no good since the air was filled with a damp kind of moisture that seemed to permeate every cell in my body. I'd gathered as many broad leaves as I could to protect us, but without the machete to cut through the stems it was mostly a futile effort. It was impossible to stop my teeth from chattering when a breeze rustled what was left of the hut's flimsy walls.

I had never known a night so dark. The canopy of trees overhead shielded even the brightest stars from view. I wished Maria's eyes would open again. The sound of her voice would help me feel less alone, but her reservoir of strength was nearly gone from the trek through the jungle and the number of contractions she'd already had. Although I had tried to minimize her concern, I was worried that her baby was no longer moving the way he had. I would never forgive myself if something happened to either of them during my watch, but I wasn't a doctor, and even my first-response training would not help much if the baby decided to make his appearance before help arrived. I had nothing to work with, not even enough water to wash away some of the grime.

I just wanted this dreadful night of fear and anguish to be over. It even crossed my mind that perhaps Agent Fielding had gone back to the compound, instead of the village, to get help. Mendoza was no longer there and what servants were left would surely help us. They might even come with him, bringing supplies and a stretcher. Perhaps some of the federal agents and local police were still there with a helicopter that could get her to a hospital where her son could be delivered in sterile, hospitable surroundings.

Over the past few hours I'd grown very fond of Agent Maria Gonzales. I couldn't rationalize her involvement with either Agent Fielding or Carlos Mendoza, but I couldn't judge her either. I just wanted her to have the chance to make everything right again. She was as strong a woman as I'd ever met, even if she couldn't see that right now, and she deserved the chance to raise the child she was carrying.

With that renewed hope, fanciful as it might be, I listened intently for the sound of her breathing. Together, we would make it though this night of horror and return to our families. I had no doubt that hers would accept whatever she had done for survival the moment she put her son in their arms, and mine would prepare a homecoming feast to rival that of the Prodigal Son returning home in the Bible. I could hardly wait to be back in my childhood home with the worn carpet on the family room floor and the pictures of relatives scattered everywhere. I had never missed it more.

But I couldn't hear the sound of breathing, even when I leaned in so close that my nose brushed her cheek. I wanted to cry out with fright and shake her, but that would only alert any wild and vicious animal in the area that we were there. So instead of giving away our location, I shoved my hand underneath the two coats that were supposed to be keeping her warm, placed my hand over her heart and waited until I felt the first weak and sporadic beat. She was still alive, but she wouldn't stay that way for long unless I did something that gave her the will to keep fighting.

Tears were stinging my nostrils when I loudly whispered her name, "Maria, can you hear me?"

I waited, shook her arm gently, and repeated her name again, "Maria, please talk to me. It's Reagan. I just need to know that you're okay."

I waited a little longer, biting my bottom lip until I could taste blood. This couldn't be happening, not after everything we'd already been through. She simply couldn't give up. Agent Fielding would be back soon, and he'd take us all to safety.

"Maria," I fiercely whispered, shaking both of her arms a little too vehemently. "You've got to fight. Jorge will be back soon."

This time, she stirred slightly, and I was so relieved I fell back on my heels. But the moment I did, I felt a drop of moisture and then another one. It was starting to rain, and the roof of the hut was partially gone. Fortunately, Agent Fielding had placed her underneath the part that was still intact.

"Reagan," she softly muttered, as if she wasn't entirely sure who I was. "Is he back yet?"

I took her hand and rubbed it gently. "Not yet, but he hasn't been gone that long."

That was a monumental lie, and not a very good one. He'd been gone for hours. Maybe he'd run into more trouble than he'd anticipated, and maybe he'd been held up indefinitely. I pushed that thought away. I would not let Satan control my thoughts when even a smidgen of hope was needed so desperately right now.

"It seems like forever," she whispered as her eyes opened ever so slightly. "Is it still night?"

"I'm afraid so, and it's starting to rain, but you're safe and warm and that's all that really matters."

I hoped she'd take comfort from my words.

"But he will never find his way in the dark and the rain," she lamented.

"Nonsense," I told her. "He knows exactly what he's doing. He's spent years in this jungle, and he's not going to let anything keep him from getting back to you and the baby. We just have to be strong until he gets here. Would you like some more water?"

I'd intentionally only had a sip or two. It would have to last until we were rescued, and Maria needed it far more than I did.

"Maybe a little," she said. "I am so cold."

I knew she was going into shock, if it had not already happened with a bullet in her shoulder, an inordinate amount of lost blood and the fear that the child she so much wanted to protect might already be gone. This night would be endless, but I had to concentrate on protecting my charges. I was glad Agent Fielding had given me a gun. It was on the ground beside me. I slid it inside the top of the backpack I'd been carrying to make sure it wouldn't getting wet.

I wasn't worried about Mendoza or his men. They wouldn't be out looking for us now, but wild animals might be. We'd already had run-ins with some of them, and the thought of something coming inside the partial enclosure terrified me. I wished I'd been smart enough to try to build a fire. There had to be dry kindling somewhere, but I'd been afraid to leave Maria alone for the amount of time it would take to find anything that might burn. Even the pieces of wood furniture left inside the hut's walls might have accepted the spark of a match if I tried hard enough.

"Reagan," Maria whispered again. "I am really scared. My baby has not moved. Are you sure he is not dead?"

"Of course not," I said, taking a deep breath for courage and hoping she didn't notice. She'd asked the same thing hours before and nothing had changed. If anything, it had only gotten worse. "He's probably resting, just like his mama."

"But I have not had any contractions for such a long time. That is not a good sign."

At least she was awake and talking. She could have so easily lapsed into unconsciousness with all her body had gone through.

"Your baby isn't quite ready to come into this world yet, or he'd already be here," I told her, trying to tuck the coverings more tightly around her, not that it would do much good. The dampness from the ground would just continue to permeate upward. I wished I wasn't so cold, but the thin shirt I was wearing did little to stave off the moist chill, and it could easily dip into the thirties before morning.

"He should not have to come into this world at all with a drug lord for a father and a disgraced agent for a mother," she bewailed. "What kind of a life will he have if he does survive?"

I almost wished I hadn't awakened her. She didn't need to start with all the negative pronouncements again.

"He'll have a mother who loves him dearly, and as soon as we get out of here, we'll find a way to get both of you to a safe place where you won't have to worry about Mendoza or anyone else finding you."

"You are talking about going into hiding. That is nothing more than a prison sentence. I would never see my family again."

"But you'd have your baby and you'd be safe. Mendoza doesn't have any reason to believe you aren't already dead."

"He will when Fernando does not show up. What if that has already happened? By morning, he could have men searching the entire jungle for bodies. He will not tolerate betrayal. He will want vengeance. Maybe he already has Jorge, and that is why he has not returned."

"We can't think that way," I said. "Agent Fielding knows what he's doing."

"No training can stop a bullet, and not many in the village can be trusted. They would sell us out in a moment if it meant they could keep food on the table for their families. Their loyalties are easily swayed."

"Maybe there are more sympathizers in the village than one would expect. Agent Fielding was sure he could find help. We need to trust him."

"Perhaps you are right," she relented, likely more out of sheer exhaustion than anything else.

"We must have faith," I told her. "There's no reason to dwell on things that can't be confirmed. I was thinking that he may have gone back to the compound, and that would take longer than going to the village. Surely there are many servants there who would be willing to offer assistance,"

She shook her head ever so slightly. "Alma would never allow it. She hated me for betraying Carlos. I think she would have killed me with her owns hands had she been given permission to do so."

"Is she really that bad?" I asked, my concerns for the children we had left behind rising. If she could confine them to their rooms when they disobeyed and feed them only bread and water . . .

"She is no better than Carlos," Maria responded, interrupting my dismal and discouraging thoughts. "Perhaps she is even worse because she is a woman and should have been born with a few motherly instincts, but there is no kindness in her."

"Do you believe she is capable of hurting Luis and Isabel?"

"Carlos would never allow her to harm them since Luis is his heir and he already has plans for Isabel's future, but now that he has run away like a coward I do not know what will happen to them. That is just another reason I never should have agreed to come with you."

"We did the only thing we could, Maria. Neither of us would be alive now if we'd stayed at the hacienda. Agent Fielding had orders to kill me at first light, and I doubt Mendoza would have allowed you to remain safety tucked away in your room when the bullets started to fly."

Her shoulders fell back against the ground. "I know you are right. I just wish I did not have so many regrets. Do you really think that Isabel and Luis are safe?"

"I can see no reason why they should have been harmed, unless the authorities didn't know they were in the hacienda."

"I gave them all the information I was able to gather, including everyone who would be of help and needed to be protected."

"Did that include Rosa and her sister?" I asked.

"Oh, yes," she replied. "I promised Rosa I would help her find work in the city once the authorities came. She is a good woman who only wants to help her family. I do not know what she will do to provide for them now."

I leaned back against a corner of the hut's wall as several huge raindrops hit my head. I had been so consumed with our flight to safety that I'd given little thought to what had actually gone on at the compound during the hours we'd been gone. All I knew was that the helicopters had arrived and the awful, lifetaking shooting had begun. There was no way of knowing who had been victorious. Mendoza's guerrillas were well-trained mercenaries with an arsenal at their disposal. They could have wiped out half the troops who were coming before they even made it over the compound walls. And even if they had survived the initial attack, getting inside the hacienda where Mendoza's cohorts had been left to take the fall for him would have been next to impossible without Agent Fielding there to lead the way.

Visions of what may have happened to innocent people who were caught unaware swirled through my head as the coldness of the night traveled inward until the real shivering began. My teeth were knocking together so hard I was afraid every animal in the jungle could hear. I had never needed hope or encouragement more but knew this was one battle I would have to get through on my own. No one would to come help us unless Agent Fielding made it back, and the length of time he had been gone only convinced me that something may have happened that had delayed his return indefinitely.

Even if he had made the conscious decision not to come back, I could hardly blame him. My being sent to the compound had destroyed the ending to a four-year mission that had required him to become nothing short of a mercenary himself so his cover would not be blown. I could hardly imagine the countless hours he had spent trying to put all the pieces of a massive and dangerous puzzle together without getting caught. I could never do what either he or Maria had done—immerse my life so completely in that of the enemy that I lost part of my humanity and most everything I held dear.

No wonder Maria felt so much concern over being rescued. The life she had known in the past was over. She could never return to her family and going into hiding where each day was spent in uncertainty and worry over when Mendoza might find her was really no way to live. It wasn't much of a legacy to leave to a child, but if she didn't make it, I doubted that I would either. That's why I had to keep fighting for both of us. She needed the chance to play out the life she had been given, and I needed the opportunity to do the same with mine. I wasn't ready to die hovering inside some partial hut in the middle of a Colombian jungle.

"We'll help Rosa," I heard myself say. It was the lamest promise yet, but Maria needed something to believe in.

"But how?" she asked. "We don't even know if Rosa survived the raid. In fact, we don't know if anyone, other than Carlos did. The shooting stopped so suddenly, and the men protecting the compound would never give up. The only thing the authorities had was the element of surprise. That was gone the moment the first helicopter made it over the top of the mountains. There is no way many of them could have survived the drop into the compound without Jorge's help."

The sudden surge in my own heart rate made it difficult to speak. "My getting caught messed up everything, didn't it?"

"No more than mine did. Jorge would have been better off to have completed the mission on his own. He knew what he was doing. You and I only got in his way and complicated things."

"Then why did the DEA send either of us?"

"I did not question my superiors about my assignment. I was young and eager to please, but I believe things were not happening fast enough for them. They knew Carlos liked beautiful women and believed I could hurry things along."

"So you weren't just sent here to teach his children."

"Carlos wanted a governess for his children. That much is true, but my only goal was to get close to him and find out where his weaknesses lay."

The bile rose quickly to my throat. How foolish I had been too believe that I could make a difference without getting my hands dirty. Assignments were given to complete an objective by whatever means necessary. I really should have listened to my father and become a teacher because I would not sacrifice my virtue for anything. It was a gift I planned to give to my husband on our wedding night—old-fashioned as that might seem to others.

"Were you able to discover anything you have not already shared with me?"

She took a deep, labored breath and began to cough. I reached out and took her hand. It was cold and felt almost lifeless.

"I tried very hard to ask questions the way I had been trained, but he would only laugh at me and say that a mere teacher did not need to concern herself with how he ran his empire. He had more money than he could spend in ten lifetimes, and he liked living at the hacienda because it was remote and he could control who came and went. It was not that way at some of his other residences where he had people in place to do his bidding. I never left the compound, but he was gone a great portion of every week. I knew when he returned if his trip had been good or bad because of what he expected me to do to soothe him."

"You don't have to talk about this, Maria," I said.

"It does not matter now what happened to me. Carlos was not always cruel. There were nights when we would sit in the library sipping wine and talking like normal people. He would tell me stories about growing up in the southern part of the country and how hard it was to survive. He wanted me to believe that he came from humble beginnings just as I had, but I never really believed him."

"Why not?"

"He did not act like someone who had ever worked in the fields or gone without food or clothing. His hunger came from greed, not from lack of what he needed to survive. I tried to find out what I could about his past and present business ventures when he was gone, but he made certain that could never happen. He placed a guard in front of my bedroom door when I was sleeping, and they were always roaming the hallways during the day. Carlos will never trust anyone but himself. I am surprised Jorge was even able to plan a raid. I just hope God can forgive me for becoming involved with

Carlos. I never meant for it to happen. I thought I could reach him some other way."

"God understand our hearts. That's what matters most. He loves us because we are his children, and he wants us to come home to him when the time is right."

"And my time is near," she sighed. "I can feel it inside."

"No," I told her. "You have to fight for life. Your baby needs you."

"But if I do not make it, you must promise to tell my son about God and the Blessed Mother. He must not grow up with hate in his heart for anyone. I am not sorry for having him. His presence is what has kept me going these past months of deprivation and fear. But I do wish he had come about in a different way. He should not have a disgraced agent for a mother or a vengeful and horrid drug lord for a father. You do not believe he is condemned because of his parents, do you?"

"Most certainly not," I replied. "Children are innocent, and they are born with the light of Christ inside. We must have faith that God's plans for us are unfolding as they should, even when the unexpected happens."

"You are very kind for not condemning me."

"There is no reason for condemnation. You are a good woman who did everything she could. Any child would be lucky to have you for a mother."

"I suppose," she replied, and then shivered almost uncontrollably. "Would you hold me? I am so cold."

The rain was falling harder now. I could feel droplets running down the small of my back where it was exposed to the open air. I made sure Maria was still completely covered and away from the downpour before picking up her head so I could cradle it in my lap. I was careful not to touch her shoulder with the bullet in it. It worried me that she was feeling no pain, but I wanted to believe that God was blessing her, and that the pain would not return until we were able to do something about it.

How naïve I was, but at that moment, I needed the assurance that we were not alone in a dark and treacherous jungle where death could strike at any moment. I brushed Maria's hair away from her face. Her forehead was hot and dry; yet every muscle in her body appeared to be trembling. Then I closed my eyes and offered a prayer for help, safety and the removal of fear. It was the only real weapon I had against the kind of danger we now faced. The small caliber gun in the top of my backpack would be useless unless I saw an enemy coming.

When I looked up again, it was growing light, and I heard Agent Fielding entering the hut from behind me. The lower portion of my body, along with my back, was drenched where the rain had come through openings in the roof. But one quick glance down at my charge assured me that she was still dry. I was trembling with cold, but he appeared not to notice my distress. He was carrying a bag that I hoped had at least some of the medical supplies we needed. He dropped it on the ground out of the mud and was by Maria's side the next moment.

"How long has she been like this?" he demanded, brushing her forehead with the back of his hand. "She's burning up."

Focusing my vision was impossible. My head ached and my brain felt like it had been frozen in a deep fog of forgetfulness that would not go away.

"I asked you a question?" he demanded in a voice empty of anything except disdain. "How long has she been like this?"

My chest heaved with feelings of guilt and horror as I realized that I must have fallen asleep while praying because I couldn't remember a thing since closing my eyes. My only task had been to watch over and protect her, and I hadn't even been able to do that. She had been conversing with me shortly before I dozed off, and now she wasn't moving at all. Even her face looks like it had been frozen into a death mask.

"I'm not sure," I admitted, knowing he'd surmise the truth anyway.

"What the hell do you mean you're not sure?"

Tears were streaking my filth-covered cheeks, and I was glad he was too busy with Maria to notice. "I'm not sure because I was praying and . . ."

"A lot of good that's done," he shot back, pulling her out of my arms. "We've got to wake her up. The infection has likely spread throughout her entire body by now thanks to your continued incompetence."

My incompetence, as he continued to label my best efforts, would not have changed the outcome of the night. He'd been gone for a least twelve hours. Even as unfamiliar as I was with the jungle, I could have found my way back in less time than that.

Still, I wished I was the one lying there, not her, but I had the presence of mind not to waste valuable time trying to defend myself against an impossible situation. I just sat numbly on the soggy ground with dozens of bugs scurrying around and watched as he leaned over and pulled a canteen out of the bag he'd brought with him. I thought he was going to try to give her a sip of water, but instead he poured a good portion of it over her face. It took a moment or two before she coughed, sputtered and shook her head until some of the water had rolled off.

"I cannot breathe . . ."

Then she opened her eyes and looked up into Agent Fielding's face and everything about her demeanor changed. His did the same, and I was filled with the complete realization that they truly cared about each other, regardless of what had happened between them or a mission that had at least partially failed.

"Oh, Jorge," she faintly whispered in a tone that conveyed both love and longing. "You did come back for me."

"What else would I do, Maria," he soothed, running his hand over her wet hair. "I couldn't leave my favorite girl out here in the jungle to deliver her baby alone."

"But he has not moved for such a long time, Jorge. I am so frightened."

Agent Fielding gave me a scathing look as if everything was my fault again, and I looked down at the ground wishing it would open and swallow me. My own self-contempt was eating away at my soul. I couldn't even keep watch while he beat his way through the jungle all night to get help. What kind of a lame excuse for an agent was I anyway?

"That's because you're very sick right now," he was saying when I forced myself to look at them again. I could feel sorry for myself later, but right now I needed to be ready for anything that was asked of me. "You've got to get up and start moving around. We need to get those contractions going again."

"But I am so tired, Jorge. I just want to go back to sleep."

"Not possible!" he told her, rising to his feet and pulling her up with him. She looked as if she'd shrunk during the night despite her protruding belly, and her feet were unable to support her weight. She slumped down against him.

"I could use some help here, Agent Sinclair," he almost snarled, but I was already on my feet, and in a moment, we were moving her around the small enclosure through the mud that sucked at the boots we were wearing. It was then I noticed that she had lost one of the slippers she'd been wearing. How long had it been gone? Possibly since our encounter with the snake and crocodiles, but it might have happened even sooner than that. I chastised myself again for not being more observant.

Maria was too weak to fight. She simply allowed us to drag her around the ramshackle hut without protest for what seemed like hours. I wished I knew what was happening. If she was burning up with fever, why was Agent Fielding so insistent that she keep moving? Shouldn't she be resting and conserving her strength, not only to fight the infection, but in preparation for the birth of her son?

And then suddenly she let out a deafening scream, her knees buckled, and she was pulling both of us down. I caught myself with one hand before landing on my face in the mud.

"I cannot do it any longer," she cried out. "It hurts too much."

"What hurts?" Agent Fielding asked. "Your shoulder?"

"No, my baby! He wants to come now!"

I looked over at Agent Fielding, but he seemed to have forgotten my presence.

"That's good, Maria," he said, reaching for the coat so he could make sure it was tucked underneath her before easing her body back onto the ground. "Do you think you can push?"

She clenched her teeth and tried, but another contraction started and she screamed again.

By now, the severity of the moment had started to sink in, and I wasn't even worried about wild animals hearing her outbursts. Agent Fielding wasn't being unreasonable or unkind by insisting that she get on her feet. He was trying to restart her contractions so her baby would have a chance if it was still alive. If it wasn't, it would act like any other foreign object attacking her body, and they would both die.

But what if she wasn't strong enough to help deliver her own child? We were not equipped to do a C-section, at least I wasn't, and I had no idea what the man with us was capable of doing or what supplies he may have brought with him. There couldn't be much if he'd gotten them at the village, but perhaps he had returned to the hacienda and his delayed return only meant that he had met with a certain amount of resistance because the raid had not happened as planned.

The only thing I knew for sure was that he cared about Maria, or he wouldn't have come back at all.

"Just go with it," he instructed as he tried to force her body into a position where a delivery could occur. She seemed to be resisting every offer of assistance, but even I could see that something was happening. "Your baby knows exactly what to do. He just needs a little help."

"But I cannot breathe."

"Yes, you can," he said. "Just pant a little bit like this."

He demonstrated, and she tried to mimic what he had done.

"It is not working," she said and then screamed again.

Agent Fielding had moved from her side and was now squatting at the foot of her makeshift bed. The furrows on his brow had significantly deepened, and I couldn't help but notice how truly tired and scared he was. This wasn't something he wanted to do, but it came as part of the job. Expecting the unexpected and knowing how to deal with it was what set the good agents apart from the dead ones.

"Oh, but it is," he encouraged as she tried to push again.

I just kneeled where I was wishing I had something of value to offer. I was a woman! I should know instinctively what to do in offering help and support during a delivery, but this was a first for me.

Maria was gripping my hand so tightly I wanted to cry out in my own pain, but considering what she was going through to give her son life I held back. The baby's head was crowning.

"Oh, Maria," I exclaimed. "Just one more push. He's coming."

"I cannot do it," she whimpered. "I do not have the strength."

She released the pressure on my hand and sank back onto the coats that had been shielding her from damp, cold earth.

Suddenly, I was no longer thinking about the mess I'd made of my first undercover mission. Maria and her child were all that mattered. I might not know what to do medically, but I could offer compassion and support.

"Come on, Maria," I coaxed, putting my hand under the back of her head and lifting it. "I know you're tired and it hurts terribly, but think about your son. You're going to hold him in your arms in a just a few moments. Won't that be glorious? Surely you can find the strength for just one more push. Please, Maria, you've got to try. I know how much you love him and how much you've sacrificed to get him here. I've already promised to do what you asked, but you can't give up now, you simply can't. You have a son who needs you so very much."

The tears in my eyes were making it hard to see any of the details of my surroundings except for the look of complete trust and acceptance on Maria's beautiful face. I would give all my strength and everything I possessed for this baby to be born strong and healthy. I didn't care that we were in the middle of the jungle, or that what she had asked of me was impossible. All we had was this moment, and if she didn't try again, both mother and child would be lost.

"You must never forget that a promise is forever," she whispered as her eyes found mine. "God will remember and so will I."

"I won't," I told her. "Now please try to push."

She just lay there as if trying to gather the strength. I glanced over at Agent Fielding. For once he didn't look impatient or hostile towards me. He just looked scared.

"Please help all of us, Father," I silently prayed.

It seemed that no sooner had the words left my conscious thought than Maria gave a loud scream and one final thrust forward. I watched as the baby slipped out into the cloth Agent Fielding was holding in his hands—a tiny, slimy scrap of humanity.

"It's a boy, Maria," he said, lifting the baby up so Maria could see her son.

I sank back in sheer relief. Had this baby really chosen to come to earth with a drug lord for a father, and a terrified, disgraced, DEA agent for a mother? What a story they would both tell someday when they related his birth in a cocaine-cutting hut in the middle of the jungle. His life would not be one of ease or safety, but I knew he would be loved.

"Poor baby," I thought as I watched Agent Fielding wipe the mucus from his mouth, nose and eyes. I held my breath waiting for a cry that would let us know he was alive.

"Come on, little guy," Agent Fielding said as he dangled the baby in the air by his feet. "You can't quit on us now."

I held my breath in fear and anticipation of what might happen. At first, I only heard a little squeak, quite like the one a mouse would make if it got caught in a trap. Then, as if he didn't have much of a choice in the cold, dankness of the hut, the baby screamed and shook so hard I thought he would break before Agent Fielding got him back in the soiled cloth he'd first fallen into.

"We've got ourselves a little scrapper here," he said. "I've never seen anything like it."

I should have looked at Maria then, but I didn't. I was too wrapped up watching Agent Fielding cut the umbilical cord and clamp it off with a wooden clothespin—the kind the women in the village used to hang their laundry up to dry in the sun when it made its rare appearance in the sky.

"Wasn't sure this was going to happen today," he continued as he worked. "I just wish we had some warm water to clean him up a bit. He should look reasonably presentable when his mother holds him for the first time, but since we don't, we'll have to use what we have. Would you mind getting one of the extra bottles of it that I brought along?"

I did as he instructed, feeling as if I was moving through an altered reality where the warm rays of the sun never penetrated, and the very insects were determined to consume our tender flesh. They were already swarming around the afterbirth and trying to get at the baby as Agent Fielding tried to protect him from being bitten.

"Hurry up," he instructed. "I wish we had something better to dress him in, but I was lucky to get out of the village with what I did."

It was another warning and I knew it, but what did he expect? We couldn't control when the baby was going to be born, even if evil men were coming after us.

"Maria has some things in her bag," I told him.

"There isn't time for that now. We need to get moving. Mendoza's men were swarming all over the village. There's a piece of cloth we can rip up for a diaper and a blanket I pulled off one of the lines. But that's the best I could do."

I handed him one of the bottles that had been filled with water. He held the baby on his knees while he tried to clean off as much blood and gore as he could, wiping the baby's face and body with a portion of the cloth he'd brought. It looked like a highly worn sheet and was rough to the touch, but then we weren't dealing with people who even knew about washers and dryers. These sheets had been cleaned on rocks with whatever could be found for detergent.

I ripped the remaining cloth into three strips and watched as he tied one of them around the baby. It wouldn't hold anything, but for a man who'd been willing to leave Maria behind the day before, he was certainly taking great care with her newly born son.

"There he is," Agent Fielding said, extending the baby in my direction. "Why don't you show him to his mother while I see if I can't do something more to stop the bleeding. He'd already shoved a towel between Maria's legs. I wondered how he knew what to do. He'd been adamant before going into the village that he knew nothing about the birthing process.

The baby he handed me opened his eyes, and I was sure he saw my face even though I knew it took time before an infant could focus on anything. He was a miracle, and I knew in that moment that I wanted children far more than I wanted the excitement and danger of the career I'd chosen. I intuitively lifted his face to my lips and kissed the top of his head. It was covered with a downy covering of dark hair.

"Look, Maria," I said with a smile I felt from the inside out. "You have the most incredible baby boy."

I held him out to her, but she was lying back on the ground with her eyes closed. I felt the chill of fear scurry down my spine.

"He's the most beautiful baby you've ever seen."

Still, she did not move. I tucked the baby under one arm and reached down and touched her shoulder, shaking it softly.

"Maria," I whispered. "Don't you want to see your son?"

It was a stupid question. All mothers wanted to see their child; even those who did not want to keep them. When she didn't respond this time, I put my hand on her chest, hoping to feel her heart beating, but there was no movement.

I turned my terrified face to Agent Fielding, but he was already on her other side lifting her arm in his hand and checking for a pulse, his face an expressionless mask.

"She's gone," he said in a toneless voice. "There's nothing we can do for her now."

"No," I whimpered. "Check again. She hasn't even met her son."

The tears were frozen in my eyes as I clutched the baby tighter in my arms. I wasn't going to leave Maria, regardless of what he said.

"It's no good, Agent Sinclair. We have to let her go."

I sat back on the heels of my feet, shaking uncontrollably. Agent Fielding reached across Maria's lifeless body and touched my knee.

"I know we both hoped it wouldn't end this way, but it has, and we have to accept it. Now, gather your things together. We have to be going."

"No," I said. "I'm not leaving her here like this. It's inhumane!"

"It's life in the jungle," he replied with an icy glare. "Mendoza's men will be coming soon. They were asking if anyone had seen

Fernando. I was barely able to avoid detection. The rain stopped them for a few hours, but now that it's let up, they'll be on their way to exact revenge."

"Why can't he just let us go? We can't hurt him now."

"Mendoza doesn't operate like that. It's a sign of weakness to let anyone who has betrayed him escape. I can't even guarantee that the friend who helped me get a few supplies won't tell them where we are. They're more afraid of Mendoza than anything else."

"But we can't . . ."

He didn't wait for me to finish my thought.

"We don't have time for niceties. We can't go back to the village, and it's very unlikely we'll make it out of the jungle alive ourselves, but we have to give it a try."

I numbly rose to my feet and then bent down and pulled the coat that had covered Maria during the night over her face. How could I leave her here all alone? It wouldn't take long until the wild animals found her body. I couldn't bear to think of what would happen then.

"Listen, Agent Sinclair," Agent Fielding said. "I know you're a good person and a very compassionate one, but life out here doesn't play by the rules of mercy. We don't have time to be sentimental."

I knew he was right, but the tears still trickled from my eyes as I looked down to where Maria's body lay so still and lifeless. Just a few minutes ago we had been talking. No one should have to be left alone like that. It tore at my heartstrings and made me want to be ill, but then I turned my attention to the tiny scrap of humanity in my arms. Maria had given her life so her baby could be born free from the tyrannical rule of the ruthless man who was responsible for her death, and she'd asked me to take care of him – to love, cherish and protect him as she had done. But I wasn't even sure I could keep him alive for the next few hours. There was simply too much stacked against us.

"If we can't go back to the hacienda or to the village," I asked, struggling to my feet with the baby still in my arms. "Then where are we going?"

"I'm not entirely sure," he said. "I only know that we can't go back the way we came, and they'll assume we're heading straight for the river since that's the quickest way out of the jungle."

"And the people in the village weren't any help?"

He looked at me without sympathy. "Let's just say that most of the natives in this jungle don't see what they're doing as wrong, and they sure as hell don't like the idea of no longer having a way to provide for their families. A lot of the people who worked the fields lost their lives during the raid. I'd say that makes us pretty unpopular."

He emptied the contents of the backpack he'd brought from the hacienda onto the ground. "I suppose you're going to insist on taking some of the things in that suitcase. There's no way we can carry it, now that we have a baby to drag along. You do know it's not going to make it. No child can be expected to after what it's been through."

"Let me worry about that," I told him as I balanced the baby on my knees and reached for the small suitcase whose outside was soaked with rain. I was not going to allow him to touch anything Maria had packed inside. Her baby would not die while I had an ounce of strength left in my body, and he would have something to remember his mother by if I had to carry it in my teeth.

The first thing I found was a small blanket that had been stitched together by hand, likely from pillowcases she'd found. I wanted to bring it to my lips, but I couldn't show sentiment in front of Agent Fielding, or he might tell me to leave everything behind. Besides, I needed the papers she had packed in the bottom. I would do everything in my power to fulfill the promise I'd made. Her son would know his mother and how she'd sacrificed everything to give him life.

"That's enough," Agent Fielding said when he saw that I had pulled two silver candlesticks from the suitcase. "Those aren't going to do us any good."

"I wasn't planning on taking them," I replied, dropping them unceremoniously. He didn't need to know about the notes or the promise I'd made to Maria right now. It would only give him more of a reason to ridicule me.

Without any warning, he ripped the backpack from my hands and zipped it shut, but while he was securing his machete and machine gun, I stuffed everything else I could reach into the top of my own backpack, making sure the papers I might need were thrust as far to the bottom as possible. I managed to grab a gold and diamond bracelet and matching pair of earrings. Not that they would ever be used or sold, but they had belonged to the baby's mother.

The tiny thing in arms started to fuss as I forced myself to my feet. I was stiff from sitting so long in the cold night air, and my knees were less than stable after the ordeal I'd just witnessed, but I couldn't ask my companion for any more leniencies, even though I knew the baby needed to eat and there was nothing I could give him.

He slung a backpack over each arm and extended the last one in my direction. "You'll have to carry this one. It's got a couple of bottles of goat's milk. It was all I had time to get."

I shifted the baby from arm to arm as he slipped the straps over my shoulders. There was no weight to him all, but at least he was still breathing.

Chapter 11

I felt numb from the top of my head to the tips of my toes as we left the confines of the small hut where so much tragedy had just occurred. If I thought about it now I wouldn't be able to move forward. Every shred of decency screamed for me to retrace my steps and insist that Agent Fielding stop long enough to dig a grave for Maria. How could I ever tell her son that her body had been left for wild animals to devour because we under a timetable that wouldn't allow it? He'd hate me, but no more than I'd hate myself.

Still, I didn't say anything. It would have done no good. Laws of decorum didn't exist in the jungle, and this wasn't a dream I could stop at will. This was unsympathetic reality, and Agent Fielding was right. We had few friends, and even those could easily turn against us after what had happened the day before. I couldn't begin to imagine the anguish and destruction that had taken place at the hacienda. I only knew that its rippling effect might be felt for generations.

Raindrops hung on the low-growing shrubs and bushes that slapped at me as I pushed my way through them. We were not following a trail, and Agent Fielding was not trying to clear a path. I knew why he was doing it, but if Mendoza's men were as close behind us as he'd led me to believe it would do little good. They'd easily see where broken branches and crumpled leaves had been disturbed.

As we walked my own clothes became damper, but the odd thing was that I wasn't so concerned about myself anymore. I was fearful for Maria's baby. He was clinging to life right now, but that wouldn't last long if he wasn't properly cared for. He needed to be thoroughly warmed and fed, not carried through the trees and damp air in nothing but a towel. Thankfully, Agent Fielding had brought two of them from the village. The one covered with afterbirth and blood lay on the floor of the hut, along with Maria's still body. The one wrapped around him was now dry, but that wouldn't last long if we stopped long enough for him to try to eat.

Cold goat's milk sounded horrid, but it was the only thing we had. I hugged him to me, feeling an outpouring of love and compassion so strong that the tears started to flow again, and I could barely see where I was going. If he got chilled, he would catch cold that could lead to pneumonia or worse, and I'd promised to guard him with my life and raise him to manhood if the need arose.

What a sobering thought that was now that the need had arisen. Even if we made it out of the jungle, I'd never get him out of the country. His dark skin was a dead giveaway that he didn't belong to me. And the legalities! No magistrate on the face of the planet would rule in my favor. He was a Colombian citizen, but he was also a child of God. If he made it . . . Well, I had to concentrate on the moment and let everything else go. There was nothing I could do about the future anyway.

As I stumbled along behind Agent Fielding, I wondered what he was really thinking. He was a man of few words, unless he was angry, but he had shown me that there was a softer side to him—one he didn't often reveal because of the kind of work he did. He wouldn't have come back for us if he hadn't cared about his former partner, despite the mistakes they had both made. It couldn't be any easier for him than it was for me to leave her alone, but he had pledged to save innocent lives just as I had done, and who was more deserving than the infant I held so tightly in my arms?

I had no idea in what direction we were heading, only that we were going deeper into the jungle. Could Agent Fielding really know where he was going? I understood that he didn't want Mendoza's men to know which way we had gone when they found Maria's body, but if we got lost deep within the interior what would it matter anyway? He carried a semi-automatic weapon with a strap of ammunition, and there was a handgun in one of the backpacks, but we couldn't keep our eyes on everything at once. Besides, I was more worried about the dangers we couldn't easily see than the ones that might be hunting or following us.

Although the insects were less ferocious than they had been the day before, I knew it was only from the amount of rain during the night. Once the sun had burned most of the moisture away, they would be back with a vengeance. I had to protect the baby from them. It no longer mattered if they came after me.

It wasn't long before the baby started to whimper. I bounced him in my arms like I'd done with my nieces and nephews when I'd been left alone with them, but he refused to be comforted. Agent Fielding was a few yards ahead when I called to him, asking if we could stop for a few minutes while I tried to feed the baby.

His jaw was set in a hard line when he turned around to face me. "Can't this wait? I'd like to put more distance between us and the hut before we stop."

"So would I, but I'm afraid the baby needs nourishment if he's going to survive."

"I already told you that the chances of that happening are minimal. We're not going to get out of here by nightfall. Hell, we might not even make it out of here at all."

"That may be true, but we still have to try. It's what Maria would want."

I wasn't sure what had made me mention her name in such a context since he'd already told me that he didn't believe in God or forever, but he still took a few steps in my direction. I knew he was about to say something else derisive, but he refrained from doing so. Even he had to know that an infant needed milk.

"Okay, but only for a few minutes," he relented, leaning his machete against a tree while he opened the backpack he'd brought from the village. "We have a long way to go, and there's no telling what we might have to face before dark."

I found a fallen log to sit on. They seemed to be prolific in the jungle. I just hoped it wasn't filled with termites, or some other flesh eating beetle, ant, hornet or bee. Then I unwrapped the baby and took a very close look at him. His tiny body was curled up, and his eyes were tightly shut. The clothespin that had been attached to his umbilical cord   before it was cut was covered with damp, oozing blood that had completely saturated the makeshift diaper I had ripped from a sheet, and it looked to be almost half as big as he was. There was no way I could guess how much he weighed, but I figured he could easily fit in the palm of Agent's Fielding's hand."

"Quit staring at him and start feeding," Agent Fielding almost snarled as he pushed a large, plastic bottle that didn't look any too clean in my direction. I was fairly certain that it wasn't meant for human consumption since the nipple was much too large for an infant, but I couldn't afford to be critical when it was all I had.

"I will feed him, but I need to change his diaper first. All that external blood can't be good for him."

"I don't know what you expect me to do about that," he replied as the baby began to wail. It was a sound that indicated pain—not just fear and discomfort.

"You could hold him for a moment while I get a gauze dressing from my backpack. I don't know why I didn't think about that sooner," I replied, hoping some of the compassion he'd displayed at the baby's birth would resurface.

He looked at me as if I'd completely lost my mind. "That baby looks just fine where he's at, and a gauze bandage won't do any good without something large enough to hold it in place. Besides, I don't care much for kids. That's one of the reasons I never married."

I knew better than to ask him a second time. He was being tolerant for now, but that could easily change. What had me confused was the way he'd held the baby up so Maria could see him. Perhaps now that she was gone, he no longer really cared what happened to either of us. He was simply doing his duty.

"That's okay," I said as I untied the knot in the piece of sheet that served as a diaper and pulled it away from the baby's skin. I couldn't afford to throw it away, and I could rinse it out with rainwater when there was more time. Then I secured another strip of dry cloth around his waist.

The man leading us to safety must have known that Maria had little chance of survival so he'd made provisions for the baby just in case. Perhaps he wasn't such a bad person after all, just a trifle too rough around the edges for me.

I nestled the baby's dark head in the crook of my arm and put the rubber nipple to his lips, but he seemed uncertain as to what he must do. The goat's milk wasn't warm, and I couldn't bear to think of all the bacteria it contained, but I squeezed the nipple anyway and then rubbed it gently back and forth until the white substance covered his lips. When I didn't get any response, I parted them ever so slowly with the cleanest of my fingers so some of the milk could enter his mouth.

"I thought babies were supposed to know what to do," Agent Fielding said as he watched my slow progress from several feet away.

"They do, but this isn't exactly the way things are usually done," I told him without looking up. "A new baby is kept with its mother until it learns how to nurse. This milk is cold and the nipple is too big for his mouth."

It was pointless to tell him that I didn't think it was safe for an infant to be drinking milk straight from an animal that had to taste awful, in addition to containing millions of germs. He might take it away from me and pour it out.

In near desperation, I reached up underneath my shirt and wiped my right baby finger against my bra, trying to clean it as best I could. Then I covered it with milk and forced it inside the baby's mouth. His lips started moving back and forth in a sucking motion, and I nearly cried out with joy. Now, if I could just get him to take the bottle. It took a few minutes of trial and error before he could latch onto the nipple that was much too large for his tiny mouth and pull some of the milk inside. He only took a few swallows, but it was a sign to me that he wasn't going to give up and neither was I.

"Can we go now?" Agent Fielding demanded once I had handed him the bottle, rewrapped the baby and tied the stained piece of cloth to the outside of my backpack.

I was angry with him because of his outward insensitivity towards an infant who'd just lost his mother, but I knew one of us had to remain grounded. My priorities had certainly become divided. All I wanted to do was protect Maria's baby. I loved him more intensely in the few minutes I'd known him than I'd ever loved anyone else. It was different with my family who had always taken care of me. I was responsible for this little person who was totally helpless without my care. It was a heady and weighty feeling, and one I had never supposed I would have until I had a child of my own.

We made slow progress during the next couple of hours. The jungle was dense and every bend in the trail Agent Fielding was trying to forge could easily be filled with danger, but with so much at stake, I no longer even contemplated complaining. I tripped over fallen logs, listened to the ferocious sound of wild animals too near for comfort and tried to keep from dropping the baby. When we stopped again, Agent Fielding didn't seem as worried as he'd been before.

"Just for a few minutes," he said. "We have to keep moving if we want to get to a safer place before we stop for the night."

I didn't say anything. I just changed the baby's diaper and got him to drink another few swallows of milk. I didn't know how much he was supposed to consume. I was just grateful that he was still clinging to life.

It was mid-afternoon when Agent Fielding stopped walking and held up his hand to silence me. I couldn't hear anything unusual except for the drip of rain as it hit the tree branches and leaves above us. I hadn't had anything to eat all day, and very little the day before. My stomach was beyond the point of growling, but I was too worried about the infant in my arms to give my discomfort much thought. We were going to get caught in another downpour; only this time there would be no shelter. Could the day possibly get any worse?

But those thoughts had barely formed in my mind when I realized that it wasn't the sound of falling rain in our green and drizzling world that had disturbed him. It was the sound of crushing branches, and they were not that far away.

Mere seconds later, I heard a voice coming through the gloom of the afternoon. "This way," it shouted in Spanish.

I then knew that Mendoza's men were following close behind, and they were not worried about giving their location away. But then, why should they be worried about anything other than getting lost or becoming a victim to something unforeseen in the jungle? They had the manpower and the machine guns necessary to stop us. The only real question was whether they would try to capture us alive or simply kill us. As long as they could offer proof that we were dead, Mendoza would handsomely reward them.

"You go," Agent Fielding whispered. "I'll hold them off as long as I can."

The sickness inside of me was almost consuming. "Where?" I asked.

"Just away! I'll find you as soon as I can, I promise."

But even as my feet started to move away from him, I knew what he had given me was a fool's promise. He would never find us if we separated, and the baby and I didn't stand a chance without him. My sense of direction was as good as any other agent's, but everything in the jungle looked the same to me.

"No!" I said. "We go together, or we perish together. There's no other way."

He looked at me with a combination of scorn and admiration. "All right," he said, pushing me to the left. Let's see if a place where we can at least attempt to defend ourselves can be found."

I moved on leaden feet trying to sidestep roots and branches that were becoming saturated again as the rain started to pound on our heads from above. At first, I wanted to complain, but it suddenly dawned on me that heavy precipitation would muffle any sounds we were making. And if it became heavy enough, it would wash away our footsteps and erase the signs of disrupted vegetation until the area had significantly dried out again. But finding adequate shelter would not be easy since we were a great distance from either the hacienda or the village, and Agent Fielding had given me little indication that he had any idea where we might find refuge before they overtook us.

The baby started to whimper, and I tried to bounce him just a little in my arms as I followed Agent Fielding through a world that blurred into an enveloping green aura that was far too astringent for comfort. I longed for a flash of vociferous color to relieve the green intensity but knew that the sudden movement of even a flock of birds overheard could give our location away. Had we truly come this far only to be lost forever in a mass of twisted green vines and undergrowth that had buried complete civilizations?

I fought back blistering tears of regret and terror as I tried to remain upright on the earth that had suddenly become slippery and shifty underneath my feet. We were moving up a slight incline and every few steps I found myself sliding backwards. Occasionally, I grabbed at vines for support, but that was usually short-lived. Their tentacles seemed to be endless, and I worried that I might latch onto something deadlier than Mendoza's men. The jungle was literally teeming with poisonous reptiles, insects, plants and animals of every variety. I wanted to remain positive. At least we hadn't been captured and killed yet, but it might only be a matter of time.

And even if we managed to evade our pursuers and other lethal creatures, pools of quicksand existed in the jungle. I wondered if we might fall into one of them during our flight through the rain and dense undergrowth. It was not unheard of, and we couldn't see where we were going.

Oh, why had I insisted on a career that was fraught with continual danger? It had seemed so glamorous and exciting before I'd left home on this mission. Now, I just wanted to be back with my family, enjoying my brother's never-ending teasing and one of my mother's fabulous meals. I was terrifyingly cold, hungry and afraid, and I had an infant in my arms that might not make it through the rest of the day.

"Over here," I suddenly heard Agent Fielding say.

He had pushed back a large clump of voracious, shinny, green-gold vines and before us stood a stone monument that rose over twenty feet towards the sky. It was about six feet in diameter with hieroglyphics of human-like faces, birds and animals etched into its surface.

"What is this place," I asked as fingers of forbiddance traveled up my spine. Beyond it stood a structure that reminded me of an ancient Egyptian pyramid, though not nearly as tall, with chiseled stone sides that at one time must have been steps. They were now worn, weathered and moss-covered and too treacherous to even attempt to climb.

"I have no idea, but it might prove useful," he replied. "Natives are terrified of sacred ground."

I didn't understand his logic. Most of Mendoza's men weren't locals, and I could see nothing in the way of protection unless the statue offered more fortification than trees would have done, but Agent Fielding wasn't as easily discouraged. He moved closer to the formation beyond the statue.

I hung back. Had this been any other time than the present I might have been overjoyed at our find. While it was impossible to date, its very existence gave credence to the fact that other civilizations had existed long before our recorded time, perhaps even as far back as the ancient people of the Bible.

But this wasn't a vacation. We were fighting for our lives and everything seemed to be going against us, even Mother Nature. I pulled the baby closer to me. I was shivering from cold, wet and fright. What if his little body could not generate enough heat to survive? The rain was falling faster now. There wasn't a dry spot anywhere around us, and I didn't even have a coat for protection.

I pushed back thoughts of what might have happened during the hours we'd been gone from the hut where Maria's body had been left. Perhaps we had been reckless in not bringing more protective wear, but then a thorough preparation hadn't exactly been possible, and I'd brought everything I could think of that might be helpful. There was another shirt in the backpack I was carrying. It might still be dry enough to offer additional protection for the baby if we ever found a place where we could open it and see.

And the medical supplies still had to be intact since I'd put them in a plastic baggie. Plus, there was another large towel and two granola bars I'd forgotten completely about in the horror of the past two days. If hope came in simple things, those few items certainly added to mine. Things were not quite as desperate as they seemed.

The overly large lips of the face of the statue that was eye level to me—and so much resembled Indian totem poles in North America—seemed to be laughing at the fact that we'd lost our way and might never see civilization again. How many other people had died out here alone and afraid? Maria might be the lucky one after all. At least she was now back home with God in a true paradise.

I shivered as more dampness from the late afternoon settled into my bones, and then I glanced around at the heavy vines and trees that seemed to be closing in on us now that the rain was beginning to fall more rapidly. There was no way we'd be going any place now.

"Agent Sinclair," I heard Agent Fielding call my name. "I think I may have found something."

I followed the sound of his voice through creeping, wet plants that pulled at my legs and made walking without stumbling every few steps impossible. His discovery was an opening at the base of the tall pyramid-type structure. Behind it was complete blackness.

"Are you sure it's safe?" I asked him.

"I'm not sure of anything right now, except that I've never seen rain like this before. It's not going to let up before morning, and if we don't take shelter now it will be too late."

He led the way inside the enclosed space. I waited while he shined his flashlight around the room. A few bats hung from the ceiling, but they only flapped their wings when we entered and didn't appear to be frightened or in any great hurry to get away. This time I held my teeth tightly together, even though they were chattering, and did not scream even when I felt something about the size of a dog move past me on its way outside.

"What was that?" I whispered when the air had quit moving, leaving behind the musty smell of wild animals.

"Perhaps it's best if we don't know," he said, taking a few steps farther inside and shining the light into every corner. It was pitch black, and impossible to tell just how deep the enclosure was, but there was room enough to sit down, and it did offer protection from the elements outside. "I'll check things out a little more thoroughly before we settle in. I'm not fond of surprises."

"Me either," I thought as I stood inside the enclosure, listening to rain as it sheeted down in front of the doorway. It never rained like that at home, even during the worst storm. This was relentless, and if it kept up all night, it could wash a great deal of soil away. But once again, I realized that I wasn't at home, and the soil in the jungle was so completely covered with vegetation that I doubted anything could move it. I felt a moment of pity for Mendoza's men, but it passed quickly enough.

The baby in my arms wasn't moving. I prayed he was just asleep. The day had been long and hard, and he was only a few hours old and had taken no more than an ounce of milk. In many ways, I was surprised that he had consumed it at all. It wasn't what infants were meant to drink, but perhaps God in his wisdom and mercy could make even the vilest of liquid seem sweet and inviting.

Wasn't that exactly what he had done with the ancient Israelites who had refused to obey his commandments? They had wandered in the wilderness for forty years feasting on nothing but manna from heaven. I was so glad to be a Christian who believed in a God of love and miracles, and a Savior who chose to die for our sins so we could all live with him again.

Coming from the darkness behind me, I heard several thuds and a little swearing, but nothing else rushed past me and there was no sound of a gun being fired. It would have echoed terribly inside the small chamber. After what seemed like forever, Agent Fielding was at my side again.

"Sorry it took so long," he said. "But I wanted to make sure we were alone, except for our nocturnal friends overhead, and a few things on the ground I'd rather not talk about."

"So, we'll be safe?" I asked.

"That's what I'm hoping. This enclosure isn't large, and there's a high ledge at the back. That's what all the banging was about. I wanted to check it out before taking you there. I had to knock a bunch of crap off, but it should be good to go now."

I followed him in silence until we came to the back wall. The ledge he was referring to stood at least six feet off the ground—

several inches above the top of my head. I wondered how he expected me to climb up there without a ladder. If I stretched to my full height I might be able to reach the lip, but even with the arduous amount of training I'd received at the academy, in my weakened state, I wasn't sure I had strength enough to pull myself up.

As if reading my thoughts, Agent Fielding said. "Give me the baby. I'll put him up there with the backpacks, and then I'll pull you up once I've gotten there myself. And don't ask me if it's safe because I've already checked. I'm not in the mood to lose anyone else."

His words were meant to be reassuring, but I felt stripped completely naked when he took the baby from my arms and moved away so I no longer had contact with anything human or comforting. Why couldn't I just wake up from this nightmare and find myself back in my own apartment with nothing to worry about, other than the bad guys who roamed the civilized streets and alleys in America?

I heard the sound of the towel the baby was wrapped in move across the surface of the rock above my head. How it had been fashioned was as big a mystery as the monolithic structure that now surrounded us. I just hoped we had found safety and wouldn't be disturbed by anything or anyone else that might be seeking shelter.

"Here, let me help you." he said, reaching his hand down towards me once he and the baby were safely on top of the ledge. "You can use your feet to help propel you up if you'd like. I know you don't really trust me yet."

"I trust you," I said as I felt his fingers close around my wrist.

The strength he possessed was unmistakable, even though I knew he was likely even more tired and hungry than I was. I'd managed a few moments of unsolicited rest the night before, while he'd spent its entirety fighting his way through the jungle in hopes of finding us still alive when he made it back to the hut.

In less than thirty seconds, I found myself on the ledge with him. My feet had barely grazed the side of the rock wall.

"Don't try to stand up," he cautioned. "I did and smacked my head."

"Where's the baby?" I asked, wishing I could really care about his head. I had to make sure Maria's son was still alive. I hadn't checked on him since the rain began, and he hadn't whimpered in the longest time.

He picked up the small, soggy bundle and placed it in my arms. I'd tried so hard to shield him with my arms and my body, but there was only so much I could do while traveling over rough and foreign terrain and trying to keep from falling in a virtual cloudburst.

"You shouldn't get so attached to a dream that's never going to see fruition," he said. "It's only fitting that Maria's son dies in the jungle with her. I should have insisted that we leave him with her. It's made traveling today so much harder, and now we have Mendoza's men on our tail again. This rain will slow them down, but they'll be ready to move again as soon as we are."

I was too angry to say anything. It wasn't "fitting" to leave an infant to certain death when there was even the tiniest chance of saving his life. I didn't know what I'd do if I lost him now. I had been fighting horrifying images of what had most likely happened to Maria's body all day as I traipsed through a merciless jungle with her infant son. She hadn't wanted to leave him, but the choice had been taken out of her hands. And even if it had been under duress, I had given a sacred promise that I would take care of him. I never went back on my pledges, and with God's help, I knew I could do it , regardless of what Agent Fielding said or what obstacles still lay ahead.

"I'm sorry, Agent Sinclair," he said, forcing me back to the cold darkness of the cave underneath the pyramid-like structure. "I was out of line. Of course, we couldn't leave Maria's son behind."

"Then why did you say it?" I asked, hugging the towel with he baby in it even closer.

"Because I was angry! And because there's little reason to believe that even you and I will make it out of this jungle. I'm a realist. We might be able to find plenty of water to stay alive for a few days, but without food and something to keep us warm ..."

"There are two granola bars in my backpack," I volunteered.

He laughed. It was a low and guttural sound. "I can see why Maria became attached to you so rapidly. You have an optimistic spirit that defies logic. I wish I could build you a fire, but there isn't anything dry to burn even if we dared risk it."

"That's okay," I told him. "I'll be fine, but I am worried about the baby."

"Of course you are," he replied. "I've never seen anyone quite so protective as you, but why don't you give him to me and then see if you can find something dry to wrap him in. I may have little reason to believe that he's going to make it, but I'm certain you're not going to give up unless there's no other option available."

I knew what he was doing, even if I didn't want to accept it. He was afraid the baby was already dead, and he wanted to spare me the ordeal of being the one to discover it. I wasn't sure anything would help if the unthinkable happened to Maria's son, but I handed him my tiny bundle anyway.

The harsh-edged beam coming from the flashlight that Agent Fielding had secured between his knees so it would not roll off the ledge illuminated the area immediately around us, casting sinister-looking shadows that made the hair covering my body stand on end. It took all the willpower I possessed to look away from him, but I managed to find the backpack I'd brought from the hacienda and drag it towards me. With numb fingers, I fumbled with the zipper but soon had the partially dry, white towel sitting in my lap.

The baby didn't make the slightest sound when Agent Fielding exposed his small body to the dank, cold air. I clamped down on the edge of the towel with my teeth when he raised the small lifeless body into the air.

"Is he still breathing?" I managed to ask as a knot of indescribable fear settled in the pit of my empty stomach. I felt like retching, but there was nothing left inside to come up.

"Not right now," he said, almost dropping the still body back onto the upper part of his legs.

I slumped back while my partner—I had to look at him in that way now—cupped his hands and blew hot air into them, and then he began vigorously rubbing the chest, arms and legs of the infant that had only been part of this world for a few hours, coaxing life back into his unresponsive body. I could only sit there in stupefied horror and watch. We had come so far only to have a precious life end on a ledge in the middle of a jungle.

But in a few moments the baby let out a whimper—not strong and lusty like it had been when he'd first been delivered—but enough of a noise to let me know that he was still alive.

"That kid's got one hell of a fighting spirit," Agent Fielding remarked. "I thought for sure he was gone."

My relief was almost overwhelming. "Can I have him now?" I asked, a little too abruptly after the small miracle he'd just performed.

"You don't waste any time on pleasantries or thanks, do you," he replied while extending the baby towards me. "But he's not out of the woods by any means yet. Most likely, we've just extended the inevitable."

"I know that, and I'm sorry for being so snappish," I said as soon as the baby was back in my arms. "I'll never forget all you've done for us."

"Never is a long time, Agent Sinclair."

He picked up the flashlight and held it so I could more easily see what I was doing while I tended to the baby.

I peeled the wet piece of sheet that covered baby's lower body away from him and then wrapped him snugly in the semi-dry towel before reaching towards the backpack that contained the unsavory bottles of goat's milk.

"You know what I mean," I replied as my fingers fumbled for the bottle that meant life for the infant I'd come so close to losing. "You didn't have to come back for us, and you certainly didn't have to save the baby's life for a second time today."

"Don't lavish me with too much praise. People like me can't afford to be sentimental. It's what gets us killed."

He suddenly lay the flashlight on the ledge beside me and moved further into the darkness. I had insulted him again for the way he conducted himself on the job without meaning to. He had been forced to make unimaginable choices to accomplish what was required, but he still cared, even if he couldn't admit it.

I held the bottle to the baby's lips. At first, he simply let a few drops of liquid slide down his chin.

"Come on, little one," I coaxed, trying to part his lips with my fingers. "I know it's not what you were meant to drink, but it's all we have for now. I promise to find something far more palatable once we get out of here."

Tears were stinging my eyes and my cheeks as they traveled downward until they were falling on the towel that was wrapped around the baby. If Maria was indeed watching us from her vintage point in heaven, like I believed she was, she needed to make her presence felt to her son. The maternal bond was strong, and I knew she would be able to get him to respond when I couldn't.

While I was still waiting for the baby to open his mouth, I heard wet clothing being removed. "Is that really necessary?" I asked.

"It is, if you don't want to die before morning. It's going to be a long, damp night, and we don't even have some of those coca leaves to chew on. We may detest how most of humanity uses them, but they do serve a purpose. I've used them to stave off hunger and dress wounds, but they're effective with hypothermia as well. But, hey, it's your choice."

It was my choice, but not a very good one if I wanted to stay where I was and survive the night. My entire body was trembling, and my teeth were rattling. I wasn't sure if it was more from cold or fear, but at the moment it didn't really matter. The baby was trying to latch onto the nipple. Someone had heard my silent prayer, and I needed to be holding him securely if I was going to get him to drink. It was foolish to think I could do that with sopping wet clothes and not undo the efforts Agent Fielding had made in saving his life, but stripping down to my underwear was not something I relished doing in front of anyone.

The light from the flashlight lying on the floor near my feet cast a harsh beam, fanning out in contorted circles that reminded me of a strobe light—only it wasn't flashing. Everything else around us was pitch back, and the musty smell of moss, dirt and lichens was nearly overpowering as it assailed my nostrils.

I didn't want to be here, but all the wishing in the world would not change the desperate situation we were in. Agent Fielding was trying to be proactive, and I would do well to listen to him since my only previous experience with roughing it was going camping with my family.

"Let me try to feed him while you get out of your wet things," he said as he reached for the baby. All I could see was his arms and legs and the bottoms of his boxers. At least he'd been considerate enough to leave them on.

I let him take the baby while I crawled a short distance away, took off my boots and attempted to remove my saturated jeans. I thought I heard him snicker as I pushed them slowly down my legs and then hung them over the edge of ledge hoping they might have time to dry before I had to put them on again. I did the same with his and then unbuttoned the long-sleeved shirt I was wearing and tried unsuccessfully to rub some of the lingering water from my hair. Fortunately, the tee underneath was still dry, except for the shoulders. It was going to be a very uncomfortable night, but at least I didn't feel nearly so cold. That surprised me almost as much as my being willing to follow Agent Fielding's orders without more contemptuous remarks did.

"Now that you've done that," he said, picking up the flashlight and thrusting it in my direction. "If you'll reach down to the bottom of the backpack I brought from the compound you'll find two solar blankets. Unwrap them and see if you can get one of them on the ledge underneath us. We can lie on it and use the other one as a covering. It's not ideal, but if we keep the baby between us and rely on each other for body heat, we might just make it through the night."

I did as he instructed, wondering why he hadn't mentioned the solar blankets the night before. They certainly would have come in handy in keeping Maria warm while we waited for his return. Perhaps they would have even helped to save her life. But even as those thoughts flitted through my head, I knew that the agent we had left behind would never have survived the birth of her son and the bullet in her shoulder without proper medical attention. Her death had been a tragedy I would never forget, but I still had hope that her son would survive, as long as Agent Fielding did not give up on either of us. He might not be the most pleasant person to be around most of the time, but I was learning to respect him as an operative who knew what he was doing. He had spent years in and around this jungle. If anyone could get us home again, he could.

"Why do you suppose this room was was built under such an amazing structure?" I asked to keep my mind from racing back to its previous thoughts as I ripped open the first package. It was hard to believe something so thin could save our lives, but science had created some amazing things, and I was glad Agent Fielding had brought them along.

"I have a couple of theories, but the most likely one is that the ground around here floods when it rains too hard, and the people needed a place of refuge or even a storage room for food and other supplies. The jungle is replete with underground rivers and caverns, and the ancient inhabitants who created this structure knew they needed a place high enough off the ground to be safe. It's really quite amazing when you consider the type of concrete they knew how to mix that was capable of withstanding the elements for centuries. Nothing modern man has been able to produce can equal it. I went as far as I dared into the tunnel behind this room but didn't want to get lost. These manmade monoliths have secret passageways that that can wind around for miles."

He had moved as far to the opposite end of the ledge as he could while I fumbled with the flimsy material in my hands until the blanket was open, and I'd spread it out as neatly as I could without the luxury of shifting my position.

"I suppose that makes sense," I replied. "I don't know much about Colombia."

"I didn't either, until I was given this assignment."

"So you're not from around here."

"Not exactly. I go where I'm needed, but I have spent the majority of my life in South America. It's a fascinating continent, and structures like this pop up everywhere. Their significance is highly religious since they believed in a great spirit who ruled both the heaven and the earth. They were trying to get closer to him. I'm afraid that's all I can tell you."

"You don't have to explain anything," I replied. "I'm just glad it's here to offer us shelter tonight."

He returned the baby to my arms the minute I was sitting down on the foil covering I'd placed over the unbroken rock that formed the top part of the ledge. The ancient Colombian natives knew more than just the components of mixing lasting cement; they appeared to be able to move smooth, massive rocks from one place to another without breaking them. There was far more to their civilization than I would ever be able to comprehend.

"Why don't you try to feed him while I check out this place a little bit more? I didn't see anything alarming at first glance, other than bats and whatever ran in front of us, but one never knows what might be seeking shelter. Mendoza's men will be looking for cover just like we were."

If his words were meant to be reassuring, they certainly missed their mark, but I was grateful to have a few minutes alone. He slipped into his boots and then went over the ledge while I held the baby close to my face and kissed the top of his head.

"I love you little one," I whispered as tears formed a covering over my eyes. "Please try to be strong. We're going to get out of this. Heavenly Father knows where we are, and he's not going to let us die away from everyone who loves us."

Once I knew he had made his way into the tunnel I knew nothing about, I closed my eyes and allowed the warm moisture to slide down my cheeks. Tears cleansed the soul and mine was certainly in need of that. If God wished for us to survive, we would. That didn't mean it would be easy, or that we would find our way unharmed, but we would make it out of this jungle of horrors. I just hoped Mendoza's men had not been able to follow us. I needed this time for mental, spiritual and physical renewal before the next part of our indescribable journey began.

My decision to be stronger made, I situated the baby so he could eat. He managed to swallow a sip or two of milk before falling back almost listless in my arms. He really had no reason to keep fighting now that his mother was gone, unless I gave it to him. But as I looked at his tiny face that was barely visible from between the folds of the towel and wondered what I could possible do to help him survive, I had the sudden impression that we were not alone. It momentarily startled me because I had not heard any footsteps approach.

Glancing up, I saw Marie's beautiful form. It seemed to be floating in front of my eyes, but it was neither disturbing nor frightening as I supposed an apparition might be. She was dressed in the most exquisite white robe, and while her lips did not move, I seemed to know intuitively what she was saying.

"Do not be afraid to love him with all your heart. My son, who is yours now, will bring great joy into your life, and I will never be far away. Just hold him, protect him and let him know that you care. He will take care of everything else. He was meant to have the kind of life I would never be able to give him."

As I sat there wondering if I was still awake or dreaming, she vanished. It took a moment or two for reality to settle again, but during that time I realized that this child was indeed a priceless gift, and as long as a spark of life continued to flicker I would not give up.

I held him to my chest and gently patted his back, murmuring words of love and comfort as I kissed the top of his head repeatedly. I could feel his tiny heart beating in time with mine. If he could just feel my devotion to him, maybe he'd give me a chance to love him. After a few minutes of holding and rocking, I laid him back in the crook of my arm and forced the much-too-large rubber nipple between his lips.

He sputtered and coughed, but then as if he knew I really meant what I had said, he started to drink. The milk must have tasted quite vile, and I worried that it would make him ill since it had received no refrigeration, but without it he wouldn't be alive come morning.

When Agent Fielding returned, he told me that the room we were in extended much further than he'd originally thought, and beyond it tunnels led in at least three directions. He had followed one a short distance over a floor of rock that was covered with a sizable amount of debris but had the distinct feeling that it was a waste of both time and effort since the labyrinth had obviously been constructed to confuse the wanderer. He hadn't run into any wild animals that would cause us harm, but signs of habitation were there.

I thought about asking him for details. I didn't like the idea of sharing my sleeping quarters with anything that couldn't be readily identified but decided against it since the ledge appeared to be safe and a six-foot rock wall separated it from the floor. Besides, the storm alone would keep anything that did not roam freely at night in its lair. We needed to concentrate our attention on the entrance and what might be coming rather than worrying about what might be lurking behind or beneath us.

"Thank you for finding this place," I told him as he pulled the additional solar blanket over the three of us. I didn't know if it would really keep us warm, but even if it did nothing but keep the cooler air from circulating over our bodies that was something to be grateful for. "Do you really think we'll be safe here until morning?"

"I hope so," he said, rolling onto his side and reaching out his arm until his hand encircled my shoulder. I was glad the baby lay between us. He'd keep our bodies from making too much contact. "I doubt Mendoza's men will keep hunting for us now. And even if they do, it's highly doubtful two parties could find this place by accident. I don't exactly believe in divine providence, but I'd say that we received our fair amount of luck the past couple of days."

I smiled into the darkness. It wasn't luck that had brought us here. God had orchestrated our finding this place to save our lives. Nothing else could explain finding the remains of an ancient civilization in a jungle inhabited by vicious animals, parasites, insects, and quite likely, a few tribes of local aborigines who would be less than happy to find us here.

My stomach growled so loudly I was afraid it would awaken the baby who had managed to drink a little milk before becoming too tired to suck any longer.

"Sorry about that," I said. "I guess there hasn't been a whole lot to eat since leaving the compound."

"I snagged a few tortillas at the village. How about you?"

"A granola bar sometime last night. I'm surprised we had the physical strength to make it this far."

"The human body is pretty amazing. When I think of what that little guy resting so peacefully between us went through to be born, and what he will yet have to go through if he survives this difficult journey, it makes me appreciate the human will more than I ever have. I'm not sure now is the time to admit this, but I almost didn't come back to the hut."

My deep intake of breath let him know that I wasn't too surprised by his admittance. "You had no way of knowing if we'd even be there when you came back."

"I knew that with your indomitable spirit at least one of you would make it through the night, but that's not exactly what I was getting at. I met some resistance in the village. Mendoza had been there earlier and had convinced everyone that we were the enemy, not him. You have no idea how much these people relied on the work he gave them to survive. Most of the men and women who were able to work had already gone to the fields before the police and members of the DEA arrived. There were a lot of casualties, and the lamentation was intense—children crying for their parents, spouses mourning the loss of the person they had hoped to grow old with, and the old ones simply shaking their heads and staring blankly into space."

"I'm so sorry. I never thought about what the raid might mean them, other than a loss of income which couldn't have been that great."

"It's often easy to overlook the real casualties in this war on drugs. The people who work the fields aren't villains. They're simply trying to keep body and soul together. I felt awful stealing what little I did from them."

"You mentioned resistance. What happened?" It was easier to ask that question than to think about the horrid scene that had been awaiting him in the village. Any normal instinct would be to stay where the most good could be done.

"Some of Mendoza's men were waiting for me. He knew at least one of us would show up there, and he'd promised a sizable reward to the person or persons who could prove that any one of us was dead. Suffice it to say that I had to shoot my way out. That's why we have another tail on us now, and I'm afraid it won't stop, even if we do make it out of here. The price on our heads will bring every bounty hunter in the country looking for us. As much as I hate to admit it, this may be the easiest part of our flight to freedom. Mendoza has a head start, and his people are everywhere."

"Did you learn what happened at the compound?"

"If you're asking about the children, that information, along with everything else that transpired, will not be known until we make it back to the embassy. But I'm confident that Alma would make sure they were safe, even if no one else survived. Her loyalty to Mendoza has always baffled me, but I suppose that even the most evil of men needs someone he can count on."

"She is a woman capable of doing just about anything," I replied, trying to let go of the images his recitation about his findings at the village had brought. If the situation there was one of grief and sorrow, it only stood to reason that it would be far worse at the compound where the initial attack had taken place. "I just wish I'd never messed up; then maybe none of this would have happened."

"You can't beat yourself up over something that wasn't your fault, regardless of the fact that I led you to believe that you had singlehandedly ruined the whole thing."

"But my incompetence made it impossible for you to bring Mendoza down."

"That may have happened anyway. Mendoza knew it was only a matter of time until the government made a move."

"That's not what he said at the last dinner you had."

"It is not a good business practice to let anyone involved in the venture know that the one in charge has any doubts or fears. Allowing you into the compound when he knew you were a plant was simply his way of thumbing his nose at the DEA. He wanted them to think he wasn't prepared, but the exact opposite was actually true. He'd been conducting drills for weeks on the best way to combat enemy fire. That's why my being there when it all went down was so important. I knew the exact placement of every man and his weapon but wasn't able to rely the final information to my superiors."

"You're not making me feel any better."

"This isn't about casting blame or hurting anyone's feelings. It's about recognizing weaknesses in both plans and people before they become a liability. I should have anticipated what your arrival would really mean. I knew a replacement for Maria had been found and that the DEA would try to use it to their advantage, if they could, but

I didn't know who you were for sure until Mendoza told me to get rid of you."

"But you had your suspicions."

"I've learned to be wary of suspicions until there's something to back them up."

Quite suddenly, my stomach growled with such intensity that I almost doubled over in pain.

"Why don't we save this unpleasant discussion for another time," he said, and knew that our time for being more open with each other was over. "I should have given more thought to finding us something to eat while I had the chance. There are a few edible berries and even some bananas in the jungle if one knows where to look, but I draw the line at slugs and beetles—unless they're roasted."

His poor attempt at levity made me smile.

"You can laugh out loud, if you want to," he said. "I used to know how to show a woman a good time. You must think I'm a Neanderthal with all my shouting and name calling."

"You had every right to be upset. The past few days have been anything but pleasant. I'm just grateful you're a good agent who wouldn't leave the women who sabotaged your operation behind."

"I may be a good agent, but I'm not a very good man, Agent Sinclair. I've done some horrible things because the job required it, but I would never desert a woman or an innocent child. I just wish I'd gotten there sooner. Maybe together we could have saved Maria's life."

His hand still lay on my shoulder, and I reached up to touch it. My boldness surprised me, but not more than feeling his fingers close over mine. "You did everything humanly possible," I said.

"Maybe I wish I was more than human. If I were, we wouldn't be trying to get comfortable on some ledge in a cave in the jungle. We'd be in some fascinating city sipping our favorite alcoholic beverages and hoping like hell that this was the worst assignment we'd ever be given."

"Is it really the worst?" I asked.

"Let's just say that I'm not in the habit of being on the losing end of anything," he paused, but only momentarily. "Now, how about us eating those granola bars you mentioned? I'd say to leave them until morning, but I'm not sure I can get any sleep with your stomach protesting so loudly."

"Do you want me to get them?"

"Nope!" he replied, and I felt a sudden letdown when his fingers pulled away. I wasn't sure how I felt about this man with so many different faces, but if I had to be where I was, I was more than grateful he was with me. "Just stay where you are, and I'll find them. What kind are they anyway?"

"Just some protein bars from the states that are filled with lots of fruits and nuts. They should be in the front pocket," I told him as the solar blanket moved and he reached above his head.

I checked the baby's breathing while he was hunting for the right backpack. I wasn't sure I'd get any rest, even if I was warm and comfortable. I had never been around such a small baby that was so in need of care. One wrong move, and he would be crushed.

"What's the real reason you're doing this?" he asked me once the silvery covering had settled over us again. "You just met Maria, and this child you're trying so desperately to protect isn't likely to make it no matter what we do. We've been lucky today, but I can't guarantee what's going to happen tomorrow."

"Tomorrow is only a myth because it never comes," I told him as I listened to the rain that was battering everything outside with even more intensity than it had previously done, making it impossible to hear anything softer than a human voice. "And Maria was my friend, even if we hadn't known each other very long."

"I guess she had that effect on most everyone," he replied, sighing heavily as he handed me one of the protein bars and then tore the wrapper off the other one so he could eat it himself. "She was the most beautiful creature I'd ever seen, so delicate and helpless-looking. I couldn't believe the agency sent her on an undercover assignment like this. It was like putting a graceful deer in a the den of a ravishing lion. She didn't stand a chance. "

"I'm sure she was well-trained and competent. I know she was fully aware of what the job entailed before accepting it."

"She told you that."

"She said she was to gain Mendoza's confidence and trust, regardless of what it took."

"I'm not sure that justified her sleeping with him, but I suppose we all do what is necessary. Mendoza was literally salivating the moment I brought her to the hacienda. He'd already killed his wife because she was not quite so diffident as she had been right after their marriage. I suppose he may have fallen out of love with her, if he had ever loved her at all. She was a very attractive woman and very kind, but I'm not sure she realized the kind of life her father had sold her into. I have to call it that because their marriage solidified a smaller cartel with a larger one until her father died, and then Mendoza took it all. Marriages of convenience are implemented here to gain power, although I'm sure the extra money came in handy. Mendoza is a man of great passion, and there's nothing more lethal than a man in lust who has no scruples and plenty of help in getting what he wants."

"I suppose murder comes easy to some people if the motivation is strong enough."

"If that's your polite way of asking just what I've been doing these past few years, well, it's nothing I'm proud of. I've been forced to kill people, but none of them were exactly innocent. Callous mercenaries are more like it."

I didn't want to think about what that meant, not with him lying so near. The oaths we had taken meant doing a certain number of things we found repugnant, but taking a life without justifiable cause was something I could never do.

"Was Mendoza's wife helping you?" I asked.

"She told me things occasionally. Nothing that would lead to his downfall, just little things that let me know where his weaknesses lay. She was a good woman in a bad situation, and I'm sorry she died. It never should have happened, especially when children were involved. I tried to convince him to send her away, but there wasn't much I could do without blowing my cover."

"So she knew who you were?"

"She suspected since, even at my worst, I was less brutal than the other men who were involved with her husband."

"And her own family did nothing to retaliate?" That seemed unbelievable after all the violence I'd witnessed over the past few days, especially if her father had run a cartel of his own.

"I'm sure her death was explained as an accident. Mendoza can be very convincing if it suits his agenda. Besides, I'm not sure they had any idea what was going on inside the walls of the hacienda. Her father met an untimely demise before I was sent to the compound, and to my knowledge, Isabella was never allowed to leave and her mother was too ill to travel."

"Surly they knew about Isabel and Luis."

He took another bite and chewed thoughtfully for a few seconds. "You're asking questions I can't answer. While I was privy to some of what went on in the house, my main focus was keeping the men on the outside in line by whatever means Mendoza thought necessary."

I wished he'd quit bringing up his sordid past as an agent. I didn't exactly feel sorry for him because he'd chosen his path just as I had chosen mine, but it was a continual reminder that the day might come when I was forced to point a weapon at another human being and pull the trigger like Maria had done.

"Are all undercover agents forced to compromise so much of their integrity just to get the job done?"

His snort of laughter left me know that he was getting tired of answering questions that had such a personal edge to them.

"It's easy to tell that you're FBI and not DEA. While we take the same basic oath, the steps necessary for completing our assignments vary greatly. I've killed more people than I can count, and Maria was a fool for falling into Mendoza's bed, even though that is where she gained her most useful information."

"She never planned on becoming pregnant, but that didn't stop her from loving her son and wanting to protect him."

"Her recklessness got her killed."

"So Mendoza really would not have let her live once her child was born, even if she had stayed at compound?"

"Mendoza is a beast. The only reason he kept her alive for as long as he did was for sadistic enjoyment. He likes controlling and manipulating people. You heard what he said about the child. He just wanted to watch her suffer."

"Why didn't she try to get away? She obviously knew about the tunnels."

"She also knew Mendoza would find her no matter where she went and exact revenge. You really don't understand anything about this life, do you? Colombia is not like America. If everyone whose life was in danger was placed in protective custody there would be no one free to wander the streets. The government is trying, but there is too much corruption. A person's life is only as safe as he or she can make it, and most of the time that means complying with the wants of every despicable force that comes along."

I leaned back against the rock wall, hoping to put a little more distance between us. He was right, I didn't understand the depths of human depravity, even though I'd studied a great deal about man's inhumanity in my classes at the university and in my training at Quantico. I had been raised with the belief that all people had a spark of truth and nobleness about them, even those who had lost their way. But my experience in Colombia had shown me how truly evil mankind had become with its greed, corruption and taste for blood. The Savior's promised return to earth could not come fast enough for me.

My lungs took in some of the heavy, dank air that smelled even more of sodden earth, mixed with the dung and sweat of feral animals, now that we were no longer moving around. It was most unpleasant but at least we were safe and dry. The ledge we were laying on was narrow, no more than five feet in the width, and Agent Fielding had insisted on sleeping closest to the edge. I was grateful for his consideration but doubted either of us would get any real sleep. Between the rock wall, the baby sleeping between us and the ledge with a six-foot drop moving from one position would be be impossible.

But as the minutes moved by at what seemed to be a snail's pace, I suddenly realized that I was no longer shaking. The heavy rainfall outside the enclosure was acting as a barrier to the cold of the night, and the three stone walls surrounding us were thick and provided insulation. I moved slightly to try to find a more comfortable way to rest.

"Are you, all right?" Agent Fielding asked. His arm was back resting on my shoulder. I wasn't sure if it was meant for comfort, or simply as a safeguard against falling.

"I'm fine," I replied. "I didn't mean to disturb you. I was just trying to get a little more comfortable."

"Try not to think about how much your body aches. Just concentrate on your breathing. I know what you said about tomorrow never coming, but whatever faces us when the sun comes up isn't going to be pleasant. Even if we manage to avoid Mendoza's men, there's a lot of untamed territory between us and any semblance of civilization."

I didn't want to get into another discussion about the possibilities, or more likely, the probabilities of what we would face during the coming hours. We were safe and dry now, albeit still hungry, despite the granola bars, and this was as good as it was going to get for now.

"Thanks for all you've done for us today. There's no way I'll ever be able to repay you," I told him.

"I'm not looking for adulation. I want to get out of this mess as quickly and painlessly as you do. I'm just not sure our journey is going to have a pleasant ending."

Despite his less than comforting assessment of our situation, I managed to doze on and off throughout most of the night. My body had been depleted of every ounce of strength, but I knew my spirit was strong enough to help me through anything I might be required to face. Nonetheless, every time Agent Fielding or the baby moved, I was startled into the awful awareness that our plight was far from over. Once the skies had lightened and the rain had lessened, we'd be forced to leave our hideaway and deal with Mendoza's men, or whatever else might be waiting for us.

Chapter 12

Just as the first fingers of a gray and dreary dawn found their way through the denseness of the foliage outside, Agent Fielding coughed and pulled himself up on one elbow. I wasn't ready to open my eyes but knew he would insist on leaving the shelter of the room underneath the monolithic structure the moment it was safe enough to do so. The storm had let up considerably. In fact, I couldn't hear the sound of anything other than his heavy breathing. He had to be even more tired than I was.

"How are you doing?" he asked as he tried to clear his throat again.

He likely assumed that I had been unable to sleep at all since I had tried to feed the baby twice during the time I'd spent lying nearly motionless underneath my edge of the small, silvery tarp. He'd managed a few more swallows, but I knew he wasn't getting nearly enough to subsist on. When I had removed the cloth that served as his diaper, it had barely been wet. I feared his kidneys were already shutting down.

"As well as can be expected," I replied. "And you?"

"Can't complain. At least I wasn't traipsing through the jungle."

"I suppose that could be considered a blessing."

Maria's son was still nestled in the crook of my arm where he had been throughout the entire night. I winced in pain when I tried to lift him.

"I should have been more help," Agent Fielding said as he sat upright, turned on his flashlight, and then took the baby from me. The light surrounding them was bright, but I couldn't see either of their faces as the towel was unwrapped.

"Is he okay?" I asked as my heart began to pound.

"Not to worry." he said after a cursory inspection. "I do believe this little one has survived the night. He's actually frowning at me."

My relief was so intense that I swung my head backwards and hit the rock wall with a resounding thud that made miniature stars explode in front of my eyes.

"Careful there," Agent Fielding responded with the first real smile I'd seen him make. "We're not out of the preverbal woods yet, and I don't need a woman with a concussion to worry about."

"I'll be fine," I replied, rubbing the back of my head. "I must have had a memory lapse as to where we are."

He pushed the baby in my direction. "You'll get past that soon enough. Why don't you see what can be done with him while I get dressed and check things outside."

I tried to avert my eyes as the tarp that had covered us during the night was pushed to the end of the ledge, but it was impossible not to notice the way his sinewy muscles rippled as he set the flashlight beside me and began to crawl to where we had left our wet clothing the night before.

"Thanks for hanging my pants besides yours. I'm sure it's the last thing you wanted to do."

He was back to his old commanding self that was less than genial, but I didn't mind. I'd learned a little bit more about him during the night. He did have a heart, even if he had to keep it hidden, and his annoyance with me was lessening. I could expect more tongue-lashings. That's just how he reacted when he was upset, but he wasn't going to leave us alone and defenseless. He'd make sure we made it to safety, if he did.

The baby was indeed still alive, but his skin had taken on an orange cast, and he looked more listless than he had the day before.

I checked his umbilical cord. The blood had dried and hardened, but it didn't look to be seriously infected yet. I took the small bottle of disinfectant I'd brought from the bathroom of the hacienda and gently applied some of it to both the end of the incision and the surrounding area. Then I replaced the cloth that was being used for a diaper with the one I had removed during the night. Fortunately, it was dry, but it needed to be washed desperately, just like the one that was still stained with blood and the slime of afterbirth. I'd make sure to do that before our day's journey began. There had to be a puddle of clean water outside somewhere.

"I'm not sure that milk is good for him," I told Agent Fielding while he struggled to pull on his still-damp pants.

"I'm afraid it's all we have, unless . . ."

"Unless what?" I prodded. I'd been diluting the last bottle of goat's milk with water, but if it had already spoiled it would only make the baby's failing condition worse.

"Unless I can find a coconut tree. The milk inside is full of nutrients and electrolytes, and you don't have to worry about lactose intolerance, if that's another of your concerns. I've even heard stories that it's been used for blood transfusions when nothing else was available, though I'm not sure I believe that."

"And there are trees like that round here?"

His snort of disdain only showed that in my anxiety I had made another geographical blunder. "This is the jungle, and there are hundreds of them. The trick is getting the coconuts to the ground without splitting the husks and losing what's inside."

"But you can do it?"

"You're not about to give up, are you?" he said, tying his last bootlace before dropping over the edge of the ledge. "No wonder the DEA agreed to let you come. What you lack in experience, you make up for in heart and perseverance. I'm not making any promises, but I'll see what I can do."

I dressed quickly once he had gone, folded the solar blankets and then shoved everything that was still laying around into the three backpacks we would take with us. Agent Fielding had taken both the machine gun and the machete with him, but I knew exactly where the revolver I had used to kill the anaconda was. The baby was beginning to whimper, but instead of trying to feed him the last of the watery, goat's milk, I simply held him tight and tried to reassure him while I waited for Agent Fielding's return.

Coconut trees were huge and their fruit easily twenty or more feet from the ground. He couldn't just hit them with a stick and hope they'd come down without breaking. He'd have to climb the tree to get them. What if he decided it wasn't worth the risk or the extra time. Mendoza's men couldn't be that far away, unless they'd retreated the way they had come trying to find shelter.

I was still sitting on the ledge in the dark when he returned. There was no way I could get down by myself with the baby in my arms, and it seemed safer to remain where I was until I knew what he'd found outside. There had been no gunfire. That didn't mean a whole lot, except that he hadn't been discovered or shot.

"I hope this will last him for a few hours," Agent Fielding said as I heard several objects hit the rock floor. It was much lighter inside the enclosure than it had been when he left, but it was still nearly impossible to see anything clearly from where I was perched. I'd packed the flashlight with the rest of our meager belongings.

"Did you see Mendoza's men?"

"No! But that doesn't mean they aren't nearby. The rain has washed away anything that might give our location away, other than my footsteps this morning, but I'd still like to put as much distance between us as possible. With any luck, we'll make it to the river by nightfall. Now scoot those backpacks over to the edge where I can reach them, and then I'll help you and the baby down."

I did as he asked without comment or complaint. It was going to be another long, emotional and possibly quite dangerous day, and there was no reason to begin it with an unnecessary argument.

"I'd like to rinse the bottles and diapers before we leave, if it's alright with you," I said as I leaned forward and two strong arms caught me around the waist and lifted me to the ground.

"You can do that while I try to split open these coconuts. There are several pools of rainwater right outside the door, but I can't guarantee that they aren't filled with millions of invisible organisms you'd just as soon not know about."

"I suppose I'll just have to take my chances," I replied, situating the baby on one hip while I moved towards the doorway with the bottle and two soiled pieces of cloth in my free hand. I would have asked for his helping in caring for the baby while I completed my tasks, but he had his own work to do.

The world outside looked quite different without the heavy rain falling. The tall, majestic trees, radiantly-colored flowers, brambly bushes and broad-leafed plants seemed as if it had been specifically planted to hide the pyramid-shaped structure that had sheltered us during the night. I felt a chill rush over my extremities as I realized that we truly had been the recipients of a great miracle in finding our way there. We were as closed off from the rest of humanity as any three people could ever be. If it weren't for the baby, I might just consider staying where we were until Mendoza's men gave up looking for us.

I knelt down beside the first puddle of water I came to and put the baby on my knees while I swished the two plastic bottles through the water and ran my fingers inside the nipples to make sure they were clean. Then I briskly rubbed the soiled pieces of sheet together. I knew they would never look clean, but at least they might be dry enough to absorb more moisture if I tied them to the strap of my backpack while we traveled more distance by foot.

"Thank you again," I replied a short time later as I watched him insert the tip of the machete into a coconut husk and tap on it with a rock. I'd returned to the enclosure and set both bottles by his feet. He'd already filled one of the them with coconut milk. I would feed some of it to the baby once he had finished.

"Don't thank me yet. We might just be prolonging the inevitable. I know you've become very attached to that baby, but you have to be realistic ..."

"Please don't say it," I replied before he could finish his sentence. Telling him about Maria's visitation the night before would be a huge mistake. He didn't believe in God or miracles, but I certainly did, and I knew she would help us from the life beyond this one if she possibly could. "I know the odds, but I happen to believe that everything is going to turn out okay, eventually."

"I wish I had your optimism," he replied as one more hit with the rock made a clear substance start to ooze from a small hole in the brown, hairy husk. "But right now, I just want to get out of here."

It took a few minutes to fill the remaining bottle. I hated that some of the contents had spilled to the ground, but it didn't seem to concern Agent Fielding. One swift hit with the machete split open the hard husk.

"We'll take some of this with us to eat. There's no time to look for anything else. Now that it's light and the rain has stopped, things could get really messy in a hurry."

I wondered what he wasn't telling me, but I still fed the baby what he would eat while Agent Fielding went back outside to make sure the way was still clear. Our brief respite was over. Once we left the enclosure, we'd be at the mercy of anything that wanted to harm us.

"I've decided to head in a slightly different direction," he said when we'd gone no more than a few yards away from the monolithic stone structure we'd found safety in the night before. It truly was magnificent with its carefully hewn edges that reached towards the sky. It must have taken years to complete. "I wasn't completely honest with you before. I saw Mendoza's men from the tree."

"Why didn't you tell me?" I asked, the fear of discovery rising like bile to my throat again. "I could have been ready sooner."

"You needed time with the baby. Besides, it's not going to be easy for them to track us after all the rain, and they looked miserable. All they had for shelter was a tree. They were trying to start a fire, but since I doubt that will be successful, they will be hunting for us again soon. If they do pick up our trail, they won't lose it again with all the mud."

I looked down at my feet. While I wasn't sinking, the tracks left by my hiking boots were clearly visible. "How many are there?"

"I saw three, but there could be more. I didn't stick around to find out."

"No, that would have been foolish," I thought as we trudged through the deep green vegetation that pulled at my clothing like sticky fly paper it was so wet. I held the baby tightly to my body in a sort of sling Agent Fielding had fashioned from the sleeve of a shirt he found in one of the backpacks. I'd torn part of what remained into shreds that could be used for additional diapers.

My gun was in my right hand front pocket. It made walking more difficult because it dug into my hip and my thigh, but it was as close as I could carry it since I didn't want to leave the baby dangling. There was too great a risk of falling.

We'd managed to condense our belongings from three backpacks to two without leaving behind any of the things I wanted to preserve for the baby, or the diary Tess had written and the papers I would need to get out of the country. I didn't know why I was thinking about such trivial things now, except that I needed a diversion from the constant threat of being overtaken by men who would be only to happy to kill us to get the reward the Mendoza had offered.

Agent Fielding had the machine gun slung over his left shoulder, along with the machete, and a gun holstered at his waist. I knew he'd do everything in his power to keep us from harm, but if Mendoza's men found us, he'd need my help.

I was trying my best to keep up with him, but for practical purposes he wasn't even trying to clear the way. We were moving at what felt like a snail's pace with obstructions materializing every few feet. I tried not to listen to the sounds around me as more than birds and monkeys moved through the jungle with us. There were moments when I felt cold, cruel eyes watching us from a distance but knew I couldn't give in to fear. I tried to stay focused on the man walking in front of me as we moved over moss-covered logs and through twisted vines that grabbed at my ankles and boots. I knew he would turn around and offer assistance if a great enough need arose.

A constant prayer was in my heart that I would not brush up against a tree and come in contact with some colorful, but highly toxic, frog or insect when I lost my footing. Despite the rest I had received the night before, I was exhausted and weak from lack of nourishment. Agent Fielding had filled his canteen from the water running off the broad leaves outside the enclose. He'd insisted that I drink as much as I could from them before our day's journey began, but any moisture taken in was quickly expelled due to strenuous exertion.

We stopped to rest only twice during the hours we walked so I could take care of the baby's needs, and we could eat a few bites of the coconut Agent Fielding had procured for us. The tiny infant, in the makeshift carrier that was far from clean or comfortable, drank an ounce or so each time I fed him, but even coconut milk with all its supposed miracle properties would not keep him alive for long once his organs began to shut down. I talked to him every chance I could, even while I was walking. He needed to know that I would l not forsake the vow I had made to his mother, and that no matter what happened, I would love him for always.

It was hard to tell how far we had gone, or even in what direction, since the sun didn't come out. It was damp and miserable, but at least we were moving downhill. There had been a few times when Agent Fielding had motioned for me to remain quiet. Sounds in the jungle were varied from the laughing, beautiful macaws to the sleek and and menacing jaguars. One time we even heard gunfire. Several shots that reverberated through the trees and made my blood run cold, but Mendoza's men didn't catch up with us.

The adrenaline that had carried me away from the compound and through the horrors of the past two days and nights was nearly spent, and I kept stumbling over even the tiniest pebble until I fell to my knees on the ground. I tried to push myself to my feet, but I couldn't seem to do.

"What's wrong?" Agent Fielding asked when he heard the thump and turned around.

I looked up at him with tears in my eyes. "I can't go any farther. My strength is nearly depleted."

He knelt beside me as the weight of my body slipped forward. A scowl creased his forehead, but there was sympathy in his eyes.

"I shouldn't have pushed so hard. You need food and rest."

"So do you," I replied, relaxing my grip on the baby just enough to relieve some of the tension in my arms. "I'm sorry for letting you down."

His hand came to rest on my shoulder. "You haven't let me down, Agent Sinclair. You've shown remarkable courage, but our bodies can only take so much. You rest, eat some of that coconut and let me do a little scouting. We shouldn't be too far from the river, and there are huts all along its banks."

"But we can't risk it. What about Mendoza's men?"

"From the shots we heard not that long ago, I'm sure they have their own trouble to deal with. I've been seeing tracks of wild animals all day. They could have easily had a run in with one of them."

My mind raced back to our encounters two days earlier with a puma, an anaconda, and two crocodiles. There was plenty to fear in the jungle, and our lives had been miraculously spared so many times it seemed almost sacrilegious to ask for more blessings, but we wouldn't make it without them.

"What are our chances of having the same thing happen to us?" I asked.

"That's what guns and machetes are for, but I'd say the good luck that seems to follow you is holding. Still, we can't afford to stop for long. I'll look for a hut, but if I don't find one, I'm afraid we'll have no choice except to make our way to the river."

"What would be the advantage of that?"

"A miracle way of getting across it without having to swim," he mocked. "If you think the jungle is bad, it only means that you haven't seen one of our rivers yet."

He helped get me situated with my back against a tree that appeared to be safe before disappearing into the dense undergrowth that surrounded us on all sides. I knew he was just trying to give me hope, but I couldn't make it any further on a promise. Without the stamina to go on, I had no choice except to keep my gun handy and pray for the best. I'd done all that I possibly could.

I unwrapped the baby and smiled down at his innocent, sweet face. His lips were making a sucking motion, and the orange tinge to his skin didn't appear to have gotten any worse. Maybe the coconut milk was helping. He'd certainly been far more willing to drink it than he had the goat's milk.

"Hey, there, little guy," I told him as I lifted his face to my lips. "We're getting closer. All you have to do is hang on for a few more hours. I know your mother is watching over you, and we will make it. I just need a few minutes to rest."

I fed him some more of his bottle with the giant rubber nipple that had doubtless been used to nurse more than one baby animal back to health. It stretched his lips and had to be most uncomfortable, but he seemed to know that it was what he needed. I thanked Heavenly Father for that.

Then I pried a few pieces of the coconut from the husk with the sturdier end of the tweezers I'd put in my backpack before leaving the hacienda, ate them, and took a few swallows of the metallic-tasting water from the canteen Agent Fielding had left with me. The strength he still possessed after all he'd been through astounded me. Any lesser man would have left us to die.

He might not believe in miracles or a higher being, but evidence of their existence surrounded us, especially the way we had found shelter the night before in human-constructed haven made by persons who had lived centuries before. I wished I had a picture that would prove it wasn't simply overstimulation of a very tired mind. Perhaps I would try to paint one once we were back to civilization. I'd taken a closer look at both the structure and the statue with the imposing lips before leaving the clearing in which they stood and was more than certain I would never forget what few eyes had ever seen.

The jarring and unrecognizable sounds around me, along with the fear of being discovered, kept me from sleeping, but I did close my eyes while I held the baby against my chest and gently patted his back with my fingertips. He was an incredible child, so strong and courageous, just like his mother had been. I would keep my promise to her, even if I had to move heaven and earth to do it.

I was startled back to the present when something touched my arm. I was about to cry out when Agent Fielding's hand clapped across my mouth.

"Don't be alarmed," he whispered, bending close to my ear. "But two of Mendoza's men aren't that far away. They don't know where we are yet, but we must keep moving. I spotted a hut. We'll be better able to fight them off from there."

"But I thought there were three men," I mouthed as he motioned for me to get ready to leave.

"There were, but the shots we heard . . . Let's just say that we're more evenly matched now. We should be able to defend ourselves if we see them coming."

He gave me time to secure the baby before pulling me upright. It was hard to stand. My feet felt like molten lead, but I couldn't give in to discomfort.

The rain of the night before had burned off, leaving nothing but a stickiness that permeated every cell in my body. I hated the green world that was trying to suffocate me, but followed as best I could, trying to dodge the obstacles that continued to materialize in front of me. I also tried to stay focused on the fact that I was not in this alone. Agent Fielding had returned to us a second time. He would not have done that if he didn't think there was a chance we could make it.

It was almost dusk when we came to the small, thrush hut. This one was in better repair than the one where Maria had given birth to her son. The door was made of planks of knotted wood, and the walls and roof were constructed of broad-leafed plants and grasses. It actually looked strong enough to remain standing should a sudden wind arise.

"We'll stop here for the night," Agent Fielding said as he pushed the door open with the toe of his boot. "It's not much to look at, but it's better than staying out in the open."

"I can go farther," I told him as the inside of the hut became visible. It was empty, except for several small rodents that scurried away and made me cringe.

"Don't worry about them. They're perfectly harmless," he responded, standing back so I could pass in front of him. "This isn't a coca processing hut. It used to be a private residence. There are dozens of them scattered along the banks of the river."

I could have asked him what they did for a living, but all I could think about was the baby's safety.

"What about Mendoza's men?"

"They're probably in worse shape than we are, and it's highly unlikely they'll come after us once it gets dark. I didn't see them carrying anything with night vision, but if they do, we'll be ready for them."

I hoped he was right because I was too tired to argue. I simply stepped inside and fell to my knees with the baby still in my arms. They throbbed from holding him near me for the hours we'd been forcing our way through the intense vegetation that had cut through the layers of clothing I was wearing. I couldn't imagine what I must look and smell like. My hands were covered with scratches, gouges and dried blood. I knew my face couldn't look any better, and if I sat still long enough, I was afraid something might make a nest in my hair. They might have done it already, only I was too numb and miserable to notice.

"I'll search for more coconuts and anything else that is edible in a few minutes," he said, closing the door and sitting beside me on the hard-packed, earthen floor.

My eyes found his, and I smiled. "I can never thank you enough for what you've done, Agent Fielding. You've been risking your life for me since the moment we met."

"Not exactly! I was hedging my own bets. You were right in saying that I could have left you at the airport in Bogotá. Mendoza would have believed anything I told him back then."

His admission shocked me. "Why didn't you?"

It was the second time I'd ask that question. Perhaps he would finally give me a truthful answer.

"Because I needed a diversion that would keep Mendoza occupied. You were an attractive girl—not what I expected—and he likes female companionship. He'd given me orders to execute Maria the minute the baby was born, and I had the final details of the raid to set in place without being caught. Your arrival bought me valuable time."

"So I was a pawn."

"Like I said last night, I had no confirmation on anything. I simply figured you knew what you were doing, federal agent or loyal employee, or you wouldn't have come."

"I'm sorry I was such a disappointment, but what would have happened if I wasn't there officially?"

"Then you would have had nothing to fear. Mendoza would have seen that you were nothing but a governess who didn't like men, and you would have been left alone to work with the children. The only thing he would have required was that you stay out of his way and follow his rules."

"I don't hate men," I said.

He laughed. "According to Mendoza you did. I doubt he's ever met a woman he couldn't seduce, provided he wanted to badly enough."

"I'm not going to give myself to any man, unless he's my husband," I told him, wondering why I felt it necessary to defend myself to someone I had barely met; albeit a man who was trying to save my life.

"Noble ambition, but not exactly a practical one considering what you do for a living," he scoffed. "Sometimes compromises are necessary. You'd be better off in a nunnery if you really believe what you just said. Most people don't live by those standards anymore. They're archaic."

I rolled my eyes, although I knew it was unbecoming. If I commented on that statement, we'd end up in an explosive battle of wills, and I didn't want that. People were entitled to their own opinions. Mine just happened to be different than those of the masses who lived for the moment and did what felt good or was necessary for survival on the job.

I watched him lift a large, green lizard with the toe of his boot and fling it out of the hut. I hoped that would be the worst thing we'd find once darkness fell. Even though we were closer to getting out of the jungle, I almost wished we were back in the rock structure behind the sacred statue where I'd felt safe, if not secure.

"There's still so much I want to know, but I'm not sure I have the right to ask."

"That hasn't stopped you before, so fire away," he responded with a look in his eyes that I could not read. "But be prepared not to like what I might have to say."

He was warning me to proceed carefully, but I was no longer afraid of his wrath. I stretched out my legs and made sure the baby was still breathing. We had another long night to endure, and I doubted we'd get much sleep.

"I guess for starters, I'd like to know why Tess Tremaine was chosen to be the new governess. From what I was able to learn, she had no practical experience with children, had quit attending a community college, and had never been out of the country before. Considering Mendoza's views on education, I'm surprised she was even a candidate. If she hadn't been selected as Maria's replacement, I would never have been sent in her place, and your mission would not have been compromised."

He leaned back against a wooden stake that was meant to support the flimsy walls and roof. I hoped it would support his weight. "Is this just another way of asking why I didn't inform you that I was your contact sooner?"

I wriggled my mouth but didn't say anything.

"That's not the way undercover assignments work with the DEA, and Mendoza had no reason to give me any explanations as to the people he hired. Certain protocols are set in place so agents will know whom they're dealing with. You didn't express any of those."

"That's because I wasn't told what they were."

"And precisely the reason I didn't give you a gun before we got to the compound. This is a hell of a place to gain field experience with another agency."

"I suppose I could have refused the assignment."

"You and I both know that's a career-ender in our line of work. Once we pin on that badge and pick up that weapon we belong to the government. What they say is law."

"And I was led to believe that everything would be ready when I got off that plane. I guess connections weren't made in time."

"You're beginning to see what I've been up against all these years. You can't afford to trust anyone when you're on your own, without a very good reason for doing so. How did you even make contact with Maria? She was under strict lockdown."

"I saw her outside the schoolroom door the morning after I arrived. I think she was surprised to see me there. She had come looking for the children."

"She was very fond of them."

"And they obviously loved her. I thought I had it made to discover what I had been sent to find out so quickly, but then the long wait came."

"She should have stayed in her quarters. Someone could have easily seen her. That may even have been why Mendoza was able to put things together so quickly."

"That's not what you said before."

"I was angry with both of you. I'm not in the habit of having my plans interrupted."

"So why didn't you just leave me behind and go on about your business? No one would have known what had happened, and justification seems to be part of the game you've been playing."

"It's no game, unless you're a man like Mendoza, and sacrifices have to be made at times," he said as his eyes narrowed. "I've spent my career learning how to infiltrate organizations without getting caught. It's not an easy life, the rewards are few and every word must be carefully weighed against the reaction it might trigger. I wouldn't advise anyone to pursue it who couldn't live without creature comforts and personal involvement for months and even years at a time. Maria wasn't seasoned enough to do that."

"She paid the ultimate price for her actions, but you were willing to give all of that up. Why?"

"That's a little personal, don't you think?"

"I suppose, but I think it's a fair one. We all have reasons for making the choices we do."

"All right, then, I'll give you an answer. I never had anything I thought was worth keeping, and I was good at what I chose to do. It earned me the respect I craved and gave me the excitement I needed. Why did you choose to become an FBI agent? You're not exactly the kind of person I expected them to send my way."

"I already told you why I was here. It was never my intention to be part of the DEA. I'm much better at the work I chose to do."

"Chasing bad guys on American soil? I can see the advantage of that, but it's not for me. I wanted to see exotic places and put my life on the line in ways few people would be willing to do. I guess in my own egotistical way I like defying death. It keeps my juices boiling."

"And you've never thought about settling down?"

"Do I detect an interest there? I can assure you that I'm not the marrying kind."

"I was just trying to have a civil conversation."

"And I suppose you have some guy waiting for you back home."

"No," I replied.

"But you'll start looking someday."

"I want to be married and have a family."

"So why the need to put your life in danger? I've watched you with the baby. Taking on the role of motherhood seems to come naturally, but I'm still here to tell you that it isn't a good idea to become too attached."

"I know how you feel about his survival, but I'm not willing to give up."

"You've made that abundantly clear, Agent Sinclair, and who am I to argue. Things seem to be working out the way you want them to, but we're getting off track. You were asking questions about the assignment you took and why I wasn't willing to give you more of a chance."

His abrupt return to business let me know he'd given me all the details about his personal life that he was willing to disclose. That was fine by me because I already knew we had little in common besides surviving our time in the jungle.

"Do you think Mendoza was aware of Tess's existence before she even contacted him about a job? He told me that he went to college in New York City. It's conceivable that he crossed paths with her parents since they were very heavily involved in the drug culture there, and he was big on expanding his business even then."

"That seems like a stretch. We can't invent facts just because they make sense."

"I'm not saying that's what happened. It's just something to think about. There's a reason the DEA had her on their radar, or I would never have been brought in at the last minute as a switch."

"You do resemble her picture. I've always been told we had a double but never quite believed it."

"So you don't think I'm crazy for thinking there may be more to this? I know I have a habit of looking for connections where none might even exist, but it's one of the things that helped me stand out at the academy."

"It's also something that could get you killed. Criminals don't like people who look for answers. That's why I told you not to ask leading questions when you got to the compound. Mendoza's astute. He's been doing this for a long time. He can spot a phony a mile away."

"I tried to be careful."

"That doesn't cut it in undercover work. You can't take anything for granted. The slightest look could give you away. I told you that you might not like what I had to say."

"As long as your comments are constructive, I won't take offense. I recognize that I wasn't prepared to come, but the DEA was looking for someone who had a chance of pulling it off, and apparently no one in your agency matched the profile closely enough."

"Then you did the only thing you could," he replied and began pushing himself to his feet, but I wasn't ready to let him go just yet.

"You said Alma had likely gotten the children to safety. Wouldn't the authorities want to have them in custody as a bargaining chip?"

"Perhaps, if they were found. My people know Mendoza isn't exactly a family man. He's not going to come looking for his children, unless he knows it's safe."

"He's an evil man and his children deserve so much better," I fumed. "Who's going to take care of them? I don't think Alma should. They're scared of her."

"That doesn't mean she isn't capable."

"What about their mother's family? Is there anyone left who could do it?"

"I can't answer that, but I wouldn't worry too much about them. The underground world is teeming with people who will do anything to prove their loyalty to the man who feeds them. The children will be taken care of."

I looked down at Maria's baby who was asleep in my arms. His father was a monster, and I'd move heaven and earth to make sure they were never reunited. But what if I couldn't keep him alive? He was much too lethargic. Even newborns should be moving around more than he was.

Agent Fielding placed his hand on my arm. "Life isn't fair, and out here is no exception. People look the other way on almost everything. It's absolute power that keeps men like Mendoza from being caught and prosecuted."

"So you really think he'll get away."

"Without a doubt! Some of his men will take the fall on this one, and he'll make his headquarters elsewhere. The compound wasn't his only base of operation."

"Do you know where he might have gone?"

"I have a few ideas, but while I did a lot of his dirty work and he trusted me, I was really nothing more than one of the mercenaries hired to protect him. What concerns me is that he isn't the only one calling the shots. I just wasn't able to figure out who his partner really was."

"Perhaps if someone went back to the compound . . ."

"That place would have been thoroughly searched and everyone there questioned. If there was any information to be gleaned, the authorities will have it by now."

I looked down at Maria's child again and thought about the beautiful woman who'd sacrificed her life to bring him into the world. It was too bad that he would never know her, but I would do my best to make it up to him.

"There's something I might need your help with once we get out of the jungle," I told him.

He let his breath out slowly and leaned back against the wooden beam that supported the hut's leafy roof. I knew that because it was starting to sprinkle again. "I think I know what you're going to say, but it's a little premature. We don't even know if the baby will be alive come morning. Hell, we don't even know if we will."

"It's not that simple," I replied. "Maria asked me to raise her son if something happened to her. She wants me to take him back to the United States. I thought it was preposterous at first, but now that he's here, I know I have to do it. He can never be exposed to his father."

"You've been through an emotional ordeal, and what you propose is admirable but completely insane. We'll try to find a good home where he won't be found, but that's as good as it's going to get. I don't think you understand just how far Mendoza's circle of influence extends. He has affiliates on every continent and supplies more cocaine to the United States than any other drug cartel in Colombia. If you had something he wanted, he'd use anything within his power to get it back."

Icy fingers of trepidation returned. Mendoza might not want the baby, but he wanted everyone to fear him, and he would not tolerate our deception if we happened to survive.

"I understand that, but I love this baby as if he were my own, and I'll do anything necessary to keep him safe."

"Give up your own life and safety?" he questioned. "That's what Maria is asking you to do. You wouldn't know a moment's peace until the day you die."

"And you think I'll know peace if I leave him here where his father can more easily find him?"

"So he becomes a casualty of this war on drugs. He wouldn't be the first one, and he certainly won't be the last. Innocent people die every day, despite our most valiant efforts. You have to pick your battles, and you have to know when to walk away."

I was glad it was almost dark. I didn't want him to see the look of horror that crossed my face. How could he even think about leaving the baby with strangers who may or may not be able to care for him or keep him out of harm's way?

"We need more coconut milk," I said, hoping the tone of my voice didn't show my contempt. He might have moments of kindness, but he was a pragmatic at heart. That's what kept him alive.

He turned to walk away, leaving the machine gun on the ground. "I'll see what I can find. I'm not trying to be insensitive, Agent Sinclair. I don't want anything bad to happen to the child either, but there's no way you'll get him out of the country. The sooner you accept that, the better. There are things in life we just can't do anything about."

I sang to the baby while he was gone, and marveled at how perfect he really was. Small though he might be, I sensed a strong and valiant spirit inside his little body, and I desperately wanted to be the one to raise him. I understood Agent Fielding's warnings about becoming too attached. What I was thinking about doing was beyond sanity, but I couldn't simply let him go into a life his mother did not want for him. If there was a way to take him home with me, I would find it.

Agent Fielding found several more coconuts and a few berries before dusk settled. We followed the same procedure for getting the precious milk into the bottles.

The silence between us was deafening, but neither of us challenged it. What was there left to say anyway? We weren't exactly on the same page when it came to religious or moral beliefs. I believed God would help me find a way to keep the baby, even if it appeared impossible. I wasn't sure what he believed, except survival of the fittest. He was a complicated man, and I had more to worry about than what drove him to accept undercover assignments where he was forced to take lives.

"Why don't you try to get some rest," he said after we'd eaten the berries and a few chucks of coconut, washing it down with some tepid water from the canteen he carried around his neck. We could do without food for several days if necessary, but water was different, and what he'd collected that morning would soon be gone.

"What about you?" I asked. We'd been sitting together in the dark listening to the sounds of the jungle for what seemed an eternity. They didn't seem quite so threatening with him beside me, and the machine gun just inches away, but that could all change in an instant. "You've had even less sleep than I have."

"Combat training," he replied. "I was a Marine before I joined the DEA. I'll sleep once I get you and the baby back to civilization."

"All right," I whispered, too tired to argue. Surely, I could afford to close my eyes for a few minutes. I'd hear a new sound anyway, and I was acutely aware of the baby resting in my lap. If I moved, he'd fall to the ground.

My own body was covered with more bites and abrasions than I'd ever be able to count, but hopefully none of them were lethal.

And my feet! Oh, how they ached from all the walking and sweating. I would never get my boots on again if I gave in to the temptation to take them off for even a moment of relief. And I couldn't even think about my muscles. I hurt in places I didn't even know existed.

As for my mental state, I'd been trained to compartmentalize, but I'd never faced such complexity before. Every part of my life had been brought into question—physical, spiritual, emotional, mental—and it was almost more than I could endure.

At some point, I must have dozed off because when I opened my eyes, I found that my head was leaning against Agent Fielding's shoulder. He'd put one of the solar blankets over me, but it covered the baby too. I immediately pushed it away so I could see if he was still breathing.

"Don't be so paranoid," he said with a heavy yawn. "I might not believe that some higher power is orchestrating our lives the way you do, but there's no reason for this baby not to make it if we do. Go back to sleep."

But I couldn't allow myself to fall into that state of oblivion again. It would be too easy not to wake up. So I bounced the baby in my arms until he was awake, and then I tried to get him to drink more coconut milk before rocking him back to sleep. I might not be his biological mother, but I was the only mother he had left, and I needed him to know that I would never leave him alone and comfortless.

Chapter 13

I didn't ask any questions when Agent Fielding put his elbow into my arm long before the sun came up the next morning and told me we needed to leave the hut. I could barely see my feet it was so dark but knew he was worried about Mendoza's men. It had been a quiet night, but our best chance for survival was to get away without a confrontation. I could use my gun to help defend us, but I'd have to relinquish my hold on the baby to do it, and having him out of my sight for even an instant wasn't an option. It would be too easy for him to be bitten by something or even carried away.

I was at a point where I really didn't care what happened to me. I was so tired and hungry and thirsty that putting one foot in front of the other seemed an arduous task almost too difficult to endure, but I wanted the baby to live. I had such maternal feelings for him that tears came to my eyes every time I even thought about him, and it was impossible not to hold him close and kiss his soft, downy head every time I had a chance. If Agent Fielding noticed my preoccupation he didn't say anything.

We stumbled through undergrowth in the near dark for what seemed like hours. I couldn't ask him how long he thought it would be until we reached civilization because I knew he couldn't tell me. Our progress was infinitely slow, and he had to hold branches for me or push aside creepers more than once so I could make it through some very rough terrain. He wasn't using his machete even though it was in a sheath slung over his shoulder. It would be a dead giveaway to the direction we'd gone. If we didn't cause a major disruption of the area we were traveling through, there was still a chance we could get away without any more violence.

He'd left the backpack he'd brought from the village in the structure underneath the pyramid. He'd encouraged me to do the same with one of the other two we still had before leaving the grass hut that morning, but I'd refused. We needed a place to carry the milk, the towels, the solar blankets, the extra ammo, and the few medical supplies I'd brought.

But I knew he wasn't referring to that. He wanted me to leave the backpack, filled with the few things I'd taken from the suitcase Maria had brought from the hacienda, behind. I wouldn't do that as long as I could still carry it on my back. It was all the baby had left of his mother, and it had the papers I would need to keep him with me. I would not relinquish that.

"I hate to bother you," I said as the first light of day came peeking through the tops of the trees. "But the baby needs to eat again."

He'd been fussy for quite some time, now he was starting to cry. The vibrations seemed to rumble through the jungle, but it didn't seem much like a baby, it sounded more like a wounded, desperate animal.

"We'll take ten," he said with a heavy sigh. He looked exhausted, even if he wouldn't admit it. I was certain he had barely closed his eyes the night before. "I'll do some scouting while you rest."

I understood his anger and frustration over the lengthy mess we were in. If it wasn't for me, he would likely be back in Bogotá reporting the success of his years of undercover work, and Maria might still be alive, despite what he had said about his orders to kill her once the baby was born. Nothing had gone right since I'd arrived at the compound, nothing except the perfect little baby I was holding in my arms.

When his feet were curled up, he was less than a foot long, but those penetrating black eyes. Whenever he looked at me, I realized just how special he was. God meant for him to live. If he hadn't, he would not have survived a difficult birth and two ridiculously long nights and days in the jungle.

Agent Fielding would find a way out. He might not believe in anything he couldn't see or touch, but I certainly did. I also believed in angels, divine intervention and personal revelation. All of those things had happened to me during the past 72 hours.

I sank down on my knees since there wasn't a log to sit on and pulled out the baby's bottle. I'd stuffed it into the top of the things Maria had accumulated. When we got to some place safe, I'd look at what I'd managed to bring along with us, and I'd find a way to use the notes she had written. They were my only real leverage, and I refused to believe that getting him out of Colombia and away from his evil, inhumane drug-lord father was as impossible as my newly acquired partner made it seem.

We walked again until late in the morning. That was when I first heard the sound of rushing water. It should have filled me with joy because it meant that our journey was almost over, but instead, I felt only dread. I could handle what we were going through now, but the future lay before me as daunting as anything we had left behind. What if someone tried to take the baby away from me? I wasn't sure I could go on without him. He had become a part of me.

"There's a small village a few miles on the other side of the river," Agent Fielding said. "If my contact was able to get word to him, Manuel should have a two-seater ready for us to use. But we must keep the baby hidden since Mendoza, and anyone looking for easy money, is still searching for us. It's best that he believes the child died with his mother or was carried away by wild animals."

I knew his concern was well founded, but how could I keep a baby from crying if he was tired, hungry or upset? Perhaps if I fed him right before we got to the village he'd sleep for a couple of hours. He was doing that now because he was almost too weak for anything else, but I couldn't exactly hide him. He wasn't a doll. He needed air to survive.

"What about the men who are following us?" They had not been seen or heard for hours.

"They're back there, fighting through all the vegetation just as we did, although their motivation might be a little stronger since a great deal of money is involved. Luckily, we got a head start, but I'd say we have less than hour to make a clean getaway. They're not going to let a body of water stop them."

The river, when we came to it, was wide, muddy and loathsome looking. Its current did not appear to be swift, but it was impossible to tell its depth. I looked anxiously around for a boat, a swinging bridge or any other form of conveyance. Certainly, Agent Fielding did not mean for us to cross it on foot.

"Is this the river with the crocodiles and snakes?" I asked him as my heart began race.

"Every river in the jungle has those, in addition to leeches, piranhas, crabs, algae, turtles, caimans and flesh-eating microbes I can't even name."

I looked up and down its banks for as far as my eyes could see. We were standing in a marshland of tall, yellowish-green grass that was swaying in a light breeze, and I couldn't be sure there wasn't something menacing close by my feet. Fallen tree trunks rose from the water's depths in frightening contortions, but distinguishing them from reptiles waiting for their next meal was nearly impossible.

"It's noon," he added, as if sensing my hesitation and fear. "Most of the animals that inhabit this area will be looking for sun. If we move quietly and quickly we should be okay."

That didn't sound like much encouragement to me, but I was left with no choice except to move forward or be left behind.

"How are we going to get across?" I asked.

"I hate to be the bearer of more bad news, but if it's too deep to walk across; we'll have to swim."

"But all those things you talked about . . ."

"Will be in the river with us, but you seem to be a pretty good shot. A croc or anything else would be crazy to come after you. Besides, it's our only option unless we want a shootout with Mendoza's men. Leaving early gave us an advantage, but that time has almost run out. I'm surprised they haven't caught up with us already. They can move much faster than we can, and they know the jungle every bit as good as I do. Perhaps, even better."

My heart, that had felt like it was sitting in my throat only moments before plummeted. I didn't want a repeat of the day when the anaconda and crocodiles came after us, and I certainly didn't want another confrontation with Mendoza's men. They had nothing to lose, but I had a baby to protect, and I couldn't carry him, swim and keep a gun in my hands at the same time.

Agent Fielding must have anticipated my thoughts. "Give me the baby. He can ride in my backpack. I'm taller and can hopefully keep him out of the water."

"He isn't a sack of groceries," I protested, horrified by what he was suggesting. One slip and the baby would drown.

"Then what do you propose, Agent Sinclair, after all your vast experience out here? We need both of our hands free. The water looks calm on the surface, but it can move swiftly in places. We're going to have to keep moving, despite what lies beneath. The only thing we have going for us right now is that no one is shooting at us. That could change in an instant. Are you willing to wait around for that?"

In answer, I gingerly handed the baby to him. It ripped at my soul, but Agent Fielding was right, he was both bigger and stronger and had a much better chance of making it across the river safely than I did. I wanted to tell him to take care of the baby if I didn't make it, but regardless of what we were facing, I still believed we were all going to survive.

He put the baby in his backpack but didn't secure the top. "Just step where I do. I'll try to find the easiest way across. It should never get above your waist, but I can't be certain. You'll have to keep your hands up if you want a dry gun."

I had never been a great fan of water, even though I knew how to swim, but as the cold current rose around my legs I shivered uncontrollably. We were in a jungle. The water shouldn't be so cold.

About a quarter of the way across, Agent Fielding turned his head and gave me a minute to catch up with him. My legs were shorter, and I wasn't nearly as confident as he was.

"I don't want to frighten you, but on the bank we just left are three large crocs. They have their eyes closed, and we should be able to make it across okay. Just don't fall into the water or make any big, splashing noises that will draw attention to where we are. You already know what else lives here."

"Sure do," I thought as I tried to keep up with him once he had started moving forward again. He could have spared me the recitation of all the dangers we faced. My body was fully covered by clothing, and we were moving too fast for anything to attach, but if I fell . . . Well, I hoped Agent Fielding would be kind enough to come back and help me. I didn't like the idea of bloodsucking leeches and flesh-eating piranhas getting anywhere near me, let alone the crocodiles that appeared to be sleeping.

My guardian angels must have been working overtime because every time I felt my feet slipping and wanted to scream, I could feel a presence helping me to remain upright and taking away my fear.

The water that had only whipped around my legs when we first entered the river continued to rise. I kept my eyes focused on the man in front of me, and the precious cargo he was carrying, but that didn't stop me from both sensing and feeling the masters of the deep as their bodies whipped around me. Nor did it stop me from being acutely aware of my other surroundings—the trees on the banks that seemed to be staring at us, the great vultures that flew overhead in anticipation of some tasty meal and the unwanted wind that kept whipping my damp hair in front of my eyes.

I held my gun above my head and tried to maintain my balance whenever I hit a sinkhole, a jutting rock, or some careless amphibian as I moved more rapidly than was prudent. Still, I was soaked to my chin by the time I'd made it to the far shore, and I fell to the earth in a quivering heap, knowing that the entire contents of my backpack were wet. I just hoped that nothing had been destroyed. Agent Fielding had been right about taking the baby. He would have been under water if I'd been carrying him.

"You can't stop now," he said, gripping my arm and dragging me behind a clump of tall grass. I was angry at his insensitivity. Hadn't I just risked everything by following him across a river? I wanted time to make sure I had brought nothing unsavory with me, but when I looked up, I saw two men standing on the other side. They were only a few yards farther down the riverbank than we had been. If we moved now, they would see us. It was impossible to know if they were aware of the reptiles sleeping so close to them.

"What do we do?" I panted, taking in great gulps of of air and wishing I could take the baby from him, but knowing that would have to wait until it was safe.

"Nothing! We stay exactly where we are while they decide what they're going to do."

"But surely they know we've made it across."

"Only if they've already discovered where we've been, and I doubt that's happened, or they wouldn't be hesitating. If they move across the river, and we're still behind them ... Well, it's a calculated risk either way. Mendoza is going to be livid if they come back empty-handed."

"Maybe they'll just run away. There's nothing forcing them to go back."

"That's not exactly true. Most of his men have families somewhere. Mendoza might forget about them for a few days, but once he's reestablished his operations, he'll figure out what happened and send someone to find them. He's not going to let us get away, and he'll think they have information he can use, even if they don't claim his reward."

"Well, they don't," I said as the insects swarmed around my face, biting at my skin and making it difficult not to swat at them. I was trying not to think about all the diseases they carried, especially so close to the water. Even if I survived the trek out of the jungle, I could still die from something that couldn't be seen – something deadly like malaria, yellow fever or any of at least a dozen other illnesses. The bureau gave each recruit a whole series of shots, but they couldn't vaccinate against everything.

Agent Fielding suddenly took my hand and squeezed it. "It's going to be okay. I've been in a lot worse situations. Maybe the crocs will find them and save us a whole lot of trouble."

I didn't exactly share his sentiment, but it would certainly solve our most pressing problem. Fortunately, it didn't come to that. After a few moments of waiting with baited breath, the two men moved back inside the jungle.

"I guess they decided the river wasn't for them," my companion said. "But that doesn't mean they won't decide to cross it once they've looked around a bit. I suggest we use this time to put more distance between us."

He pulled me to my feet and led me a fair distance away from the smells and the sounds of the river before stopping again. We were in a sort of meadow, and the dismal clouds were not as heavy as they had been. We seemed to have left the dense jungle behind, at least momentarily. I was not going to miss it, but hills rose all around us, and it was impossible to see what lay beyond them.

"You did well again today," Agent Fielding said as we walked side by side for the first time ever. "I might just have to change my opinion of you."

I no longer cared how he felt about me. All I wanted was to know that the baby, my baby, was safe. He hadn't even offered to return him to me. I was afraid he knew something I didn't.

"Can I take him now?" I almost demanded, planting my feet on the ground and refusing to go any further until he complied with my wishes. "He's been in that backpack far too long."

"It was the only way. I hope you realize that," he said as he took the pack off his back and held it out for me. "There you go, safe and sound."

But I couldn't take his word for it. I had to see for myself that the child I already loved more than life itself was still alive.

I knelt down on the ground and loosened the knot that had kept the baby from falling into the river. Unlike the backpack I'd been carrying, this one was basically dry. When I pulled the towel from his face, he wrinkled his nose and stretched. It was a most heartwarming sight.

"I told you he'd be all right," Agent Fielding said, joining us.

I didn't reply. I simply took the baby out of the towel, rubbed his little body and talked to him until he was forced to open his eyes. He would never remember what he had gone through, but when he was older, I would tell him everything. He needed to know just how much two women had loved him. He accepted a little coconut milk from the bottle before closing his eyes again.

During the time I'd been busy feeding and changing the baby, Agent Fielding had been scouring the area for any kind of life. I knew he hated being out in the open and wished I would hurry with my ministrations, but some things simply couldn't be rushed.

We walked along in silence, our clothing still heavy from all the water it had absorbed. I had been wearing the same thing for the past four days and couldn't imagine how awful I must look and smell, even though the water from the river had washed most of the grime away. I stole several glances at my companion. He was walking erect, but I knew he carried a tremendous weight not knowing what might happen when we arrived at the village. If what he'd said about Mendoza's bounty had spread, we could be walking straight into a trap.

A short time later, we came to the top of a ridge. I can't explain the relief that took away the cold of the river and the fear of the jungle. Before us, on the other side of a small valley, the tops of grass covered huts were clearly visible.

"We should be there in under an hour, but we have to keep the baby hidden. HIs only chance for survival is if people believe he's dead. I can't stress that enough," Agent Fielding said, giving me an incredibly stern look. "Mendoza's people are everywhere, and they will tell him anything they discover, even if they don't try to apprehend us or take our lives."

I was tired of all his warnings. By now I knew exactly what was at stake, along with the fact that we couldn't really trust anyone but each other. But how was I going to hide the baby unless I returned him to the inside of a backpack? I didn't even have a jacket with which to cover him.

"Let me try to feed him again," I replied. "If he's full and dry, he should sleep."

I sat down on the grass and looked behind me at the thick underbrush we'd come through—at the trees and bushes that had torn my skin, leaving it scratched, bruised and bleeding, and beyond that lay the deadly river that could have so easily claimed our lives. Gratitude filled my heart as I thought about all we'd endured, but I knew our journey was far from over. If anyone discovered the baby's presence before I was able to get him out of the country; his life truly would be over.

After pulling the last bottle of coconut milk from the backpack, I unwrapped the baby. His large, dark eyes were closed, but his little limbs twitched at the sudden burst of cooler air. The towel that covered him was damp. I changed his diaper, cleaned the entire area as best I could with the last of water from the canteen Agent Fielding had been carrying, and then checked for signs of infection at the site where his umbilical cord had been cut. When I was sure that nothing had invaded even the smallest crevice of his body, I replaced the towel with one that was somewhat drier.

Agent Fielding just stood there with his machine gun and machete and watched. I knew he understood my need to take care of the baby, but that didn't underscore his belief that I was battling something that would not have the outcome I desired.

But when I looked at the tiny scrap of humanity in my arms, I knew I could never relinquish him to a life without me in it. It didn't matter what I might have to face in the future; he deserved the life Maria wanted for him.

"How's he doing?" Agent Fielding asked as I secured him in my arms and put the nipple of the bottle to his lips.

"Good," I replied, biting my bottom lip and looking up at him.

The strength of the human spirit truly was mind-boggling. By all rights, none of us should have survived the entirety of the past few days. Even without Mendoza's men following us, there were literally thousands of wild animals and poisonous amphibians, reptiles and insects that could have claimed our lives, but somehow, we'd managed to avoid all of them.

"I'm glad he seems to be doing so well, Agent Sinclair. I have to give him credit for being a scrapper."

He was trying to be sincere, but from harsh contours of his face I knew that something more than my desire to keep the baby safe was bothering him. It seemed highly unlikely that anyone would know who we were and where we had come from since we were miles away from the compound, and news of our unlikely escape still couldn't be proved. But perhaps people from most everywhere in the region knew him by sight since he'd been with Mendoza for nearly four years.

"You look like a thunder cloud," he suddenly said, looking down at me as I tried to force some of the nearly clear liquid into the baby's mouth. "I thought you'd be happy to be out of that damned jungle."

"I could say the same thing about you," I responded. "I am happy to be closer to civilization since the baby's not responding even as much as he was last night, but I know you're worried about more than someone discovering who we are."

He shrugged his shoulders. "My problems are my own. I just wish I could get you to understand that deathbed promises don't count. You said what you did to bring Maria peace. The baby will go into the system if he survives, and a home will be found for him here in his own country. We can only hope Mendoza thinks he perished along with his mother. It's the only real chance he's got."

Now was not the time to fight with him over my intentions. Maria's son was coming home with me. I didn't care what obstacles I had to overcome for that to happen. This precious child of God would not become a casualty in the war against drugs.

"You're one fierce, little mother," he said as he watched me hold the baby over my shoulder and try to burp him. "I could almost believe he was yours."

"He feels like my own. There isn't anything I wouldn't do to keep him safe, and I do mean anything."

I looked back at the baby because I didn't want to see Agent Fielding's intimidating eyes leveled at me again. He had the right to believe what he thought was right, but so did I. My outrage at all the injustice I had witnessed had been kept in check because of the dangerous circumstances we were in, but once we got back to Bogotá, he was going to have a fight on his hands if he thought I was going to leave Colombia without Maria's child.

The trek across the valley floor was easy compared to what we had already endured, but before we even got close to the village, a man dressed in a red and gold, striped woolen poncho and a worn sombrero stepped out of the tall brush and stopped us. It startled me so much I felt my heart race to my throat, but Agent Fielding was clearly relieved when he spoke.

"It is good to see you, Jorge," the man told him. "Your message only arrived an hour ago, but it gave me time to get the plane ready. It is good you got here when you did. Most of the people in the village are taking a siesta. There has been a reward put out for your capture. Mendoza knows what happened to Fernando in the jungle. He will not let it go unpunished."

"We've heard as much. I was in the village below the compound three nights ago and had to shoot my way out. Some of the men who were once under my charge figured they'd found an easy way to move up the organizational ladder."

"Then you must know that there is no place where you will ever be safe."

"My life's not over yet," Agent Fielding said. "I'm more concerned about you, Manuel. What I've asked this time is far more dangerous than anything in the past."

"Do not worry about me. I do too much to help the people here. There is little that could turn them against me."

I was interested in what they might say next, but the man suddenly turned his attention to me. His eyes narrowed, and I felt a moment of both judgment and apprehension.

"I had hoped I would be meeting three people, but since there are only two of you, it must mean that Maria did not survive the gunshot wound and the birth of her child. I secured a few things for the baby, just in case, and some blankets since I knew you would be coming across the river."

"The baby is with us," Agent Fielding said.

The man looked surprised. "How is it possible the child survived?"

"It was a difficult birth, but the woman with us would not leave him behind, even though he was more dead than alive."

I grimaced, but was grateful he had not mentioned my name. If there was a price on his head, there would be one on mine as well, even if Mendoza didn't know my affiliation was with the FBI and not the DEA.

"Sometimes a little hope is all it takes," the man said.

Agent Fielding gave him a small wad of damp bills. "For your trouble. We appreciate all the sacrifices you have made."

It suddenly occurred to me that they would never see each other again. If we made it back to DEA headquarters, Agent Fielding would be assigned to another case. He would never leave the bureau and go into hiding, even if it meant he would be a visible target for the rest of his life.

"It was my pleasure," I heard the man say. "There was not time to secure much, just a little fresh, goat's milk and clean cloth for the baby, and some tortillas for you. No one must ever know he survived."

Agent Fielding took the offered supplies and stuffed everything but the blankets into the backpack that had recently held the baby. "How is the rest of your family?"

"They are well, and the little ones just keep coming. I wish I could offer to take the baby for you, but I am afraid my wife would not agree."

"That certainly isn't necessary. We'll find a place for him. Just be careful. It appears that no one can be trusted right now."

"I will do my best," he replied. "I am in no hurry to return to God."

"None of us are," Agent Fielding replied, and I couldn't help but notice the look of sadness in his eyes. He'd lost far more than we had.

It was decided that I would put a blanket over my head and around my shoulders in a way that would cover the entire front of my body. That way, I could keep the baby close to me, and if he didn't fuss, villagers would only think that I was pregnant or overweight if they happened to see us. He was used to me now and would feel safer that way.

My legs were none too steady, and I kept my head down as we followed him into the village. True to his word, very few people were moving about, mostly children who were playing outside the small huts. They looked our way but didn't approach as the little ones in the village by the compound had. There was nothing that gave any clue as to how they supported themselves - just a few goats and chickens wandering aimlessly around.

Perhaps the small, vintage aircraft that sat on a dirt runway at the end of the row of huts did more than carry supplies and an occasional passenger. That was the only way news could travel rapidly in the jungle since I hadn't seen any carrier pigeons.

The man named Manuel held the passenger door open for me. "Thank you for being so kind to Maria's baby. He will not be safe for as long as he lives, but at least you have given him a chance."

"I will make sure he survives and has a good life," I told him, not caring if it was inappropriate of me to speak.

He slammed the door shut, but not before I heard Agent Fielding ask him what he knew about Mendoza and his men. Then I strained to hear his answer.

"He got away, but this you already know since he found you in the jungle. I do not know where he is now, except that he has no intention of getting caught. He will likely move on to one of his other compounds in the southern part of the country where the authorities are not so intent on finding him. The hacienda is still filled with people burying the dead and trying to figure out how he escaped and where he will go. Something might be learned if the price is right."

"Perhaps," Agent Fielding said. "I just wish I had been there. Things did not go as I planned."

The hard edge to his voice made me shudder. My presence had cost him over three, long years of undercover work, but it wasn't completely my fault. He could have let me return to the states instead of taking me into the mountains, but he'd used me as a decoy to get what he wanted.

"Be safe," Manuel told him. "I am afraid that you have made an enemy for life - one who has the resources to follow you to the ends of the earth if he so desires. The sooner you get out of Colombia the better it will be for you. However, there is a little clinic on St. Peter's Street where you can take the baby. No questions will be asked, but you cannot stay there long. We often need their help, and we do not want their work to be compromised."

"We'll stay no longer than is necessary," Agent Fielding assured him. "Thank you, my friend. I hope this favor has not cost you too much."

"As long as Mendoza thinks I am loyal to him everything will be fine. We both knew the risks when we chose this life. I have told the people in the village that someone from the jungle is going to get supplies. They seldom question anything as long as their bellies are full. Just make sure you send back enough supplies to last for a week or two. One of our replacement pilots will be waiting for you."

"You'll get everything you need and more."

"Thank you," Manuel said, then he bowed his head and made the sign of the cross. "I will make sure a marker is erected for Maria inside the jungle. It might not be where she lost her life, but she will know that her sacrifice has not been forgotten."

The threat of tears burned my nostrils again. No one who knew Maria would ever forget her, especially not her son. I had a few of her belongings in a backpack that would go to him when he was older. I was thankful I had not been intimidated into leaving them behind.

The two men hugged, and then Agent Fielding got into the plane and started turning knobs. Manuel stepped away so we could take off. I was glad he had not said anything about what had happened to Maria's body. I wanted to go on deluding myself that her remains were still underneath the coat where we'd left her.

I clutched the baby even tighter as I heard the engine engage. Poor little guy! He didn't deserve to come into the world like this, but I was going to make certain he had a happy life, and when the time came to tell him about his biological parents I would make sure he knew just what his mother had sacrificed for him. I didn't care if he ever learned about his father.

We taxied down the dirt runway and before long we were in the air. The clanging and banging of the rustic plane awakened the baby, and he began to cry. But I simply held him securely in my arms and tried to get him to drink some of the fresh goat's milk Manuel had brought. He refused it at first, but suddenly he seemed to change his mind and began pulling at the nipple with as much strength as his little body could muster. He was a fighter, but if we didn't get him the help he needed, his little body would simply give out.

As I watched him eat, I felt my stomach tighten and start to churn. Nothing in the way of refreshment had been offered to us before leaving the village, but Manuel had mentioned including some tortillas for Agent Fielding and me. I would look for them soon, but right now both of my hands were full. So I settled back in the worn, leather seat with prickly, frayed edges and glanced out the small and filthy window to my left. The green foliage below had become more of an emerald, hazy blur than distinct trees and bushes. It gave me a moment of relief, but I knew it wouldn't last long. Once we were on the ground, we would be in grave danger again. Mendoza would not stop looking for us until he knew we were dead.

Agent Fielding kept his eyes focused on the sky in front of him, giving me plenty of time to think. I was glad Manuel was going to erect a cross for Maria. It was hardly worthy as a reminder of all she'd sacrificed, but it was a start. In my eyes, she was a true hero, sacrificing everything for a cause she believed in. I didn't even care that Mendoza was her baby's father. I wanted to remember her as a beautiful, kind and gentle woman who loved children.

And she was brave. She had killed a man to save our lives, and she had fought to remain alive long enough to give her son life. Yes, he would know all the good things about her, and the many lives she had touched in a positive way, including mine. She had given me the only thing of true value she had. I would keep her son safe, and I would fight anyone who got in my way.

I looked over at Agent Fielding's profile, but he didn't notice. I could understand how conflicted he must feel losing his partner and not being there to see the cartel brought down. He would never forgive me for Mendoza's escape, but his attitude towards Maria's baby still baffled me. He'd been the one to bring the child into the world. He'd cleared his airways and breathed life into his lungs. How could he relegate him to an existence of fear and uncertainty by committing him into the hands of the Colombian government where dirty officials ruled no matter how hard the good ones tried to clean up the hierarchy?

"What happens when we get to Bogotá?" I asked him when I could stand the silence no longer.

"You'll drop the baby off at the clinic, and then you'll be on the first plane out of here. I trust you have the necessary papers with you."

"I do, but I won't go without the baby. I already told you that."

"And I told you that it's out of the question. This is no longer your problem, Agent Sinclair. The faster you get out of Colombia the better, though I'm afraid something will have to be done about your passport. Mendoza knows you're still alive by now, and we don't want to give him any advantage in tracing where you've gone. Your best chance for survival is to get back to your life as quickly as possible and forget this little adventure ever took place."

That wasn't going to happen. My mind was replaying an almost constant kaleidoscope of grizzly snapshots that was impossible to stop. It wouldn't matter how many miles I traveled or what other assignments I was given, this experience would never be forgotten with or without the baby in my life. My decision would be my own once we parted company anyway.

"What about you?" I asked.

"I'm afraid the powers that be may insist that I leave the country until things cool down a bit."

I refused to take full blame for the debacle any longer. If I'd been given a chance, I might have been able to help, but I still told him that I was sorry for being instrumental in spoiling the raid.

He shook his head, but didn't look at me. "I played my own part in what happened by trying to buy more time. I just wish our collective efforts hadn't put a price on both our heads. I'm the one who needs to be tracking Mendoza since I know more about him than any other agent in the country, but like I just said, I'm fairly certain they'll send me packing until things cool down a bit. He's going to let his partners run things until he feels like it's safe to surface again."

"How many partners does he have?"

"That's hard to tell. I've met a great many of them, but if the cartels aren't actively warring, they're working together. The compound was his main base of operation and some of the men he brought there were pretty high up the food chain, but I know he'd never risk having all the key players in one place at the same time."

"That makes sense. If a few get caught, at least the entire operation wouldn't fold."

"Our biggest hope was to cripple him enough that others might become careless. The war we're fighting will never be over as long as men like Mendoza are still alive."

"You'd actually stay here and hunt him if you could?"

"In a heartbeat! Wouldn't you?"

Giving him an immediate answer was impossible. The events of the past few days had stripped me of nearly every reserve. Perhaps I would feel differently if I had been trained by the DEA and had been allowed to be more of a participant in the operation I'd been assigned, but I wasn't even sure about my own job now that I had the baby to consider.

"I'm not sure what I would do if our roles were reversed, and not because I don't believe in the work you're doing. I'm just not sure I'm cut out to be an undercover agent. There's too much compromise and uncertainty."

"And you don't have that with the FBI?"

"As you already know, my experience as a field agent was almost non-existent until I came here. I was still riding with a training officer."

My admittance must have amused him because he smiled again. "So you really are a newbie."

"Yes, and when we go after the bad guys it's usually with an arsenal of support behind us."

"I suppose our support is limited, and we're often put into situations where we're forced to make concessions, but you'd make a good undercover agent, given a little more experience and time."

I looked at him with what amounted to stunned amazement. My cover had been blown before I even arrived.

"Don't give me that look," he replied. "I know you got off to a rough start, but you've proven that you can make confident decisions under pressure. I'm glad I got to work with you. It's nice knowing that not everyone is as jaded as I am, but I do wish you'd take my advice about Maria's baby. You're young. You have a long life and a fulfilling career ahead. Why would you want to destroy that over a baby that doesn't even belong to you? In any event, he could have a multitude of health issues, not to mention that price on his head."

I looked out of the window before answering. Maria's baby deserved a chance, and no one would give it to him but me. This wasn't just an ethical or a moral issue. I believed he had come into my life for a purpose. Perhaps my being sent on this mission was solely to meet him since everything else had turned out so poorly.

"I know you don't agree with what I'm going to do, Agent Fielding, and I'm not sure I could explain it to you if I tried. But sometimes we just need to act on faith. The end can't always be known from the beginning."

"Even if it destroys the rest of your life? You haven't dealt with men like Mendoza. He's not going to give up just because you want him to."

"None of us are here by chance, Agent Fielding. I'm the only one who knows this baby's needs, and who loves him unconditionally. No worthy person in Colombia will adopt him if they know about his past. Please don't ask me to turn my back on him. I may not know exactly what I'm getting into, but I do know that I'm the best chance he's got."

Agent Fielding looked out at the vista in front of us with the heavy cumulus clouds that made visibility almost impossible. If a plane as old as the one we were in could stay in the sky, I could certainly take care of one sick little baby, even under some very dubious circumstances.

We flew for some distance in silence. I changed and fed the baby again; grateful for the things Manuel had given us. By the things he had said, he appeared to have known Maria personally. I didn't even have a picture I could show to her son. The Colombian government and the DEA would have more information, but I doubted that I would be allowed to see any of it.

"How much do you know about Maria's past?" I asked Agent Fielding as he sat in the seat next to me brooding.

"Why should that interest you? She's gone! Nothing is going to bring her back."

"Because her son will want to know about her when he gets older."

He shook his head as his jaws clenched. "I wish you'd just give up."

"Well, I won't," I replied.

"Then you'll have to discover on your own that the Colombian government will not relinquish him, and the United States will not eagerly embrace a refugee with such clear ties to the Mendoza Cartel. What you're asking could take months, if not years, to accomplish, if it can be done at all."

"I think you misjudge the goodness of others, but I will take what you said under advisement."

"That's just a polite way of telling me to mind my own business because you're going to do what you want anyway. All women are the same. They think they can handle anything. Maria found out the hard way that isn't true, and you seem determined to do the same."

There was no point in fueling hostilities, but I needed as many answers as I could get, regardless of what the future brought. "Please tell me about her. I know so little, and Manuel seemed very fond of her."

"They came from the same little village outside Villavincencio. It's southeast of Bogotá. When he found out she was going to the compound, he offered to go with her, even though he's not an agent."

"He must have cared for her dearly."

"They knew each other as children, though neither of them mentioned any personal involvement. She asked him not to come near Mendoza, but one day he showed up at the hacienda bringing supplies. I know she used him as a means of getting information to the authorities."

"Then he has been a valuable asset."

"There are hundreds just like him. We give them what we can, but it is never enough. Most of them come from very humble backgrounds. Maria's family worked the coffee fields and sometimes picked bananas. She was the oldest and felt it her responsibility to do more than add just a few pesos a day to the family coffers. They lived in a small hut, not unlike the ones in the village where we first landed, but with the money she sent, they were able to buy a modest house, and her father opened his own produce stand."

"How did she get involved with the DEA? It seems so unlikely considering her beginnings."

"The local priest saw something in her. Perhaps it was her beauty, and perhaps it was her spirit, but he arranged for her to attend school where she was recruited by the DEA when she was sixteen."

"That's so young. I'm surprised her family let her go."

"It's an honor to go to school when a family cannot afford it, and much better than being sold to the highest bidder. Surely you are not so naïve as to believe that young girls with few options can still have good lives?"

I clenched my teeth until my jaws ached. Even in the United States, some of the FBI's most intense cases involved human trafficking and prostitution.

"I wish everyone had the chance to grow up the way I did," I said.

"And what way would that be?" he asked.

I could have taken his response as just another attempt to put me down, but he needed to know that there were still families in the world who had high values and who supported each other. "I grew up with four brothers and two wonderful, loving parents in a home filled with warmth and laughter. What about you?"

"I make it a point never discuss my personal life. It's easier that way."

Tears clouded my vision as I looked down at the sleeping baby in my arms. No matter what obstacles stood in my path, I would not allow Maria's baby to be given away to the highest bidder or be left in an orphanage because no one wanted him. There had to be someone who would be willing to help me.

Chapter 14

It wasn't much longer until we began our initial descent onto a landing field at an obscure airport on the outskirts of Bogotá. This trip had taken far less time than the one when I'd arrived, but we had started much farther down the mountains. There were two metal sheds instead of a lone hut, and another small plane like the one we were flying in was sitting on a bare strip of land next to them.

"Don't look so worried," Agent Fielding said as I held the baby securely in my arms while we bumped along another dirt runway until we came to a complete stop. "Our people know what they're doing."

I glanced around to see if I could detect any movement in the brush surrounding us. We might be close to the capital city of Colombia, but that only meant people could easily get lost in any number of subcultures, and we could be walking into a trap, despite what Agent Fielding believed.

I doubted I would ever feel safe again. With Mendoza on the run and angry, he'd be more dangerous than ever, but I couldn't let fear override faith. We were out of the jungle, and in what I hoped would be a short amount of time, Maria's baby would be receiving medical help.

A man in a tan shirt and darker tan pants came out of a white stucco building to greet us. There was a small tower on top, and I wondered if flight plans were ever filed for the kind of planes I had been in since they could easily be traced. Perhaps they flew low enough that they didn't need to worry about other aircrafts and certainly no one in their right mind would go anywhere near the mountain jungles without a specific reason for doing so.

Agent Fielding must have noticed my hesitancy in getting out because he came around the nose of the plane and opened the door.

"Don't give up on me now, Agent Sinclair," he said. "You're almost home free."

I climbed out with the baby while he took charge of the two backpacks still in our possession. He had his gun in the holster around his waist. A long wool poncho covered it, but he left the machine gun and the machete inside the plane. I felt oddly exposed leaving them behind, but their presence would only arouse suspicion. From the way we looked after four days in the jungle, anyone who saw us would assume we were some indigent couple of the mountainous regions looking for help. That misconception was what would keep us alive.

"We have been waiting for you," the man said. His face was covered with pox marks. I'd noticed that quite often since arriving in the country. People could not always afford to be vaccinated, and the results of childhood illnesses often left scars. "I have a truck ready for you."

I kept my head down, the blanket secure and didn't say anything. It would be much easier to disappear if no one remembered seeing my face or hearing my voice.

"Thank you," Agent Fielding said. "I guess you know what to do from here. Manuel wants enough supplies to last a week or two."

"Already arranged," the man said.

"Have you heard anything about the raid? I must say that I'm mad as hell that Mendoza slipped away again."

"Only rumors," the man answered. "He knows you and the other agent are still alive. His men radioed back after finding the hut."

"And the baby? Does he think it survived?"

"Who can tell what a madman thinks? The remains were pretty much gone by the time they got there. I take it you were able to allude the men who followed you back into the jungle, or you would not be here now."

I didn't want to hear anything else. Visions of what had most likely happened to Maria's body were swirling through my head making me more than a little ill. I stayed a discreet distance behind the two men as they walked away from the plane.

"They were at the river when we crossed over earlier this morning, but it won't take them long to make radio contact again. That's why we have to hurry now."

"Understood," the man replied. "But you will be happy to know that all of the fields have been burned and the processing huts destroyed. The authorities seized hundreds of pounds of cocaine. It will take Mendoza time to recoup his losses."

"Not nearly long enough," Agent Fielding replied, and I could hear the vehemence in his voice again. "He would be in prison now if things had gone according to plan."

The man nodded but didn't say anything. He led us past what I assumed was his office to a battered green truck without offering anything with which to refresh ourselves, not even the use of much-needed facilities. I kept the baby hidden. It seemed like the right thing to do.

"You don't need to look so severe," Agent Fielding said to me as we rattled along the two-way road past fields of maize and coffee that led to the outskirts of the city. "In no time at all you'll be on your way back to the states, and this will be nothing more than an unpleasant memory."

"You don't know me very well if you think I'll ever forget what happened here, or that I'll give up trying to take the baby with me. As long as he stays here so will I."

"Then you're more of a fool than I thought. It won't take Mendoza long to find us, and I plan on staying ahead of him, for the time being anyway. There are hundreds of cartels that need to be brought down. As soon as I make my report, I'll be on my way to another assignment. You'd be wise to follow my lead. No baby is worth being killed for. Someone will take care of him, and there is plenty of work that needs to be done by both our agencies."

Arguing with him until I had a plan of my own was futile. What I was contemplating wasn't even logical, but some things had to be taken on faith. If the baby were meant to leave the country with me, as I believed he was, God would provide a way.

We drove for nearly an hour before stopping in front of a weather-beaten stucco building in a very unsavory part of the city. It looked more like tenement housing where drug pushers resided than a hospital or a clinic, but I had to take what was offered.

Agent Fielding didn't bother to come around the truck to help me out, so I held the door with my foot while I stepped onto a sidewalk with grass growing between the cracks. A cool wind had picked up, and I involuntarily shivered, grateful for the heavy wool covering I had been given before reaching the village. It shielded my face and completely covered the baby. There were a few rose bushes lining the walkway to the building, but it was too cold for much of anything to be blooming.

A ceiling fan inside the front door did little to lessen the feel of moisture in the air. I noticed from the corner of one eye that there were three other adults and one little girl in the waiting room. They appeared safe enough, but one could never be sure. The two women in light blue uniforms looked up from behind the counter.

Agent Fielding walked briskly towards them, leaving me to follow along behind.

"And what might we help you with today, senõr?" one of them asked in Spanish, while the other one put notations on a chart. I wasn't sure Agent Fielding even knew that I understood, but now was not the time to enlighten him.

"My wife is very ill with an unexplainable growth, and we were hoping to find help. We have no money, but I am willing to work."

"This clinic is free to anyone who needs help and cannot afford to pay. Please be seated. There is one patient in front of you."

The baby was beginning to move around. I would not be able to keep him hidden for long. As if sensing the need to hurry things along, Agent Fielding asked the receptionist if there was a place where I could lie down. It had been a long and tiring trip.

"Of course," the woman said. "You may wait in one of the examination rooms. Please follow me."

We followed her down a dimly lit hallway with several closed doors on each side. The smell of antiseptic was strong, but then so was the stench of decay and disease. It was not a place I wanted to stay for long.

"We have been waiting for you to arrive," she told Agent Fielding as soon as the door was securely shut behind us. "I did not want it to seem that you were being given special privileges in case someone was watching. Dr. Perez will be with you shortly. He will want to see the baby as soon as possible."

She advanced towards me with her arms held out.

"I can manage," I told her, not wanting the baby out of my sight for even a moment.

"As you wish," she said, reverting to much-practiced English. "But your wounds will need to be cared for, and there are some precautionary shots you will need to have."

Up until then, I hadn't truly considered how frightful I must look to someone who didn't know what we'd been through. But looking into the mirror that hung suspended above the bed, I hardly recognized the woman staring back at me. My eyes appeared much too large for my hollow-cheeked face, and there were cuts, insect bites, bruises and deep abrasions underneath the dirt that was everywhere. Twigs and dead insects were matted in my hair. I looked a hundred times worse than any homeless person I'd ever seen. Not at all like the beautiful Maria, even in death.

"I understand," I told her, lifting the covering so she could see the baby.

She took him from me and laid him on the white paper that covered the table. He trembled and started to moan. It was the sound of an injured animal, and it shook me beyond belief with its mournfulness, but I maintained my distance giving her the space she needed to assess the damage that had already been done.

I glanced at Agent Fielding from the corner of my eye. He stood in front of the window looking out. He wasn't sure of our safety even yet. No one had followed us into the city, and unless our destination was already known, there was no reason to believe we had been compromised. But I couldn't fault his diligence. I'd tried to act like a fully trained agent at the compound, even though I'd failed miserably, but my emotions had taken over almost completely the past few days. Now it was time for me to begin assessing the situation in light of the confines of the reality that would now determine my future. There were people around willing to offer assistance, but no one I had met had the authority or the resources to help me keep my promise.

I wished he could understand how desperately I wanted to keep the sacred vow I had made to Maria. I would love to share my insecurities with him now that they were beginning to surface, but he would only repeat what he'd already said. I was being foolishly naïve if I thought I could outwit two federal governments and one of the most stealthy drug lords in the business. We may have made it back to Bogotá, but we weren't out of the woods yet.

Dr. Perez was short and dark-skinned, but he had very kind eyes, and I knew instinctively that I could trust him. Agent Fielding disappeared when he arrived, but I didn't much care where he'd gone, or even if I saw him again. I was much too worried about the baby, and if he wouldn't help me get him out of the country, I had to find someone who would.

The baby's moan turned into a howl as Dr. Perez put a cold metal stethoscope on his bare chest. I immediately moved closer to the table.

"Babies cry," he told me in a gentle voice. "It is a good sign."

The doctor weighed and measured him and then began cleaning up the umbilical cord that looked like it might have become infected. It was not easy for him to remove the clothespin that had been put in place after his birth. Dried blood encrusted it.

"Is he going to be all right?" I asked as he made an incision and lifted the wooden object away from the baby's body. There was a spurt of fresh blood, but deft fingers repaired the damage. The nurse was holding the writhing baby down. I wanted to do it myself, but her body blocked me.

"It is too soon to tell, but he appears remarkably healthy considering what he has been through. You have kept him hydrated, but he is jaundiced and is going to need to stay here for a few days until we know that his vital organs are functioning properly."

I must have looked terrified because he put a reassuring hand on my arm.

"Babies are far less fragile than we might think. I am just being cautious. It is not every day a baby is born in the jungle to one of our own and survives. His life is important to me as well."

"One of our own." Those words filled me with an incredible amount of hope. Dr. Perez was not going to give up on Maria's son. Maybe he would even be willing to help me get him out of the country when the time came.

"Thank you, doctor," I said with a weak smile. "I've been so worried about him. He only drinks a few sips at a time. Mostly, he's had goat's milk, but when we ran out, he was given coconut milk. Nothing was refrigerated. I couldn't even sterilize the bottles, and they hadn't been used by humans."

"He was taking liquid. That is what is important. You may find many of our ways unsanitary and even a little uncivilized, but life is not easy in many parts of our country, and people do what is necessary. The challenge might be getting him to accept something that was meant for him."

"I'll do whatever it takes, Dr. Perez."

"I am sure you will," he replied. "It is apparent that you have bonded with him. It is important for a baby to feel safe and loved no matter the circumstance. I would say you have accomplished the impossible already. I am going to have Nurse Juana take him for some additional tests, make sure he is cleaned up and given his first bottle of formula. You can trust her. She has been working for the cause for ten years. We will let you know as soon as there is something to tell."

I wanted to protest, but I had to trust someone if I was ever going to get out of the country with the baby, and Agent Fielding had already told me that he wasn't interested in my reckless plan. So I allowed the nurse to take him from the room. I'd have him back in my arms soon enough, and then I would never let anyone take him away from me again.

"Now, climb up on the table," the doctor instructed. "You look in far worse shape than the baby."

He took my pulse, listened to my heart, and then he told me to undress and put on the gown that was lying over the back of a chair. He pulled a light blanket from a cupboard that I could use if I got cold and then left the room while I changed. I struggled to even get a grip on the laces of my boots they were so filled with debris. My clothes had dried from our time in the river, but they were still caked with mud, and the stink left from the water was insufferable. I needed a hot shower and some clean clothing to wear, but none of that mattered as long as the baby was being cared for. This was the first time we'd been separated since his birth.

Dr. Perez knocked on the door before entering the room again. "I will make this as easy on you as possible. There are so many microscopic insects and organisms in the jungle that can make you ill or even kill you. I know what to look for. You can keep the blanket if it will make you more comfortable."

I mumbled my thanks as he began looking up and down my arms and legs, turning them this way and that so he could see better with the aid of the strong light bulb that hung suspended from a metal arm over the table. He chatted amicably as he worked, removing things I could not see with tweezers and even checking out the crevices I'd been taught were private. I hated every moment of it, but knew it had to be done. I didn't want any lifelong health problems because of my short adventure in the Colombian jungle.

"Your clothing protected you amazingly well," he said, helping me sit up so he could check my back. "I can see nothing to be overly alarmed about, except that you are critically dehydrated, and I doubt you have had much to eat the past few days."

"It wasn't so bad. We had a protein bar and some coconut to eat."

"I can only imagine what you have endured these past few days. You are a brave young woman for risking your life for a baby that had very little chance of survival."

"Everything I did was worth it. Maria's baby deserves a chance to live."

He didn't respond to that, he simply asked me to lie back down so he could check the front of my torso. I knew he wouldn't be pleased with what he saw. While I had been trying to mask the pain brought about by several cracked ribs, dark, repugnant bruises covered the entire area where Fernando had kicked me with his boots.

"Why did you not tell me that you had been severely injured?" he asked when he saw them.

"It seemed like the least of my worries once the baby was born. Besides, no permanent damage was done, or I would have been unable to carry him."

He touched the bruises tenderly while I tried not to wince. Now that the adrenaline had quite pumping so hard, I was in a great deal of pain.

"Unfortunately, I do not have the equipment necessary to take an x-ray, but I do not feel any protruding bones. I will have nurse Juana wrap them once you have showered and see that you have something for the pain. Sadly, it is the best I can do."

"Just make sure the baby is okay. That's all that matters to me."

"You are young and strong but do not believe that you are invincible. It will take time for your ribs to heal, and you must be careful not to reinsure them. I have instructed our housekeeper to prepare a room for you on the third floor."

"Thank you," I replied. "When will I be able to see the baby again?"

"After you have had something to eat and drink. It would be dangerous to force anything too fast. Your body has been severely depleted, and you will need to take things slow for the next few days. Rest assured that both you and the baby will be safe here until you are well enough to leave."

It felt marvelous as the warm water cascaded over my bruised and bloodied body, and it felt even better when I'd been able to get everything out of my hair. I combed it slowly as the doctor had instructed me to do. It was important that I take notice of anything that hadn't been there before our escape into the jungle.

After Nurse Juana had bandaged my ribs and given me a bottle of painkillers and a glass of water, she escorted me to my room and gave me a short, flowered housedress to wear. It was more like a robe so it would fit just about anyone.

Oh, how inviting the bed looked. I felt I could easily sleep for a week once I climbed underneath the covers but knew that could never happen until a great many things had been settled. I wanted to know where Agent Fielding had gone and when he would return. Now that we were back to a semblance of civilization our relationship would most certainly change, but what that meant was the least of my worries since he'd already decided that I needed to go home without the baby.

The kind doctor met me in the hallway outside my assigned room shortly after seven that evening. "This way," he instructed. "The housekeeper has prepared a small meal for us."

I followed him to a suite of rooms he used as a private residence. It wasn't fancy by any means, but the walls had been painted and there was carpet on the floor. He pulled out a chair so I could sit down at a table that had been prepared for two.

"I wish I had better accommodations to offer, but I gave up a more luxurious lifestyle when I decided to work for the cause."

"How long have you been doing this?" I asked as a woman brought bowls of warm broth with a little meat in it.

"Fifteen years. There is so little anyone can do to stop this dreadful epidemic, but my services are often needed. I try to do what I can."

"I'll never forget what you've done for the baby and me," I replied.

He looked at me from over the top of his spectacles. "This is a war we have very little chance of winning, unless people are willing to sacrifice for the greater good. I am only doing one small part of what needs to be done. The ones we should be thanking are people like Agent Fielding, who put their entire lives on hold, and who take personal risks few people would even consider. Why did you come from America to work with him?"

I felt a moment of panic. I knew instinctively that I could trust him, but letting out any personal information wasn't wise.

"I was given the opportunity to help, and I took it," I replied with a smile. "I wish there was more I could do."

"You saved a child's life. What more could anyone ask?"

We ate most of the small meal in silence. It seemed there was little we could talk about without divulging more than was necessary or prudent. I longed to ask him questions about his work, the kinds of people he met and what had prompted him to walk away from a lucrative business to live on the third floor of a rundown building in a very undesirable part of the city. But secrecy kept him alive, and I didn't want to do anything to jeopardize his unselfish work.

Nurse Juana walked into the room as we were finishing our meal. She smiled at me, but her whispered words were meant only for Dr. Perez. He listened intently, and then rose to his feet.

"I am sorry I cannot stay longer. A situation has arisen that demands my immediate attention. Nurse Juana will take you to see the baby. Do not be alarmed when you see him. We have put him under a light to help with the jaundice, and he is getting oxygen and fluid. It is just a precaution. He is breathing on his own quite well."

"He has taken a full ounce of formula, and is resting comfortably," Nurse Juana added as she stood by the side of my chair with her arms folded in front of her body.

"I don't know how I can ever repay you," I replied, not caring that tears were beginning to surface. "You've been so kind."

"We each have our part to play," Dr. Perez said. "But I must leave you now. I have instructed Nurse Juana to give you an IV to slowly help replace the fluid you have lost. You will be better able to care for the baby once you have had some rest."

"But I'm used to having him in my arms while I try to sleep."

"A necessity as well as a comfort, but things are different now that he is here. I have put him in a room with a connecting door."

I almost kissed him for his thoughtfulness but thought better of it. Then I followed him into the hallway and watched while he hurried down a flight of stairs without looking back.

Nurse Juana escorted me to the room where the baby was sleeping in a crib with clean clothing and a soft blanket. His eyes were closed, and I felt a moment of alarm as I realized that the doctor's warnings about his appearance had not been exaggerated.

He looked so tiny and helpless with an oxygen mask covering most of his face and tubes running into his arm. There was a bright light shining on him.

"Are you sure he's okay?" I asked Nurse Juana.

"He is doing very well," she replied. "I know it is hard to see him like this, but you must try not to worry. He will not be left alone, and by tomorrow everything will seem much brighter."

I touched the baby's arm. He twitched but didn't open his eyes.

"Please," Nurse Juana said. "You must do as the doctor ordered if you are to get well."

"But I feel perfectly fine," I assured her.

"You are still running on adrenaline, but your body will crash. It is best to be resting when that happens."

I knew she was right, but I fought leaving the baby's side.

"Your bed is just through that door. I promise to awaken you if there is a change in his condition."

I didn't touch the baby as I left his side but silently hoped that he could feel my presence. It was going to be a very long night, and I wasn't sure I could stop myself from checking on him, but Nurse Juana followed me into my sleeping quarters and slid the needle of an IV into my arm.

"Please do not worry about the baby. He is in good hands and will get the care he needs. Just try to sleep. Your body must be ready for whatever comes tomorrow."

The two backpacks had been left on the floor near the bed. Had I known what was going to happen first thing the next morning, I would have taken a moment to go through them. But exhaustion was stronger than curiosity, and since I knew I'd be able to hear the baby if he cried out during the night, I allowed myself the luxury of laying between clean sheets on a mattress that reminded me of a fluffy, white cloud.

A sedative must have been put into the first bag of my IV because I slept soundly, not hearing the baby or even dreaming. I awoke to a loud rapping on my bedroom door, and nearly tore the IV from my arm as my feet hit the cold tile. It took a moment or two before I realized where I was, and then I gripped the metal frame for support.

When I pulled the door open, a woman in a black dress was waiting for me with a letter on a silver tray and a brown paper package underneath one arm. Her presence in such austere surroundings surprised me.

"Agent Fielding sent these," she said in broken English.

"Thank you," I replied. "Is he here this morning?"

"I give you these. He explain everything."

I took both the bundle and the letter and closed the door behind her. This was most unusual. It had been over twelve hours since he'd slipped out of the examining room without saying anything to either Dr. Perez or me.

Pushing the stand back to the bed, I sat down on the edge of it and began fumbling with the covering on the package. My hands were incredibly stiff, as was every other part of my body, and the IV was getting in my way. Without a thought to the advisability of what I was doing, I carefully removed the needle from the inside of my elbow. Watching it withdraw from my skin brought the nausea to my throat, but I needed the freedom to move around at will. Something was incredibly wrong. I might not be Agent Fielding's favorite person, but I felt certain that he would not leave without saying goodbye - unless something unforeseen had arisen.

The package contained a yellow sundress that had obviously been worn before, a light gray jacket with three-quarter length sleeves, sandals that wrapped around the ankles, a blonde wig and a pair of sunglasses. It had to be for a disguise, but why did he feel I needed to completely change my appearance? I took a deep breath in hopes of steadying my nerves. The costume and what it might represent was disturbing, but jumping to conclusions prematurely was useless.

The note began without even a simple salutation. *"I'm leaving the country tonight and will not see you again. Mendoza knows that only one person in our party did not survive. That puts you in more danger than I had anticipated. I hope you're professional enough to walk away and not look back.*

"The director will meet you at the American Embassy at ten to arrange for transport out of the country. Forget your heart. It will only get you into more trouble. Take only your papers with you."

That was it! Unemotional and detached! He'd said nothing about the baby, not even if Mendoza believed he was still alive. Well, Agent Fielding might be able to live without looking back, but I couldn't. Maria's son would not become another casualty. I'd given her my solemn promise. No one else might understand why I felt as I did, but God knew, and he would prepare a way for our delivery.

I crumpled the paper in my hand. It was almost eight. I didn't have a plan and there was very little time to devise one, but I would not leave the baby behind, even if it meant I had to go rogue. I wasn't entirely sure what that meant for me in my present circumstances, except I would be on my own without any help from either government, but Maria's son deserved a chance.

Perhaps I was a little naïve when it came to bureaucracy, but my faith was in God, not man, and I believed that he would show me the way. So after kneeling and thanking my Maker for his many blessings and promising to be ready to act when guidance came, I slipped into the dress and went into the bathroom to put the wig on. There were three sewn-in combs to keep it in place, and it made me look like an entirely different person.

Once the sandals were on my feet, I unzipped the bag I had brought from the hacienda and dumped its contents onto the floor. It was too damp and grimy to be set on the bed, and there were only a few things I needed anyway - the passport I had been given, the small amount of American currency I had left, and Tess's diary. I couldn't leave that behind, although I doubted I would be able to read any more of it since it had been completely submerged in the water when I'd crossed the river the day before.

I contemplated taking the things Maria had prepared for the baby but knew that if I truly believed Heavenly Father was helping me, I needed more than simple faith. So I left everything else where it was in the backpack Agent Fielding had carried, including the letters Maria had written. It was dry and should be perfectly safe.

But I couldn't leave without seeing the baby again, so I went through the connecting door to his crib. He was sleeping soundly, and tears filled my eyes as I watched as his tiny chest move up and down. He was safe now and needed more time to recover, so I pushed back the urge to snatch him from his bed and take my chances. I loved him too much to risk his life. I would find my way back to the clinic to get him.

Since there was little time left, I bent down and kissed the top of his head. He really was the most beautiful baby ever. Now that he'd been cleaned up, and I could see him in the light of day, his skin was almost the color of light, burnished copper, but then Maria had been light-skinned. I didn't want to think about his father's dark, swarthy complexion. That man would not rest until all of us were dead. I left the baby sleeping and hurried down two flights of stairs to find the kind doctor.

He was waiting for me in his office.

"You read your letter," he said. "I had one also. Since there is not much time, I will drive you to the embassy myself."

"Thank you," I replied, rubbing my hands briskly together. It was too early to involve him in plans that had yet to be formulated, but I needed him to know that I wasn't simply going to disappear. "I will be back for the baby. Please keep him safe until then."

"He will be safe here," Dr. Perez promised. "Those of us fighting this seemingly unstoppable war must stick together. However small or large the sacrifice, it is duly noted in heaven. I saw how much you love the baby. I lost my own wife and child. We need to protect the innocent."

I wanted to reply, but he didn't give me the chance. He led me down a short hallway and through an outside door into a back alley that was strewn with trash and stray animals. I thought I saw a torn curtain at a window above my head move but couldn't be certain.

"People here do not live an easy life, but most of them are honest and hardworking when jobs are available," he said as he opened the door to a late model car so I could climb in. "That is why I chose to open a practice here. People with money can afford the medical attention they need."

I watched as he walked in front of the car on his way to the driver's seat. I didn't want to be heading into the unknown again, but there was really nothing I could do, unless I took the baby from the clinic and tried to disappear on my own. That thought was totally laughable since it was doubtful I would make it out of the city on my own and remaining at the clinic would only jeopardize what Dr. Perez was trying to do.

"I'm sorry about your wife and child," I told him as he pulled to the end of the alley and looked both ways before driving onto the street.

"They were in the wrong place at the wrong time," he replied. "It does not matter where one lives. The battle between good and evil will continue as long as there are men who value money and power more than life. I chose to go where I could do the most good."

He took a series of back roads until we were on a freeway with hundreds of other people heading towards the heart of the city. The difference between the wealthy and poor had never been more apparent, and once again, I wondered why Dr. Perez had chosen the kind of life he was living when it was obvious he had been used to more gracious living. The silver tray the letter from Agent Fielding had been delivered on was not the only sign of luxury I had seen at the clinic.

"Is there a way I can contact you?" I asked as the miles we drove took me farther away from the precious gift I had left behind. My hands were clutched tightly together in my lap, and I wanted nothing more than to demand that we return to the clinic and get the baby. My faith was taking a horrid beating, and I wasn't sure I could follow thorough with what was expected of me.

"I am afraid not, but I do have someone there who can get a message to me if it is necessary. Her name is Maria too. She lived in the apartment building where my wife and I used to reside and has been at the embassy for many years. She also lost someone she loved."

"How did your wife and child die?" I asked, hoping my question was not too personal or impudent since we had just met.

He looked over at me and smiled, but his eyes were filled with tears. "They were hit by a member of the Mendoza cartel while driving to pick up presents for my son's third birthday party. He was trying to escape from the authorities. It was the most dreadful day of my life. I knew I could not go back to the home we had shared, so I opened a clinic in the worst part of the city hoping to show God that I was not angry for having them taken away from me."

"That was a very selfless thing to do."

"It was my only means of survival. I could no longer walk the streets where it had happened and knew it was what my wife would want. She was the most courageous and loving woman in the world."

I looked away from him as moisture filled my own eyes. Family was the most important thing in the world to me as well. Was I doing what was right for mine by defying Agent Fielding's recommendation that I walk away? Bringing the child of a powerful drug lord to the United States would do more than just disrupt my life. I could be placing everyone I loved in unnecessary danger. Suddenly, I felt more powerless than I had in the middle of the jungle. My decision could not be made lightly, despite the promise I had given to a dying friend.

Dr. Perez must have noticed my change in countenance.

"Please do not worry about the baby. Whatever happens, I will do my best to see that he is properly cared for. He will not be returned to his father, but for now, we must follow orders. It is imperative that you leave my country just as Agent Fielding has done."

"I'm not sure I can do that," I replied as the fear inside erupted like a once-dormant volcano. "I know you mean well, Dr. Perez, but there is no one here who can keep the baby safe if Mendoza decides to come after him."

"You must not concern yourself with that right now. My orders were explicit - deliver you to the United States Embassy. What happens from there is up to both of our governments."

"And you don't think they will help me get the baby out of the country?"

"I think it would require a miracle. While the life of one child is important, sacrifices must be made. You are young. You will understand more as you get older. Go home. Get married. Raise babies of your own. Try to forget what happened here. It is the only thing that will bring comfort."

I wasn't convinced, but without a viable plan, it was best to remain silent. The people I'd met had relinquished so much personal freedom already, and it wasn't fair to involve them in something that would not further their cause. They needed to remain as inconspicuous as possible.

When we arrived at the embassy, I bid him a brief farewell and exited the car. My jaw was locked as I walked towards the gate without looking back. I was on my own, and in a very real way, so was Maria's baby. I had no doubt that there were people in Colombia who would take him in and try to keep him away from Mendoza, but I couldn't simply forget the promise I had made to his mother.

I held Tess's passport up to a man in uniform who sat behind a barred, glass window in a concrete booth and repeated what Dr. Perez had told me to say. I was an American citizen seeking asylum at the embassy. He told me to back away from the window and wait on the sidewalk while he gained permission for the gate to be opened.

Being left in the open on a street with numerous people passing by and no discernible means of defending myself made my heart race, but it also gave me a few moments to think. My chosen career meant I would never be truly safe from people who broke the law and didn't want to be held accountable. My parents understood that. It was one of the reasons they had tried so hard to get me to change my mind and pursue something else. Would bringing a baby into their lives really change anything if Mendoza didn't know where we were? Certainly he had more pressing things to do than look for me since there was nothing I could do to hurt him, and the baby meant less than nothing to him. He'd ordered Fernando to kill his mother before he was even born.

While I stood in the damp, morning air with my brow knit in confusion and my teeth biting down on my bottom lip, the heavy, iron gate creaked open, and a man with a rifle in his hands escorted me to a small room where a uniformed woman told me to put the bag that held the passport, the money and the diary on the table and raise my arms. She ran her hands quickly over my body and then emptied the few contents from the bag.

"I am sorry this is necessary, but we cannot have weapons smuggled into the embassy."

Her face showed no emotion, and I knew she was simply doing her job, but I had never been on the receiving end of a pat-down before. It was humiliating emotionally and uncomfortable physically since my ribs still throbbed and every other part of my body was bruised, scratched and tender. When she had finished, she led me along a sidewalk lined with low-growing shrubs and beautiful, scented flowers. I noticed that several guards stood along the parameter of the property. They were also armed, and I knew they were well-trained and would not miss their mark if the embassy came under attack.

A short flight of steps led up to the elaborately-carved, wood doors of a three-story, white stucco building with a gleaming, metal roof. The windows were large with balconies, bars and heavy draperies. She stood aside when a man wearing a dark suit and an earpiece pulled them open for us.

"Thank you," he said. "I'll take it from here."

She nodded her head and disappeared through one of the doors on the ground level while he led me up a marble staircase, through several other sets of doors and over a large symbol of the United States Government that had been etched into the floor. I was safe now, but that didn't bring much comfort. Armed men were stationed at intervals along the hallways, and none of them spoke to us. Their job was to protect, not provide an atmosphere of familiarity and home.

We came at last to a single door. This too was drawn open, but not until an invitation to enter had been given.

"The woman you requested to see is here," the agent accompanying me said to a man sitting behind the desk. On either side of him stood men wearing dark suits. They were strong and muscular, with regulation haircuts and eyes that missed nothing. I would recognize fellow agents anywhere - as long as they were not undercover and very good at their job like the reluctant operative who had delivered me from the dangers of the jungle.

"My name is Director Stevens. I'm head of the DEA here in Colombia. I'm sorry our movements have to be so cautious and surreptitious, but we couldn't take any chances. Agent Fielding gave me a complete report last night. He said you acted admirably, despite the way the mission was compromised."

I shook the hand he extended without saying anything. Agent Fielding must have told him about my part in allowing Mendoza to escape. I would not be receiving any accolades from him.

"Please sit down, Agent Sinclair," he instructed. "There are a few things we need to discuss."

"Yes, sir," I replied, easing myself into the nearest chair with the brightly-colored, cloth bag - that had a strap so it could be worn over the shoulder - clutched security in my hands. Thankfully, it had been returned to me, along with everything I had brought from the clinic.

I knew what was coming next, and his questions brought out the entirety of my time at the compound and in the jungle. I answered them with every detail I could remember. He nodded his head at times and took notes, but he never smiled, and the men stationed on each side of him didn't move. They just stood silently with their feet planted parallel to their shoulders and their hands clasped together in front of their bodies.

After what seemed an eternity of delving into both sad and traumatic remembrances that brought occasional bursts of emotion I couldn't hide, Director Stevens was ready to dismiss me. He told me that he appreciated the work I had done and had already been in touch with my boss who concurred that getting me out of the country on the first available flight was best for both agencies. I was to remain at the embassy until arrangements could be made, but I couldn't just walk out of his office as if I'd completed a routine mission, albeit one that could have gone much more smoothly had I been given the information I needed.

He seemed to know everything about Maria's affair with Carlos Mendoza and the child it had produced, but what he didn't know was how strongly I felt about the baby, and my great desire to take him home with me.

I would never reveal the fact that Agent Fielding and Agent Gonzales had been more than partners, but I was still having trouble understanding how he could walk away from what had happened in the jungle without looking back. That might be the mark of a good agent, but to me, it made him a very insensitive man.

"What is going to happen to Maria's baby?" I asked.

Director Stevens frowned. "This was your first undercover assignment, Agent Sinclair, so I do not expect you to understand how things work. Suffice it to say that the child will be cared for. Agent Gonzales knew there were risks when she went undercover, but no one forced her to get into bed with Mendoza. She did that of her own volition. It's unfortunate that liaison led to the birth of a child, but from what Agent Fielding told me, there is little reason to believe the child will survive for long, despite all you did to protect him."

My fury with the man who had brought us out of the jungle, only to leave us at the mercy of a government who had no desire to help, rose to the surface again with such intensity that it almost frightened me. I tried with all the willpower I possessed not to raise my voice or glare at the man who was sitting behind his desk looking so smug and sure of himself. I couldn't afford to be insolent or disrespectful, but I would not leave until he knew just how much I loved the baby. I was the only mother he had known during his brief life.

"I understand that certain lines were crossed, Director Stevens, but there is an innocent baby to consider. I've been with him since the moment he was born, and while his condition is tenuous, the doctor and his staff have done some incredible things the past twelve hours. He's much more responsive, and there's every indication that he will make a full recovery. I know there could be latent complications associated with his birth, but I want to be around to watch him grow up."

His impatience with my impertinence was instantaneous. "Impossible!" he almost roared. "My orders are to see you on the first plane home. Nothing will stop that from happening."

"But I want to take him with me and raise him as my own child."

"I'm afraid that's out of the question, Agent Sinclair. That baby is a Colombian citizen, not to mention the son of one of the most feared drug lords in the country. He will not be allowed to leave the country."

"But I made a promise to his mother. She did not want to see him reunited with his father. I can give him a home and a family away from what he might have to face here. All children should be allowed to have love and security, regardless of who their father is."

He leaned back in his chair, and I suddenly knew that I was on the verge of receiving a severe reprimand for actions unbecoming a federal agent when speaking to a superior.

"You give a passionate speech, Agent Sinclair, but Mendoza has people everywhere, and you have a target on your back as well. He could easily find out where the baby has been taken and dispose of you at the same time."

"I'm prepared to deal with that," I told him. "I love that baby with all my heart and vowed to Maria on her deathbed that I'd take him back to America and raise him as my own. She wanted him as far away from Mendoza as possible."

The way his eyes narrowed let me know that he was having trouble not laughing in my face, but he wasn't my boss, and this was the only chance I had to state my case.

"I know what I'm asking is highly irregular, sir," I hurried on before he had time to shut me down again. "But Mendoza is a monster! He gave orders for all of us to be killed. Does that sound like a man who should be allowed even the most remote chance of finding his child? I'm not deluding myself about the risks involved. If Mendoza ever discovers what really happened, he'll do everything in his power to exact his revenge."

Somewhere during my tirade, I had moved closer to his desk until I was almost on the edge of my chair, but I didn't move back. I couldn't, not until he told me that hell would freeze over before my wish was even considered. Then, I'd just have to find another way.

"I don't suppose you have anything to support what you've told me."

A burst of relief caused my heart to race, but I managed to pull my thoughts together enough to make a coherent reply. "Other than what she asked me in person, she said she'd written everything in a letter before we left the compound. She knew she might not make it and wanted to make sure her son would be loved and cherished if she wasn't allowed to raise him herself."

"And where is this letter?"

"In a backpack at the clinic. I could bring it to you."

"That's out of the question. We can't compromise the clinic's existence. It's too important to our operations here. Everything you brought with you is to be destroyed."

My hopeful respite disappeared, and I sank back in my chair. This couldn't be happening. I would never see Maria's baby again. He would never know anything about his biological mother, or the mother who had loved him from the first moment she held him. He would only know that everyone who really cared had left him alone to fend for himself, and he wasn't even five days-old yet.

"Don't look so stricken, Agent Sinclair," Director Stevens' said. "It's obvious that you care about this child."

"I do, sir. I would do anything to protect him."

"Even if it means walking away? I know Agent Fielding has already told you to leave this situation alone."

"Yes, he did," I admitted. "But he also told me what happens in cases like this. Maria was willing to leave the compound so he could be born free, and she killed Fernando after Mendoza had shot her to protect us. She died a tragic and painful death, and her body was left in the jungle to be eaten by wild animals. She never complained or blamed anyone for her fate. She accepted the consequences of her actions and was true to her oath to the very end. She died as a hero so others could live. How can I not fight to see that her only request be granted?"

I took a quick breath but hurried on before he could interrupt me. "There are only a handful of people who know the baby survived, and not one of them would wish him any harm. If he is put into an orphanage, he will become a number and never know the kind of love I can give him. And if by some miracle a home is ever found for him here, there will be the constant worry that someone associated with Mendoza will discover who and where he is. That means certain death for both him and the family who has taken him in.

"What I propose might be difficult to accomplish, but it's what Maria was willing to die for, and it is in the best interest of her son. He could have died at any time during our journey, but he chose to live. That kind of strength and will needs to be rewarded. I'm not afraid to take him home and love him, regardless of what the future might bring. She gave me a most precious gift, and I gave her the promise that I would see it fulfilled."

I sank back too emotionally drained to say anything more. I no longer cared if I was perceived as being unprofessional or insubordinate. Maria's son deserved a fighting chance.

He just sat there and looked at me for the longest time. He had every right to tell Assistant Director Bridges what I had done. That could mean dismissal from the FBI for me, but I'd come to Colombia as a favor to the DEA without the proper training or the information I needed to be successful. The least Director Stevens could do was listen to me.

"I am not an unreasonable man," he finally said. "I feel the depth of your devotion to the child, but what you are proposing is both unethical and illegal."

"Perhaps, but a mother's dying wishes should be considered," I interjected. "If he was older, he would be placed in protective custody so his father could not harm him. That's all I'm asking to do. It would cost the government nothing. I would assume every responsibility."

"You are very young, Agent Sinclair," he said. "And while I applaud your loyalty to Maria and her son, I'm not sure I can grant your wish. However, I have two sons of my own and would hate to think that any man in my position would risk their fate if there was another alternative. Why don't you wait in the library while I make a few inquiries. I'm not going to make any promise because it might already be out of my hands."

"Thank you, sir," I said as I rose to my feet. My knees were wobbly and I felt sick to my stomach, but I managed to make it out of his office without collapsing. I couldn't believe that he was seriously considering my request. It was just another manifestation that God truly was in charge. If Maria's son was meant to come home with me, it would happen. Not everyone was as indifferent to our plight as the man who had led us out of the jungle.

The library at the Embassy wasn't nearly as ornate, or as well-stocked, as the one at the compound, but there was a fire burning behind an iron grate, computers sitting on tables and chairs with reading lamps. My mind was too consumed with worries to take more than a cursory look at anything. Director Stevens could have dismissed my wishes as utter foolishness, but he hadn't. I wasn't bold enough to think that my impassioned speech had changed his mind. His job was to make difficult decisions, not please an inexperienced agent who had messed up his one chance at bringing a wanted drug lord and terrorist into custody. Still, something had made him reconsider his original stance.

I suddenly wished I had asked him about Isabel and Luis. Despite his job, he appeared to care a great deal about children. Were they still at the compound? Had they been flown into Bogotá or taken to one of their father's other compounds? Was the sly Alma still watching their every move? They were too young to understand what had happened, and too frightened of the adults in their lives to ask any questions. They would be heartbroken if they found out what had happened to Maria, and they would believe I had voluntarily deserted them just like everyone else who had offered the least bit of love and compassion. But there was one thing they would never know—the existence of their little half-brother.

"So many innocent lives have been needlessly destroyed," I thought as sat in a chair near a window and looked through the black, iron bars into a gray and somber sky. Like the beautiful children in the village below the compound, Luis and Isabel were blameless of any involvement in the cocaine industry, and yet they were paying an incalculable cost for the lives their parents were leading. They needed to be protected just like Maria's baby, but there was nothing I could do to help any of them. I hated to think of my former charges being with Alma. I had never liked, nor trusted, her. Her loyalty to Mendoza was apparent, and she knew everything that went on in that house.

Her name had only been mentioned in passing during our entire interview. Perhaps we were all dismissing her too lightly. Mendoza would never have left the children and staff under her sole direction if he didn't trust her implicitly. He would also need someone who could destroy any information left behind that might disclose his hiding place while he regrouped.

The more I thought about it, the more certain I was that Alma was far more involved in what went on in that house than anyone knew. She appeared to have complete freedom and seemed to materialize everywhere. I knew she listened at the doors. I'd heard her soft footsteps in the hallway during both the day and the night. She would be the perfect accomplice for Mendoza. She intimidated everyone around her and never let anything slip. She might even have been the one who disclosed Maria's real identity. If she knew that much, she may also have known about the brief indiscretion between Maria and Agent Fielding.

I wasn't sure if I was just grasping for straws that might help my present situation, but when I talked to Director Sevens again I would relay my observations and suspicions about the illusive, intimidating and frightening Alma. Nothing about her place at the compound made sense, unless we were all missing something important. At the very least, she held the key to where Luis and Isabel were. I would rest much more comfortably if I knew they were still okay, and that Alma was in a place where she could no longer torment them.

Unable to remain sitting for any longer, I paced the library while my mind jumped from topic to topic like a kangaroo with free range of the outback. I wanted to be able to accept whatever decisions were made regarding Maria's son, Mendoza's children, and the disruption that could possibly come to my family's life if my wants were realized. But I understood that while faith with works could move mountains, nothing that I was worrying about would change without some kind of mortal intervention. In a few hours, I would be on a plane heading for home, and the past would be lost to me forever.

The man who had escorted me to both Director Stevens' office and the library finally opened the door and stuck his head inside the room.

"Is there word?" I asked him.

"Not yet," he replied, giving me a very grave look. "I just came to see if you'd like some tea or coffee while you wait."

"Some water, please," I responded, remembering the doctor's orders to rehydrate. I might have asked for something to eat since breakfast had not been offered to me at the clinic, but I wasn't sure my stomach would cooperate. It seemed to be lurching everywhere.

"I'll be back in a few minutes. Try not to worry. The director is a good man."

I smiled my thanks. He might well be a very good man, but what I was asking could jeopardize his position, not only with the agency, but also with two governments. He could even end up in prison. I doubted he would be willing to risk that when he had a family of his own to consider.

The man returned a short time later with the promised water, but he'd added some cold meat, fresh fruit and crackers to the tray.

"It's almost two, and I thought you might be hungry."

"Thank you," I told him. "I haven't had much to eat the past few days."

He set the tray down on a table that had a bouquet of fresh flowers in the center. "That's understandable. I was with Agent Fielding when he gave his report. He was impressed with the way you handled yourself - this being your first field assignment and all."

I looked at him with surprise. "I got the impression he blamed me for everything that went wrong."

"Sam can be a hard-ass, but it's only because he believes so strongly in what he's doing. If you stay on the job long enough, you'll have plenty of disappointing moments that can make you act a little uncivilized at times. Try not to judge him too harshly."

"I am trying to be fair, but it's all so complicated. How well do you know each other?"

"We've worked a few cases together, but I'm a desk-jockey while he likes being in the field. Nonetheless, I'm well acquainted with Mendoza and his operations. You can rest assured that we won't give up until he's behind bars."

I tried to eat a few bites of fruit and cheese after he had gone, but my mind kept swirling. If Agent Fielding had not been totally dissatisfied with the way I'd conducted myself why couldn't he be a little more understanding when it came to Maria's son? It's not like he would have to see either of us again, and his support of my plan would have gone a long way in convincing Director Stevens that I was not some newbie nutcase who had lost sight of what she had been sent to do.

Fortunately for my sanity, it wasn't long until the door opened again, and I was led back to Director Stevens' office. He wasn't smiling when he motioned for me to enter, but then anyone involved in the game of espionage couldn't afford to get personally involved. It was too easy to make mistakes. My own experience over the past few days had proven that.

The two men who had been in the room with him when I first arrived were no longer there.

"Agent Sinclair, thank you for your patience," he said as I resumed my place in the chair I had occupied earlier. "I do have some limited information."

As much as I wanted to hear what he had to say, he needed to know what I had been thinking first. I wasn't some civilian they'd picked up off the street. I was an FBI agent who had been gifted with the ability to see relationships others might miss. If I'd had the information I needed going in, I might have been able to prove my worth instead of botching almost everything.

"There's something I need to tell you, sir, before my attention becomes divided again."

He raised his eyebrow, but gestured for me to continue. So I told him about Alma, and what I had observed and felt during the relatively short time I'd been at the compound. How she was present everywhere, and how Mendoza seemed to defer to her more than he would to an actual servant. He listened attentively, and after my narrative, he asked me to describe her.

"Physically," I began. "She was a woman who could easily fade into the background. She was a little taller than me, maybe five-feet eight, with black hair pulled severely back from her face and coiled at the nape of her neck. It was a plain face, rather angular, nothing distinctive except three moles along her right jaw. Her eyes reminded me of a reptile; cold, small and dark."

"How old was she?"

"That's hard to say. Appearances can be deceiving, but she had to be in her late forties or even her fifties. She wasn't young, but she wasn't old either."

"Would you recognize her if you saw her again?"

"Without a doubt! I saw her several times, although no one, except for Mendoza, ever dared to look directly at her."

Director Stevens fingered through the stack of folders on his desk until he came to one that was near the bottom. He opened it and then extended a photo in my direction.

"Is the lady you described in this photo? I know she would have aged. That picture was taken over thirty years ago."

I took it in my hands. There were six people in the photo who looked like they had to be related, most likely parents and their children, two boys and two girls. I studied it carefully and ruled out the mother figure immediately. She was too old to be the Alma I had met at the compound, but when I looked into the face of the oldest daughter, I gasped.

"That's her," I exclaimed as the now familiar coldness of fear snaked its way inward.

"You're sure?" the director asked. "Take another look to be certain."

I held the picture up to the light and studied it more closely before looking at him again. "I could never forget those eyes, and if you look closely, you can see the three moles. Who is she?"

"Mendoza's oldest sister. She was ten when Carlos was born, and she was supposed to have died with the rest of the family in a boating accident not long after that photo was taken."

I looked down at the picture in my hands again, doing mental calculations. The youngest child must have been Carlos when he was a boy of two or three, not yet distinguishable from the masses. I would never have picked him out, but his sister! When one had seen eyes as cold as hers, it was never forgotten.

"Is the smallest boy Mendoza?" I asked.

"From what we've been able to establish, yes. He was at home at the time of the accident and went to live with an uncle on his mother's side that was quite well-known in the underworld. We assume that's where he honed his skills and made his contacts."

"What happened to the uncle?"

"Killed in a raid. Mendoza must have taken over his entire operation when he was no more than a teenager."

"He said his father was a poor man."

"That's highly unlikely, but who knows what goes on in the mind of a criminal. Perhaps he simply wanted to aggrandize himself to impress you. He's been known to have quite the way with women."

"Not with me," I said with an acidic laugh. "I found him reprehensible, but that doesn't explain what happened to Alma. Surely, she would have gone to live with the uncle too, if she'd survived."

"Her named wasn't Alma. It was Catherine, and this is the first time we've learned anything that would indicate she was still alive. A fifth body was never recovered, but the lake the boat capsized in was deep and large. The authorities assumed that the body had simply submerged too far to be found since Mendoza was the only child found at home. The technology we have today didn't exist back then, and I'm sure that after the initial search she was simply forgotten. A young girl would hardly seem like a threat to anyone, and she was included at the service that was held for the rest of the family."

"Bt she obviously survived."

"It could be that she was with another relative or a family friend. She may even have managed to make it to shore undetected after the boat turned over. The cartels are notorious for deception, and they would plan for every possibility, even during a short, family vacation. If they didn't, they wouldn't be in business for long. Do you have any idea where she might be now?"

"I don't think she ever left the compound. Since the authorities had no idea who she was, she could remain hidden in plain sight indefinitely. And no one who works there would give her away, even if they knew her identity. She would kill them herself before being taken into custody. What will happen to Isabel and Luis if she's apprehended?"

"I know you don't like the idea of children being put into the system, but sometimes there are no alternatives. You can't rescue everyone, Agent Sinclair. Still, you can rest assured that we'll act on the information you've supplied with haste before Mendoza has time to move anyone to a safer location. You've got good instincts, not even Agent Fielding picked up on their possible connection. We could use more people like you in the DEA; should you ever decide to leave the FBI. But there's still a baby whose fate needs to be decided. Are you still determined to raise him?"

"More than ever, sir," I said as goose bumps sent cold rivulets of trepidation up and down my spine.

"Then you'll be pleased to know that I've made a few discreet queries without revealing any of the specifics. It may be that political asylum is an option—as long as no one discovers his identity first. That could unleash a tidal wave I would never be able to stop."

"Oh, sir," I replied. "I don't know what to say."

"It's a little soon to start arranging for his transport. This is all subject to proof of what his mother's wishes really were and his condition in making such a long journey when he might be too ill to leave the clinic. But Agent Gonzales was a member of this team, and that takes precedence over a lot of different mandates. I hope you understand the risk I'm taking, but I don't want to be held responsible if something should happen to the child. Have you actually read the note you told me about?"

"No, sir," I replied. "I held it in my hands, and we talked at great length about her desires for her son's future. I'm sure Agent Fielding overheard part of our conversations."

"That's a moot point since he isn't here. All he said about the baby was that he hoped he'd be okay. He was more concerned with seeing you back on American soil as soon as it could be arranged."

"Then I don't know what to do, sir," I replied. "You said that the things I left behind were going to be destroyed."

"That might have been a little premature. We do try to clean up so there will be no surprises, but a direct order has not been issued yet. I'll see what I can do about having the note delivered to the embassy, but you must understand that nothing we've talked about in this room can ever be repeated. That's why we're alone now. If we do get proof, and you take him out of the country, this office will not be held accountable for anything that happens in the future. You will be acting strictly on your own volition. Director Bridges will be notified of the situation, but what he decides to do about it from his end is out of my jurisdiction. Are we clear?"

"Completely," I replied as tears of joy and relief tickled the end of my nose. He had given me than just hope. Political asylum couldn't be granted to anyone in need. It was done all the time.

"There are still many legalities to circumvent, and we have other more pressing matters to deal with right now. The Colombian government wants to see Mendoza put away as much as we do, but if they find out he has another child, they could use that as leverage."

I shuddered at the implications. Mendoza didn't care what happened to his son, and he'd already put a price on my head.

"Try not to concern yourself with things that have not happened yet, Agent Sinclair. I will take care of this matter personally and will only involve people I know I can trust. Now, leave me to my work. I'll contact you again when I have more information."

I was given a room on the top floor of the consulate. It was light and cheerful, but I was too preoccupied with the baby's safety and whether or not Director Stevens could accomplish what needed to be done to care much about my physical surroundings. I mainly sat on the edge of the bed or in a lime green chair that faced a white wall with a crucifix on it. I stayed away from the window. Even though I knew I was safe within the high walls that were guarded on every side, I was fearful that someone with evil intents would discover my presence and betray it.

My head was literally spinning. How could I keep the entirety of this secret from my family and closest friends if Director Stevens followed through on granting the baby political asylum? I could tell acquaintances that I'd been fortunate in adopting an infant who had lost his parents while I'd been in South America on business, but my family had the right to know how he had come into my life, and the danger he brought with him. What I was still hoping to do had far-reaching consequences, and nothing about it was going to be easy.

The backpack arrived from the clinic in less than an hour. Nothing inside of it had been disturbed. I dug through the contents until I came to an envelope. Several pieces of paper had been folded together. The first one looked like the document necessary to begin generating paperwork that would give my baby asylum in the United States. It had been hastily written, but was still easily readable.

My baby! It seemed odd referring to him as such, but in truth, I'd felt that way from the moment I knew Maria would not be around to raise him. What a glorious example of hope, faith and courage she had been to me. I might not be able to relate facts and specifics about her life, but the child I raised would know every amazing quality she possessed.

"We are leaving the compound. It is doubtful I will survive the journey. If my son should live, I want him to be raised by the agent who is helping me escape from a life of torture and despair. His father must never find him. That is my dying wish." Maria's signature was hastily scribbled at the bottom. But it was the postscript that made my unease return. *"He is to be named Samuel after the man who befriended me when there was no one else around who could."*

The second sheet of paper contained personal information and must have been written before she decided to leave with us. She had known her impending death was near, regardless of what she did, and wanted to be prepared.

"My name is Maria Elizabeth Gonzales, and I was born on April 23, 1976 in Villavincencio, Colombia to Pedro and Magdalena Sente Gonzales. I am a DEA operative assigned to the Mendoza case. I violated the oath I had taken by becoming involved with Carlos, but my baby should not be punished for my sins. Despite my less than honorable actions, I have never been disloyal to my oath. If this letter is found, it means I have not survived. Carlos has vowed to have me killed for betraying him, but it is my hope that he will allow my child to survive. I am O negative and there are no inherited family illnesses that I am aware of. Carlos is an evil man who has many weaknesses and perversions. He should never raise any child. I have been unable to find out anything about his family, only that his blood type is the same as mine. I find that quite ironic."

That was where it stopped. Either she had been interrupted or felt she had time to finish it later. I didn't know whom she thought would acknowledge its existence. Perhaps Rosa had become her friend as I had.

I lay back on the bed and watched specks of sunlight dance across the ceiling. Agent Fielding needed to know what she had written about her son's name, if only to bring a sense of closure, but he was gone now, and it was doubtful our paths would ever cross again.

My heart constricted with pain as I pictured that tiny, innocent baby lying in his crib at the clinic with oxygen running into his lungs, fluid being forced into his veins, and a light hanging over his body. It would be inhumane to leave him behind, but that decision was out of my hands.

I took both letters with me when I went down to see Director Stevens.

"I assume you have what we need," he said, after I'd knocked on his partially open door.

"I have proof that she wanted her baby to be with me. I'm not sure what other information you're going to need."

He took the letters I offered, read through them quickly, and handed both of them it back to me.

"If the signatures match, I'd say it's as much proof as I need to proceed," he replied with a pucker to his brow. "But what we are doing is not without risks to more than just you and a baby. It will take a few key people to set things in motion, and while I trust everyone on staff at the embassy, that's not to say that someone might not divulge pertinent information that could get into the wrong hands. You must take the utmost care until you are on American soil again, and then I'm afraid you will be on your own."

"I can accept that, Director Stevens, and I can't thank you enough for what you're doing."

"Don't thank me yet. There is still much to be done. I have a man working on creating new passports and the documentation you'll need to get the baby past security. Any child born on Colombian soil becomes an automatic Colombian citizen, regardless of where his parents were born, but the only way our deception will work is if it appears that he belongs to you."

My stomach lurched. The baby could very easily have a native-born father who had either gone ahead or was staying behind, but the laws surrounding initial citizenship had not entered my mind. "Will that even be possible?" I asked.

"Let's hope so," he replied. "If they find anything wrong, you could end up in prison, and I don't have to tell you how hard it will be to get you out. South American Governments are not known for their leniency. People have been forced to stay here for years against their wishes. Some of them have even been executed, and there's often nothing we can do about it. Agent Fielding understood those risks. Are you sure you want to proceed?"

My heart was beating so rapidly I thought I might faint, but I knew what I had to do. "Yes, Director Stevens, I am willing to take the risk."

"Then it's decided. Our paperwork must be flawless, and we'll have to anticipate every contingency, but try to get some sleep. We should know a whole lot more in the morning. I'll have Agent Adams bring a light meal to your room. The fewer people who know you're here, the better it will be for all of us. I can't tell you how much we appreciate the information you brought."

I pushed back the thought of everything that could go wrong. I would worry about that when I was alone. "Then the information I supplied was helpful?"

"Oh, more than helpful, but it complicates things a great deal. I need you on a plane by tomorrow afternoon, with or without the baby, and I'm going to suggest to your superior that you be put in protective custody until Mendoza is captured. People are going to want to know who made the connection between him and his sister. When that happens, all hell will break loose. But try not to worry; we're doing everything we possibly can. Perhaps a delay in your leaving has been helpful. I'm sure Mendoza's men have been watching the airport closely."

I ate as much of the dinner that was provided, but it was impossible to sleep, although the bed was comfortable with its white sheets and lavender-scented pillows. My mind was racing with concerns about the future. The thought of motherhood excited me, but this wasn't exactly the way I had envisioned it happening, and my family's reaction might not be one of pleasure. I was bringing danger into their lives, something I'd promised would never happen when I joined the agency.

And what about my career? Being an FBI agent was my dream job, and I'd worked incredibly hard to get where I was. Would I be able to juggle motherhood and work? And what about Director Bridges? He certainly would not be pleased that one of his rookie agents had created such havoc within another agency by demanding to take a citizen from one country to another, even under the guise of political asylum. Would I even have a job to return to once I'd been debriefed?

Those concerns didn't include dating, marriage and providing even the meager necessities a child required. I was twenty-five years old, and the complications I was heaping on my shoulders were beginning to feel like a giant boulder instead of a tiny pebble. I had only been working for a few months, was still paying off student loans, and my government health insurance hadn't even kicked in yet.

But how could I not do what I'd promised? Tears formed as I thought about the Savior. He was the embodiment of love and sacrifice. He would never question the chance to save an innocent life, and he loved children most of all.

It had taken nothing short of many miracles to get the baby out of the jungle, and now I was harboring misgivings about God's ability to help me sort out the future. Was my faith really that weak and my resolve that flimsy? I had to be cautious and realistic, but I couldn't afford to spend an inordinate amount of time worrying about things that hadn't happened yet. If the baby was supposed to be with me, things would work out.

Chapter 15

I was on my feet as soon as the sun came in through my barred, bedroom window. There was no sense lying in bed any longer. I had fought for sleep to come for hours but had only managed to doze briefly a time or two. I'd spent the entire time the sun had been gone mulling over my decision to become an instant parent and the consequences it would bring, but anyway I looked at it, my life had already been irrevocably altered. Having the baby with me would be hard; not having him with me would be impossible.

The bathroom I was using had been stocked with the essentials so I'd been able to shower, brush my teeth and comb my hair, but I didn't even have a tube of lipstick or a mascara brush to help disguise my less than attractive appearance. The gashes that covered my face and most of my body were still red and most of them surrounded by bruises, but the swelling of the insect bites was less noticeable than it had been the day before.

I knew that the physical abrasions and cracked ribs would eventually heal—even though they might be a little difficult to explain—but I wasn't so sure about the emotional wounds. I would never forget the birth of Maria's baby, being hunted like an animal, or the people who'd risk their lives to help us. It was all part of the life I had chosen, but certainly not something for which I had been adequately prepared.

Dressing quickly was easy because there was no choice in what to wear. All I had was the yellow dress and light sweater I'd been given at the clinic. Not knowing how long it might be before I learned anything new, I opened the backpack that contained the items Maria had prepared for her son. It seemed almost sacrilegious to disturb anything, but I needed to know which things I might be able to get through customs. I couldn't afford to take any chances once we made it to the airport.

Circumstances had not allowed her to do much, and I felt a rush of emotion as I lifted a blanket that had obviously been constructed from pale, green sheets to my lips and kissed it. She must have learned how to crochet in her youth because it was edged in a delicate trim. There were several small animals made from scraps of fabric with buttons for eyes and felt for ears and an embroidered a set of pillowcases, along with a table runner.

At the bottom of the backpack was the bracelet and earrings she'd escaped with. Attached to them were a couple of diamond rings I'd missed seeing when I grabbed what I could at the processing hut. Each piece was gorgeous, but easily traceable and not worth the risk.

I put what I could in the shoulder bag, along with the American money. I wouldn't need the fake passport I'd arrived with if a new one was being prepared, but I was hesitant about leaving Tess's diary behind. There might be something more I could learn from it, so I ripped out the front page with her name on it. No one had seen it but me, and now there was nothing to connect it to her.

Shortly before eight, Agent Adams rapped lightly on my door. I jumped out of the chair I was sitting in while reading more of Tess's story. I was wearing the blonde wig and felt totally unlike myself.

"I've brought you some breakfast," he said, looking as if he'd had very little sleep. "Director Stevens wants you in his office at half past eight so there won't be time to eat much."

"Not a problem," I told him as I took the tray from his hands. "And thank you for your kindness."

"Just doing my job," he replied, backing a step away from me. "I hope you were able to get some sleep."

"A little," I said, realizing just how fragile I felt and how nice it would be to have someone sympathetic to talk to, but I had to stay focused. I'd consider the consequences of my actions more fully once I was back on American soil. "You look like you didn't get much sleep."

"It's been a long night. I'm sure you'll learn all about it during your meeting."

He turned abruptly and walked away. I pushed the door shut with my foot. It was going to be another long, emotional and scary day.

Director Stevens was seated in front of a stack of manila folders when I got to his office. I was carrying Maria's jewelry and the passport I'd already been given. I'd shredded the page into a dozen little pieces and flushed them down the toilet.

"Good morning, Agent Sinclair," he said, looking up from his work and pushing his glasses to the top of his head. He looked exhausted, and I wondered if he'd even been to bed. His suit was rumpled and his hair a mess. "Please sit down. There's much to discuss and not much time."

I took the chair across the desk from him where I'd sat the previous day.

"I know you're anxious to know what's happened, but I'm afraid the wheels of justice move rather slowly, especially in Colombia," be continued.

"No," my mind pleaded as my hand shot to my mouth, stopping the outcry of protest that was waiting there.

"Don't look so stricken, Agent Sinclair. Our first priority is getting both you and the baby out of the country today, provided he is well enough to travel. Your information yesterday has proven reliable. Alma Mendoza is still at the hacienda, and we'll be taking her into custody as soon as my men get to the compound."

"What about his children?" I asked.

"I've had no word on them, but once we have Alma in custody, Mendoza will know and start making connections. You must be gone before that happens. Word can never get out that you have been here, or it could jeopardize everything we have set in place. Despite my best efforts, your travel plans could be accessed and interpreted by someone with connections to the cartel. We haven't talked about the price on your head, but you can rest assured that his people will not be the only ones who might come looking for you."

"I'm ready," I told him.

"That's good because your new passports will be here within the hour, along with the paperwork necessary to prove that the baby is leaving the country legally. I have you booked on a flight to Dallas, Texas at two this afternoon. There will just be enough time to get you to the airport. You won't have anything except one carry on for the baby. I've been assured you'll have everything you need for the trip, but I can't caution you enough about keeping his identity hidden, even when you get home. I contacted Assistant Director Bridges earlier this morning; he'll take care of things on his end. He is the only person who must ever know what happened here. From this point on, the baby is your son and you, alone, will be responsible for his safety."

I hoped he didn't notice that my jaw was trembling. I wanted the baby with me more than anything, but my doubts and uncertainties still ran deep.

"Thank you," I told him. "I understand my responsibilities, and I'll be very careful. Maria's baby will be safe."

"That is the last time you can refer to him in the way, Agent Sinclair," he said, and his eyes were dark and determined. "Maria is no longer part of your life if you want to stay alive. One little slip could bring Mendoza's men to your doorstep. I am only allowing this to happen because I don't want the baby to become a pawn for anyone. His only chance, if we proceed, is your ability to maintain this cover for the rest of your life. If you can't do that, then we'll stop this arrangement immediately. I'm not in the habit of putting agents at risk, and I don't want to lose another one, even if she does not belong to my organization."

If I had any doubts, now was the time to voice them. Once I walked out of this room no one could ever know who the baby's parents really were, or how he had come into my life, unless I disclosed it.

"I can do it, sir," I told him. "I love the baby, and I would never do anything to bring him harm."

"That's good," he said. "Are you ready for your cover story?"

"Yes," I replied.

"You are Angela Bastif, widow of George Bentley Bastif, who was an American-born citizen of Colombian parentage and whom you met while you were both attending the University of Arizona. You were here visiting family with your small son, Rafael Bentley Bastif, when you were in an auto accident that your husband did not survive. That will help explain the cuts and bruises on your face—should anyone ask—and should give you enough sympathy not to be hassled. You're on your way home so your family can help you through this difficult time. Present the passports, and any other documents they ask for, but keep the baby hidden as much as you possibly can. According to his birth certificate, he is two months old. That won't fly if anyone gets a good look at him."

I swallowed back a fresh onslaught of fear. I had never realized how complex my request had been. No wonder Director Stevens had told me it would not happen the first time I asked.

"Anything else?"

"Yes," he promptly replied. "Remain alert and vigilant and do not take anything for granted. You will have no one there to back you up once the baby is handed over to you. If the authorities suspect anything, you will be taken to jail, possibly prison. If that happens, my hands are tied. Now, I have a few last-minute details to attend to. Go back to your room and be ready to leave when I send for you. The baby will be taken directly to the airport. I'll let you know when and where the switch will take place. You'll have to be very convincing if there's a hiccup in the plan."

"I can do it, but there is one more thing I need to ask."

He looked up at me and frowned.

"Maria brought some jewelry from the hacienda." I handed him the tissue I had put it in. "I'm not sure what I should do with it."

He looked down at the rings, the bracelet and earrings. They glimmered brilliantly in the light cast by the lamp on his desk. After a few moments of speculation, he spoke.

"I'd tell you to take them with you since Agent Gonzales' son most certainly deserves something after his mother's sacrifice, but they could lead Mendoza directly to you."

"That's what I thought, so I'll leave them with you."

"Just know that they will be put in a safe and used when necessary."

"Thank you, sir, for everything," I responded.

The phone rang, so I left his office without looking back, but by the time I was back in my room, my knees were trembling, so I fell to my knees and did not stop praying until a degree of calm filled my soul. With God's help, I could do what I had promised. I would keep the baby safe for now and always. My responsibility was not to deviate from the plan that was being laid out for us. I might be on my own in certain respects for the rest of my life, but I would never be totally alone. My faith assured me of that.

It was nearly ten-thirty when I was summoned back to Director Stevens' office and told it was time to leave. I took nothing but the small bag with me. True to his word, there were two passports waiting, along with the other paperwork that would be needed to clear security. I didn't question how many laws had been broken. Governments did illegal things all the time. I had just never imagined myself being part of them.

"When you get to the El Dorado International Airport, you will go directly to the women's restroom on the main floor by Avianca Airlines Check in. A woman will meet you there with the baby. You'll have to make sure no one is around when the switch is made. The woman will be wearing a yellow dress similar to yours and a blonde wig. Keep your head down as much as possible. There are security cameras everywhere. You will be flying into Dallas where you will pick up another ticket at United Airlines that has been reserved under the name of Erica Bowles. You must make a complete change in your appearance. From there you will fly into JFK. Assistant Director Bridges has assured me that someone will be there to meet you."

He rose from his chair and walked around the desk to shake my hand.

"It's been a pleasure meeting you, Agent Sinclair," he said, placing an envelope of money in my hands. "You'll need this, and I can't thank you enough for the job you've done. You have a very bright future. If you ever decide to leave the FBI, there will always be a job for you with the DEA. And remember, agents can have families and still do what needs to be done."

"Thank you again," I replied as I took the envelope without opening it. Whatever was left when I got home would be placed in a bank account for my son.

I was led through a back door, down a series of staircases, not unlike the ones at the hacienda, and put into the back seat of an unmarked car. The driver didn't speak to me, and I was glad. There was nothing to say anyway, so I settled back and tried to regulate my breathing. The memories of the past few days momentarily seemed like nothing but an incredibly bad dream.

When we arrived at the airport, I was dropped off at the entrance to building 1, with only my bag slung over my shoulder and a very uncomfortable wig on my head. Not exactly the way I had come, but it was far better than going home in a body bag or not at all. Every trace of Tess Tremaine had been left behind, except for her diary, and I made a solemn vow that if the chance ever came when it was safe enough to pursue more about her, I would take it.

I hurried inside to where thousands of people were milling around. The El Dorado International Airport was one of the 50 busiest airports in the world. It would be easy to get lost in the crowd if I did nothing to call attention to myself.

I found the women's restroom and went inside to wait. My mind was so preoccupied with what was supposed to happen that I was hardly aware of the other women and girls who came and went. A woman pushed a baby stroller into the room, and my heart immediately began to race, but it was only a false alarm because she left right after checking her flawless makeup in the mirror.

That was certainly something I didn't have to worry about. All the abrasions on my face made my cover story believable if no one asked any pointed questions, like why I had no luggage to check, and why I didn't appear to be the least bit concerned about my appearance.

I leaned against one of the sinks and folded my arms across my chest. How was I supposed to stay calm when things could go south at any moment? I had two forged passports, a fake driver's license from Arizona and a bunch of phony documents I hadn't even looked at. I also had a plane ticket and a boarding pass. What I didn't have was the baby who was the only reason such a complicated and potentially dangerous plan had been put together in the first place. I was still having trouble believing that Director Stevenson had willingly put his career on the line to do it. He owed me nothing since I'd accepted the assignment to come.

After chewing on my thumbnail for a few minutes, a lady wearing a yellow dress and a blonde wig, both quite similar to mine, walked into the restroom carrying an infant car seat in one hand. She had a large, tan diaper bag with blue piping around the edges slung over her shoulder. I literally felt my heart skip a beat when she gave me a warm smile.

"I guess yellow is today's color," she said in English, but with a very pronounced accent.

Cold chills of excitement and trepidation scurried down my arms and legs as a burst of emotion rushed to throat. Maria's baby— my baby—was being returned to me. She crossed the tile floor to a pullout changing table on the wall, put the transporter on the floor, unzipped the hood and pulled back the blue quilt and cream-colored receiving blanket just far enough that his face was exposed. I was standing a few feet away but could clearly see my little man asleep with a pacifier in his mouth. He looked so small and his skin was definitely tinged with yellow, but he was breathing normally and appeared to be quite content.

She looked around the room and when she was certain we were alone for the amount of time it would take to make the switch, she motioned for me to join her.

"Everything you need is in the baby's bag," she whispered. "I cannot believe what you are willing to do for a child."

"He's worth it," I responded.

She smiled again and touched my arm reassuringly. "Check his diaper and give me enough time to exit the building before leaving the restroom. And good luck, you're doing a very brave and courageous thing."

Oh, how I wanted to take the baby out and cover his sleeping face with hungry kisses, but the restroom was becoming busy again. We'd been lucky to find a moment alone. I waited with the baby still on the floor in his carrier while she stepped inside a stall and closed the door. When she emerged, the wig was gone and she was wearing leggings and a long top—an outfit that could easily be concealed underneath the sundress and top. She deftly slipped a plastic bag into the nearest trashcan, tapped her lips and then walked out of the room without glancing in my direction.

While she was making the change, I checked the diaper bag to see what it contained. Besides a stack of disposable diapers and a package of wipes, there were two cans of powdered formula, three bottles, an extra change of clothing for the baby, some diaper rash ointment, a rectal thermometer and another receiving blanket. I certainly hoped I had everything I would need for the long flight since there would be no chance to purchase anything once we were in the air.

But instead of pulling the baby out and checking his diaper as the woman had suggested, I decided to wait until I was closer to the gate from which my flight would depart. I didn't trust the rush of emotions that would come when I held him in my arms again. I was barely holding it together now and wanted to be able to enjoy our reunion.

So I recovered his sleeping face, put the two bags I would be carrying through the terminal over my shoulder and picked up his carrier. My heart was beating so loudly I was afraid anyone within a few feet would hear. I felt awkward and uncomfortable but couldn't let my unease show. I knew how to take care of my baby. I had done it since the moment he was born.

When a left the restroom, I looked around to make sure that the woman who had brought him to me was no longer visible. My next step was to make it through the first checkpoint. If there were any imperfections on the passports, or with any of the other paperwork, it would most certainly be discovered. Then I'd be on my way to prison, and the baby would end up in some orphanage where he'd likely spend his entire youth, unless Mendoza found him first. I had to be convincing and strong. Kidnapping was a serious crime in any country, and forged documents wouldn't protect me. I'd destroy them once they were no longer useful.

"Good afternoon," the guard, whose security checkpoint I had been directed to said as I set the car seat on the floor and pulled the passports I'd been given out of the diaper bag.

"Good afternoon," I replied, forcing what I hoped was a convincing and confident smile. There had been a long, waiting line that snaked its way back and forth, but I'd kept my head down and tried not to make eye contact with anyone. Fortunately, the baby hadn't awakened, but I'd still checked on him to make sure he was still breathing.

It seemed like it took the guard forever to read every line and make sure all the stamps were in order, but he didn't call anyone over to double-check information, and he didn't motion for additional guards to take me into custody, but I knew I could be stopped at any number of places before actually making it to my plane.

I had thought about my cover story enough that I was ready to play the bereaved widow who just wanted to get home to her family, but I hoped no one would need convincing. Not many people, even security guards at an international airport, would want to see a grown woman fall apart, unless they were darned sure there was a reason for it.

"Have a nice flight," the man responsible for letting me through the first checkpoint finally said after a very lengthy pause where he looked into my face as if he was searching for something.

I thanked him, took the passports back, picked up the car seat and headed for the conveyer belts feeling more light-headed than when I had been standing in line. I'd always prided myself on being honest and trustworthy, and now I would spend the rest of my life lying to the people I loved most and looking over my shoulder. I pushed back a sudden wave of nausea as I set the baby's infant seat back on the floor, took off my sandals and put them in one of the plastic tubs along with the shoulder and diaper bags.

The reality of my future was hitting me hard and heavy now, but I wouldn't change the decision I had made. However long and hard my future journey might be, the baby I was taking to his new home would keep me strong. I loved him with all of my heart and would be there to protect him until the day I died. He deserved everything I could possibly give him.

I must have looked a little overwhelmed and frazzled because the elderly gentleman who was standing behind me gave me a clue as to what to do when traveling with an infant. "It's ridiculous that you have to remove a sleeping baby from its carrier just so it can go through the metal detector, but I guess terrorists will use anything. I can certainly offer my assistance if it would be helpful."

His suggestion was alarming, but I realized that not everyone I met would turn into an enemy, and it was better to appear friendly and weary than like I had something to hide. Besides, his voice let me know that he was an American too.

"Thank you," I replied, bending over and unfastening the straps that held the baby in place. I looked around to see who might be watching as I lifted him into my arms, but the people in uniform were busy with their own tasks. They likely wouldn't bother me as long as I kept him hidden, but if I had to uncover his face, his size and the yellow tinge to his skin might necessitate answering a few questions.

The man lifted the carrier onto the conveyer belt. "I wish we'd had these contraptions when my own children were little, but in those days, cars weren't even required to have seat belts."

"I'm afraid that was a little before my time," I replied as he followed me towards the metal detector. He'd been carrying a briefcase but seemed too old to still be working.

"Times do change," he continued as we waited in short line. "My wife, God rest her soul, gave me a son and a daughter. Bill, that's my son, has been working here in Bogotá. He's an engineer. I wasn't going to come to see him at first since I've never done much traveling, but he finally convinced me that I needed to do something to get out of the rut I've been in. It's not easy to lose a spouse of over forty years."

"I'm sure it's been very hard," I replied.

It was my turn to step into the enclosure, and I could feel the heat in my body rising. I felt totally naked and exposed, but before I could enter the enclosure with the baby held tightly against me, the woman standing near it motioned for me to move to side. She had a gun holstered at her waist and didn't look all that friendly.

"Please come with me," she said.

On unsteady legs, I followed her behind a partition where she told me to lay the baby on the bench and raise my hands in the air. It took all the strength I possessed to do as she requested, but I knew it was simply part of her job, just as it had been for the guard at the embassy. Her hands ran quickly up and down my arms and legs, but when she came to my torso that had been wrapped in tape, I winced.

"Is something wrong?" she asked.

Now was the time for my act to begin in earnest. "Yes," I replied. "I have a few cracked ribs. My husband and I were in a horrid automobile accident a few days ago. He did not survive. I am on my way home to my family with our son."

She studied me with narrowed eyes for a few seconds while I let the tears come. They were my best defense right now.

"I am sorry for your loss, but regulations must be followed," she said.

I thought she might ask me to unwrap the baby so she could make sure I wasn't carrying something else, but his arms and legs started to move and he began to whimper. That seemed to help her change her mind about any further invasive procedures, and she turned to leave.

My arms quickly found their way around my son, and I hurried back to the conveyor belt hoping our few belongings would not be difficult to find. Without them, I would be left with no recourse except to contact the police in the building, and that would lead to nothing short disaster.

People were swarming everywhere like locusts to honey, and I felt a moment of panic, but the man who had been helping me earlier had retrieved my bags. He was waiting for us on a bench not far from the body scanner.

"I suppose this is where we part company," he said. "Unless you're heading to Chicago. That's where I live."

"No," I replied. "I'm from Arizona."

It was the first intentional lie I'd told anyone without justifiable cause, but I knew it wouldn't be my last. My life of duplicity over a promise made in haste—when I'd taken an oath to defend the truth —had just begun.

He rose to his feet. "I hope you have a safe trip. It sounds like your little one needs his mother. Traveling is never easy for them."

My heart was warmed over what he had said. The baby I had with me was my son in every way that really mattered, and I would move both heaven and earth, if necessary, to make sure no one took him away from me.

"Thank you for taking care of our things. We would never make it home without them."

"It was my pleasure. You looked like you could use a friend."

When he had gone, I put the baby back in his carrier and secured the straps of the sandals around my ankles. From there, I took an escalator to the upper floor and then traveled along several moving walkways to the end of the terminal. My plane was scheduled to depart from gate 103. I still had forty-five minutes to wait until the first call to board was announced.

It wasn't until I was seated with my face to a wall that the baby gave his first sound of real complaint. I pulled back his blanket and smiled down at him. His black eyes were closed against the harsh fluorescent lights, but he was letting me know that I had neglected him long enough. He needed to be changed and fed.

"I missed you so much," I whispered, without reaching in to touch him. He was dressed in a blue onesie with a frog on the front, and I wanted nothing more than to hold him in my arms. But I had been given orders about not letting anyone see him for a reason. I might have made it this far, but I still had to board the plane, and it had to be in the air and headed north before I would really believe that we had made it out of the Colombia without detection.

The airline personnel were already at their counter, and people were standing and sitting everywhere. No one seemed particularly interested in me, and I knew it would be nearly impossible for unauthorized firearms to be brought in from the outside, but a few regulations wouldn't prevent a man like Mendoza from having people inside the terminal to do his bidding. Death wasn't the only punishment he could inflict. Anyone interested in detaining me would be able to do it with little resistance.

I was inside one of the stalls where a changing table had been built into the wall before I lifted the baby out of his carrier. How good he felt, but how small and helpless he looked. I pulled off the little, blue suit and checked his diaper. It was soaked, so I made the change. Then I just looked into his tiny, trusting face. How I had missed not having him with me.

It would not be easy changing my life to meet his needs, but this precious infant—a direct gift from God—was my responsibility for as long as I lived. That frightened me a great deal, especially since I wasn't even sure I'd have my own government's help if we made it home. Assistant Director Bridges had been informed about the decision being made, but there had been no mention of the kind of reception or help I might receive once I was standing in his office. Maybe he'd be like DEA Director Stevens and tell me I was on my own. He certainly had no obligation to help in my continued charade.

But what I would be doing to my own family was even more concerning. They deserved to know the entire truth surrounding the baby's birth, and I would only be able to tell them that he had been granted political asylum, and I'd volunteered to raise him. Knowing each one of them as I did, there was little chance that such a blatant misrepresentation of the truth after what I'd put them through to join the FBI would ever be accepted. I had belittled every other career suggested and driven home—on more than one occasion—the fact that I wasn't ready for either marriage or family.

Perhaps I had taken on more than I would ever be able to handle. Parenthood was a privilege, not just an act of nature, but I couldn't doubt the rightness of what I had committed to do. I would give my life, and even association with the rest of my family, to protect him and give him the love he deserved. But raising a child was more than just taking care of physical needs and offering support and devotion. The baby I'd promised to cherish was sick and should be in a hospital, not getting on some plane. If an emergency occurred during the flight, or at any time thereafter, I would be held legally and morally responsible.

After leaving the restroom, I found a chair as far away from the rest of the travelers as I could and began feeding him while he sat in his car seat. I would have preferred holding him but didn't want to risk anyone asking to see him. Every so often I scanned the room to see if anything unusual popped. I had been taught to notice even the slightest irregularity, but I knew I wasn't at the top of my game professionally and hadn't been since leaving Assistant Director Bridge's office to begin this fateful assignment. My work had been sloppy because I hadn't been adequately prepared or informed, and that information would be included in my file. The most redeeming thing I had done was figuring out the relationship between Alma and Carlos Mendoza. I hoped it would bring about his capture and the dismantling of his cartel.

The baby finished part of his bottle before falling asleep again. I knew his little stomach couldn't hold much, but I had to keep forcing what I could. I wished Dr. Perez had sent a note outlining the precautions I should be taking until I was able to get him home, but I understood the need to keep his cover intact, and a paper trail might endanger that. I didn't even know the kind of antibiotics he had been given, or if he'd received enough prior to this journey. There were hours to go and thousands of miles to cross before I had any of the answers I needed.

I tried not to think about Alma as I waited for boarding to be announced. She would be furious learning that such a carefully guarded secret had come to light, and it wouldn't take long for her to figure out who was behind it. The thought of the kind of retaliation she could unleash frightened me even more than the threats her brother had made against both Agent Fielding and me. As long as I lived, I would never forget the cold look in her eyes and the way everyone feared her. What if she wasn't just a silent partner, but the ringleader? She might be a woman, but age, personality and opportunity told me that she was capable of doing most anything.

And what about Luis and Isabel? Without other family members to take them in, they could end up in foster care, protective custody or even be given to the highest bidder. I could hardly bring myself to think about the turmoil my interference had brought into their lives. They'd lost their mother, Maria and a baby brother. How would they ever learn to trust when every compassionate adult they had ever associated with had disappeared?

Fortunately, the call for passengers traveling with infants was made, or I may have given in to the unrealistic desire to leave the airport and return to the embassy where I'd seek shelter until I knew the baby's life wouldn't be further endangered by traveling, and where I could find an answer as to what had happened to his siblings. Maybe a way could be found to get all of them out of the country if I looked hard enough.

I checked my surroundings before moving to the front of a line that had already formed. While I was waiting next to a man and a woman with two small children in tow, I saw another man, dressed in camouflage, hurrying my way and felt a moment of alarm, but he stopped before reaching me, threw his arms around a girl in a short, leather skirt and kissed her soundly. I averted my attention quickly. The best way to be spotted was by watching someone else.

The agent at the gate swiped the barcode on my ticket but frowned when she saw the smallness of the bundle in the carrier. I knew what she was thinking - people with infants that little should not be traveling.

But she only told me to have a nice flight before allowing us to pass. I made my way down the long hallway that could be moved in and out at will. It seemed cold and damp, and I involuntarily shivered as I wished I'd been given something warmer to wear. When I reached the plane door, I left the infant carrier with the flight attendant who tagged it and said I could pick it up once we landed in Dallas.

I'd put all the documents I needed in a side zipper on the diaper bag where they would be easy to access and less likely to disappear should someone try to grab my smaller bag. I wondered how I would receive my new identity once I made it stateside, but if all else failed, I could rent a car under the identity I now possessed and drive part of the way home before calling Neil to come and get me. That might be the safest course anyway. If I didn't follow the protocol I'd been given, it would make it even more difficult for someone to find me.

Since few passengers had already boarded, I didn't have to worry about ramming anyone with the diaper bag as I proceeded down the narrow isle to my assigned row. I shoved the baby's bag underneath the seat in front of me and then laid him on my knees while I buckled my seat belt. I was next to the window, and a man and his son soon occupied the two seats to my left. Neither seemed interested in a baby which suited me perfectly. I just hoped he would sleep for most of the trip.

My brow furrowed as I glanced out of the window at the gray, cloudy sky and a tarmac that was wet with rain. Men were scurrying around making sure the luggage was loaded, food was aboard and the way clear for the plane to back out of its stall and head down the runway where the pilot would be given clearance to take off.

It was a true miracle that we'd made it this far, but the uncertainty that loomed ahead made me quiver. I'd been gone from home for less than two weeks, but during that time the course of my entire life had changed. I didn't want to think about Agent Fielding and all the angst he'd caused over the past few days. He was an enigma I would never understand. His emotional outbursts could change at the drop of a hat, but the fact remained that his expertise had kept us alive. When I really thought about it, I owed everything to him, but it was doubtful we would ever meet again so I could tell him thanks.

The baby squirmed as we left the ground but didn't open his eyes. This wasn't his first plane ride. We'd come out of the jungle in a two-seater that was far less safe and comfortable than the one we were in now. Oh, what a story I would have to tell him when he was older.

I closed my eyes when we were far enough off the ground that nothing but sky and clouds could be seen and thought about the experience I'd just survived and what the next leg of our journey might bring. I would never forget the time I had spent in Colombia or the people I'd met while there. The evil, the innocent, the proud and the ones willing to give their lives for the greater good. It was truly the adventure of a lifetime, but I didn't want to go back. I would be perfectly content disappearing into the heart of Washington D.C. and living my life as an FBI agent while taking care of my son. How good it felt to have him back in my arms.

Chapter 16

The flight was uneventful, even though it was personally stressful. While most people slept, watched movies or read, I worried that the something might happen to the baby before we landed and I was able to find proper medical care. I kept him tightly bundled against the chill of the air flowing through the cabin of the plane, and when I fed or burped him, I made sure no one could see his face. But he drank very little and seemed more lethargic as the time passed slowly onward. I had to keep reminding myself that newborns slept most of the time, even when they were perfectly healthy.

I excused myself twice to change his diaper. It was only when I had him on the changing table away from prying eyes that I could open my heart to him and express my undying love while the tears fell. He was a miracle baby, filled with the Light of Christ and a future that had yet to be written. For a reason I might never understand, I had been chosen to take care of him. I would never forsake the promise I had made to his dying mother.

Still, my heart ached that he would never know the beautiful Maria with the kind heart and fierce devotion to making sure her son survived. She hadn't held him or even looked into his beautiful face, but I had no doubt that she had helped us along the way to safety. She would be the baby's guardian angel. That belief gave me a great deal of comfort because I knew we would, in a sense, be raising him together.

It was well after dark when we landed. I inwardly shouted with joy as the plane's wheels touched down with a bump and force that propelled me slightly forward in my seat. The baby didn't make a sound, so while the boy in the seat next to me was putting his cell phone away, I lifted the edge of the blanket to make sure he was still okay. The way he squinted his closed eyes let me know that he was still alive, but the tinge to his skin had deepened. He even looked like he might be running a fever, but there was no way I could check unless I used the rectal thermometer the doctor had sent. I wasn't sure I could insert it property, so I place the back of my hand on his forehead like my mother had done to me so many times when I was small. It was warm to the touch, but then I had been holding him close, and my own body was given off the extra heat of a woman who was more than a little scared.

It seemed an eternity passed while I waited outside the plane for the car seat to be brought from the cargo hold. No one spoke to me except for the flight attendant that offered to help me get the baby situated once it arrived. I declined her offer knowing that her curiosity had been aroused during the flight because I'd been so intent on making sure he wasn't seen. She'd stopped in the aisle several times to ask if there was anything I needed.

While I knew she had just been doing her job, I couldn't overlook the fact that she was a native Colombian, and I had been told to trust no one. She could easily have ties to the cartel, and my lack of openness, along with all the cuts, bruises and abrasions on my face and lower arms would not go unnoticed by anyone who was watching for me.

But in due course, I made it inside the terminal and was relieved to find that no one appeared to be waiting for me. I paused long enough to stop the adrenalin surge before continuing down the long hallway that was lined with chairs, departure and arrival signs hanging above my head, and hundreds of people pushing or carrying suitcases and overnight bags.

I was alone in an unfamiliar city with a sick baby. Every inclination told me to call home, let my parents know what had happened, and ask for some much-needed advice. They would never betray my trust, but I'd been told that arrangements were being made for the completion of my assignment and including anyone in what had happened wasn't an option. Tears tickled the end of my nose as I thought about all the lies I would now be forced to tell, but from this point on, no one must ever know the entirety of what I'd done. Too many lives depended on my ability to be deceptive while trying to go about my life as I had always done.

Only one little shop on the concourse was open, and there wasn't much clothing to select from, but I had to change my appearance before getting on another flight. So after a short deliberation, I purchased a pink Dallas Cowboy's oversized sweatshirt and matching sweatpants. It was hideous and something I would never wear outside of a gym, and even that was a stretch, but it was the only thing available.

I went directly from the shop to a restroom where I took off the wig that had left my head itching and changed clothes. It was good to see my brown hair again as it hung down my back the way it did whenever I wasn't at work. Then I discarded the yellow dress and light sweater, but I had no choice except to keep wearing the sandals since no shoes were for sale.

I felt ridiculous, but after making sure the baby was okay, I went to find a place to wait while I decided what I would do if plans had fallen though. If I left the airport, I would definitely be on my own, but if I remained inside without another ticket and different identification, I could be putting both of our lives in danger again. I wasn't used to working without a plan, and notwithstanding my relief at having made it back to America, I was a little apprehensive because I was still a long way from home.

Just as I was about to look for a pay phone, if such things still existed in airports, I heard the name Erica Bowles announced over the intercom. It seemed to reverberate throughout the entire airport. "Please come to the courtesy desk at the end of concourse A."

I rose to my feet, put the two bags over my shoulder and picked up the infant carrier just as the announcement came again. That was the name I'd been told would become my next identity, so I checked my location and hurried off to the right.

"I'm Erica Bowles," I said, arriving at my destination and hoping I hadn't made a colossal mistake. It didn't release me from being careful just because I was no longer on foreign soil.

The girl at the desk looked non-threatening and smiled when she glanced at me, regardless of my less than attractive appearance. With no makeup, my injuries were clearly evident, and I had done no more than run my hands through my hair. "I was told to give you this when your flight arrived."

She handed me a white envelope with the name "Erica Bowles" printed in bold letters on the front.

"Thank you," I replied, taking it from her.

"Perhaps I shouldn't ask, but there are people who can help if you're in trouble."

Her kindness was moving, but I couldn't afford to involve anyone. "It was just a small accident," I told her, remembering the cover story I'd been given in Colombia. "I'm perfectly fine, really."

"Are you sure? I could get someone to help with the baby. That's what customer service is for."

"We'll be fine," I replied, reminding myself that Carlos Mendoza's influence went far beyond Colombian borders.

I moved away from the courtesy desk before tearing the envelope open and watching a small key fall into my hand. It belonged to a locker that was likely located somewhere inside of the terminal, but I had no idea in which direction to even look. The baby was starting to fuss. I knew he wasn't hungry or wet. He just needed to be held and reassured. I understood because that's exactly how I felt.

I hesitated talking to her again, but I couldn't waste time hunting around for something I might never find on my own, so I took a step back towards her desk.

"Could you tell me where are the lockers? This is my first trip to Dallas."

"On the ground level, next to entry 4," she answered, trying to be pleasant after my slight rebuff. "Just take the escalator at the end of the concourse. The lockers will be to your left. Is there anything else I can help you with?"

"No, but you've been very helpful," I replied, shoving the envelope and key into the side pocket of the diaper bag next to the documents I needed to dispose of.

She was trying not to be obvious, but her scrutinizing look told me that she still had plenty of questions I wasn't at liberty to answer.

I quickly joined the travelers who were making their way to ground floor. Inside the locker, I found a Texas Driver's License under the name of Erica Bowles and a first-class ticket to JFK International Airport that left in less than two hours. I was instructed to take the pair of scissors that had been included and shred the forged passports and anything else I had been given in Colombia and deposit the remains in different trashcans before going through security again.

So I found the nearest restroom, secluded myself in a handicap stall because it was the only one large enough for both the baby and me and cut what I could not tear. I flushed the smallest pieces, put some in the container where dirty diapers were to be placed and dropped the remainder in receptacles at each end of the room containing sinks and blow dryers.

I had to remind myself that as hard as everything was for me, there were other people calling in favors and pulling strings to make the baby's extraction possible. I couldn't give in to uncertainty now. What we did mattered in more than a global way. It mattered individually. All I had to do was look inside the baby carrier to know that people working together could make a difference. If I still had a job when I returned, I'd recommit to doing it with all the passion I'd felt when my badge had first been given to me.

Once all traces of my recent past had been destroyed, I left the restroom feeling somewhat more confident, but I still had to pass through security under another assumed name before boarding the plane. I was heading towards the long line that led to the checkpoint where tickets and driver's licenses had to be produced when I saw two uniformed officers heading my way. Their guns and badges were clearly visible, but it was their determined gait and the harsh looks on their faces that made me start to shake.

"Don't move," one of them said. I couldn't believe he was talking to me, but it was impossible to look away. I'd followed my directives precisely. How could I ever explain what had happened without incriminating people I'd promised to protect? This wasn't what I'd signed on for but running wouldn't help. For the first time since this debacle had begun, I wondered how far God's mercy would extend when he'd already done so much. Sometimes people were left to get out of difficult situations on their own.

To be continued ...

Enjoy this excerpt from

Resilience

Book 2 - Reagan Sinclair, FBI

by JS Ririe

"Welcome home, Agent Sinclair," Assistant Director Bridges said, indicating the chair he wanted me to sit in once we were alone. "It's good to have you safely back. I understand you've had quite an experience for your first field assignment."

"Yes, sir," I said trying not to frown. I had the distinct feeling that he was being extra nice to me for a reason. I'd put him in an intolerable situation having to back a decision he never would have made if it hadn't been forced on him. Perhaps he wanted to meet with me before the work day officially began so I could be dismissed and have my desk cleaned out before any of the other agents arrived. It would certainly make life easier for him. "I learned a great deal."

"As we all do when we're given new challenges. First, I want to tell you that your Intel has led to Alma Mendoza's arrest. It's a big coup for the DEA since no one had made the connection before. They're very pleased with your work and asked me to relay their thanks. I guess a fresh pair of eyes really paid off for them this time."

"Thank you, sir," I replied, remembering to keep silent until my opinion was solicited.

"She's not talking obviously, but they aren't giving up. They're convinced she knows where her brother is and what his next move will be, and they want to be ready. Mendoza won't let her stay in custody for long. She's too valuable to his operation, not to mention the family ties."

"I'm glad my information proved useful."

"You have the makings of a fine undercover agent. You improvised and managed to get away alive. That was your mission."

My mind inadvertently rushed back to those terrible days at the compound and in the jungle: Mendoza's ambition and cruelty, Alma's cunningness, Isabel and Luis' longing for love and attention, Marie's desperate situation in carrying the child of the man she'd been sent to take down. And that was just the beginning. There was also the feel of the barrel of a gun shoved against the back of my head, Agent Fielding's constant threats and putdowns, and a sick baby's survival to contend with. None of those things would ever be forgotten, and they could never be adequately explained.

"I'm just sorry that my presence cost Agent Fielding the arrest he worked so hard to get. If he'd been able to do his job, Mendoza would be in custody now."

"You were placed in an impossible situation, and there were no guarantees that Mendoza wouldn't have escaped anyway. Men like that have plans for every contingency. You can't blame yourself for the way things turned out."

"I'm not sure everyone would agree, but I didn't have the information necessary to do much differently."

"It's not the way I run things, but I suppose they figured that the less you knew the safer you'd be. I'm sorry the baby's mother didn't make it. I've been told she was a good agent."

"From what I observed, she was," I replied, realizing that now might be the only chance I had to state my case. "I can't thank you enough for helping me get her son out of the country. It was her dying wish, and after what she'd been though, one I felt I couldn't disregard."

Assistant Director Bridges did not let his eyes move away from my face. "I hope you understand that a lot of strings had to be pulled for that to happen. I'm still not sure it was the wisest thing to do since I'm not in the habit of making unnecessary enemies, but I do understand the need to protect the child. From what Director Stevens told me, Mendoza doesn't know he's alive, but you still managed to convince him that the baby would not survive in his own country. That tells me a great deal about the tenacity of the agents we train. My greatest concern is what will happen when Mendoza finds out you were the one who made the connection between him and his sister. Things could go south in a hurry, but it was still a job well done, and I suppose you deserve a little consideration."

I wasn't sure quite how to answer. My job had plunged me into a world I knew little about – a world filled with evil men and women who would stop at nothing to keep from being exposed. Having Alma in custody was a great first step, but it opened the door to more trouble than I cared to contemplate. I sank back in my chair wondering what he was going to say next.

"How is the baby?" he asked, surprising me.

"Quite well, considering the adverse circumstances. I hope you won't blame Agent Southwick for anything. I'm the one responsible for not coming directly back to D.C. after he picked us up at the airport."

"Agent Southwick told me your concerns for the baby's health and safety, and I hope meeting with the doctor at the Naval hospital helped. He'll make sure your records are kept confidential. That said, Director Stevens informed me of your desire to keep the baby. I'm not sure that's advisable."

"Please, Assistant Director Bridges," I said. "I know it's against every conceivable rule, but I made a promise to his mother."

"A promise made under duress. I'm sure she didn't expect you to keep it."

"Begging your pardon, sir. You weren't there, and I take the oaths I make very seriously."

He cleared his throat. "I understand your moral convictions, Agent Sinclair, but we're dealing with facts here; not beliefs. The best solution would be having him taken in by someone not affiliated with the government. That would make him harder to find and would free you to go on more undercover assignments."

A wave of nausea washed over me. There it was! The DEA wasn't through with me, even though any further involvement with them could lead a member of Mendoza's cartel straight to my front door. I was living on borrowed time, and anyone associated with me might already be at risk. I wasn't sure how I could protect Neil from any backlash. I only knew that I wasn't going to change my mind about keeping the baby.

"I made a promise to a friend," I told him. "I know it's not going to be easy, and sacrifices will have to be made, but I love the baby with all my heart. I'm the only one he's got. I can be his mother and still do my job."

His sigh was heavy and showed his displeasure. "I try to stay out of my agent's personal lives as long as it doesn't affect their ability to do their work, but you are young and inexperienced, and your actions have relinquished the right for me to remain neutral to a certain extent. I would not be doing my job if I didn't let you know the serious reservations I have."

"I appreciate your concern, sir. I know having him with me isn't going to be easy, but I am in the best position to protect him should the need arise. That is, if I still have a job."

"Your position with the agency has never been in question. You are not the first agent who has asked for help in granting someone political asylum. I just don't want you to regret an impulsive decision based on an emotional response to a difficult situation. You have a very bright future - if you don't do something to mess it up."

"I am committed to both my work and the baby," I said without flinching.

"Then I hope you understand that it's not going to be easy living a lie for the rest of your life. No one can ever know the baby's true parentage. It will be dangerous enough just knowing that he's been granted political asylum. If adoption is your ultimate goal, your cover story must be impeccable. Have you thought about going into witness protection until Mendoza is caught? It might be worth considering."

"I think it's a little premature. Mendoza assumes I'm a DEA agent, and it would be nearly impossible for him to trace me back to the FBI after all the precautions that were taken."

"It only takes one slip, Agent Sinclair."

The crushing pain in my chest made it difficult to breath, but there was no way I'd relinquish the baby to anyone else. I'd find a way to raise him or die trying. I was taking that leap of faith, and it was every bit as difficult as some people claimed it to be.

"I understand, and I will be careful. Mendoza is a cold-blooded psychopath, and I doubt his sister has any compulsions about eliminating anyone who gets in her way either. But I'm really of no concern to them as long as they believe the baby is dead. I wasn't there long enough to find out anything that could hurt them."

"You figured out a family connection no one even suspected before."

"Only because certain things didn't add up at the hacienda, and because Director Stevens showed me a thirty-year-old picture. I would never have made the connection if it hadn't been for her eyes and the three moles on her chin. I don't know that she's ever spent much time in public. It comes as no surprise to me that no one else saw it."

"All the more reason for you to watch your back. You're the only one who realized they are siblings. That will put you in greater danger than having the baby with you."

I pushed back another round of fear. "Then it doesn't really matter what I do about the baby, does it? And I'm far better off being around fellow agents than going into hiding. At least here, I will be advised of any changes."

"We'll do everything we can, Agent Sinclair, but we can't control what goes on outside this office. What do you know about the other agent you were working with?"

My brows automatically wrinkled. "Relatively little! He helped us escape the compound when he should have been able to see a nearly four-year mission through to completion. I suppose that says something about his character and his commitment to fellow agents, but I haven't seen or heard from him since he dropped us off at the clinic in Bogotá. I understand he's already been assigned to a new case. He left Colombia before I did."

"Do you think he can be trusted?"

"What are you saying?" I asked, knowing I was on the verge of being insubordinate again. Nothing about the explanations I'd been given by anyone associated with the DEA rang completely true, but I'd just assumed that everything was on a "need-to-know" basis, and I didn't have the right clearance.

"I'm just thinking out loud," he replied. "There is no reason to believe anything is amiss. I'm giving you the next two days to get your affairs rearranged. You'll be expected to report back to work first thing Monday morning. I hope that's sufficient time."

"More than adequate," I replied.

This certainly wasn't the debriefing I'd expected, and I had a bad feeling that he wasn't telling me everything I needed to know. No one got off that easily after they'd been out of the country for ten days on an assignment with another agency. If nothing more, reports would have to be written.

Still, four days was an unexpected blessing and would give me time to make some very difficult decisions. The hardest would be trying to figure out how to explain what I had done to my family without being able to truthfully answer any of the questions I knew they would ask.

"Then it's understood that nothing we've talked about leaves this room," he said, forcing me back to the present. "Agent Southwick has been apprised of certain aspects of the situation, and I have no doubt that you've told him what you felt was necessary, but watch your words and actions carefully. We don't want an international incident."

"No, sir," I replied. "I only want to keep the baby safe."

"Then, we'll see you back here on Monday morning." He rose to his feet. "I have some work to do and trust you can find your own way out. You can pick up your things before leaving the building."

"I hope you don't mind that Agent Southwick might be a few minutes late. He's at my place with the baby."

I thought I detected a hint of a smile. "Tell him to get here as soon as he can. I'm sure his partner will be waiting for him."

"Yes, sir," I replied as I left his office. He'd made no mention of future plans for me, other than the fact that I still had a job. For now, I had to be content with that.

See Book Two: **Resilience - Reagan Sinclair, FBI** for more of Reagan's story.

Other Titles From Jan Hill Books:

Indecision's Flame - Book 1: by JS Ririe

Brylee Hawkins was prepared to enjoy a bright, hopeful future until her fiancé convinced her to return to the Australian Outback to confront the father that had driven her away. On her own again in a harsh and unforgiving land, she is forced to face a mottled and unsavory past and an even more disturbing and dangerous present. As unrelenting lies, secrets and cover-ups – including a family she never knew about - continue to unfold, Brylee soon learns that both decisions and indecision are bringing her closer to a point of no return. Will she find the strength to fight the darkness, or will it seep into her soul and take away everything she had come to treasure?

Lost - Indecision's Flame - Book 2: by JS Ririe

Torn between her family and the obligations of a promise made to her father, Brylee longs to return to the United States and to her fiancé who is patiently waiting for her, but fate seems to have other plans. Jake, the brother of her father's wife, decides to take her under his wing and teach her the ropes of running the ranch - mostly in an attempt to get rid of her. His mockery and ridicule are only enhanced when she learns of her father's legacy and the part she is to play if she wants to help keep it alive. Unable to make a decision about leaving, she is left to wonder if the outback will consume her before the next harsh blow comes.

Exposed - Indecision's Flame - Book 3: by JS Ririe

With LeAnn gone from the ranch because she is unable to accept her husband's death, and the aftermath of the flood to deal with, Brylee is forced to assume more responsibility than she is prepared for in raising her little brother, Trevor, and trying to keep the family heritage intact. Her troubles deepen when a secret she was keeping from her fiancé is revealed through an unexpected source, and she must learn to accept the fact that her feelings for Jake, the incorrigible, yet handsome ranch hand and family member who has the uncanny knack for seeing into her heart as no one else has been able to do, not even Ben, are beginning to change. A chance encounter on the beach proves just how much she has to fear. Uncle Ned delivers unsetting news about the fate of the ranch, and LeAnn learns about a priceless gift that turns the family upside down and causes Brylee to accept the reality that her life may never turn out the way she planned. Could a bleak present become an even more desolate future?

Betrayal - Indecision's Flame - Book 4: by JS Ririe

Despite a fractured heart over Jake leaving the ranch, Brylee must forge onward in support of her cousin, Molly, who has suddenly decided to get married, inviting Beth to be her maid of honor. Helping to plan an unexpected wedding is prickly, but the reception is even worse when Jake's appearance confirms what she has known all along. Tension and violence quickly ignite in the outback when a nugget of gold is found on a neighboring homestead and a man is killed for not revealing its source, forcing Brylee and Jake to put aside their differences and pretend to get along as they are pulled deeper into a web of misunderstandings, cover-ups and danger. A desperate ride down a mountain on a saddle less horse helps Brylee arrive at an important deduction that could alter her future, but will providence intervene before she can make good on a promise? Every hope for her future is put to the test.

Reawakening - Indecision's Flame - Book 5: by JS Ririe

Jake's cryptic note, when leaving the sinking ranch for a second time, forces Brylee to reconsider the advisability of remaining in the outback where personal heartbreak and unrelenting responsibility are reducing her to a shell of the woman she had once been. But fate intercedes in a most curious way, bringing with it an old aborigine from her past who sincerely believes in the mythical Rainbow Serpent and whose revelations about her childhood and omens about the future of her family shake her fledgling beliefs unmercifully.

A short holiday in Sydney to see her ex-fiancé, Ben, surf in a national competition comes to an end with an unexpected moment of closure and news that both Beth and Jake are in a hospital in

Brisbane after a critical car accident. Part of Hawkins' family livelihood is destroyed by a pack of marauding dingoes, and Brylee contracts a mysterious illness that even the experts at the disease control center are unable to accurately diagnose. Her near death causes a recovering Jake to re-evaluate his priorities and decide what he really wants to do with his life.

Unraveling - Indecision's Flame - Book 6: by JS Ririe

After months of disastrous confrontations and ill-fated choices, Brylee and Jake are finally at a place where the future doesn't seem quite so grim, but navigating through the maze of obstacles that have already set in place to keep them apart isn't going to be easy. It's a test of survival, heart and commitment as they race against time, elements and devious plotting to rescue Trevor from the hands of a deranged madman, search for answers and try to keep LeAnn from becoming a sacrificial lamb. Unforeseen circumstances force Brylee to the edge of a precipice where the decision she makes will determine if everything she believes in and holds dear is worth the sacrifice she is about to make.

Destiny - Indecision's Flame - Book 7: by JS Ririe

Beth's arrival at the ancestral home effectively ruins what Brylee and Jake hope will be the beginning of many happy Christmas days, but the much-anticipated holiday turns to complete ruin when Raymond Tucker interferes in a most galling way. It's a battle against family feelings of betrayal, sinister alliances and catastrophic news as NJ returns to the outback armed with a plan that has the potential of upsetting the very balance of nature. Ongoing confrontations and unmitigated pressure force LeAnn to rethink what is right for her and her children, and Brylee wrestles with feelings of self-doubt and a very uncertain future while trying to keep the family together. Will Jake's final decision bring her the closure and peace she so much desires, or will it turn to ashes everything they have been trying to build?

About the Author

JS Ririe is the pen name for Jan Hill who spent her youth in the country where she learned to appreciate solitude, making her own fun, and reading romance novels from some of the masters like the Bronte sisters, Louisa May Alcott, Victoria Holt and Phyllis Whitney. She penned her first novel as a teenager but never pursued what is now her greatest passion until becoming the lead witness in a federal case brought against the school district where she taught broadcasting and journalism. Reagan's story is her second series after writing Indecision's Flame and its sequels as she waited two years to testify. She lives in Utah and has two children and two living grandchildren who bring meaning and joy to her life.

A Note From Jan

Thank you so much for reading this novel. I'd love to stay in touch with you. Please consider joining my MAILING LIST so I can send you periodic newsletters about upcoming book releases, special offers and more. The link to sign up is: http://eepurl.com/dCPYVf . I promise not to spam you or sell your email information to anyone. It will be treated with care.

One last favor: Your rating/review of this book helps promote my work and encourages me to keep writing. A short, but honest review would mean a lot. It shouldn't take more than a minute or two. You can reach the page directly at http://bit.ly/IFReview

Thank you again.
JS Ririe

www.JanHillBooks.com
For contacting the author: JSRirie@JanHillBooks.com

www.ingramcontent.com/pod-product-compliance
Lightning Source LLC
Chambersburg PA
CBHW020240200626

46816CB00001BA/54